MADELINE CAIN: ADVENTURES IN FASHION

MADELINE CAIN: ADVENTURES IN FASHION

EMILY CRAVEN

Craven Publishing

Australia

Please note all spelling is in English (Australia).

Madeline Cain: Adventures In Fashion Cover Design
By Kit Foster Design

Website: http://www.kitfosterdesign.com

Contact

Facebook: *http://www.facebook.com/EmilyCravenAuthor*

Website (bookmark me!): *http://www.cravenstories.com*

Twitter: *@cravenstories*

Instagram: *@imagesforjoy*

My Email: emily (at) cravenstories (dot) com

Other Novels By Emily Craven

Madeline Cain: The Adventure Begins

The Grand Adventures Of Madeline Cain

Jake's Page

Original Fantasy: A Practical Guide To Writing Genre

Dedication

To my darling Josh.

Here's a dedication just for you.

All my love.

Madeline Cain: Adventures In Fashion

Your Un-Invitation To The Annual I'Anson Charity Ball!

EVENT INVITATION> Suggest your friends [Edit Event]

You are Attending. Private event

Time: 16th June at 18:30

Location: NYC

Created by:

Madeline Cain, Jarrah Annelli, Jade Annelli, Josh Anneli, Richard Arnoou, Cain Michaels, Victoria Zeng.

More Info:

The 2012 class from Jason I'Anson's School of Photography, cordially un-invite you to the Annual Charity Ball. The Ball, being only for important rich people and good-looking volunteers such as ourselves, is the star studded photography event of the year. Not only will some of the world's best photography (*cough**cough* ours *cough**cough*) grace the halls of Manhattan's elite, but vast sums of money will be raised for the Children's Camera Drive, a charity that provides orphans and street kids around the world with a chance to express themselves through photography.

Why would we bother to un-invite you? Well, we're a generous lot, we know you'd kill to be there, so we thought we'd throw you a bone and let you feel like you're involved. Hey, an un-invitation is better than being ignored.

Write something… [Share]

Kathy Bloomingdale So you're inviting us, to not be invited, to an event I wouldn't be able to get to without a teleporter? *Posted Saturday 16th June at 15:18* [Comment . Like]

Madeline Cain NYC Cinderella I'd like to point out you're not invited not because we hate you, but because you're poor. *Posted Saturday 16th June at 15:20* [Comment . Like]

Tim Gleeve Teleporters are science fiction Kathy, if they were real I'd have one in my basement. However, that doesn't strike me out of the race! I could probably get there with a space shuttle sized jetpack! I'll just get dressed in my zero-G space suit and grab my pack from the shed. *Posted Saturday 16th June at 15:23* [Comment . Like]

Tim Gleeve Shit, jetpack's too dusty, guess I'll have to miss this gag-tastic ball. *Posted Saturday 16th June at 15:25* [Comment . Like]

Madeline Cain NYC Cinderella Wolverine was there. *Posted Sunday 17th June at 11:13* [Comment . Like]

Tim Gleeve Flaming Barf Balls!! Seriously? Right, new genie wish: go back in time to my high-school self, convince him to gain your romantic trust, follow you to New York AND MEET WOLVERINE!! *Posted Sunday 17th June at 15:30* [Comment . Like]

Kathy Bloomingdale All to meet an actor?? Why can't you do that to meet a girl? *Posted Sunday 17th June at 16:14* [Comment . Like]

Tim Gleeve How dare you downgrade his legend to the piddly title of actor! *Posted Sunday 17th June at 16:17* [Comment . Like]

Kathy Bloomingdale Well at least you're crushing on comic book characters now and not electronics. *Posted Sunday 17th June at 17:05* [Comment . Like]

Mike Cain We all know an un-invite is just a sneaky invite. You've just got to prove you're worthy enough to decipher the real instructions. I noticed that the actual address of your event is missing. It is but a tiny hurdle for my awesome genius. *Posted Saturday 16th June at 15:18* [Comment . Like]

Madeline Cain NYC Cinderella And only sending the un-invite three hours before the event? *Posted Sunday 17th June at 11:17* [Comment . Like]

Mike Cain Stopping time is a slightly larger hurdle. But, I will prevail! *Posted Sunday 17th June at 12:20* [Comment . Like]

Josh Annelli That was a more eventful than I thought it would be... *Posted Sunday 17th June at 20:20* [Comment . Like]

Richard Arnoou You mean nerve-wracking don't you? I think half a cup of spit ended up on the Mayor's shirt before I could get out my first word. *Posted Sunday 17th June at 21:07* [Comment . Like]

Jade Annelli We had no idea you were staring in your own version of Cougar Town, Bro. *Posted Sunday 17th June at 21:12* [Comment . Like]

Madeline Cain NYC Cinderella At least you didn't end up with a penis icicle in your drink when you were introduced to a curator at the Guggenheim. *Posted Sunday 17th June at 23:00* [Comment . Like]

Josh Annelli Sis, I can handle frisky middle aged women, what I was referring to was the scene Maddie managed to orchestrate, though the phallic icicle is an addition I was unaware of. I was there when you spoke to the curator too, no idea how I missed *that.* Good to see you balance the public moments with the private ones, Maddie. *Posted Sunday 17th June at 23:05* [Comment . Like]

Madeline Cain NYC Cinderella You were probably too busy ogling the curator's PA. She was MILF age. *Posted Sunday 17th June at 23:07* [Comment . Like]

Jarrah Annelli What?? How did you manage that? So it wasn't double trouble for you yesterday, it was the triple nipple? *Posted Sunday 17th June at 23:09* [Comment . Like]

Madeline Cain NYC Cinderella Sure was. I do everything in threes: injuries, bad luck, embarrassment. Why don't you ask Cain how it got there? *Posted Sunday 17th June at 23:11* [Comment . Like]

Cain Michaels The ice sculptor was clearly female, no male artist would have carved a set of the family jewels that poorly. *Posted Sunday 17th June at 23:13* [Comment . Like]

Madeline Cain NYC Cinderella The only way you could tell that was by touching them?? *Posted Sunday 17th June at 23:17* [Comment . Like]

Cain Michaels The proportions were all off! The real David was a master piece and she butchered it. *Posted Sunday 17th June at 23:21* [Comment . Like]

Madeline Cain NYC Cinderella So you decided you would butcher her centrepiece by removing the offending member? *Posted Sunday 17th June at 23:26* [Comment . Like]

Richard Arnoou Classy. *Posted Sunday 17th June at 23:32* [Comment . Like]

Cain Michaels No! I told you, it just snapped off. *Posted Sunday 17th June at 23:34* [Comment . Like]

Kathy Bloomingdale Geez Maddie, what the hell happened? *Posted Sunday 17th June at 23:53* [Comment . Like]

Kate Nikle joined the group **Wouldn't It Be Ironic If You Choked On A Life Saver?** and 20 other groups.

Kathy Bloomingdale -> Cliff Wheeland So, some hardcore writing over summer and then experiment time? *Posted Monday 18th June at 06:23* [Comment . Like]

Cliff Wheeland Experiment time is my favourite part; it's where I can compare how stupid I think people are to how stupid they *actually* are. I didn't go deep enough for my last book and it flopped, never again will I be lazy! *Posted Monday 18th June at 07:40* [Comment . Like]

Madeline Cain NYC Cinderella So you'll reply to Kathy's message but you won't answer a knock on your damn door? I thought you'd be happy I finally have a moment longer then a sneeze to say hi. *Posted Monday 18th June at 10:10* [Comment . Like]

Tim Gleeve Who will be your nursing home friends? Use the first seven friends on the left of your profile.

- Has the title of Captain Underpants for most undie changes: **Mike Cain**
- Wheelchair races you across the car-park: **Jack Fox**

- Steals your dessert: **Derek Chan**
- Vaselines your walker handles: **Madeline Cain**
- Steals your false teeth: **Virginia Lowe**
- Has the booze stash: **Kyle Traybna**
- Still has honey for some bunny: **Kathy Bloomingdale**

Posted Monday 18th June at 10:55 [Comment . Like]

> **Kathy Bloomingdale** Do I *want* to know what honey for some bunny means? *Posted Monday 18th June at 12:05* [Comment . Like]
>
> **Jack Fox** Hell yeah! I'll still be doing the Rabbit when I'm a wrinkly stud. *Posted Monday 18th June at 13:10* [Comment . Like]
>
> **Madeline Cain NYC Cinderella** You can count on me being ready with the Vaseline buddy, promise. Think you got Kathy and Jack switched though… *Posted Monday 18th June at 15:19* [Comment . Like]
>
> **Tim Gleeve** Don't know, seems the Facebook randomiser is pretty accurate on this one. *Posted Monday 18th June at 16:11* [Comment . Like]
>
> **Kathy Bloomingdale** You wish Grandpa. *Posted Monday 18th June at 17:10* [Comment . Like]

Richard Arnoou My doctor just suggested I smoke a joint or two. *Posted Tuesday 19th June at 12:00* [Comment . Like]

> **Madeline Cain NYC Cinderella** I suggest you get a new doctor. *Posted Tuesday 19th June at 13:30* [Comment . Like]
>
> **Josh Annelli** The doc is right… the chronic maybe your tonic. *Posted Tuesday 19th June at 13:48* [Comment . Like]

Cain Michaels Sign me up! Where do I find him? *Posted Tuesday 19th June at 16:00* [Comment . Like]

Victoria Zeng Hope it's not to deal with the pain of a terminal disease. *Posted Tuesday 19th June at 16:22* [Comment . Like]

Richard Arnoou To help with the stuttering. *Posted Tuesday 19th June at 16:33* [Comment . Like]

Josh Annelli Just relax, or as the doc says, 'Just play it cool'. *Posted Tuesday 19th June at 17:03* [Comment . Like]

Madeline Cain NYC Cinderella Dear Karma, please work quickly, I am losing my patience. *Posted Wednesday 20th June at 09:00* [Comment . Like]

Sorry, Madam Chair

NOTES > My Notes [Write a note]

By **Madeline Cain NYC Cinderella.** Wednesday, 20th June 2012 at 11:00.

This Ball was supposed to be the start of an illustrious career. I thought I was taking the right steps, that I could throw away my back up plans (model architect horse whisperer accountant car saleswoman) and become a Pro photographer. That I could follow the creative wind.

Instead, it seems I'm just an unfocused wannabe who causes chaos at parties.

As you'd expect from me, the chaos started pretty much immediately. Standing on the curb as my cab driver sped away, I craned my head to take in the two story banner with, 'I'Anson Charity Ball, 16th of June 2012' emblazoned in gold across the bottom. The massive dragon head reared up behind the two 'lovers' (or adulterers if you preferred accuracy), dripping fire from its mouth. Shapelle's hair rippled like lava down her back and the handsome young man's black hair seemed to absorb the light, a void balancing her radiance. They were kissing desperately as though the dragon would eat them in their last moments.

That banner has basically guaranteed me free entry into The Dragon's Den for life. Anytime I need to feel like a VIP, all I have to do is approach the bouncers, Bob and Keith, and I become a person of envy to hundreds of party goers. Well, at least on the nights when Giovanni wasn't sending me to the four corners of Manhattan delivering pizza to New York's eclectic inhabitants.

My phone reminder buzzed, letting me know how abominably late I was. I took a step forward and to my surprise dropped six inches, my foot stuck fast as though gripped by quick-dry cement. Teetering,

I managed not to face plant into a cluster of chewing gum on the sidewalk, but couldn't stop my momentum entirely. A sharp crack joined the city sounds and I stumbled forward, six inches shorter on my left side than my right. Limping around I saw a sparkly gold heel wedged in one of New York's infamous, shoe destroying grates.

The thought of what Jarrah would do if I worked grime into her silky red, floor-length dress stopped me from kneeling to pry it out. It was a ridiculous impulse, I wasn't bloody MacGyver, I didn't waltz around with superglue in my handbag, how did I think I was even going to reattach it? I thought about just going barefoot and shuddered at the mental image of me stepping on the hem of my super long dress, ripping the fabric and showing my undies to the world. No thank you! Jarrah was taller than me, it was the only reason why I risked my neck in six inch heels.

"Madeline!" Jason's deep voice broke me from my panic. "Come on Bell-of-the-Ball, I only want to give instructions once. Let's go, let's go!"

There was nothing left but to pray for balance, rise to the ball of my left foot and climbed the stairs as though I had two perfectly ordinary heels. I attempted to pat a stone lion on the rump as I passed, hoping to pass off the motion as youthful exuberance when I was really using it to stop myself falling.

To fill in the silence I called, "Sorry boss, old Simba's a bit of a talker."

A funny look passed Jason's debonair face, his eyebrows crinkling over almond eyes as he followed my erratic progress up the stone steps. "Right there sailor?" He raised an eyebrow.

Before I could stop myself I gave a wobbly salute at the top of the stair. "Tip top. They don't teach you how to wear heels in the Navy."

Still watching me suspiciously he said, "Alright then. Just refrain from drinking the hard stuff before your welcome speech, ok?"

Crap! I'd forgotten I was launching the auction. The night was getting more complicated by the minute.

Jason led me across the gray flagstone terrace, still radiating warmth after a bright summer's day, towards a second set of steps covered in lanterns. The flickering tea light candles inside cast flares of light like a living rainbow down the stairs. Three massive stone arches dominated the top terrace, supported by six, three-story high columns. Each archway had a door with a patterned window reaching from the top of the door to the arched ceiling high above. In his considerate way, Jason took me to the safety of a metal handrail to battle the final flight of stairs and we passed between the columns, under the central arch, through the middle door and into the most elegant reception hall I'd ever seen. Seriously, the royal wedding was a ho-down in comparison.

The hall was dominated by tall columns and sandstone archways. Two large staircases led off to the left and right climbing to a balcony that overlooked the cavernous room. Spotlights lit the banners that hung down the columns with captivating photographs of snarling animals, giant trees, ancient temples, spectacular sunsets and my dragon banner which hung prominently from the balcony. The banners were mainly Jason's work, but work from dozens of other photographers also graced the room on large stretch canvases balanced on easels. Richard's masterpiece of mirrors and water was projected onto the roof, changing from blue to green to purple to red to orange every couple of seconds.

Circular orange couches, ruffled in velvet material, were scattered around the space like fancy oversized footstools. I gave them but a passing glance at the time, but I should have studied them under a magnifying glass. In the middle of the room a long table held finger food, vases of orange tiger lilies and a metre high ice sculpture, which on closer examination turned out to be a replica of the Statue of David.

The rest of my classmates were waiting at the drinks station behind the stage and dragon banner. Cain and Josh looked suave in navy and black suits (respectively, they didn't mix and match like M & M's); Richard looked like less of a mountain hermit than usual in black dress pants, white shirt and a red and orange bow tie; Jarrah and Jade were in 50's style cocktail dresses, one navy blue and the other a green and orange flower pattern; and Victoria was wearing a purple and blue tutu with an emerald green dinner jacket with coattails. Trust our eclectic group to dress like a fireworks display on New Years.

Jason was describing our role as drink providers and

conversationalists when Jade sidled up and elbowed me in the ribs. "Had a couple before you came, hey? We've got to teach you where the line is between relaxed and pissed puppeteer."

Jarrah nudged me on the other side and hissed, "You're walking like a ballerina off her tits."

"Or a zombie," said Jade.

"I'm not drunk," I snapped when Jason turned his back to demonstrate champagne pouring techniques. "It's these stupid—" I shut up as Jason turned back.

"Remember, you're not waiters! You can eat food, you can drink drinks. The drink trays are an excuse for you to talk to people, so network; the industry's top photographers are here, pick their brains! The regular benefactors know you're my students. If you get any rude newbies, politely excuse yourselves and send me their way. Josh, Madeline, take a pile of auction lists and pamphlets on the charity and hand them to the guests as they enter. The rest of you grab a tray and array yourselves. It's show time!"

Jarrah wiggled her eyebrows at me and Jade pretended to stagger to the right as she fetched a tray. Thanks for all your support ladies; I couldn't have made it through the evening without your suggestive mimes. Not.

I managed to keep my feet when Jason dropped a five kilo bundle of paper in my hands. "At eight o'clock I want you to go to the stage, and flick the 'on' switch for the microphone. All you need to do is welcome the crowd, tell them who you are and where you're from, show them your beautiful banner, then introduce myself and tonight's main benefactor Ms Bellgrave to start the auction. Sound good?"

"Miss Bellview, got it," I replied, distracted, as each of my classmates did their own special rendition of how I'd supposedly walked, as they carried their drinks into the hall.

"No, *Ms Bellgrave,*" Jason repeated, "Don't worry, I'll remind you again before you go on. Handing those out for an hour should give you some time to sober up."

"Really, Jason, I would never—"

Mind already on other things he patted my shoulder almost tipping me to the side. "No need to explain, I was the same at my first show. Just use the wall as a tipsy pole, you'll be fine. Don't move that canvas there! There isn't enough light!" Jason half-ran to the overzealous event planner leaving me with a grinning Josh.

"My lady," Josh said, offering me his arm. It was only after I slipped my arm through the crook of his elbow that he said, "Let me be your tipsy pole to the door."

"You're not a very effective tipsy pole if you're the size of a dwarf," I shot back; my 'heels' made me almost half a head taller than him.

"That makes you a dwarf too then, as soon as you come off your vampire-stake stilettos."

He left me several metres back from the closed doors and moved to grab the handles as light orchestra music started up behind us. The windows were blacked out but we could hear a storm of noise coming from the other side. Josh heaved the two doors towards us, the edge of the left door just grazing my elbow (a fairly unstable tipsy pole if you ask me) and the fun began.

Event planners took the tickets as I greeted every socialite and her pet husband north of 59th Street. I don't think I've ever seen that much jewellery in my life, we could have funded the Camera Drive for five years and not needed another fundraiser. I'm pretty sure we were also responsible for half the city's hairdressing and makeup appointments; it was as though they were attending a wedding, not a charity event. The men reminded me of Penguins One and Two from the FBI, dressed in their black suits, hair slicked back or spiked up, half with the Agents' physique, half looking like they were smuggling beach balls under their dinner jackets. Every person made a b-line for our classmates and their tray of drinks, mobbing them in clouds of perfumed bodies.

"The way they act, you'd think they'd only just been let out of rehab," a high, child-like voice tittered.

I snorted, turning to a giant golden beehive. Looking down I saw a pretty, petite woman in a black, beaded cocktail dress, blond ringlets falling down from her fluffed up hairdo which gave her an extra foot of height.

"The more they drink the better our photographs look," I replied with a grin. "Welcome, I'm Madeline, one of Jason's students."

"Ah, the dragon hunter," she said taking the pamphlets I offered, my last set.

"Ha, I doubt you can hunt a dragon with a camera."

"No, but you can give it body image issues."

I laughed. "The Dragon's Den would be mortified if I turned their name sake bulimic."

She stepped back, hands on hips as she studied the banner with wide, green eyes. "It's a beautiful shot; you've got a real eye for portraits."

My heart fluttered a little at the praise. "Thanks, you're the first to say that. Are you one of-" I stopped myself short of saying *the rich ones*, "-the budding art collectors?"

She laughed a high-pitched giggle and laid a perfectly manicured hand on my arm. I realised from the deep dimples in on her cheeks as she laughed that she was a lot older than I'd first assumed, perhaps late thirties rather than twenties. "Goodness no! I'm not one of the walking jewellery boxes! I'm Natalie West, I do wedding photography. Though between you and me, I wouldn't mind getting a little A4 print of your photo for my apartment. I'll get in touch later so the money comes to you, the charity will get enough tonight. How does that sound?"

I opened and closed my mouth several times before I managed, "That would be great."

When really I wanted to pick her up, hug her like a little child and scream, '*First Sale! First Sale!*' Someone wanted my photographs for *art*! Not promotion, not black mail bribes, not FBI evidence, ART!

She clasped her hands together. "Wonderful! I love taking photographs of people in love, don't you? When you shoot weddings around the world you realise no matter how different the ceremonies are, love makes everyone the same, you know? It's hard to have a bad day when everyone around you is smiling and drunk as a skunk. Oh, there's Jason! I must say hello. We'll chat again soon." She wiggled her fingers at me and like a whirlwind, she was gone, leaving me strangely full of energy.

Josh closed the doors after the final stragglers and came over, hands in pockets. "Wow, fast talker; a fire cracker to balance out the snobbery, I like it. Come on twinkle toes, drink and food first and then we'll grab a tray and get some rich people drunk enough to bid their first born at the auction."

Dodging around the human cheque-books almost undid me, my ankle was on fire as we skirted elbows, canvases and candelabras, and I'd lost all feeling in my left toes. I have no doubt Josh and I looked like some bizarre, crab-like conga line.

"Perhaps I'll leave you near the food. Fill your belly with more than air and Chanel Number Five fumes," said Josh.

We approached the central table, already stripped of half the food. The area was clear of patrons, except for Cain who stood with his back to us, his normally perfect posture contorted as he thrust his upper body over the platters. The icy mist from the sculpture hung like a halo around his head.

Josh rapped on Cain's shoulder with a finger and thrust me next to him. "Tag! You're it."

Cain jumped as Josh melted into the crowd. A sharp crack, sounding very much like a heel snapping off, made me flinch. But my legs hadn't collapsed, so I knew it wasn't my right shoe packing it in.

"Shit shit shit!!!" hissed Cain.

"Broke a heel?" I joked. "You wouldn't be the first tonight."

He whipped his hands behind his back and suddenly I felt like I was facing my brother Mike, he had the same sour-lemon look on his face of an experiment gone wrong. "Don't be absurd, I'm a man, I don't wear heels."

I narrowed my eyes, hunting clues in his facial expression. With Mike the giveaway was always in the face, a treasure map to an expert in white lies such as myself. A necessary skill to learn when keeping your kid brother off the terrorist watch list.

"What did you do? What's behind your back?"

"Nothing!" His eyes flicking to the sculpture beside us.

"Nothing my Aunt Myrium." I turned my attention to the statue.

"No, don't!" A moist, freezing palm gripped my arm and I shrieked. At the same time I noticed David's most famous… feature, was missing.

"You turned the Statue of David into a Sh-im! What is wrong

with you?" I hissed shaking free of his clammy grip and almost up-ending a plate of fruit on the floor.

"Not on purpose! It just snapped off." He pulled his hand from behind his back and thrust the slick, transparent… *member* in my face.

I slapped his hand away. "Get that away from me! You're taking your love of the…the… hot-dog, a little too far, don't you think?"

A smirk briefly chased away his alarm. "Seriously? That's the euphemism you're going with? Hot-dog?"

"I can call it whatever I like, I wasn't *fondling* it!"

"I wasn't—" he cried, then realising how loud his voice sounded, dropped it to a growl, "I wasn't fondling."

"So what, it detached itself with the power of your mind? Did you melt it off with your laser vision?"

"It didn't look right," he whispered, trying to hide the thick, dripping representation between his hands.

"So you touched it?" I pressed, "In the middle of a room full of three hundred people?"

"Christ sake Maddie, it happened! Ok? Can we drop it?"

"Well apparently *you* can," I said, pointedly staring at the partially visible joy-stick.

"At least I'm not making up stupid similes in my head so I can avoid saying the word penis," he shot back.

God damn it, how do these people know me so well?

"What are we avoiding?" asked Josh expertly offering a tray of beverages. "The biggest glass is yours, Maddie. Ginger Ale. I've got your back." He winked.

I breathed a sigh of relief, lifting the large glass from the middle of the array. I wasn't sure I wanted to touch a drop of alcohol when my feet felt like they were on fire. The ache had taken on the qualities of an electrical current, all rippling spasms and pins and needles.

"Cain was just explaining to me why he—"

"This cannot be happening," groaned Cain. His face had drained completely of colour; it looked as though he had bleached his lips ivory.

"Always the melodramatic," I said.

"Ah!" said Jason's voice behind me, "Here's a drink station Bill, maned by not by one but three of my talented side-kicks. Cain, Josh, Madeline, this is Bill Greene, a curator at the Guggenheim."

I turned, my drink making as unusual *plop* sound as sticky Ginger Ale splashed down my knuckles.

"Ooh, such a hard choice, what a selection," said the non-descript man before me. He flicked his mouse-brown fringe from his eyes. "Look! That one even has a swizzle stick in it." He pointed to my hands.

That was how I found out I was the proud drinker of Ginger Ale with a splash of penis icicle.

Seriously, what the hell?! Then Cain hangs back like he'd taken a vow of silence. Cain, I didn't expect you to tell him that you'd accidentally broken off the statue's old-fella, but an 'oh that's just a bit of ice, we thought it was strange too, looks like a finger bone' would have been nice. Instead, nothing.

The big busted brunette beside him leaned forward with a frown, her boobs just kept in check by the super tight corset of her dress. Her eyes widened and she shook her head, leaning forward to the point where I thought she would topple into my cup.

Arranging my hands awkwardly, finger tips to the palm of each hand to obscure as much as possible, I said, "I think it's just a quirk of the ice machine. Sorry to disappoint. Puts me in mind of a fish though."

Which of course made them look closer. All I wanted was to get away, or some plausible reason to drop my glass. My half numb foot twitched and a burst of bubbles hid the specifics of the icicle.

It was enough to snap the curator out of his contemplation. "Always thought an exhibition of cocktail accessories would be fascinating."

Cain, the coward, murmured his agreement.

"Jason tells me you took the dragon portrait. Any chance we can use the shot for a Romeo and Juliet installation in the fall?"

"Ah..." I replied, distracted by the brunette moving slightly to the right for a better angle of my glass.

Mistaking my pause for hesitation, he said, "Oh don't worry, the exhibit won't have any *rude* bits, so to speak. We don't want to tarnish the reputation of artists who prefer not to be associated with erotic works."

I swallowed hard trying not to look down, the gulp sounding like a brass band to my ears.

Then Jason, my wonderful saviour, jumped in. "I think Madeline's hesitation comes from the donation to the charity from The Dragon's Den. Am I right?"

Not sure where he was heading, but glad the attention was off the glass, I nodded enthusiastically. I opted for the vaguest sentence I could. "That's right. I wasn't sure how your kind offer would be affected by that."

"Part of their condition for the large donation was the exclusive use of the banner and photo for a year. Unfortunately that would exclude Madeline from your fall exhibit, but around the same time next year the exclusivity will lapse," Jason said.

Bill sighed. "Shame. Commercialism always seems to get in the way of world culture. Well, I can wait. It was a pleasure to meet you all." He gave a bow bringing him within inches of my glass. He looked up as I tried hard to push down dread. "It really does look like a mould of something phallic, doesn't it? Strange how the world's randomness is sometimes more artistic than man-made art."

Jason winked at me as the curator and his confused PA left. "You're photo is making quite a splash tonight. The charity is in your debit."

I could fell a flush spreading up my neck to my cheeks. I was involved in more splashes than Jason knew. Pain flared in my ankle again and the drink splashed across my palms as I wobbled. That was it, I had to sit down before I fell down, and dress be damned I was going to abandon those shoes under one of the ridiculously plump footstool-couches.

"Here!" I snapped, thrusting my glass into Cain's hands.

Staggering as gracefully as I could, I headed to the closest patch of orange velvet, a sanctuary of rest and relief. The final, unsteady step was my undoing. I stumbled and reached out a hand to lean against the bright fabric. The soft surface ripped and with a sound like a bandaid pulled from a hairy leg, I pitched forward tumbling to the ground. I was in a sea of orange fuzz, my hand entangled up to the elbow in plush fabric. A high pitched shriek like nails on a chalk board echoed around the room.

I rolled from knees to butt, my eyes focusing on a pudgy ankle which merged into a wide calf and massive, cellulite dimpled thighs that disappeared into a pair of lacy blue knickers with black polka dots. Above the underwear, orange velvet encased a round belly and ample bosom of a woman. A moon of a face stared down at me, horror setting her mouth in a big 'O'. It was her scream that had turned the bubbling room of conversation into a tomb of silence.

As I looked from the enormous woman with only half of her skirt attached, to a nearby orange couch, to an abandoned bag, to the woman's knickers bared to a room of Manhattan's elite, I realised a very important fact. A large, squat woman, who bends down to pick up a dropped handbag, is about the same height and width as a large circular seat.

I understand you may be puzzled at how I mistook a woman's dress for a chair. All I can do is assure you that large Cinderella skirts the same colour, texture and ruffage as a dozen circular couches littering the room, only invites the inevitable.

"What are you doing?" Bewilderment seemed to have taken over the woman's natural instinct to cover herself, her hands hanging at her side like salami rolls at a butcher.

What are you supposed to say to that? I'm sorry, I thought you were a chair?

Pain was dulling my normally ready wit. As soon as my weight had come off my feet it felt as though I had tried to beat out a house fire with my soles, or tried to climb Mount Everest with no shoes. Pins and needles drove me to distraction.

The eventual words my mind landed on were, "My, that's a bright orange. Don't worry, it's definitely stain free, I checked." Because, of course, pretending you were looking at a woman's arse for imaginary stains is preferable to calling her a chair.

"Madam Chair! Are you ok?"

A hysterical burst of laughter bubbled in my throat as Jason swooped in. There was no way I heard that right, surely my mind was so horrified it was replacing random words of conversation with 'chair'.

He put a hand on one of the woman's thick shoulders and several event staff encircled us.

"Ms Bellgrave? I…" He paused, taking in the whole scene. "Odd place for a rest, Madeline, why didn't you just find a…" His eyes widened before he said the c-word, flicking a look to one of the nearby footstools-of-hell and back.

I didn't have time to be proud of my super-quick mentor; I was too busy giving the woman above me a horrified stare for horrified stare. Licking my suddenly numb lips I managed, "Not *the* Ms Bellgrave?"

She nodded, mouth pressed in a wavering line.

Holy Shit. I had just mistaken the Chair of the Charity Board and benefactor of this whole God damn party, for FURNITURE! I had just disrobed one of New York's most wealthy and compassionate women. I had just turned her (probably) thousand dollar dress into a thousand dollar top and throw rug. Daring to glance at my watch I almost had a seizure. It was 7:55pm. We were both supposed to be on stage, in five minutes, starting the charity's biggest fundraiser for the year.

What had I done in a past life to turn the city of New York itself against me? I must have been a banker, or a rogue knight, or a really bad soap opera actor.

"Why do you only have half a shoe?" Tiny hands, blessedly cool, gripped first one ankle then the other, levering the instruments of torture from my feet.

Victoria, never before has your attention to footwear ever been as sorely needed as in that moment. Magically, I turned from a kamakazi fashion plane, condemned for my part in destroying the layer cake monstrosity of a dress, to pitied victim of poorly made footwear. All claims of stain inspection and accidental booty watching were forgotten as several pairs of hands hauled me to my aching feet.

"Well, as long as it was an *accident…"*

"It was, I'm so sorry," I replied, abandoning my previous excuse and grovelling for all I was worth.

"At least I'm not the only one with a wardrobe malfunction," said

Ms Bellgrave with a tremulous smile, as she gathered the mess of fabric in shaking hands.

I've got to hand it to the woman, she was plucky.

"Come this way Phyllis, we have a staple gun that will fix that up, and in the morning we'll get it tailored," soothed Jason. He looked at me over his shoulder as they moved away. "Stall the auction please, Madeline."

"It can stay stapled for all I care." Ms Bellgrave's voice drifted back towards me. "I told Russel I looked more like the pumpkin carriage than Cinderella in this circus tent."

"Or a couch," muttered one of the events people, shaking their head.

Awkward doesn't begin to describe my speech. After initial jokes including a comparison between wearing heels and the little mermaid dancing on knife points, I think I went on to describe Adelaide like it was the root of all photographic inspiration, summarised the good work of the Camera Drive charity by reading (discretely) from a spare pamphlet I found on the lectern, and finished with *very* imagined accounts of the 'touching' reactions from various disadvantaged children around the world to receiving their cameras. I believe I ended on a description of one imagined deaf child who showed their appreciation through interpretive mime. If Jason hadn't turned up at that moment with a newly patched up Ms Bellgrave I'm not sure where my imaginings would have taken us. Would I have started to explain about the whole black mail incident behind the dragon banner just to fill the silence? We'll never know.

Finally, I got my longed for rest as Jason launched into full auction mode. I didn't need to hear the numbers to know Jason was *very* good at convincing the tipsy attendees to part with their money. I think the uncertain smile and awkward hand movements of Ms Bellgrave as she introduced each piece added an extra five hundred dollars to each photograph. A kind of pity/encouragement payment if you will.

As the auction wrapped up after forty five minutes I thought I had made it. Three bouts of drama in a two hour period was a personal record, there was no way even I could trump that. I could relax, safe in the knowledge that the night would end calmly and I could go home and burn the broken shoes-of-chaos in revenge.

Then the Pros showed up.

"Well you've had an interesting night."

There were three of them in total dressed to the nines, one women and two men all looking at me like a curious exhibit in a museum. It was only Cain, staring at me opened mouthed from across the room that galvanised me into lifting the hem of my dress, standing and plastering a smile on my face. My feet stayed stable beneath me and I breathed a sigh.

"Indeed. I should probably thank the chaos though; it's gotten me some interesting shots this year. I'm Madeline, pleasure to meet you."

They blinked at my outstretched hand for several seconds, like a single entity with three heads. A slow smile stretched across the face of the 'tall, dark and handsome' man on my far right, as though I had just amused him. If he was recalling the previous hour, I probably had.

His thick eyebrows were just short of a mono-brow and wiggled slightly as he took my hand in a mild grip. "David Havelock."

I couldn't stop my hand flexing; he winced. "Sorry! It's just, are you *the* David Havelock? Right-hand man of the National Geographic editor? Wildlife photographic guru?"

The short, stocky man next to him with a perfectly manicured goatee elbowed David with a smirk. "You've got yourself a fan."

"No need for jealousy, Justin," he said, grin broadening. Pointing to the Justin he said, "I'm sure you've heard of Justin Barlew too, NG's urban landscape genius."

"Seriously?" I asked, cringing at the squeak that had found its way into my voice. Feeling a flush creep up my neck, I forged on, who knew when luck would find me in a position to talk to some of the world's best photographers again? "I'm a huge fan, of both of you. My mum bought me National Geographic subscriptions for my birthday. Meeting the men whose names I've been seeing in print for years is amazing! You're like, in the top ten of guests I'd invite to my imaginary dinner party."

Stunned silence greeted me.

"Oh that's so cute! I've played that game too!" A giggle

accompanied the sweet voice of Natalie West, as she joined our circle. "Where you have to pick a guest list for the dinner party of your dreams. Were you allowed to invite dead people?"

It felt as though my face was on fire. The woman opposite me raised an eyebrow. Her angular cheekbones, pure white skin, fiery hair and floor length green gown put me in mind of the Queen of the Faerie.

I stammered, "Ah, no. The undead and I don't go well together. The idea of inviting ghosts is just too creepy."

"Fair enough, it's better to keep dead presidents out of it, right?" she said with a wink. "I just wanted to say goodbye, I've got an early morning wedding so I'm for the Land of Nod."

"It was so wonderful to meet you." I smiled.

She gripped my hand briefly in her small one and said to the others, "It was lovely to see you again David, Justin, Sorella. Until next year!"

They said goodbye with less enthusiasm than I'd expected, the flame haired woman in the middle, Sorella, flashing a dazzling smile for only a couple of seconds before dropping it as soon as Natalie had turned away.

"Urrgh," said Justin. "I can't think of anything more degrading than shooting weddings."

David nodded. "Sure, do it when times are tough, but not for a career. It's like the hospitality sector of the photographic industry."

"Little skill, no creativity. I'd die if I couldn't express myself through my work," agreed the spectacularly tall Sorella. "Please, tell us you weren't thinking of taking it up, Madeline."

I swallowed. Like most forms of photography, I'd considered it, maybe even had the odd day dream or two about meeting the guy of my dreams at a small affair on the beach. I'd take his photo as best man, he'd look deep into my eyes and...whatever. It was just many of the imaginings in my daydream closet. In any case, I had never been adverse to the idea. I'd just never realised it was at the bottom of the photographic pyramid, probably along with the people who photographed furniture or dog food for catalogues. In fact, I'd never had a preference to any particular type of photography. I just love how a camera can help you capture a moment so you can share how you see the world with other people, because we all see it differently.

"Well, I've never really thought about wedding photography specifically but-"

"You're right, it's not worth thinking about," said Sorella with a delicate shudder. "Give me a sex charged fashion portrait any day."

Then it clicked. I was standing before the Queen of female photographers, Sorella Fontain, fashion photographer. I had literally landed in the middle of a third of the guest list of my imaginary dinner party. If I was a cartoon character my eyes would have popped out of my head and exploded. As it was, I think I just stood there with a manic smile and crazy eyes.

"What is your specialisation then, Madeline? Portraits?" asked David.

They were interest in me. ME! I spread my hands wide, shrugging in what I hoped was a nonchalant manner. "I don't really have one. I love all forms of photography; I don't think I could ever possibly choose. I'm only young, there's plenty of time to experiment, figure out what suits, what's me, you know?"

I'm not sure what I expected, maybe agreement, a spirited conversation on the awesomeness of photography, or stories of their youthful experiments. What I didn't expect was silence. All three stared at me equally horrified.

"But, you're already six months through Jason's course," said Justin.

"That's the fast track to poverty," said David shaking his head.

"How do you plan to make money?" asked Sorella.

It felt as though a ball of ice had formed beneath my rib cage. "I don't understand..."

David put a heavy hand on my shoulder. "Don't get us wrong, we're artists, we couldn't live without our creativity, but you can't just flit from one thing to the next. You can't make a living like that. You can't create a career or a reputation that way. We're known for our specialisations."

Justin ran a hand through his wavy mop of hair with a sigh. "Jason's course puts you leagues beyond the rest of the wannabes, but if you don't build up a portfolio by the end of the year, *this*," he turned around gesturing to the hall and my banner, "This, comes to nothing. You've blown your best chance, the easiest, most painless path to a stellar career. I can guarantee you, it took all of us two decades to get to where we are now, and we knew exactly what our passion was. God, where we'd be now if we had Jason at the start of our careers."

My whole body felt as though it were wrapped in bandages. I couldn't move. "I have to decide now? I don't even think I've tried half the different types out there."

"If you want to earn enough money to pick your own assignments, you need to get focused," said Sorella, her green eyes intense. "If you're known as one of the best at what you do, like we are, people will pay what you tell them to pay. And they'll thank you for it. But as soon as you become one of the many photographers who live in this city, then you are at the mercy of the client's terms."

Justin took a step forward and lowered his voice. "Jason could be teaching dozens each year, but he doesn't, because he knows if he's not selective, his course is worth no more than any other photography course."

"If I were you, I'd figure out what you want fast," said David. "Then I'd build a portfolio of shots in your spare time over the next six months."

"At the same time you've got to scout out jobs and internships in your specialisation," chimed Sorella, inspecting her nails. "Even Jason's course won't give you enough experience to start your own freelance. It *will* get you into the top jobs though, so start making a list of your dream employers, magazines and companies."

"Three or four years in a top company or internship and you won't even need to look for jobs, they'll come to you," said Justin. He snapped his fingers. "Wallah!"

I forced myself to loosen my aching jaw before I broke a tooth. "That all seems very specific."

Sorella shrugged. "You could do it your way I suppose, use the next couple of years to get it out of your system. We'll see your banner on the walls in another decade or so. We're just telling you the easiest way. Maybe I won't have listened to this advice when I was your age."

"Who are you kidding?" David laughed. "All you wanted was to be a world class photographer, you would have followed it to the letter!"

Sorella winked. "That's why they pay me the big bucks!"

What have I been doing?? Seriously! Why hasn't Jason said anything? I thought we're all at the same point, just learning about photography and techniques and… I don't know, just having fun! Taking steps! Slowly making breakthroughs. Tell me I'm not the only daisy in the field of I-don't-know-what-I-want-to-do-with-my-life-yet.

Nothing has ignited an all-consuming passionate Hindenburg-esque fire in me yet. Am I slowly destroying my career before it's even begun? How am I going to choose? How do I even get an opportunity to try them? I can't just ask major companies if I can tag along to see if I like what they do, I'd be burning my bridges faster than Mike eats hot-dogs. Do I even have time to try them all AND build up a portfolio?

I still have work at Giovanni's, I'm barely scraping by as it is. My piggy bank is so anorexic it's probably going to implode and form its own black hole. My specialisation needs to be one that can bring in a reasonable amount of dough. I don't know if I could live a life of poverty, the first half of the year has been a nightmare of stress. If stress was energy, I'd be able to power Tim's computer usage.

How do I do this? How do I decide?

I DON'T KNOW!! And time is running out while I freak out.

[Comment . Like . Share]

Alexa McMarshal and **70 others** like this.

Madeline Cain NYC Cinderella What sort of cruel friends are you that you would 'like' this? You should be ashamed of yourselves… *Posted Wednesday 20th June at 14:05* [Comment . Like]

> **Josh Annelli** Calm down there homicidal Cinderella. You don't think we'd leave you in the lurch, do you? Sure we're

out of the country for a couple of weeks of the holidays, but that's no reason to go crazy on us. It's time for a Facebook PM conference with your classmates. Until then, just be cool, ok? Don't slay anyone with your stilettos. *Posted Wednesday 20th June at 14:40* [Comment . Like]

Jade Annelli No need to freak out. Between the six of us we cover most photographic fields. We'll get you sorted. *Posted Wednesday 20th June at 14:45* [Comment . Like]

Madeline Cain NYC Cinderella What do you mean you have all the fields covered? Do you already have specialisations?? Am I the *only* one who hasn't had a clue this whole time? *Posted Wednesday 20th June at 15:00* [Comment . Like]

Cain Michaels All you need to know is portraits of celebrities = big money. Fashion Photographer for Vogue = big money. Gay guy who takes portraits of underwear models = happy + big money. I'm sure we can find an equation that suits you too. *Posted Wednesday 20th June at 15:37* [Comment . Like]

Madeline Cain NYC Cinderella You've not only chosen your specialisations but you've gotten JOBS in them?! *Posted Wednesday 20th June at 15:40* [Comment . Like]

Josh Annelli You're forbidden from obsessing about this until the weekend. We'll organise a time on Sunday to all get on Facebook and knock this on the head. You will not magically gain clarity on the future by bashing your head against a desk. Can you do that, or do we need to get you drunk for real and tie you to a tipsy pole? *Posted Wednesday 20th June at 17:30* [Comment . Like]

Tim Gleeve I remember the number of times I've needed a tipsy pole… Don't worry, you're not unfocused, it's just your conscious and subconscious differ on what to focus *on.* The subconscious wants to focus on chaos, the conscious on photography. It's going to make for some wacky art. I say, just let it happen. *Posted Wednesday 20th June at 19:29* [Comment . Like]

Kathy Bloomingdale Maddie, how many times have I told you? You have the balance of a suicidal tight rope walker. It didn't work when we were ten and really, your co-ordination appears to have only decreased since then. *Posted Wednesday 20th June at 20:10* [Comment . Like]

Madeline Cain NYC Cinderella I'll tell you where you can shove your tipsy poles and it's not in my Ginger Ale! *Posted Wednesday 20th June at 20:15* [Comment . Like]

Madeline Cain NYC Cinderella Look I'm sorry, that was inappropriate. It's just when your idols are telling you that you're running out of time, you can't help but freak out. *Posted Wednesday 20th June at 20:25* [Comment . Like]

Kathy Bloomingdale Pfft, they sound like a group of pompous asses anyway. Not all your idols can live up to your expectations like Jason. You heard what he said, the charity was in your debt and your photo was a hit. Sounds like they're jealous. Listen to Jason, not the imaginary tea party. If he hasn't mentioned it's important, it probably isn't. *Posted Wednesday 20th June at 20:35* [Comment . Like]

Madeline Cain NYC Cinderella What would they have to be jealous about? Their photographs sold three times more than mine in the auction. They were trying to help, it might seem abrupt but that's because I was paraphrasing, they said it really nicely and were super concerned. That's why I know I'm in trouble, if they were nasty I'd just ignore it. What if the reason Jason hasn't said anything is because it's assumed knowledge? Like everyone was supposed to know the Moon causes the tides. But up until the final year of school I just thought tides happened. What if this is just like the moon thing, Kathy?! Then I'm the idiot. *Posted Wednesday 20th June at 20:47* [Comment . Like]

Kathy Bloomingdale All I'm saying is it's the opinion of just one group of people, not the only way. Your classmates are right, have a chat to them. All will be well. *Posted Wednesday 20th June at 20:50* [Comment . Like]

Cain Michaels Now that's wrapped up, let's talk about me. It's fine to expose your own failings on Facebook, but can you keep the rest of us out of your notes to the public? *Posted Wednesday 20th June at 22:40* [Comment . Like]

Madeline Cain NYC Cinderella You lost that right when you penis icicled my drink in front of a fine-art museum curator. So did the rest of you with your suggestive mimes. *Posted Thursday 21st June at 08:52* [Comment . Like]

Jarrah Annelli Always happy to help the night along with a suggestive mime or two. *Posted Thursday 21st June at 10:11* [Comment . Like]

Cain Michaels I maintain it slipped from my hands before I could hide it under the table. It was like a bar of soap I couldn't control, don't punish me for fate. *Posted Thursday 21st June at 10:16* [Comment . Like]

Jade Annelli If it was fate, I'm a turnip. You panicked Cain, no use denying it. Why'd you describe its shape as a fish, Maddie? Why not a tea spoon? *Posted Thursday 21st June at 10:59* [Comment . Like]

Richard Arnoou Or a sword, a pen, a poker, a caterpillar, a wand, a sausage, a lightning bolt… *Posted Thursday 21st June at 11:15* [Comment . Like]

Mike Cain It's a penisicle, no! A cocksicle. You were always squeamish around simple words like the p-word and the v-word. I never understood it. By the way, I don't like it when you refer to a man's junk as a hot-dog and then comment at my perchance for devouring hot-dogs. NOT COOL. Also, can't believe you didn't know about the moon, *shakes head*. *Posted Thursday 21st June at 11:24* [Comment . Like]

Tim Gleeve If you were the Hulk, your green rage monster would have decimated half of NYC. In this instance you were probably lucky. That would be the aim of my imaginary dinner party. To get the Hulk to crack. *Posted Thursday 21st June at 11:49* [Comment . Like]

Madeline Cain NYC Cinderella That's your contribution to this crisis? Comic book heroes? Do you even interact with real people, or are Kathy and I the lucky ones? You know you can't invite imaginary people to your imaginary dinner party, that's too many imaginaries for one event. It would probably cause a black hole in the universe or something equally retarded. *Posted Thursday 21st June at 11:58* [Comment . Like]

Jarrah Annelli That's a question, who would be on your dinner party list? *Posted Thursday 21st June at 13:21* [Comment . Like]

Jade Annelli I'd go for dead people, the really weird ones too, you know like Edgar Allan Poe, and that guy who invented the vibrator, and Cleopatra and Gandhi. Just as long as I could send them back to the grave after, I don't want a zombie apocalypse on my hands. *Posted Thursday 21st June at 13:53* [Comment . Like]

Richard Arnoou I'm not even sure what any of those people have in common. *Posted Thursday 21st June at 14:03* [Comment . Like]

Victoria Zeng They'd make an ethnically diverse zombie apocalypse? Add Genghis Khan in there too, by all definitions he was insane. Made boots out of skin. He'd probably be leader of the undead. *Posted Thursday 21st June at 15:19* [Comment . Like]

Mike Cain Thanks Sis, your bizarre life has helped me to decide my future chair. I've decided I'm going to take film at university so I can be your personal documentary chair. Someone has to film you stumbling through chair, because frankly half of the chair that makes it into your notes needs to be seen to be chaired. Personally, my chair response to El Chair would have been, "Do you double as furniture often?" She of course would have replied with chair and everything would have been chair. Chair solved. *Posted Wednesday 20th June at 16:08* [Comment . Like]

Madeline Cain NYC Cinderella Very fricken funny, guess the word Madeline's brain replaced with 'chair'. If you'd read the post properly, you would have seen that every 'chair' I heard was actually real, not a mental breakdown. I'm sure your response would have gone down real well with Miss Bellgrave, just like Laani's latest – "If I had a face like yours, I'd trade it in for a new model." That little diamond almost got Kim punched. There's no way I'd have you anywhere near me with a camera. You'd sabotage my shoes and replace any spares with embarrassing things from adult stores. *Posted Wednesday 20th June at 16:17* [Comment . Like]

Tim Gleeve I would have chaired with, "Sorry, I thought you were a jumping castle." *Posted Wednesday 20th June at 17:01* [Comment . Like]

Mike Cain That's so chair. How about, "Sorry, you looked like the world's tastiest orange, I had to have a bite." *Posted Wednesday 20th June at 17:17* [Comment . Like]

Tim Gleeve "Sorry, you looked like a soft place to park a bottom." *Posted Wednesday 20th June at 17:23* [Comment . Like]

Mike Cain "Sorry, it's midnight, I lost my shoe looking for my pumpkin." If I broke a shoe I'd fix that baby in ten seconds flat. I would be a hero – New York MacGyver. *Posted Wednesday 20th June at 17:33* [Comment . Like]

Tim Gleeve Girls would swoon at your... chair. *Posted Wednesday 20th June at 17:35* [Comment . Like]

Mike Cain Basically, I'd be Tony Stark with an Australian accent. *Posted Wednesday 20th June at 17:40* [Comment . Like]

Madeline Cain NYC Cinderella The only thing you and Tony Stark have in common is a spectacular ability to misunderstand women. And a well prepared look of innocence when one of your big experiments wanders up shit-creek. *Posted Wednesday 20th June at 19:20* [Comment . Like]

Mike Cain I am a fortress of innocence, if an experiment goes wrong ye will never know! *Posted Wednesday 20th June at 20:16* [Comment . Like]

Madeline Cain NYC Cinderella I will always know. Your poker face has so many holes I could use it as a sponge. *Posted Wednesday 20th June at 20:20* [Comment . Like]

Richard Arnoou Have to say I was very surprised to hear your detailed description of one child who now apparently makes a living taking photos for Japanese Tourists. *Posted Wednesday 20th June at 18:48* [Comment . Like]

Victoria Zeng And the one who makes a living doing photo-mugs for upmarket hotels in Bangkok. *Posted Wednesday 20th June at 18:55* [Comment . Like]

Cain Michaels And the one who does photographic day tours around the Angkor temples. *Posted Wednesday 20th June at 19:19* [Comment . Like]

Madeline Cain NYC Cinderella I'd like to see you do better under pressure. None of you had to stall an entire auction after your resting spot turned into a person. *Posted Wednesday 20th June at 19:31* [Comment . Like]

Kim Enuik On the plus side, entry to The Dragon's Den for life and a possible showing at the Guggenheim! Not doing bad for an unfocused wannabe. Also, made your *second* sale with that wedding lady, the first was with the Den. Even if you didn't get the money yourself but donated it. That's what happened right? You weren't mugged by a charity were you? *Posted Wednesday 20th June at 19:40* [Comment . Like]

Madeline Cain NYC Cinderella No, I wasn't mugged by a charity. Too bad free entry into the Den doesn't equate to free food from the Den bar. Maybe an offer to exhibit at the Guggenheim is enough to boost my portfolio... *Posted Wednesday 20th June at 19:50* [Comment . Like]

Tim Gleeve It depends on how racy the Romeo and Juliet display is. I don't know if exhibiting your banner with other rude art work is going to tarnish your reputation any more than that porn set incident... *Posted Wednesday 20th June at 19:59* [Comment . Like]

Madeline Cain NYC Cinderella Thanks for bringing that up when I'd almost wiped it from my memory. *Posted Wednesday 20th June at 20:50* [Comment . Like]

Tim Gleeve Social media and best friends never forget. *Posted Wednesday 20th June at 20:51* [Comment . Like]

Kevin Doherty Those NYC grates are dangerous, babe! They eat change, watches, belts, even homework. You've been lucky. *Posted Wednesday 20th June at 20:00* [Comment . Like]

Madeline Cain NYC Cinderella I don't feel lucky! Not after all that chaos and having to cancel our dinner tonight. *Posted Wednesday 20th June at 20:54* [Comment . Like]

Mike Cain Babe? Oink oink. *Posted Wednesday 20th June at 23:00* [Comment . Like]

Kevin Doherty Chaos? There was more? Sorry, I didn't get a chance to read it all, I had to duck out for more filming. Will get to it soon, promise. The plus side of missing tonight is the pilot episode is looking awesome! Um, who the hell is Mike? *Posted Thursday 21st June at 10:35* [Comment . Like]

Madeline Cain NYC Cinderella He's my idiot kid brother. Ignore him, he was dropped on his head as a baby. *Posted Thursday 21st June at 15:00* [Comment . Like]

Nadine Cain I'm so proud! You'd be able to see that banner from five hundred metres away! That's how much Jason likes your work. If only we'd been there to celebrate. I'd have shooed those up-start photographers away from you. I'd teach them to bully my daughter; a penis icicle would be the least of their worries.

I wish you'd been sensible enough to remove your shoes before you head butted that poor woman. Once at a party, your father let me wonder around a room for a whole hour with my dress tucked into my knickers. It's much worse when your own underwear's on display. Don't you worry about money any more love, things are finally starting to pick up with your father's business, we're far enough ahead to be able to give you seventy five dollars a week now! How wonderful is that? *Posted Thursday 21st June at 07:48* [Comment . Like]

Madeline Cain NYC Cinderella Wow Mum, that comment was like its own essay. You could have told me all that over the phone. Phones are great for telling people long stories. Thanks for the help; I'll still have to keep all my work with Giovanni but that seventy-five will stop me having to eat baked beans and alphabet spaghetti every night. Also, thanks for the overprotective rant, but I'd prefer it if you didn't penis icicle the people who were giving me helpful career advice. *Posted Thursday 21st June at 15:12* [Comment . Like]

Nadine Cain As long as they weren't being nasty… I do think *some* of their advice made sense darling, you need to think about what is going to make money. You're doing really well but maybe you should keep this as a hobby until the right opportunity. By the way, what happened to that lovely Cliff friend of yours? He hasn't made one peep at this post at all. *Posted Thursday 21st June at 17:00* [Comment . Like]

Madeline Cain NYC Cinderella Mum this IS the right opportunity! Only seven people get in a year. Seven! Out of hundreds of applicants. If I let this be a hobby I'll never be in the right place at the right time. This is what I want. And I don't know where Cliff is. *Posted Thursday 21st June at 19:13* [Comment . Like]

Kim Enuik I do, he's off writing in some cabin in the woods for two months over summer. How cliché. *Posted Thursday 21st June at 19:20* [Comment . Like]

Madeline Cain NYC Cinderella God damn it, how come everyone else knows what he's up to but me? Do I give off some sort of digital stench? Am I the Piranha of our social media circle? *Posted Thursday 21st June at 19:23* [Comment . Like]

Nadine Cain I think the word you're looking for is 'pariah', love. Alright, if it's your dream, it's your dream. Daddy and I will support your life choices whole-heartedly. As long as you don't end up like your beggar friend who yells at Mexican's with traffic-light-mind-powers. *Posted Thursday 21st June at 19:47* [Comment . Like]

Madeline Cain NYC Cinderella You've got to be in it to win it. You can't make a career in arts by halves. And I'm IN it! *Posted Thursday 21st June at 19:52* [Comment . Like]

Madeline Cain NYC Cinderella What did you do with those shoes, Victoria? *Posted Thursday 21st June at 20:30* [Comment . Like]

Victoria Zeng Buried them. *Posted Thursday 21st June at 22:57* [Comment . Like]

Madeline Cain NYC Cinderella likes **Awkward Family Photos.** *5 hours ago.* [Like]

Kate Nikle joined the group **Nightmare on Elmo Street** and **What NOT To Wear.** [Like . Join]

Mike Cain On viewing today's solar eclipse:

Attempt 1: Try various materials as viewing filters. Fail Miserably. Now require eye patch.
Attempt 2: Pirate look cultivated – decide to build a pin-hole 'camera'.

- Step 1: Wail at lack of building resources.
- Step 2: Construct the most amazing pinhole camera in the history of the universe, using scientific principles to relate the length of the tube to the size of the projected image. You know, the basics.
- Step 3: View Eclipse – puny now in comparison to the awesomeness that is my engineering genius.
- Finally: Deliver camera to Mother for her viewing pleasure. Spend rest of the day grounded for using pool-pump plumbing to construct said eclipse camera. Some people are just ungrateful.

Posted Thursday 21st June at 17:00 [Comment . Like]

Madeline Cain NYC Cinderella Serves you right you little sod. Bet you made her take you to the doctor too. What's the damage? Can I now refer to you as One-Eyed Mike or is this only a temporary road block in your plans to take over the world? *Posted Thursday 21st June at 20:31* [Comment . Like]

Mike Cain Nah, temporary, it's just a retina burn. I'll be right as two wrongs in a week. *Posted Thursday 21st June at 20:47* [Comment . Like]

Madeline Cain NYC Cinderella How can a person as stupidly smart as you continuously put yourself in danger without any serious repercussions? Bet at the end of the week that eye will come out with laser vision or some other ridiculously positive outcome. Why God bothered to pass the luck gene to you I'll never know. I'd make much better use of it. *Posted Thursday 21st June at 20:50* [Comment . Like]

Tim Gleeve I would have stolen a down pipe from one of the school buildings myself. That way, you're Mama's golden boy and your parents are none the wiser. You should have known better than to attack your Dad's pride and joy for spare parts though. *Posted Thursday 21st June at 21:00* [Comment . Like]

Madeline Cain NYC Cinderella Stop giving him ideas! Or when I get home I'll be giving you the two fisted Pirate Patch. *Posted Thursday 21st June at 21:03* [Comment . Like]

Tim Gleeve I'd like to see you try little stick arms. Unless you've been hitting the weights recently, I'll be sleeping easy tonight. *Posted Thursday 21st June at 21:07* [Comment . Like]

Madeline Cain NYC Cinderella I haven't been telling you half of what goes on in NYC, I'll leave the specifics up to your imagination. *Posted Thursday 21st June at 21:09* [Comment . Like]

Mike Cain Pfffft, we don't use the pool in winter, what's the problem? Plenty of time to put it all back together. *Posted Thursday 21st June at 21:12* [Comment . Like]

Tim Gleeve Dude, just because you're not using the pool doesn't mean the pool pump stops turning on once a day. *Posted Thursday 21st June at 21:15* [Comment . Like]

Madeline Cain NYC Cinderella See, stupidly smart. *Posted Thursday 21st June at 21:16* [Comment . Like]

Kim Enuik I can't, sorry. My pet rock died. *Posted Thursday 21st June at 21:20* [Comment . Like]

Madeline Cain NYC Cinderella Let me guess, your latest excuse to your parents as to why you won't join them in the Peruvian Amazon for summer holidays. *Posted Thursday 21st June at 21:22* [Comment . Like]

Kim Enuik Bingo. *Posted Thursday 21st June at 21:24* [Comment . Like]

Madeline Cain NYC Cinderella You need to ask yourself, what would be MORE catastrophic, you going there and chilling in a hammock, or them coming to New York and knowing everything you do... *Posted Thursday 21st June at 21:26* [Comment . Like]

Kim Enuik Aww Mad, that's not fair, why did you put that in my head? Right after my pet rock died too. *Posted Thursday 21st June at 21:30* [Comment . Like]

Kevin Doherty Duncan is their child too, they deserve the chance to say goodbye. *Posted Thursday 21st June at 21:40* [Comment . Like]

Cliff Wheeland Duncan is the lizard, not the rock. Best way out I can see is trading your big holidays for your little ones. Tell them you can't get away this summer but you CAN do a week in the mid-semester ones. You're going to have to see them sometime if you don't want them to know what really goes on here. May as well be for a week rather than a month. *Posted Thursday 21st June at 21:49* [Comment . Like]

Kim Enuik Fine, fine! Has anyone told you, you should be a lawyer rather than a writer? You'd be good at it. Not that I don't appreciate the advice, but shouldn't you be holed up in the woods somewhere writing? *Posted Thursday 21st June at 21:57* [Comment . Like]

Kevin Doherty Yeah, I know dude, just trying out my comedy. Better face to face I think, people take me too seriously in text. *Posted Thursday 21st June at 21:59* [Comment . Like]

Cliff Wheeland Right. Funny. Just had to duck out to the local town to send off some pages. Last connection with the outside world for a while, so don't let Duncan and Madeline be together alone while I'm gone, who knows what part of New York they'll break. *Posted Thursday 21st June at 22:01* [Comment . Like]

Madeline Cain NYC Cinderella Wait! Cliff! *Posted Thursday 21st June at 22:46* [Comment . Like]

Madeline Cain NYC Cinderella Gah! Who wants to talk to a know-it-all anyway? *Posted Thursday 21st June at 23:00* [Comment . Like]

Alexa McMarshal The naughty police made me post this... *Posted Thursday 22nd June at 04:30* [Comment . Like]

Jack Fox Yeeeahhh they did! *Posted Thursday 22nd June at 04:34* [Comment . Like]

Alexa McMarshal You got keys to these handcuffs officer? *Posted Thursday 22nd June at 04:40* [Comment . Like]

Madeline Cain NYC Cinderella Ok, seriously, we need to channel this somewhere where I don't have to see it. *Posted Thursday 22nd June at 07:59* [Comment . Like]

Kathy Bloomingdale Or dam it. *Posted Thursday 22nd June at 08:05* [Comment . Like]

Jack Fox I already dam it, if you know what I mean. *Posted Thursday 22nd June at 08:08* [Comment . Like]

Madeline Cain NYC Cinderella Damming it is *way* too dangerous; if it burst I think my eyes would spontaneously combust from the flood of innuendo. *Posted Thursday 22nd June at 08:21* [Comment . Like]

Tim Gleeve Maddie knows some film makers in NYC who need good dialogue… *Posted Thursday 22nd June at 08:59* [Comment . Like]

Kathy Bloomingdale likes the page **Bookshelf Porn.** *2 hours ago* [Like]

Claire Holderness has added you as a friend. [Confirm . Not Now]

Madeline Cain NYC Cinderella Holy Crappolla you're on Facebook!! What happened to 'I'd rather die a thousand deaths by flaming homing pigeons than set up a Facebook account'? *About 2 hours ago* [Comment . Like]

Claire Holderness I have not willing join yet somehow this fake account has amassed supporters like flies. No matter, this forced transition and uprising will be crushed. Vengeance will be mine. Facebook will know no ruler but me! #StormTheCastle #TrojanHorse

#TheOnlyWayToBringItDownIsFromTheInside *About 2 hours ago* [Comment . Like]

Tim Gleeve You need look no further for Minions than us! #AmassTheMinions *About 2 hours ago* [Comment . Like]

Madeline Cain NYC Cinderella You may not be excited you're here but I am! Though I don't know how I feel about you trailing Twitter hashtags with you like a bad smell. *About 2 hours ago* [Comment . Like]

Claire Holderness #FacebookWILLbeTheNewTwitter #TheTakeOverHasBegun. *About 2 hours ago* [Comment . Like]

Tim Gleeve likes the page **When I Die, Friends Will Go To The Funeral & Good Friends Will Cry. But Best Friends Will Change My Status To "Chillin' Wit Jesus".** *1 hour ago* [Like]

Did You DO It? Is That Why You're Holding Out On Me?.....[New Message]

[Back to messages. Mark as unread . Report spam . Delete]

Between **Kathy Bloomingdale** and **You.**

Kathy Bloomingdale 22 June 2012 at 09:00 [Report]

Why haven't I heard about your first date with Kevin yet? I was expecting a juicy story of lust, love and sexy times *days* ago. Why are you holding out on me? Was it because I told you I wouldn't be there until September? Or because Cliff managed to say hi to me for the five seconds he was online? I may have told you to be careful, but that doesn't mean I don't want a piece of washboard-abs-pie.

Madeline Cain NYC Cinderella 22 June 2012 at 15:35

Because there was *no* sexy time. The date didn't happen. Apart from the fact I was nursing blisters bigger than my face, Kevin couldn't make it; an opportunity came up to start filming his TV pilot. He was so excited I didn't want to ruin it for him. Also, I may have drunk a bottle and a half of red wine with Kim after the Ball. I wasn't capable of long conversations anyway.

Kathy Bloomingdale 22 June 2012 at 16:12 [Report]

He blew you off for TV? Typical male. First it's life and death duelling over the remote, then the next thing you know it's sucked them inside that little square box. It would have been horrible hangover time for you, but at least you'd have broken the date-bubble and moved on. That first-date-cherry is the worst.

Madeline Cain NYC Cinderella 22 June 2012 at 16:15

Huh? Date bubble cherry? Sounds like a new flavour of gum for single ladies. When have you been breaking date-bubbles?

Kathy Bloomingdale 22 June 2012 at 16:20 [Report]

First–date-cherry, get it right. And I've been out with plenty of guys, it's just the first date cherry was made of titanium. Hence being alone and getting my kicks from your relationships.

Madeline Cain NYC Cinderella 22 June 2012 at 16:22

So many guys I haven't heard a peep about them, hey? Anyway, Kevin didn't blow me off, he asked me to come. He said he felt really bad and still wanted to do the date. But I said I was pretty beat and would let him enjoy the filming of his Japanese game show thingy.

Kathy Bloomingdale 22 June 2012 at 16:29 [Report]

Huh? Japanese game show? He speaks Japanese? Ok, I need to reassess my mental image of him.

Madeline Cain NYC Cinderella 22 June 2012 at 16:35

No, it's *like* a Japanese game show, crossed with Thank God You're Here. It's called 'Your Job Or The Money'. Kevin goes to a contestant's work place in some random disguise and starts making a scene, if they play along and do the silly things they're asked to they win the jackpot that night. As a result the past couple of days have been bizarre; Kevin has greeted me on the landing between our apartments as no less than five different characters: an English Knight, a special forces army general, an astronaut, a pig farmer and a Power Ranger. If he had to speak Japanese too I think he would've melted. Can you develop Schizophrenia from immersing yourself in method acting?

Kathy Bloomingdale 22 June 2012 at 16:44 [Report]

Not that I've heard but method acting covers all kinds of neurosis. The show sounds like something Tim would watch. Ok, so Kevin was a no show (ha! Pun). Other than disrobing dignitaries, anything new with you?

Madeline Cain NYC Cinderella 22 June 2012 at 16:47

Thankfully my life has been as boring as daytime TV. It appears I used all my weird on the Ball. Giovanni has family over, a niece from Rome who's come for the 'American Dream'. Can't say my American Dream is working in a pizza shop. She tried to explain it to me, I think she said, "Meet Hunk, get hitched," but the accent was a little too thick to hear clearly. Oh, and get this, Giovanni has a son! His name is Dom.

Kathy Bloomingdale 22 June 2012 at 16:50 [Report]

He's Italian, of course he has a family. Probably taking over the family business.

Madeline Cain NYC Cinderella 22 June 2012 at 16:59

I don't know, I think Giovanni was ashamed of him. That's what it seemed like the other day when he visited the restaurant. He's so short I think he could have doubled as an Oompa Loompa, his slicked back hair only just made it to my eyebrows. He wore the most perfectly tailored suit I've ever seen, and had a stereotypical Godfather-esque hooked nose, a beak really, like a molehill on his face. I could have camped in there. He strutted in like he was John from Saturday Night Fever but with sex appeal in the negatives.

What he lacked in height he made up for in confidence, like he was channelling the personality of a six foot four sumo wrestler. He leaned against the front counter, flashed a slick smile and said, "How you doin'?"

I felt like I'd danced into a time-warp. Perhaps that's why I exchanged, "Welcome to Giovanni's," for, "It's not every day you play Russian Roulette on a scooter with a cab driver, but I'm alive, with only slightly elevated blood pressure, so I guess that means I'm doing fine."

If you had a sound track of a donkey braying crossed with the shrieks of chimp who'd just stolen his zoo keeper's pants, you would get Dom's laugh. It conveyed a type of manic glee that had me certain I'd misjudged yet *another* customer and I was going to get my own public version of *The Apprentice*. Potentially pants-less.

"You're funny! She's funny," he said to a passing waitress. He turned back to me, tapping a finger on the counter, a smile dimpling his face. "I like you. I like YOU! Not many people make me laugh, kid. Most of the jokers here are the polite and boring kind that stab you in the back. Bam! Like a viper. Know what I mean?"

Ummm, no…

"Anyone here ever gives you trouble, you let me know, I'll sort them out. Now, be a darl and get my father. He owns the joint."

Then he pressed a fiver into my hand. If I got five dollars every time I was a smart arse, I'd be a millionaire. Come to think of it, Mike would be a billionaire.

Kathy Bloomingdale 22 June 2012 at 17:10 [Report]

Where did he think you were? 1920's New York?

Madeline Cain NYC Cinderella 22 June 2012 at 17:16

Or Casablanca. Who'd he think he was, calling me kid? I'm not the one who looks like I need platform shoes to ride the rollercoaster at Disneyland.

But here was the strange thing, Giovanni went white when I told him. Well, being an olive skinned Italian that's impossible, but definitely paler than usual.

"Thank you Bella, I'll move him."

'Move' him? Giovanni was all thumbs as he dropped his handful of topping on the counter and raced to the entrance. With arm waving and shooing motions he ushered Dom into the small office near the back. He looked like a demented sheep herder, and he didn't touch Dom once. I've never seen him so eager to get someone out of the restaurant.

Kathy Bloomingdale 22 June 2012 at 17:20 [Report]

Dom sounds like a sleaze. Maybe he scares away customers with the monkey noises. Maybe he *refused* to take over the family business. That shit does not go down well in Italian culture.

Madeline Cain NYC Cinderella 22 June 2012 at 17:25

Maybe... I don't know, he was perfectly polite, even if he was smoozy to all the ladies. Kind of like a wannabe CEO: he dresses the part, acts the way he thinks a big business man would act and comes off looking slightly ridiculous. There's only so much you can play the part when you're that vertically handicapped. I kind of just wanted to give him a hug and some tea and biscuits. Maybe sit him on my knee and tell him a bedtime story.

Kathy Bloomingdale 22 June 2012 at 17:30 [Report]

Kind of like a guy who has the 'top job' in name, but the advisor is the puppet master? Bet Giovanni wants a 'real' boy for a son. Get it? Pinocchio?

Madeline Cain NYC Cinderella 22 June 2012 at 17:40

Ok, you *really* need to get better, all this daytime television is rotting your brain.

Kathy Bloomingdale 22 June 2012 at 17:42 [Report]

Did he say what he does? Surely I can count on your nosy curiosity.

Madeline Cain NYC Cinderella 22 June 2012 at 17:47

Not really, he was super vague, like Man of Mystery vague.

I asked, "So you're Giovanni's son? Do you run another pizzeria for him? Or are you taking over this one?"

He leaned in close, his chest pushing the menus off the counter. Only my lightning quick reflexes saved them. "Ah Bella, a pizza shop is too slow paced for me! I like the high life, I like to be *connected.* This little room can't give me that. So I spread my wings, I found my calling."

I nodded, but was as confused as Duncan near a Hawaiian shirt. "And, ah, what's that?"

He winked and tapped his nose. I didn't realise people actually did that in real life. "I bring people together. I make sure they know what's right for them, what they need, even if they don't know they need it yet."

Maybe he's a butler?

Kathy Bloomingdale 22 June 2012 at 17:50 [Report]

Maybe he's a stripper who spends his money on suits? They look bigger on stage I hear.

Madeline Cain NYC Cinderella 22 June 2012 at 17:52

Eew! Though in saying that, maybe he's a pimp?

Kathy Bloomingdale 22 June 2012 at 18:03 [Report]

Well, I can see Giovanni being ashamed of that last one. It certainly 'brings people together'. That phrase sounds more sinister than a good time though.

Madeline Cain NYC Cinderella 22 June 2012 at 18:07

Meh. Either way he gave me another ten 'for my trouble'. He's loaded and willing to share, that makes him a good guy in my book.

Anyway, I've got to get ready for work. Another hair pulling night of teaching Rosa, the niece, how not to drive a scooter through red lights like she's in her own version of Fast and the Furious.

Kathy Bloomingdale 22 June 2012 at 18:09 [Report]

Gah! You're never objective when people give you money. It's like they've handed you the secret formula to everlasting gobstoppers. Suddenly they can do no wrong.

Sad face on having to go to work. Can Rosa at least take phone orders?

Madeline Cain NYC Cinderella 22 June 2012 at 18:11

What can I say, the way to my heart is with gifts. No, Rosa didn't stay half an hour in that job, not after the deliverer came back covered in pizza. An irate meat-loving football team got the Vegetarian Supreme...

Kevin Doherty Listen to me. This is important. You're gonna find yourself in a closet one day screaming at whoever passes by it that you're a burrito. It's fine. It's cool. It's part of the package. Don't delay, get in your application for Your Job Or The Money today! *Posted Friday 22nd June at 19:12* [Comment . Like]

> **Kim Enuik** While that sounds epically appealing I'm afraid my schedule is piled up with schedule-ly stuff. Good luck finding some rhyming burritos for your show. *Posted Friday 22nd June at 19:20* [Comment . Like]
>
> **Kevin Doherty** Boo yeah, that last line did rhyme! And that one! I'm a lyrical genius. *Posted Friday 22nd June at 19:24* [Comment . Like]
>
> **Madeline Cain NYC Cinderella** I too shall pass on this, only

because I don't want to outshine you :p Also, Giovanni's is the thin line between me and living off dust bunnies. *Posted Friday 22nd June at 19:32* [Comment . Like]

Kevin Doherty Outshine me all you want babe, it's your right as my lady. *Posted Friday 22nd June at 19:46* [Comment . Like]

Lulu Tanaki When destruction becomes creativity…

Beanie (age 4): I need to break these bricks.
Me: Why's that mate?
Beanie: Because I'm an ARTIST!
… Fair enough.

Posted Friday 22nd June at 20:20 [Comment . Like]

Claire Holderness Happy Mother's Day to all the mums out there! Don't be too depressed you're not my mum, your kids are fine too, I guess… #MyMotherTaughtMeSelfConfidence #ItsOnlyRightTheBestMumGotTheBestKid. *Posted Friday 22nd June at 22:16* [Comment . Like]

Tim Gleeve #YouAreWeird. *Posted Friday 22nd June at 23:00* [Comment . Like]

Claire Holderness #Its1:20am #IJustSawSupermanForTheThirdTimeInFourDays #ThisIsNotNewInformation. *Posted Friday 22nd June at 01:20* [Comment . Like]

Virginia Lowe You do realise Mother's Day was a month ago right? *Posted Saturday 23rd June at 08:25* [Comment . Like]

Claire Holderness #ClearlyYoureDeluded there's a Mother's Day in every month, or do you #HateYourMum? #MyMotherTaughtMeToBeGrateful #NoWonderImTheBestKid. *Posted Saturday 23rd June at 08:50* [Comment . Like]

Virginia Lowe Way to help capitalists like Hallmark use our sentimentality against us. There're so many made up holidays you can't see where the capitalism ends and the *true* meaning begins. *Posted Saturday 23rd June at 08:52* [Comment . Like]

Tim Gleeve #Scrooge. *Posted Saturday 23rd June at 09:12* [Comment . Like]

Kathy Bloomingdale All holidays were made up at some point Vee, religion/tradition doesn't make one holiday more valid than another. *Posted Saturday 23rd June at 09:15* [Comment . Like]

Madeline Cain NYC Cinderella Your Mother wishes she could claim me as her child. *Posted Saturday 23rd June at 09:42* [Comment . Like]

Mike Cain #ILaughedSoHardIAlmostDied. *Posted Saturday 23rd June at 09:51* [Comment . Like]

Claire Holderness #ShameYouDidntSaidAngryCat Sorry, Maddie #YoureNiceAndStuff but #IAmTheBest. *Posted Saturday 23rd June at 09:54* [Comment . Like]

Ken Holderness I thought about debating you over who's the better kid…but I'll allow you your delusions #WereOnFacebookYouTool #HashtagsAreStupid #YeahIGetTheIrony. *Posted Saturday 23rd June at 09: 58* [Comment . Like]

Claire Holderness #WhoCouldntRememberMumsAddress #FunnyYouLivedThereToo #HashtagsAreAmazeballs. *Posted Saturday 23rd June at 10:02* [Comment . Like]

Mabel Holderness I love youse all!! *Posted Saturday 23rd June at 10:10* [Comment . Like]

Claire Holderness #ButMostlyMe. *Posted Saturday 23rd June at 10:12* [Comment . Like]

Mabel Holderness Yeah mostly you, xo. *Posted Saturday 23rd June at 10:14* [Comment . Like]

Ken Holderness The only accurate word there, was balls. *Posted Saturday 23rd June at 10:16* [Comment . Like]

Claire Holderness #HowAreYouEvenAlive #HashtagsAreAmazeballs #GoPragueorGoRome. *Posted Saturday 23rd June at 10:18* [Comment . Like]

Madeline Cain #HashtagsAreGrowingOnMe #LikeFungus. *Posted Saturday 23rd June at 10:25* [Comment . Like]

Mike Cain #MmmDeliciousFungus #IKnowHowYouFeelAboutFungusMad #IveAlwaysKnown. *Posted Saturday 23rd June at 10:50* [Comment . Like]

Claire Holderness #HashtagsAreTheFuture #BetAllOfKirksCaptainsLogsAreHashtags #CaptainKirkIsTheMan. *Posted Saturday 23rd June at 10:53* [Comment . Like]

Virginia Lowe Lord! Save me from this generation who think *everything* is a joke. *Posted Saturday 23rd June at 11:09* [Comment . Like]

Tim Gleeve #ActivistsHadHumourRemovedAtBirth #ShitHappensJustChill. *Posted Saturday 23rd June at 12:00* [Comment . Like]

Tim Gleeve No party is complete without a piñata. *Posted Saturday 23rd June at 15:00* [Comment . Like]

Derek Chan -> Tim Gleeve Dude, epic night last night. Seen the pics? *Posted Saturday 23rd June at 15:00* [Comment . Like]

Tim Gleeve Whoops, I wasn't meant to poke my tongue out. *Posted Saturday 23rd June at 15:00* [Comment . Like]

Derek Chan I understand, it's difficult to keep it in your mouth. *Posted Saturday 23rd June at 15:00* [Comment . Like]

Madeline Cain NYC Cinderella Wow gents, that went downhill quickly… *Posted Saturday 23rd June at 15:00* [Comment . Like]

Kim Enuik Laani the abusive umbrella strikes again: "Did you know you look like an angel? No, really, cherubs are short and fat as well." Next time I go to borrow Maddie's stuff, I'll choose something that isn't inhabited by a poltergeist. *Posted Saturday 23rd June at 16:17* [Comment . Like]

Mike Cain Don't know how I haven't been picked up by a talent scout yet. *Posted Saturday 23rd June at 17:16* [Comment . Like]

Madeline Cain NYC Cinderella Or thrown out a window. *Posted Saturday 23rd June at 17:20* [Comment . Like]

Cain Michaels and **Kevin Doherty** are attending **Stare Dramatically Into The Distance During The Middle of A Sentence Day**. *Posted about 15 hours ago* [RSVP to this event]

Madeline Cain Jobless I actually give up. Life can suck a fat one. *Posted about an hour ago* [Comment . Like]

77

Help! I'm Going To Live Off Dust Bunnies.....[New Message]

[Back to messages. Mark as unread . Report spam . Delete]

Between **Josh Annelli, Jade Annelli, 4 others** and **You.**

Madeline Cain Jobless 24 June 2012 at 13:00

How can this be happening? I won't even get a *chance* to try anything new. I'll just be surviving, Bear Grills style, toothless and eating dog food from a dumpster which will double as my shelter from the harsh elements.

Josh Annelli 24 June 2012 at 13:05 [Report]

Ok Maddie, slow down. I thought we were trying to find your 'passion'. Why are you suddenly talking about living in a dumpster?

Madeline Cain Jobless 24 June 2012 at 13:07

Giovanni cut my hours to one night a week! What sort of cruel boss has you train your replacement? Mike always said you should never trust a man with a Luigi moustache. I should have let her crash the scooter. I should have let her deliver to Screech and his merry band of OCD misfits. I shouldn't have shown her my secret to perfect cheese distribution! She is the destroyer of bank balances, the harbinger of homelessness, the job version of a body snatcher.

Jade Annelli 24 June 2012 at 13:09 [Report]

At least Giovanni didn't fire you. Why did he hire another person though? Were you delivering pizzas one slice short?

Madeline Cain Jobless 24 June 2012 at 13:12

As good as fired me, it's a quarter of my hours! How can I look for a job, complete our assignments and build my portfolio all at once?

Apparently blood is thicker than hard work, loyalty and constant praise from Manhattan's eclectic pizza orderers. He cut my hours so he could give his niece, Rosa, full time work. I'm not even sure she has a green card, or even understands the word 'work'.

"It's family, Bella, you understand, you'd do the same for your brother."

Actually, no, no I wouldn't. Mike could go eat dirt for all I care. With all the shit he's pulled.

Jarrah Annelli 24 June 2012 at 13:16 [Report]

It's not the end of the world, hon.

Cain Michaels 24 June 2012 at 13:18 [Report]

It might be if she has to eat the cardboard of her Cheerios packet to feel full.

Jarrah Annelli 24 June 2012 at 13:20 [Report]

Not helpful ice machine! Look, there's six of us here, if we can't figure something out I'm sure Kim could. That boy would eat his own shoe before he'd introduce Duncan to a potentially sex crazed, beer pong playing, lizard hating, medical student.

Richard Arnoou 24 June 2012 at 13:21 [Report]

Just in case, start dropping hints about your bank balance situation…

Victoria Zeng 24 June 2012 at 13:22 [Report]

I love shoes but I don't think eating them is good for digestion. We need to do this to save Kim from blocked intestines as much as to help Madeline.

Madeline Cain Jobless 24 June 2012 at 13:30

Maybe you don't understand how dire this situation is:

- In three weeks my meagre savings run out and it's two months until my next scholarship payment.
- The seventy-five a week my parents are giving me basically covers my toilet time for the month. Or perhaps one square metre of my room.
- I am wasting the biggest career opportunity I have every minute I'm not building a portfolio.
- A second job will cut my assignment time to zero, zip, zilch. Unless I luck out and get Peter Parker's job photographing super heroes, I doubt I could find a job that covers all the haphazard topics Jason feels are essential for our education. Which means crashing and burning at college, which equals Jason giving up on me, which equals penniless artist on a plane back to Australia for which the ticket was paid for by the auctioning of her immortal soul on Ebay.

How can I possibly manage all three at once? I can barely manage one thing without causing a national incident!

Richard Arnoou 24 June 2012 at 13:33 [Report]

I'd bid for your immortal soul, no use wasting talent on a Satanist.

Kim Enuik 24 June 2012 at 13:35 [Report]

Giovanni's sucked all your spare time away; I thought you'd be happy at a chance to break free? Or will you miss all you strange new delivery friends?

Madeline Cain Jobless 24 June 2012 at 13:36

How did Kim get added to this conversation?

Kim Enuik 24 June 2012 at 13:36 [Report]

Doesn't matter how, what matters is keeping creepers away from Duncan.

Josh Annelli 24 June 2012 at 13:37 [Report]

Guilty.

Jade Annelli 24 June 2012 at 13:40 [Report]

I've never been good at multitasking, it makes you grey-skinned and bony. So I always look for a way to combine everything into one. It's what writers do, go on one trip and write articles from a million different angles.

Madeline Cain Jobless 24 June 2012 at 13:41

I suppose…Though merging that lot sounds like trying to juggle three puffer fish and a sashimi knife. How do you suggest we do this?

Jarrah Annelli 24 June 2012 at 13:42 [Report]

Right, so we're aiming to get paid for assignments, while building a portfolio for each photography type so we can help your poor brain decide where to funnel your creative juices.

Richard Arnoou 24 June 2012 at 13:43 [Report]

You make her sound like a car.

Cain Michaels 24 June 2012 at 13:45 [Report]

If she tries to do all three separately she'll be guzzling fuel faster than a Chrysler. So, to put it into terms your beard will understand, we're trying to metaphorically compact Madeline into her pizza scooter.

Richard Arnoou 24 June 2012 at 13:45 [Report]

Got ya. Too bad we're not doing you; I could metaphorically fit your clean shaven baby-face into a bicycle seat.

Kim Enuik 24 June 2012 at 13:46 [Report]

Alright boys, settle down, you're both the wittiest bullies in the playground. Right, let's nail this! How many assignments do you have?

Richard Arnoou 24 June 2012 at 13:46 [Report]

Six.

Madeline Cain Jobless 24 June 2012 at 13:47

You sure? It seems like Jason springs one on us every time we see him.

Cain Michaels 24 June 2012 at 13:48 [Report]

Earth to Giovanni's Pizza Slave, we see him for one week once a month. Six months left gives us six intentionally confusing, non-specific assignments.

Victoria Zeng 24 June 2012 at 13:49 [Report]

Yeah, you can mould those assignments into anything. For the last one I did a feature on tea cups.

Richard Arnoou 24 June 2012 at 13:50 [Report]

That was good, very relevant.

Madeline Cain Jobless 24 June 2012 at 13:50

It was?

Jade Annelli 24 June 2012 at 13:51 [Report]

See this *was* a good thing. You missed half the catch-ups we had showing each other our photos. Now we can hang out more in person. Facebook time doesn't count.

Kim Enuik 24 June 2012 at 13:53 [Report]

Focus people! My chameleon's future mental health is at stake. Six assignments – do you know what they're about?

Josh Annelli 24 June 2012 at 13:55 [Report]

If you have the ability to look at a tree and photograph a pig (*not* as hard as it sounds) then Jason's assignments are a piece of cake. They're made to be applied to anything that takes your fancy. All his descriptions sound so vague, but that's only to get you desperate enough to understand. You think outside the box, and outside the box around *that,* to get your photo.

Cain Michaels 24 June 2012 at 13:56 [Report]

I've never had to resort to ugly subjects so it keeps me happy.

Kim Enuik 24 June 2012 at 13:56 [Report]

To survive and ace your grades you need at least a job a month so you can incorporate your assignments into the thing you get paid for.

Madeline Cain Jobless 24 June 2012 at 13:57

At least six jobs, but how are we going to get something that allows me variety AND builds my portfolio? I can't just get a part-timer job again, it won't be broad enough, and before anyone suggests it, I REFUSE to be a taxi driver.

Kim Enuik 24 June 2012 at 13:58 [Report]

I would trust you behind the wheel as much as I would trust Duncan behind the wheel. If I ever suggest that to you, admit me to the asylum immediately.

Josh Annelli 24 June 2012 at 13:59 [Report]

That's where *we* come in. We have five different photography jobs among the six of us. Plus, there's Fashion Week.

Cain Michaels 24 June 2012 at 14:01 [Report]

Bah! Fashion Week, all that work for no pay. Sure, perving is food for the soul but it doesn't pay the bills.

Jade Annelli 24 June 2012 at 14:02 [Report]

Yeah, but it's one less assignment we've got to worry about because Jason said it's mandatory to attend.

Madeline Cain Jobless 24 June 2012 at 14:03

More worried about those bills. I have nightmares of them growing teeth and slowly gnawing my legs off…

Jarrah Annelli 24 June 2012 at 14:04 [Report]

We can be one of your six jobs. Jade and I get our modest side cash with tabloid work.

Madeline Cain Jobless 24 June 2012 at 14:04

You're paparazzi?

Jade Annelli 24 June 2012 at 14:05 [Report]

It's amazing what a pretty face and a promise of a nude portrait can do to jog a doorman's dialling thumb.

Madeline Cain Jobless 24 June 2012 at 14:05

You're portrait paparazzi?

Jarrah Annelli 24 June 2012 at 14:06 [Report]

We don't make money off the portraits yet – we're building our portfolio.

Jade Annelli 24 June 2012 at 14:06 [Report]

But we like the celeb invasion work, gets us into all the right parties.

Jarrah Annelli 24 June 2012 at 14:06 [Report]

Plus a good shot of a hot personality going commando is worth 5g.

Madeline Cain Jobless 24 June 2012 at 14:07

Five grand! Are you serious? What does drunk get?

Jarrah Annelli 24 June 2012 at 14:07 [Report]

Pfft – Five hundred. They're a less classy lot than they pretend, we get a lot of those.

Richard Arnoou 24 June 2012 at 14:08 [Report]

'Secret' dinners?

Jade Annelli 24 June 2012 at 14:08 [Report]

Fifteen hundred.

Cain Michaels 24 June 2012 at 14:08 [Report]

Gay love affair?

Jade Annelli 24 June 2012 at 14:08 [Report]

Affairs = seven or eight grand.

Kim Enuik 24 June 2012 at 14:08 [Report]

Hotel trashing?

Jarrah Annelli 24 June 2012 at 14:08 [Report]

Three thousand.

Josh Annelli 24 June 2012 at 14:08 [Report]

Out with the kids?

Jade Annelli 24 June 2012 at 14:09 [Report]

One thousand, surprisingly those photos are like Mummy fly-paper. Two thousand if it's a shot of her new lover playing Dad.

Cain Michaels 24 June 2012 at 14:10 [Report]

Attack of the Paparazzi by irate male hunk?

Jarrah Annelli 24 June 2012 at 14:12 [Report]

Oh, we never run with the Pack, they turn up, we leave. Photos are worth nothing if there are ten of you, you're lucky to get two hundred bucks. That's why we groom our own loyal sources.

Victoria Zeng 24 June 2012 at 14:12 [Report]

So red carpet photos...

Jarrah Annelli 24 June 2012 at 14:12 [Report]

All the mags have their payroll photographers there, isn't worth it.

Jade Annelli 24 June 2012 at 14:13 [Report]

Topless photos and celebs with cellulite apparently sell for twenty-five grand, but there's not much chest baring in New York. Such a shame...

Cain Michaels 24 June 2012 at 14:13 [Report]

Except in your studio.

Jarrah Annelli 24 June 2012 at 14:14 [Report]

? Indeed.

Jade Annelli 24 June 2012 at 14:15 [Report]

So, we'll bring you in on any juicy tips and put you in contact with our buyers from the mags. You can do it as often as you need.

Jarrah Annelli 24 June 2012 at 14:16 [Report]

It's not for everyone, there's a fair bit of hiding, generally in the cold...

Jade Annelli 24 June 2012 at 14:16 [Report]

We go full stealth mode – scrap our big cameras for little hidden cameras in hats and accessories.

Kim Enuik 24 June 2012 at 14:17 [Report]

Who are you? Maxwell Smart and 99?

Jade Annelli 24 June 2012 at 14:17 [Report]

That's Maxwella to you!

Madeline Cain Jobless 24 June 2012 at 14:18

For that kind of money, I'm there! Maybe I should just do *that* for a living.

Richard Arnoou 24 June 2012 at 14:19 [Report]

Keep your eyes on the prize. You need to try all types to find your passion (*and* make money), which is why you're working my next concert gig with me in August.

Cain Michaels 24 June 2012 at 14:19 [Report]

Who's on this time?

Richard Arnoou 24 June 2012 at 14:20 [Report]

Lost in Transfusion.

Kim Enuik 24 June 2012 at 14:20 [Report]

OMG! Take me with you! Maddie, seriously, I'll take the snaps and you get the dosh. I've been known to take good shoots.

Madeline Cain Jobless 24 June 2012 at 14:22

Yeah, about 5% of the time. The rest of the time it's just blurry frames of colour because you couldn't stop dancing for long enough. You are *not* representing me, my reputation would be buggered.

Josh Annelli 24 June 2012 at 14:23 [Report]

Where are the concerts?

Richard Arnoou 24 June 2012 at 14:23 [Report]

Most of mine are in Madison Square Garden.

Victoria Zeng 24 June 2012 at 14:23 [Report]

They have concerts in a garden?

Kim Enuik 24 June 2012 at 14:24 [Report]

Heck no – Madison Square Garden is that massive round building on Pennsylvania Plaza. It's a stadium.

Victoria Zeng 24 June 2012 at 14:24 [Report]

But if it's round, why call it a square?

Kim Enuik 24 June 2012 at 14:25 [Report]

I don't know!? Because the block is square, because there's a square outside. Who cares? Lost in Transfusion is playing and I need in!

Josh Annelli 24 June 2012 at 14:26 [Report]

So you work for the Garden as part of their paid media package?

Richard Arnoou 24 June 2012 at 14:26 [Report]

Basically. It's one of the major places a band can have their concert filmed and captured. Sometimes, they want backstage shots and I get to meet them.

Kim Enuik 24 June 2012 at 14:27 [Report]

Dsfahbuswe$&ofrtdpsljvbgehwj&#@%okld;s]zx'cm^,njghwe2orfe

Cain Michaels 24 June 2012 at 14:27 [Report]

Alright dude, check yourself before you wreck yourself.

Kim Enuik 24 June 2012 at 14:28 [Report]

I'm not *that* bad, it was Duncan.

Madeline Cain Jobless 24 June 2012 at 14:28

Sure, blame the Mexican horror show.

Kim Enuik 24 June 2012 at 14:28 [Report]

Giant moon-babies, how many times do I have to tell you he's from Madagascar?! There's nothing horrifying about him.

Madeline Cain Jobless 24 June 2012 at 14:29

I'm not here to pick a fight with you Kim, but… I did wake up to a white lizard on my chest yesterday morning. After freaking out that I had somehow rolled over, crushed Duncan and this was his ghost back to haunt me, I find that he'd just decided to roll in a bag of flour. He deserves the name calling.

Richard, that sounds amazing, are you sure they'll go for two photographers?

Cain Michaels 24 June 2012 at 14:29 [Report]

They will if we tart you up a bit.

Jade Annelli 24 June 2012 at 14:29 [Report]

Cain! If you weren't gay I'd call you a pervert.

Richard Arnoou 24 June 2012 at 14:30 [Report]

Easy, this is a *big* gig.

Kim Enuik 24 June 2012 at 14:30 [Report]

Better not let Madeline near it then.

Josh Annelli 24 June 2012 at 14:30 [Report]

If we're not letting her near concerts then taking her along to my school portrait gig is probably bad, right?

Cain Michaels 24 June 2012 at 14:31 [Report]

She may get mugged by eight year olds.

Madeline Cain Jobless 24 June 2012 at 14:31

Alright, enough! I'm here for solutions, not insults for imagined scenarios. I haven't screwed up yet! Josh, you're proposing I work with children? Do they even do photos without a peace sign or the KISS tongue? Are they sanitary?

Josh Annelli 24 June 2012 at 14:32 [Report]

School portraits are a fine art between being a photographer, an entertainer and your scariest school teacher, the one you were sure had eyes in the back of their head.

Jarrah Annelli 24 June 2012 at 14:32 [Report]

You're forgetting to mention 'parent smoozer'. The more you charm the single ladies, the less discipline you have to do.

Josh Annelli 24 June 2012 at 14:33 [Report]

I do like the Mums.

Richard Arnoou 24 June 2012 at 14:33 [Report]

Moms. M-O-M. Bet it's that bloody English accent that has them hooked.

Victoria Zeng 24 June 2012 at 14:33 [Report]

Ah yes, your own episode of the Bachelor but with single moms.

Cain Michaels 24 June 2012 at 14:34 [Report]

The term you're looking for is MILF.

Josh Annelli 24 June 2012 at 14:35 [Report]

There are perks I get that aren't afforded to teachers, it's true. But really, they're needed to offset the shear mayhem that is school photo day.

Madeline Cain Jobless 24 June 2012 at 14:35

I'll leave the charming of the MILFs to you Josh, I'm more into Kevin.

Cain Michaels 24 June 2012 at 14:35 [Report]

Don't let the chaos turn you off. I'm sure there are plenty of DILF's to offset all the odd children you'll attract.

Madeline Cain Jobless 24 June 2012 at 14:36

Again, Kevin.

Josh Annelli 24 June 2012 at 14:36 [Report]

Once, I had a kid give me a glass of milk and a cookie like I was some ginger version of Santa. He told me I couldn't do good work on an empty stomach, 'Elephant Juice' would help. He proceeded to tell me the biological process of milk production via elephant trunk. Very well thought out, don't know how they missed it in my school lessons.

Jarrah Annelli 24 June 2012 at 14:36 [Report]

Then there are all the young boys who think you're good for sex advice.

Jade Annelli 24 June 2012 at 14:36 [Report]

One classic one liner was: Tell your wife she looks pretty, even if she looks like a truck.

Josh Annelli 24 June 2012 at 14:37 [Report]

Solid advice. But it was the kid giving *me* counsel, not the other way around. I also had one kid tell me you could tell Mrs K and Mr X were married because they yelled at the same kids. Then he rugby tackled me around the groin.

Madeline Cain Jobless 24 June 2012 at 14:38

This is convincing me to do this, how?

Josh Annelli 24 June 2012 at 14:38 [Report]

I got three phone numbers and some good nights. Plus, the school bought extra expensive prints to make up for boisterous behaviour. It's a lucrative industry managed by pulling faces, guilt trips and lightning fast reflexes that miss poked tongues and peace symbols every time.

Richard Arnoou 24 June 2012 at 14:38 [Report]

Besides, you know you want your own glass of Elephant Juice.

Victoria Zeng 24 June 2012 at 14:39 [Report]

If you say Elephant Juice to someone across the room it looks like you're saying 'I love you'.

Madeline Cain Jobless 24 June 2012 at 14:39

Who can say no to snotty noses, milk from a trunk and love filled lip syncing? Done. When's the next one?

Josh Annelli 24 June 2012 at 14:39 [Report]

Two weeks. Just in time to save your bacon. Basically, it's portrait photography with little barbarians. Make 'em look like angels and you have a high turnover Manhattan career.

Richard Arnoou 24 June 2012 at 14:39 [Report]

Hold on, that's in the middle of the school holidays? How does that work?

Josh Annelli 24 June 2012 at 14:40 [Report]

Elite day-care centres for ages of two to twelve close for no man! The centre wants a record of how fantastic they've been at rescuing socialites from their three month summer jail service. I'll be flying in from London the day before; jetlag helps with the mum-sympathy.

Kim Enuik 24 June 2012 at 14:41 [Report]

Unless those kids have got the moves like Jagger, you've just described my hell. Thank you for pulling Maddie from the depths of the spagettio tin fort she has erected in our cupboard. Now she'll be able to buy food that hasn't been preserved. Three down, three to go, until my reptilian life companion can roam safe in the knowledge he won't be dropkicked by some uneducated jock demonstrating his latest technique.

Madeline Cain Jobless 24 June 2012 at 14:42

Rather than messaging from the room across the hall, you should come and extract said reptilian life-companion from my laundry basket. It appears a fearsome set of socks has challenged him to a wrestling match.

Kim Enuik 24 June 2012 at 14:42 [Report]

He knows fate could snatch you from him at any moment. He's demonstrating what he'll do to those who wish to separate him from his food source. Spagettios aren't a good source of vitamin for him, you really should buy something else.

Madeline Cain Jobless 24 June 2012 at 14:43

He's been eating my food?! Does he have a can opener for a jaw?

Cain Michaels 24 June 2012 at 14:43 [Report]

That's nasty Maddie, how long have you been a walking spaghetti bowl? Good thing you get that horrible child episode out of the way so you can focus on what's really important, your Lifestyle Photography session with Mwah!

Richard Arnoou 24 June 2012 at 14:44 [Report]

Isn't that just a fancy version of a bikini girl showing off a Ferrari at a car show? You're an ad-man without the creative control.

Cain Michaels 24 June 2012 at 14:44 [Report]

Don't know if you've been living under a rock the size of Minnesota, but have you heard of a little thing called 'Mad Men'? This shit is classy.

Richard Arnoou 24 June 2012 at 14:44 [Report]

Mmm, photos of glasses and kids playing with Tonka Trucks.

Cain Michaels 24 June 2012 at 14:45 [Report]

I can do that shit in my sleep, that's pocket change for me. The real work is in the travel mags, the women's mags, and the celebs in their homes looking for a piece of class. None of this stock-background-with-sponged-on-blue-paint nonsense. I show who people *are* in these photos as well as their pretty, Photo-shopped faces.

Victoria Zeng 24 June 2012 at 14:45 [Report]

Why are you Photo-shopping people, aren't they too far away from the lens for it to matter? The whole point of Lifestyle being to include the background and all.

Cain Michaels 24 June 2012 at 14:45 [Report]

Most people need help; the quality of make-up application is, quite frankly, appalling. Also, some part of the face is always asymmetric. I just apply the cosmetic surgery they always wanted.

Madeline Cain Jobless 24 June 2012 at 14:45

That is both offensive and enticing. I'm not sure if I should slap you or have you to do my profile pic. Don't know if taking photos of people pretending to enjoy things in a fake scene is really my thing…

Cain Michaels 24 June 2012 at 14:46 [Report]

Seriously? Making shit look awesome should be any photographer's *thing*.

Kim Enuik 24 June 2012 at 14:46 [Report]

Also, spagettio tins.

Richard Arnoou 24 June 2012 at 14:46 [Report]

You can't be picky when you're cupboard is stocked for a zombie apocalypse.

Cain Michaels 24 June 2012 at 14:47 [Report]

Excuse me?! Did you just insinuate my passion to be some kind of lower class photography? In comparison to a room full of six-year-old terrorist wannabes? I've seen the inside of more mansions than you've seen the outside of!

Richard Arnoou 24 June 2012 at 14:47 [Report]

So have those six-year-old terrorists.

Madeline Cain Jobless 24 June 2012 at 14:49

Cain, cool the fire before you set your pants alight. It doesn't sound like my thing, but then again I might do it and think it's better than blue cheese. So I'm in.

I think this is going to work! I feel like the giant snake that's been constricting my chest has just been attacked by a venomous version of Duncan and wrestled into submission. At this rate, with Victoria's potential gig, I'll only need to find one more job to make it through. Alright, Victoria, lay it on me.

Victoria Zeng 24 June 2012 at 14:50 [Report]

How do you feel about giant inflatable blimps?

Madeline Cain Jobless 24 June 2012 at 14:50

Positively?

Kim Enuik 24 June 2012 at 14:50 [Report]

Not me, those things go down in fiery balls of flame.

Madeline Cain Jobless 24 June 2012 at 14:50

Are we going flying?

Victoria Zeng 24 June 2012 at 14:50 [Report]

What are you two talking about?

Josh Annelli 24 June 2012 at 14:51 [Report]

What are *you* talking about?

Victoria Zeng 24 June 2012 at 14:51 [Report]

Thanksgiving Day parade... You know, giant blow up Snoopy's and the like. I do event photography. I have a ton of events before then but after you're finished with the rest of these guys sounds like you'll need something near the end of the year. And I have those loveable giants booked!

Madeline Cain Jobless 24 June 2012 at 14:52

Thank God! I thought it was some kind of metaphor.

Cain Michaels 24 June 2012 at 14:52 [Report]

For what? Bloated giant.

Richard Arnoou 24 June 2012 at 14:52 [Report]

A hot air balloon ride to the moon?

Madeline Cain Jobless 24 June 2012 at 14:52

Don't you give me that traitors! I know you had visions of cartoon characters blown up like a bowling ball and talking like pubescent Donald Ducks when comically popped.

Victoria Zeng 24 June 2012 at 14:52 [Report]

You're not too far off. The guys who blow them up have squeak wars.

Jade Annelli 24 June 2012 at 14:53 [Report]

If only we could capture that on film. Maybe they'd inhale enough helium to have one of those floating tea parties in Mary Poppins.

Madeline Cain Jobless 24 June 2012 at 14:53

Back to the matter of my sanity and ability to be able to eat something other than cardboard, what does event photography involve?

Victoria Zeng 24 June 2012 at 14:53 [Report]

Anything from brochures to newspapers to capturing the crowds enjoying the show. We'll be doing all of those things for the parade.

Kim Enuik 24 June 2012 at 14:54 [Report]

Describe it in one word please.

Victoria Zeng 24 June 2012 at 14:54 [Report]

We 'chronicle'.

Cain Michaels 24 June 2012 at 14:54 [Report]

I imagine a lot of full bodied shots are involved. You know, to take in the shoes.

Victoria Zeng 24 June 2012 at 14:54 [Report]

Don't insult me! I'm a professional. I take the shoe photos when I tell them I'm checking the lighting. Got a whole album, wanna see?

Madeline Cain Jobless 24 June 2012 at 14:54

Maybe next time, but that sounds amazing. I can't believe it, we did it! We managed to cover assignments AND portfolio jobs AND get paid. I could smother you all in kisses right now. Just one more job to see me through. Wait, you all get paid well, right?

Josh Annelli 24 June 2012 at 14:55 [Report]

Save the drool for the lizard. I told you it could be done and yes we do. We'll tackle the assignment topics when we know them, it will be a cinch.

Jarrah Annelli 24 June 2012 at 14:55 [Report]

With all that free time off from Giovanni's you can try out the more specialised types for fun. I'm sure Cliff can hook up another session, he seems to know everyone. Then there's wild life photography at the zoo… sport photography…

Richard Arnoou 24 June 2012 at 14:55 [Report]

Weird arse, self-obsessed arty-farty photographs with Cain.

Cain Michaels 24 June 2012 at 14:55 [Report]

At least it fills a gallery with people rather than filling a CD case booklet no one will buy. Every hipster these days is a pirate!

Madeline Cain Jobless 24 June 2012 at 14:56

Stop ruining my happiness with your crazy, boys. I'm going to make this! This is happening! Surely I'll find my passion from one of these.

Victoria Zeng 24 June 2012 at 14:56 [Report]

What if you don't? What if you like them all equally? How will you choose?

Kim Enuik 24 June 2012 at 14:56 [Report]

Aaaannnnddd we're done here. No more of this undoing all our good work thank you very much.

Madeline Cain Jobless 24 June 2012 at 14:57

Oh god. What if Victoria is right? What if I'm as undecided at the end of the year as I was at the ball? Goodbye baseball-of-opportunity, Madeline has hit a home run and you're out of the park? I'll have to go home. I'm not ready to go home yet!

Josh Annelli 24 June 2012 at 14:57 [Report]

Calm your horses. At least you'll have a solid portfolio to show for it. Then you'll be like every other young person, applying for jobs that kind of fit your degree and seeing what sticks. All that work won't go to waste.

Jarrah Annelli 24 June 2012 at 14:57 [Report]

Don't forget to trust the Universe. You're *doing* stuff now; you're letting the Universe know you're ready. At some point in the next six months a massive opportunity will appear and you'll *know*, you know?

Richard Arnoou 24 June 2012 at 14:58 [Report]

Think you're taking the yoga stuff a little too far. Biggest copout ever.

Jarrah Annelli 24 June 2012 at 14:58 [Report]

Your beard's the biggest copout ever. Do you even have a face?

Madeline Cain Jobless 24 June 2012 at 14:58

No Richard, she's right. Every time I've opened myself to life, something amazing has happened. What about the double whammy at the start of the year? I pulled myself out of a creative black hole and found myself the photo that headlined the ball! And in a round-about way, I got Kevin. I've just got to put the signals out there.

Kim Enuik 24 June 2012 at 14:59 [Report]

There we go, good on you! Now everyone else shut it. Duncan is finally looking less green about the whole situation.

Madeline Cain Jobless 24 June 2012 at 14:59

If you want him to look less green then get him out of my facemask. It only works on people, NOT amphibians!

Cain Michaels 24 June 2012 at 14:59 [Report]

I'm gonna leave you two to your domestic, first world problems. We'll talk deets when I'm back from holidays. Byyyeee.

Richard Arnoou 24 June 2012 at 14:59 [Report]

Amen. R out.

Jade Annelli 24 June 2012 at 15:00 [Report]

Byeee! Got a date!

Jarrah Annelli 24 June 2012 at 15:00 [Report]

We've got a date. See you in a few weeks.

Victoria Zeng 24 June 2012 at 15:00 [Report]

See ya. I'm for a design class. Get to make my own shoes!

Josh Annelli 24 June 2012 at 15:00 [Report]

Catch ya on the flip side.

Kim Enuik 24 June 2012 at 15:03 [Report]

I feel kind of abandoned.

Madeline Cain Jobless 24 June 2012 at 15:03

Yeah. I feel like I've been attacked with a meat tenderiser. Bam! We've got a plan. Bam! May not work. Bam! Sorry. Bam! Gone. Guess I'll just have to wait on the Universe. At least I've got some jobs. Come-to-Mama fresh fruit and vegies! I'm gonna have salad fun times!

Kim Enuik 24 June 2012 at 15:04 [Report]

Bloody Universe. Waltzes around like it's made of gold but when it comes to sharing a bit of the good fortune it refuses to break off a finger. The Universe has never helped me out; everything I have is all because of Kim-awesome-sauce-Enuik. My advice: Fuck the Universe. Get shit done yourself.

Madeline Cain Jobless 24 June 2012 at 15:04

Right… I think your whole Universe concept is a little more warped than mine.

Kyle Traybna "Oak not only hits the spot, it goes to the spots funeral dressed in inappropriate clothing." You had me at 'chocolate milk'. *Posted Tuesday 26th June at 09:14* [Comment . Like]

Tim Gleeve Trying to end a conversation with an old high school acquaintance is like battling a sea-monster with an infinite capacity to revive itself. Face, meet Palm. *Posted Wednesday 27th June at 10:20* [Comment . Like]

Kate Nikle likes the page **Get Real, No One Is Going To Form A Single Line If The Building Is On FIRE.** [Like]

Madeline Cain Jobless My life works better in theory than it does in practice. *Posted Wednesday 27th June at 11:00* [Comment . Like]

> **Mike Cain** What's so theoretical about it, you breathe for a while then you die. I'd say you're heading in the right direction. Being an ideas man, I'm working on a philosopher's stone so it's gonna work out different for me. I promise to remember you for like, a century or two after you kark it. *Posted Wednesday 27th June at 17:00* [Comment . Like]

Madeline Cain Jobless Chances are you'll end up exploding yourself in alchemic experiments long before I die in the arms of my twenty year old toy-boy. *Posted Wednesday 27th June at 17:30* [Comment . Like]

Kathy Bloomingdale What's theoretical about it? *Posted Wednesday 27th June at 17:49* [Comment . Like]

Madeline Cain Jobless Theoretically, I have jobs with career building work set up on the horizon. In reality, I just ate a tray of ice cubes for breakfast to feel full. Theoretically, I have a boyfriend. In reality, all I have is a Facebook status with a heart, some very sweet text messages and a lack of someone else's cooties in my mouth. Theoretically, I'm in the city that never sleeps taking part in a once in a life time opportunity. In reality, I just delivered a pizza to a woman who looked like a goth fairy – all blue and pink hair, leather studded dog collar and lizards tattooed up one arm – who tried to convince me to take payment in... wait for it... beans. *Posted Wednesday 27th June at 18:02* [Comment . Like]

Tim Gleeve As in magic beans? *Posted Wednesday 27th June at 18:20* [Comment . Like]

Madeline Cain Jobless She didn't specify. I think she thought I would fill in the blanks after being dazzled by her candy cane hair. *Life fail* *Posted Wednesday 27th June at 18:25* [Comment . Like]

Kathy Bloomingdale Was she on something? Why don't you have any food again? Haven't you told your parents you don't have any food yet? They'd help your prideful arse in two seconds flat, you know that. *Posted Wednesday 27th June at 19:18* [Comment . Like]

Tim Gleeve Maybe she was the New York version of the

Hansel and Gretel witch. Was her door covered in candy? *Posted Wednesday 27th June at 19:24* [Comment . Like]

Madeline Cain Jobless You have been watching way too many movies. Her apartment *was* covered in shit, and by that I mean piles of random stuff not *actual* shit. Potentially she was luring seagulls with her rubbish tip. I didn't tell them Kath because I was supposed to get paid by Giovanni's today but he assigned El-cannot-speak-English-but-look-like-an-eighties-pop-star to the payroll and it didn't come through on time. I didn't tell them about the job thing because with Mum these things are best kept on the down-low. *Posted Wednesday 27th June at 19:30* [Comment . Like]

Nadine Cain What haven't you told us about? What happened to the money we gave you? Have you turned to drugs? Oh god, were you mugged at GUN POINT!? Why isn't that new boyfriend of yours looking after you? Please let me know you're alright. *Posted Wednesday 27th June at 19:32* [Comment . Like]

Madeline Cain Jobless Mum, calm down before you blow a fufu valve. Everything is fine. Let's not do this on Facebook, I'll call you. *Posted Wednesday 27th June at 19:40* [Comment . Like]

Madeline Cain Jobless -> Mike Cain Keep your nose out of my life. I don't need Mum and Dad checking up on me when I have one bad week, ok? *Posted Wednesday 27th June at 21:00* [Comment . Like]

Mike Cain Sheesh, don't get your nose out of joint. Last time I ever try to go all Wonder Brother to the rescue. *Posted Wednesday 27th June at 21:42* [Comment . Like]

Madeline Cain Jobless An image of you dressed as Wonder Woman has gone half way to appeasing me. *Posted Wednesday 27th June at 21:50* [Comment . Like]

Mike Cain And a Photo-shopped image? *Posted Wednesday 27th June at 21:55* [Comment . Like]

Madeline Cain Jobless May get me the rest of the way. But I can't promise I won't wedgie you next time we meet. *Posted Wednesday 27th June at 21:59* [Comment . Like]

Tim Gleeve Fire up Netflix and its top recommendation for me is Zombie Strippers. How did it come to this? *Posted Wednesday 27th June at 22:05* [Comment . Like]

Madeline Cain Clearly Netflix knows about your love for faulty toasters. What's one step more to zombie strippers? *Posted Wednesday 27th June at 22:12* [Comment . Like]

Kathy Bloomingdale We're in Australia, how did you manage to get Netflix? *Posted Wednesday 27th June at 22:16* [Comment . Like]

Tim Gleeve How did Jobs become better than Gates? He got tech savvy monkeys and stole other people's ideas through misdirection and magic. I am Jobs. *Posted Wednesday 27th June at 22:22* [Comment . Like]

Madeline Cain Jobless What exactly did you steal? A plot of land in the US? *Posted Wednesday 27th June at 22:26* [Comment . Like]

Tim Gleeve Sigh. How can you guys be my friends and yet such tech retards? *Posted Wednesday 27th June at 22:28* [Comment . Like]

Kathy Bloomingdale Friend is a bit of a stretch. Unwilling confidant, maybe. On awkward turtle watch, most definitely. Self-appointed normaliser and overseer of social integration, yes. *Posted Wednesday 27th June at 22:30* [Comment . Like]

Tim Gleeve Whatever, either way you keep coming back. You redirect your I.P. address through a US server. Makes it look like I live in the same city as Magic Beans over there. *Posted Wednesday 27th June at 22:33* [Comment . Like]

Kathy Bloomingdale Hey, that could be your porn name, Maddie. *Posted Wednesday 27th June at 22:37* [Comment . Like]

Madeline Cain Jobless Tim's the one with Zombie Strippers on his TV and *I'm* getting the porn name? *Posted Wednesday 27th June at 22:38* [Comment . Like]

Kim Enuik This computer sounds as if it's being powered by a hamster wheel. *Posted Thursday 28th June at 11:14* [Comment . Like]

Madeline Cain Jobless Probably is. But using a chameleon slave instead. Duncan's been looking a bit fat lately. Maybe you can connect his hamster wheel to some disco lights and we can have a party. *Posted Thursday 28th June at 12:07* [Comment . Like]

Madeline Cain Jobless Just had a spam email asking if, "You or a loved one have ever had robotic surgery…" Ummm, what? *Posted Thursday 28th June at 12:30* [Comment . Like]

Tim Gleeve Didn't you know? All your family and friends are bionic. Your mum is a Cylon and I'm a Borg. Thought the metal arm with killer lasers would have given it away. *Posted Thursday 28th June at 17:42* [Comment . Like]

Madeline Cain Jobless The only reference I understood there was 'killer laser arm'. *Posted Thursday 28th June at 18:22* [Comment . Like]

Kathy Bloomingdale If it was spam, what did they want? *Posted Thursday 28th June at 18:47* [Comment . Like]

Madeline Cain Jobless As far as I can tell, robotic surgeons have been very careless and they want to support you to sue these people. Maybe they've been replacing the wrong gangrenous limb. Or they only put version 2.0 fibre optics in a new artificial eye and not version 2.3. Maybe people have been pooping wing nuts. *Posted Thursday 28th June at 18:55* [Comment . Like]

Tim Gleeve You know what a wing nut is but you can't place a Borg?? *Posted Thursday 28th June at 18:58* [Comment . Like]

Kathy Bloomingdale Why were you reading spam in the first place? *Posted Thursday 28th June at 19:08* [Comment . Like]

Madeline Cain Jobless Only free activity I could think of to pass the time. Kevin invited me to come to filming with him at 5am. Being someone who loves getting up at the crack of noon I said, "Yeah, alright." And promptly slept through all early morning wake up knocks. *Posted Thursday 28th June at 19:13* [Comment . Like]

Kim Enuik Correction, you got up. But after stumbling around in cow print pyjamas and tripping over EVERY PIECE OF FURNITURE IN THE HOUSE, Kevin kindly agreed to re-bed you. Safer for his crew that way. *Posted Thursday 28th June at 19:20* [Comment . Like]

Kathy Bloomingdale Are you mad? You're in NYC, girl! Stop reading ridiculous spam emails from the future, go out and photograph randoms in Central Park or something. *Posted Thursday 28th June at 19:23* [Comment . Like]

Madeline Cain Jobless Do you know how *long* it takes to walk to Central Park from my place? *Posted Thursday 28th June at 19:25* [Comment . Like]

Kathy Bloomingdale Clearly you've got nothing else to do. I'm sure a square near you will have just as much variety in the human zoo department. Start your own personal portrait project or something, or heck, revisit your spy photography days. Anything is better than contemplating your half robot, half human family members. *Posted Thursday 28th June at 19:27* [Comment . Like]

Tim Gleeve Before you go, could you forward that email to me, these laser beams have been playing up. I think I can get a compensation for sawing the roof in half during a particularly bad robot-army dream. *Posted Thursday 28th June at 19:30* [Comment . Like]

Madeline Cain Jobless Would love to hear their response to that tale... *Posted Thursday 28th June at 19:35* [Comment . Like]

Cliff Wheeland That moment when you're playing Scrabble with a 92 year old and have to decide between picking up a respectable 28 points with 'VAGINA' or sacrifice it all to keep her from being scandalised. *Posted Friday 29th June at 10:19* [Comment . Like]

Kevin Doherty Do it! Mind if that goes in the next show? That's TV gold! *Posted Friday 29th June at 10:42* [Comment . Like]

Kim Enuik Tough call... She probably already has 'phallus' up her sleeve because she doesn't want to corrupt a 'nice boy like you'. Free each other, Mr Wheeler. But be gentle. *Posted Friday 29th June at 11:00* [Comment . Like]

Kathy Bloomingdale She has one and chances are she's used it (unless she's a nun, is she a nun?), so at least she wouldn't have to pick up a dictionary to make sure it wasn't made up. Is she related to you? That's the line in the sand between you and

Scrabble greatness. *Posted Friday 29th June at 11:10* [Comment . Like]

Cliff Wheeland No I didn't, and no she wasn't (times two). Bloody well lost too, which cuts deep when she wins with the final word of 'tits'. "We can use modern language can't we, Son?" She was eyeballing me like a ball-busting homicide detective. I think she knew. She was daring me to call her out on 'tits' when she *knew* I was planning 'vagina'. *Posted Friday 29th June at 11:50* [Comment . Like]

Kim Enuik Told ya! She was more foul mouthed than I thought. I imagined she would have gone for a more classy 'breasts' or 'mammary gland'. *Posted Friday 29th June at 11:53* [Comment . Like]

Kathy Bloomingdale If she wasn't related all bets are off. *Posted Friday 29th June at 11:57* [Comment . Like]

Kim Enuik It's game on old lady. *Posted Friday 29th June at 11:58* [Comment . Like]

Diana Lynal Best way to find out if you can trust someone… Is to trust them. *Posted Friday 29th June at 14:16* [Comment . Like]

You and **three others** like this.

Claire Holderness Gonna miss my Bruceniums and his naughty-sounding FB posts. #EveryThingSoundsDirty #GrandmasChickenSalad. *Posted Friday 29th June at 15:11* [Comment . Like]

Jack Fox I love your grandma's chicken salad! *Posted Friday 29th June at 15:26* [Comment . Like]

Alexa McMarshal Yeah you do! *Posted Friday 29th June at 15:41* [Comment . Like]

Madeline Cain Jobless I could do with a bit of grandma's chicken salad. If it came with abs and an accent. *Posted Friday 29th June at 15:49* [Comment . Like]

Tim Gleeve Not as good as your great aunt's mango chutney. *Posted Friday 29th June at 15:50* [Comment . Like]

Claire Holderness #TooFarNoTurningBack. *Posted Friday 29th June at 16:00* [Comment . Like]

Cliff Wheeland joined the group **That Awkward Feeling When You Realise You're Chewing On A Borrowed Pen** and three other groups. [Like . Join]

Tim Gleeve likes **Sharks With Laser Beams Attached To Their Heads....** *30 minutes ago* [Like]

Kevin Doherty Hope you're all getting ready for the Greatest Show On Earth! I've barely had time to fart this past week but the filming is going awesome. I'm slam dunking this time management thing, I even managed to use a spare five minutes to do a waltz with my lady down the hall. *Posted Friday 29th June at 21:00* [Comment . Like]

Madeline Cain Jobless What a romantic five minutes it was ? You sure know how to make a lady feel special, even on a time budget. *Posted Friday 29th June at 21:15* [Comment . Like]

Kevin Doherty I call it Five Minute Love. Sorry I've been so swamped, things will calm down soon, and your man will be a star! *Posted Friday 29th June at 22:12* [Comment . Like]

Kim Enuik Especially when you could have spent that five minutes getting in some good quality farting time. *Posted Friday 29th June at 22:22* [Comment . Like]

Madeline Cain Jobless This is why your lover is a lizard. *Posted Friday 29th June at 22:43* [Comment . Like]

Madeline Cain Undecided How do normal people make decisions? *Posted Saturday 30th June at 11:11* [Comment . Like]

Mike Cain I think they take acid? This seems to be the story of how Mum had you. *Posted Saturday 30th June at 15:47* [Comment . Like]

Tim Gleeve Explains a few things. *Posted Saturday 30th June at 15:58* [Comment . Like]

Madeline Cain Undecided Hardy-ha-ha. That was so funny I forgot to flash. At least I don't live in Dad Joke Land. *Posted Saturday 30th June at 16:00* [Comment . Like]

Mike Cain Being on Acid is now a Dad joke?? *Posted Saturday 30th June at 16:04* [Comment . Like]

Cliff Wheeland Normal people? You know some 'normal' people? *Posted Saturday 30th June at 16:17* [Comment . Like]

Madeline Cain I know you don't I? Your typing hands finally recovered enough to let us know you're alive? *Posted Saturday 30th June at 16:20* [Comment . Like]

Victoria Zeng Use an Ouija board. Maybe flip a coin? *Posted Saturday 30th June at 16:30* [Comment . Like]

Kathy Bloomingdale Badly. Like abnormal people. *Posted Saturday 30th June at 16:45* [Comment . Like]

Cain Michaels Magic Eight Ball. *Posted Saturday 30th June at 16:53* [Comment . Like]

Jarrah Annelli Oooh! Jade and I 'Paper, Scissors, Rock' to decide who lets the latest bad date down gently. *Posted Saturday 30th June at 16:57* [Comment . Like]

Kim Enuik Outsource. I know a really cheap guy in India

who does some… stuff, for me. He'd be able to make that decision for you in two seconds flat. For three hundred rupees. *Posted Saturday 30th June at 16:58* [Comment . Like]

Madeline Cain Undecided You can learn fashion sense right? *Posted Saturday 30th June at 17:13* [Comment . Like]

Cain Michaels Hold on, what decision requires you to have fashion sense? Because if it's important, we need to talk about tuition. My consultation fees are on my website. *Posted Saturday 30th June at 17:22* [Comment . Like]

Madeline Cain FULL STEAM AHEAD Doesn't matter, the Universe spoke in a much more reasoned voice than you jokers. Wait until you have to make a decision. My advice is going to involve blood rituals and reading entrails. *Posted Sunday 1st July at 13:31* [Comment . Like]

Kathy Bloomingdale If you insist on capitalising your name changes, I'm de-friending you. This falls under the same category as excessive use of exclamation marks. *Posted Sunday 1st July at 13:36* [Comment . Like]

Madeline Cain Full Steam Ahead It's only because you're my friend that I'm acquiescing to your request. You don't understand the internet. *Posted Sunday 1st July at 13:41* [Comment . Like]

Kathy Bloomingdale I know enough to know 'screaming' in a text based medium is both ironic and superfluous with correct punctuation. *Posted Sunday 1st July at 13:44* [Comment . Like]

The Universe Has Spoken: Saving A Man's Life

NOTES > My Notes [Write a note]

By **Madeline Cain Fashion Star.** Sunday, 1st July 2012 at 16:20.

The Universe has spoken, basically shouting me down like a PE teacher. I've had not one but *two* signs in less than twenty-four hours! It has deemed fashion to be my life and I willingly submit to its persistence. I'm not sure what I did to flip my Life Switch from normal to dramatic, but it now seems permanently stuck.

The first sign came on Friday. I mentioned to Jason's gallery receptionist, May, that I'd been eating my way through a fort of spaghetti tins and she must've taken pity on me. She asked me what I was doing that afternoon as the darkroom technician had fallen sick and they needed someone to help the socialite mothers class develop their photos.

Then the Universe put the magic words in May's mouth. "We can pay you cash."

I stood there like an idiot, potentially delusional from spaghetti preservatives, so overwhelmed with excitement at eating things with colours other than red.

Mistaking my silence as hesitation, May said, "I know these women are a box of cats. But Ted's got them today; they're pretty docile after ten minutes with him."

Anyone is docile after ten *seconds* with Ted. Finally finding a voice, I agreed. Half an hour later I found myself in the dark room and the recipient of life changing information.

The dark room is in the basement. You have to enter via two doors, waiting until the outer door is closed before entering the inner door. The room is dark except for a dim red light so the film isn't destroyed before it's developed. I figure this is how it feels to be in a spacious, rectangular and air conditioned womb. Washing lines run along the two longest walls and the far end has shelves of developing chemicals and tools. In the centre of the room is a long rectangular table divided into tanks with chairs scattered around. To create prints you need four separate tanks, one to develop the image, one to stop the print over developing, one to fix the image to the page and then a final clean water bath to wash the residual chemicals away before pegging the paper to the drying line.

The socialite women were almost comatose by the time Ted announced it. The news was so covered in his monotone it almost escaped my notice too. I only came to after running into the corner of a developing tank.

"Sweet lemon Fruit Tingle!" I cried.

Six faces turned to stare at me blankly.

Ted, his face so average it barely registered disapproval, said, "As I was saying, for those interested in taking your photography into more specialised fields, the talented Sorella Fontain, a fashion photographer and legend in her own right, is offering a one year internship for a photographer in her high end fashion studio. Sorella is the top choice to photograph the catalogues for dozens of fashion labels and is offering to open her doors for the first time in five years. Portfolios are due for submission in the first week of December. Now please, remove your prints from the 'fix' solution, rinse and hang them on the line. They'll be available at your next lesson."

The women milled around me as I stood open mouthed. Sorella? Another of my idols, second only to Jason, encourager at the Ball to pick a specialisation and go hard, was giving some lucky person the opportunity to learn one on one, every day, for three hundred and sixty five days.

Imagine, it would be like the Devil Wears Prada except without the crazed Merrill Streep. The clothes, the models, the connections, the glamour. Visions of me sporting sunglasses as big as my face and shoes so pointy I could stab muggers, danced around my imagination. Just as I was letting my daydreams get the better of me, a little voice in my head coughed.

You want to become a fashion star when most mornings you put your shirt on backwards and inside out. You wouldn't know style if it came swanning in on a unicorn and turned Duncan into a daisy. Oh, and your visa runs out in December. Are you going to become an illegal immigrant for this? Couple that with the FBI sleep over in April and suddenly you've been banned not from a pub, or a club, or a hotel, but from an entire COUNTRY!

"I hope you heard that last part Madeline." Ted's monotone came from right beside me. I jumped. Crafty bugger moves like the Flash. "You're one of our brightest and Sorella is most particular about talent, even if that talent regularly disrobes dignitaries."

You know you've achieved infamy when even Ted starts cracking the jokes. "It comes with a green card for Australia bound photographers," he says, almost as an afterthought.

How can Ted be the most boring, yet most amazing person I know? I wanted to both kiss him and take a nap. Fearing that a combination of those might end up with me licking his cheek, I used the rest of my energy reserves to mumble, "You've made my day." And grinned like a Botox injected celebrity.

"Fashion photography is a competitive game, only go for it if you're committed to both photography *and* style."

"Won't the fashion minions do the styling?"

The look he gave was almost identifiable as pity. "You're the master of the frame, you should know better than anyone what will look good in it. *Trust no one*," he hissed, quite suddenly, then trudged off.

Okay then... Unfortunately, the little devil of negativity came back with a vengeance. Enough was enough. The constant thought storm was getting me nowhere except nauseous.

So I asked myself: what would Mum do?

The answer? A pros and cons list.

PROS & CONS

PRO: Sorella is awesome-sauce on wonder-bread. If you could

crack her brain, gold would surely fall out. You'd be rich. In knowledge that is, not golden brains.

PRO: Lots of money and prestige.

CON: Ted just told a room full of women who have nothing else to do with their time, about an opportunity that allows them to get high-end fashion for free. Competition is going to be like a cage fight with a chimera.

CON: How are you going to build a portfolio of fashion snaps when your wardrobe consists of broken high heels and jackets worn by waiters at a pizza store? You've got five planned gigs, but can't guarantee all your subjects aren't going to be colour blind, let alone wearing underwear. To turn this to a PRO, you *need* clothes that make people look good, rather than look like an 80's boy band.

PRO: You're not done with NYC, not even close. Leaving the city after a year is like licking the outside of a chocolate ice cream and never taking a bite. This job gets you a green card so you can go past licking and crack open that chocolate casing to suck on that sweet, sweet creamy centre.

PRO: Your boyfriend is hot, he's not camera shy, and is one model that will get a kick out of you fussing over him for hours. Perfect for underwear modelling. Use this gift wisely.

CON: Not really committed to fashion. Doesn't mean it won't become an obsession that sees me horde hundreds of Jimmy Choos, but just that I was never that girl who cut out outfits from my Mum's magazines and made them for my Barbies. I had mud pies that needed making and smooshing in my brother's face. To turn this into a PRO I need to learn how to *make people look cool.* You can learn fashion from watching America's Next Top Model right?

CON: Having to listen to Tara Banks on America's Next Top Model.

PRO: Clothes. Lots of them.

CON: Models. Lots of them. Could end up in a situation where I give into the urge to bludgeon them with a camera.

PRO: You would have a real photography job, one that supported a healthy diet and regular bowel movements. One that makes use of everything you've learnt this year, making you an expert, a player, a person of interest but for the *right* reasons, not because you were followed by a man with a fake moustache. It would give you some direction, a clear path, a strong mentor, a specialisation rather than playing 'hobbies' like you use to play 'dress ups'.

CON: You could cock it all up.

The last one killed the list making. Not that it was helpful, I still couldn't answer the question, 'should I go for it?' I didn't have a photographic preference, but what if Fashion was the calling I had missed? Like the sweet nectar of red wine that Kim introduced to me six months past. Once I knew the power of its fermented goodness I couldn't fathom how I passed it by.

Looking back at my 'Cons' I realise there was really only one thing holding me back from hugging this opportunity like an anaconda, and that was my lack of access to clothes. It was the brick wall, the one hurdle I couldn't fix with my winning smile and devilish charms. If I was going to build a fashion portfolio, complete Jason's assignments and tackle my classmates' jobs, I didn't have time to source models. So I'd have to use bystanders at the gigs and bring my own clothes. Unless they were magically brought by elves with an aversion for being thanked, I had to shelve the opportunity.

To which the Universe replied, "Oh no young Madeline, done with you yet, I am not."

Let me explain how the Universe took my plans to not pursue a fashion career and put them in the middle of a Wild, Wild West gun battle. The means magically appeared during a moment of dramatic good luck.

If you're thinking, "Yeah right, good luck is as likely for Madeline as a mermaid tail is for Mike," then I invite you to read the below sentence three times just so it sinks in:

I saved a man from a gun-wielding cross-dresser.

Because that's how good luck and I roll.

It all began on a Saturday morning… Every time I mope around the house, Kim sits me down on the couch, Duncan in his lap, stroking him like Dr Evil's hairless cat. I always expect him to lift his little finger to his mouth and demand I pay *One Hundred, Million Dollars* to take my next dump. But no, in true ritual form, he pulls out his inner diva and asks in his most serious voice, "What have you done today, to make you feel proud?"

The answer has been varied over the months. Previous answers include: I've built a TimTam fort; I've been building my ideal life and it now lives like a perfect gleaming unicorn fart in my head and; I taught Duncan how to fetch peanuts without eating them. Today's response was, "I made a list."

Then, with all the solemnity and gravity of the Godfather, Kim declared as he did upon receiving all my deranged and slightly pathetic answers, "Then let us celebrate that achievement with a visit to the Den of the Dragon."

Thing is, as crazy as it sounds, I don't mind being bailed up by the Dr Evil Godfather because Kim's prescribed medicine – the placebo for all over-thought Pros and Cons lists – always ends up in a good night that makes the perfect unicorn fart of a life in my head achievable.

Before you say, "Madeline, where is this secret money tree you've been swiping cash from to go out?" know that: a) I have free entry into the Dragon's Den for life and; b) I can't legally drink in public in the US so the bar staff don't mind slipping me drinks of the non-alcoholic variety.

So Godfather Kim and I decided to dance our woes away. We organised to meet out the front of the Den.

I got there first. The outside of the Den looks like it can't decide if it wants to be a Parthenon or Gotham City. A dark grey in colour, gothic buttresses arch out and gargoyles leer from the upper two levels of the four story building, while a series of five Greek columns loom out the front of the lower two stories, supporting the upper mantle of a massive iron doorway. I'd never seen the main door open; most patrons were let in via two smaller doors cut into the mammoth ones. My banner covered the centre bank of windows on those upper two floors, long enough to just brush the doorway mantle.

Two lines extended out from the doorway, down the street in each direction. The one on the right was for general public (where you could wait for hours and never get in) and the one on the left was cordoned off with sumptuous red silk rope and golden posts with a ruby carpet five metres long. This was the VIP line and moved ten times faster than the one on the right.

For shits and giggles I'll sometimes join the VIP line while waiting for Kim. You can't help but get a massive kick when some weedy metro guy pulls you out of the line and you go swanning past Bob the security guard like you've suddenly found fame on the sidewalk.

But this time as I meandered along the already ten metre long line (at only 9:30pm mind you) I spotted someone I actually knew. Hair still slicked back by half a can of oil, a nose that could coat-hang muggers in the throat and wearing a suit that I swore I'd seen walking past Versace not twenty minutes ago, Giovanni's son Dom certainly knew how to look like a mobster. It also looked like he'd gained an inch and as I approached I saw boots made for a giant with (not so) cleverly hidden disco platforms of epic thickness.

He was having a conversation with two women, clearly his company for the evening as he was standing right next to them rather than in front or behind. The one in the centre was a petite, pretty blond in the tallest heels and the shortest disco-ball dress I have ever seen. The pretty blond paled in comparison to the smoking hot sexpot of a brunette next to her. Boys, this woman wore sex appeal like a coat; she was a black widow spider luring man-flies. Gorgeous olive skin, deep brown eyes and hair enough for five bald men, she towered over her friend and Dom.

Dom was giving the blond the minimum amount of polite attention, but his A-game was trained on the glamazon, and from what

I could hear, his A-game was like Josh's F-game. They were the worst pickup lines I'd ever heard.

"Do I know you? Because you look a lot like my next girlfriend. Bet your legs will hurt from running through my dreams all night. Really, if beauty were time, you'd be eternity."

Maybe they were more like Josh's Z-game. The brunette said nothing, eyes narrowing more with each new pass. Dom was clearly the kind of guy who was so confident in his supposed ability to charm that he saw each non-comment as an excuse for more ridiculous declarations, rather than seeing them as the silent smack-downs that they were. Rejections that were going to turn into a physical smack down soon judging by the woman's face.

"I'm not a photographer, but I can picture us together, sugar. You know what I'm saying?"

The blond woman was smirking so hard at each flip-off by the brunette that I was surprised her cheeks hadn't split. Someone had to save Dom from himself.

Wandering closer I called out, "Hey, Dom right? Working on the whole 'bringing people together' thing I see."

He looked at me in confusion. Apparently my face/accent combination was more forgettable than I hoped. I walked the final couple of metres to stand next to them. "You may remember me from such locations as your father's red bricked pizzeria wearing a fairly snazzy green jacket," I hinted.

To my relief (because frankly I was flying the awkward turtle flag there) the confusion cleared and he snorted his laughing-track laugh. "Right, the Aussie kid who cracks the funnies!"

"Madeline," I supplied.

"Madeline, that's it. How you doin' sugar? You look good out of green." He winked at me. But before I could start feeling uncomfortable at his sleazy line, his eyes strayed once again to the bombshell. Yep, it was pretty clear he wasn't interested in sleazing on me. Not sure how I feel about that, I'm no glamazon but I'm good enough to deserve at least five perv-seconds.

The brunette casually reached down and scratched at her panty line. Up close the object of Dom's desire was all legs, taller than me by a foot and a half, she was basically a torso on stilts. Yet when she reached down to adjust herself again I realised, like a turkey slap to the face, that she was packing the biggest front-bum I'd ever seen. Maybe it was the angle I was at, maybe it was because most men in that line were at the same height as her very impressive rack and didn't bother to look further. But if 'she' was a woman, I was a rainbow coloured badger. That front area was all male.

I wondered how he could miss it or if he in fact knew and didn't care. It was like a wand, a Frankfurt and it wasn't a soft swell, it was a 'hello boys, check out my lego blocks', clearly defined, hard edged swell.

'Her' gaze skittered off Dom's, unable to hold it. For that matter 'she' wasn't able to hold any man's gaze. Her eyes darted around, as though looking everywhere without actually looking at anyone. At the time I thought it odd. Maybe, she was a new transgender woman on her first outing and was nervous. Suddenly the pretty blond woman's smirking made more sense. There were politics at play I couldn't begin to understand.

The blond said, "I thought this was the VIP line. We've been here *forever*, how much longer?"

I cast a practised eye down the line. "Twelve minutes max, fifteen if any very, very special VIP's come in first."

"How do you know that?" she asked, startled out of her smug superiority.

I tried hard not to let it come out like a brag but was only half successful. "I come here a lot. Bob and I have an understanding." I gave Bob a little upward nod. He returned it with one of his own. God, Bob's a dude.

"So you could get us in?" asked Dom.

Ah, now I had their attention. The bombshell looked like she'd swallowed a chainsaw, as she looked frantically between Dom and myself. My first thought was she hadn't quite psyched herself up for her first dress wearing adventure. Boy did I have that backwards.

I shrugged, feigning regret but secretly revelling in my power. "Sorry, not yet, I'm waiting for a friend. But when he gets here I'm sure we can work something out."

Now the bombshell looked like she'd only swallowed a ninja star. Curiouser and curiouser. A whistling gust rushed past, a premonition if I ever believed in such things. Like a walking cliché I said, "Burr!" rubbing my bare arms suddenly alive with gooseflesh.

It was at this point Dom regained the politeness he'd shown at the restaurant last week; shaking off his jacket in one smooth motion he draped the silkily lined garment around my shoulders. He was a smoother operator than I gave him credit for. It figures, the first time this happens the guy isn't even remotely interested in me.

"Where are my manners? This is my *friendly* rival Ivana and her stunning second in command, Camilla, the magnet to my tin man heart. This is Madeline, she–"

I cut him off before he could lower my street cred. "I'm a photographer. I know Dom's father. I also took that." I pointed upwards. I tell you, nothing beats a billboard size photo of awesome if you want to impress.

Or horrify; all the blood drained from Camilla's face the minute I said 'photographer'. She spun around turning her back without apology or explanation.

Dom's eyes flickered to her arse. Then he saw me looking, eyebrows raised and he blushed. It was clear he had it bad, and wasn't all sleaze, he'd just given me his jacket with genuine concern. Someone had to let him down gently. Ivana had already rolled her eyes and dived into the depths of her phone, probably Facebook.

So I moved closer and whispered, "I'd give up on that one mate. Unless you hold a flame for the gents," I added as an afterthought. I have a solid gay-dar and Dom wasn't giving me that vibe, but my Bi-rometer wasn't accurately tuned and you can never discount the bisexuals.

He looked at me in horror. "What? No! How dare you!" His voice was low, with a menacing undertone I wasn't expecting. His New York accent had thickened and it felt like I had somehow landed myself in a gangster film scene.

I held my hands out in a placating gesture, almost losing the jacket. "Hey now, don't get upset, I had to be sure you didn't prefer the Bros. No point on warning you off something you actually want."

His brows furrowed over that beak of his. "What do you mean?"

"You may not have noticed but 'she'—" I did some air quotes with my fingers. "–Is sporting a man box, a treasure chest, a Mars Bar, a little soldier, a vertical log, a double scoop ice cream cone, a wood pecker. You know what I mean." I gave him a wink, wink and a nudge, nudge with my elbow trying to lighten his mood.

His face broke out into a dimpled grin as soon as he realised I wasn't questioning his manhood, but hers. "I've known that brawd for a while, she ain't no tranny."

I lowered my voice even more. "I'm certain. And I think you'll find transgender is the appropriate term. When she turns around take a look. Maybe you've never seen her in clothes that tight—"

By then he was actually chuckling. "Why wouldn't she wear tight clothes? She's a fine filly, you know what I'm saying. Don't let your jealousy make you see things."

"Look!" I said, exasperated at his insistent denials, "Either 'she' is smuggling a budgie or it's a gun! There's no other possible explanation."

That's when I start remembering things in slow motion. The crunch of tires as a car pulled up in the street behind us, the excited mummer of voices as some recognisable person got out of the vehicle, Dom's body facing his 'rival' companion while he looked over his shoulder, flashes reflecting off the building as cameras phones go nuts, Camilla spinning like a ballerina her tight dress up around her hips exposing lacy white knickers, her thin, coco coloured hand reaching in and pulling out a small, silver gun and holding it level with Dom's head.

"Her penis is a gun!" I shriek.

Dom's turning but too slow. Her voice plays in my head like a record on half speed. "Mo-o-o-ve! I wa-a-nt him-m yo-o-u b-"

A bag hits her square in the face. It's bright pink glow mesh, the same bright pink glow mesh that was in my hand a second ago.

Slow motion ended, Camilla, the assassin, the maniac, the very real *woman*, disappeared like a magician. It was then I became aware of the burn in my shoulder. I'd just over arm bowled my handbag at a killer, instinct taking over, throwing the only projectile I had. A silver gun skittered past me coming to rest in the gutter. Savage animalistic squeals cut the city noise and I looked down to see a human sandwich with Dom on top.

Camilla hadn't disappeared, she had been rugby tackled by Dom, who hadn't bothered to dive around Ivana, but just collected her on the way, squashing her between him and the beautiful assassin who was out cold.

"Get off me!" Ivana's scream burrowed into my brain.

"You tried to have me killed! You wanted my position so bad you'd murder me for it! Murder!" Dom's shrieks were almost as high as her own.

"It wasn't me, I'm innocent!"

"Bullshit on liar toast!"

"I'm not that crazy!"

"What were you going to give her? Your old family position while you took mine?"

"You're not as grand as you think you are *Dominique,*" she retorted with a sneer.

"Dominic, bitch," he said, trying to head butt her and missing.

What the hell was going on? Both their bodies flailed on top of the unconscious woman, Ivana landing slaps wherever she could, Dom trying to grab her hands and pin them down. Bob and Keith the bouncers, swooped in hauling the human sandwich apart. The sound of tires squealing and kicked up gravel drowned the argument between Dom and Ivana, both pinioned in the arms of the bouncers.

I hadn't moved from where I'd been standing when the gun first came up, my body only unfreezing for the winning pitch.

Hands grabbed me roughly and pulled me into a bear hug. The smell of strong aftershave and cigarettes told me it was Kim finally arrived. "Are you ok? Why didn't you duck you stupid Aussie? You could have been shot!"

"They tried to shoot him."

"They tried to shoot me!" Dom parroted, legs flailing like they were possessed by the Lord of the Dance.

"Even that reality TV star who just arrived had the sense to dive back into his car. But not you, you had to throw disco accessories. At a gun! Why don't you try flowers next time? Deflect a speeding bullet with your shoe, MacGyver."

I was a rock to Kim's shaking leaf. Feeling quite irrationally invincible I said to Bob, "Let him go, he was the one she was aiming for."

The bouncer stood as immovable as an anvil while Dom continued air aerobics. "I'll let him go little lady, when I know he won't go making things worse with a brawl," Bob said firmly.

Dom quietened immediately. "I'll be a real gentleman if you cuff the gun-wielding brawd before she wakes up."

"We don't have hand cuffs, we're security." He dropped Dom like a sack and went to stand over Camilla, phone in hand.

"Anyone gives us trouble we have other means. Crushing the chest like an wrecking ball for example." Keith bared his teeth in a parody of a smile.

I extracted myself from Kim's killer grip and swooped under the red velvet rope to snatched my 'weapon' from the pavement. I had to smile at the rash like octagonal patterning on Camilla's cheek. I had a bowling arm like a 'real boy' my Dad always said. Served her right, the boob. Who hides a loaded gun next to their lady parts? Seriously?

"Hey Darl," said Dom. I looked up into the most earnest face I'd ever seen on a man. "You saved my life. You knew something was odd from the beginning. I should've known something was up when Ivana was so eager to bring *her* out. How can I ever repay you? I owe you my life, a blood debt that must be repaid."

"It's not a big deal. You see a gun, you make sure it doesn't turn anyone into Swiss cheese."

"No! It was so much more. You cared about my reputation as a *man*. When I didn't pay attention you tried to save my honour, when that didn't work you saved my life. You must let me help you in some way. Italian's always repay their debts."

By this time he had grasped my hand and was on one knee as though proposing. Trying to politely extract your hand when it's in a death grip is impossible. So I searched for a repayment that would satisfy and not offend with its pettiness. Anything to reclaim my hand from that cement grip.

My eyes fell upon the now rumpled suit jacket in his hands, rescued from the ground during my bag-bowling demonstration. I don't know what made me say it. I blurted it out never thinking Dom would be able to help. I didn't count on the Universe. "Well, there's this fashion photography internship I want to apply for but I don't have access to clothes that would make my application stand out. Don't suppose you could help me?"

A grin split his hawkish face and he placed a smacking kiss on the back off my hand. Tapping the side of his nose like a cliché spy, he stood. "I think I've got the means, sugar. You rescued the right man, a man with connections. Some of the gang owe me sizable favours."

His face alternated blue and red as the police finally arrived. He gave me one more suggestive wink before striding toward the gun in the gutter and waving down an officer with a practised hand.

I'm not certain what it is that I have apparently asked for, I thought it was clothes (hey, don't judge me!), but with all this winking and whispering I wasn't quite sure. But I wasn't about to look a gift horse in the mouth, particularly when it was clearly being inhabited by the Universe bent on making fashion my life.

Kim, ever a collector of gossip, loitered near Dom as the police questioned him. I still blame you, Kim, for leading the then frustrated cop to me to be questioned for over an hour.

"For a guy who has just been shot at, he's incredibly elusive with his answers. I trust you will be more forth coming," said the officer.

"She's an open book, so am I," chimed Kim.

Thanks heaps Kim, that was not how I wanted to spend my night out.

It was well past 1:30 am when everything was wrapped up. Camilla had been taken by Ambulance under police guard, Ivana was put in the back of a police car still claiming innocence.

Dom left in a taxi. "I'll be in touch about the first of our little exchanges. Who are we 'shipping' for?"

"Children?" I replied, not sure how to answer that. "My first gig is at a school."

He winked again. "Consider it done, li'l lady."

What did I do then you may ask? Well despite hours of

questioning, I was still on a high from preventing a shooting. So rather than partying for making lists, I partied to celebrate the Universe's very clear sign, and my ascent to fame and fortune as a fashion photographer.

[Comment . Like . Share]

Claire Holderness and **71 others** like this.

Kathy Bloomingdale I'm so glad you're safe! I would take a cross-dresser over a gun wielding model any day. Almost getting shot sounds like an extreme way for the 'Universe' to get its point across. Are you sure you're not just seeing signs in the sand? People grab onto a lot of things when they've been through a near death experience. I just don't want you to be consumed with something before you've figured out which photography type you like better, even if it doesn't make as much money or have as much prestige. Give yourself some time to play. Just not with guns, ok? *Posted Sunday 1st July at 18:12* [Comment . Like]

> **Madeline Cain Fashion Star** I'm hoping me and guns will only be very distant fifth cousins, three times removed, and living on separate planets. I know you think I'm jumping the gun (pun intended) but it's come together so perfectly. How can I ignore it? I'll still be experimenting. Hell, I can't live off air for six months and my classmates have been awesome in helping me organise gigs. But the last time I ignored the Universe – aka List Making Friday – I ended up in the middle of Shoot Out Saturday. I don't want to see the next level if I ignore it again. Message received! Mission locked in! *Posted Sunday 1st July at 19:00* [Comment . Like]

Jarrah Annelli It sounds a lot like you just saved him from a mob hit… *Posted Sunday 1st July at 18:30* [Comment . Like]

> **Jade Annelli** If he was a mobster why would he be waiting

in line? Wouldn't he be more connected than Maddie and have like a helicopter pad on the roof for private entry? *Posted Sunday 1st July at 18:38* [Comment . Like]

Josh Annelli Don't be stupid, how's he supposed to woo the ladies if he hasn't done the 'getting to know you' dance first? Beer smell and that God-awful music they call 'dance' only gets in the way (spoiler alert: as does the sound of helicopter rotor blades). Get to *know* them, let them see your good qualities and it's guaranteed you'll get to do the horizontal tango. *Posted Sunday 1st July at 18:57* [Comment . Like]

Madeline Cain Fashion Star Thanks for that dubious dating advice, but what I want to know is why Jarrah thinks it was a MOB HIT!? I mean Dom being Winky McGee was just odd right? Not sinister? *Posted Sunday 1st July at 19:08* [Comment . Like]

Tim Gleeve Observe: very expensive suit, Italian, Godfather mannerisms, a lot of cash, smoozing women way hotter than him, has gun pulled on him by a 'friendly rival', is evasive in police questioning and then owes you a 'blood debt' which must be 'repaid'. I'd say you've enslaved a very grateful mobster. *Posted Sunday 1st July at 19:23* [Comment . Like]

Kathy Bloomingdale He's right; remember you telling me his father, a straight laced immigrant running a thriving business, is ashamed of his son for no obvious reason? It all fits! *Posted Sunday 1st July at 19:31* [Comment . Like]

Madeline Cain Fashion Star Are you seriously saying I just saved someone from a Mob hit? *Posted Sunday 1st July at 19:39* [Comment . Like]

Josh Annelli Better than letting a mobster get shot and them *knowing* you didn't say anything. Just stay on his good side and don't do any meetings in dark alleys. *Posted Sunday 1st July at 19:51* [Comment . Like]

Madeline Cain Fashion Star He just doesn't seem…I mean, I don't know him well but he's just… odd is all. I never looked at him and thought, you know, Mob Boss. He's so short! I feel like there's a bit of stereotyping here. *Posted Sunday 1st July at 19:53* [Comment . Like]

Jarrah Annelli The Irish mob come in all sorts of funny shapes according to those true crime shows. Italians are just the more tanned version. Look, he may just be some unlucky guy who really pissed off a business rival. But stereotypes exist for a reason. So, hope for the best but expect the stereotype and there'll be no surprises. My womb-buddies do have something right; the big boss wouldn't be standing in the Den line, even if it was the VIP line. If you can get in without lining up I'm sure a Mob Boss could too. I submit to you that Dom is potentially a mob underling rather than the Godfather. *Posted Sunday 1st July at 20:17* [Comment . Like]

Jade Annelli Right stereotype with a position downgrade. I'm happy with that. I shall support your claim for mob hit. *Posted Sunday 1st July at 20:18* [Comment . Like]

Richard Arnoou I bet Camilla looked like she'd swallowed a chainsaw when you said you'd get them in because she knew she couldn't shoot him inside the club; too many layers of meat – I mean, witnesses. You accelerated her plans, surprised her; it's probably why she couldn't dodge something so pink and shiny. *Posted Sunday 1st July at 20:20* [Comment . Like]

Madeline Cain Fashion Star So if we suspect mob, should I be telling someone? A cop? *Posted Sunday 1st July at 20:21* [Comment . Like]

Tim Gleeve What are they going to do? He hasn't done

anything to *you*, and you haven't seen him do anything to anyone else (except hit *on* them which is different to ordering a hit). All you know is he's very grateful to you and you couldn't stop him from thanking you with gifts of clothes. You won't be telling the police anything they haven't already figured out. Enjoy it. Embrace your functional body with no bullet wounds. *Posted Sunday 1st July at 20:34* [Comment . Like]

Madeline Cain Fashion Star You amaze me with your sensitivity… You know what? I won't stereotype for the moment. I'm going to trust the Universe has not dropped me in a pile of dung but in a pile of beautiful outfits for a fashion shoot. I shall keep you all informed and use you as my mobster gage. *Posted Sunday 1st July at 20:40* [Comment . Like]

Richard Arnoou On a scale of one to ten how gangsta was Dom's latest breakfast? *Posted Sunday 1st July at 20:41* [Comment . Like]

Victoria Zeng Five, he ate alone. *Posted Sunday 1st July at 20:42* [Comment . Like]

Richard Arnoou On the Gangsta Scale, how was Dom's visit to the race track? *Posted Sunday 1st July at 20:43* [Comment . Like]

Victoria Zeng Eight point five, envelopes were exchanged. *Posted Sunday 1st July at 20:44* [Comment . Like]

Richard Arnoou Today's average Gangsta Score is six point seven-five. Veering toward gangsta but not conclusive. Until tomorrow. *Posted Sunday 1st July at 20:45* [Comment . Like]

Madeline Cain Fashion Star Richard, you jest, but Gangsta rating is probably going to happen. *Posted Sunday 1st July at 20:48* [Comment . Like]

Mike Cain Sis, that 'letting him down gentle' was about as subtle as a cactus to the face. *Posted Sunday 1st July at 20:55* [Comment . Like]

Kim Enuik You know how she gets when you make her talk about the junk in the trunk. She goes on these elaborate mental image rampages until you're not quite sure what it is you're supposed to be packing in your pants. I'm fairly impressed her final guess happened to be accurate. *Posted Sunday 1st July at 21:00* [Comment . Like]

Tim Gleeve 'Hello boys want to see my lego blocks' was particularly imaginative. I feel she should have lead with that. *Posted Sunday 1st July at 21:09* [Comment . Like]

Mike Cain I'm still trying to get over, 'Her penis is a gun'. *Posted Sunday 1st July at 21:11* [Comment . Like]

Madeline Cain Fashion Star At least my warning was direct and accurate. You couldn't misunderstand it. *Posted Sunday 1st July at 21:15* [Comment . Like]

Kim Enuik I think you should have titled the note, 'I Saved A Man from A Gun-Wielding Cross-Dresser'. I feel it would have gotten way more likes and is far more interesting than a piddly Pros and Cons list. You need to give people a reason to read in the first place. *Posted Sunday 1st July at 21:20* [Comment . Like]

Madeline Cain Fashion Star I'm not a bloody novelist Kim, I'm a photographer. You're all reading this because you know I only write Facebook notes when random funnies go down. So quit your complaining. You saw the whole thing happen anyway, why are you reading about it? *Posted Sunday 1st July at 21:23* [Comment . Like]

Kim Enuik Your perspective is often vastly skewed, I like to know what lies you're telling yourself. *Posted Sunday 1st July at 21:24* [Comment . Like]

Tim Gleeve Did you walk out that morning saying, "Look, I don't think I can get clothes with my good charm and wit, but I think being a human bullet vest could do the job." There are easier ways to use your body that result in less damage. As an aside, I would like to see Mike with a mermaid tail. *Posted Sunday 1st July at 21:40* [Comment . Like]

Kathy Bloomingdale I was just thinking that. *Posted Sunday 1st July at 21:50* [Comment . Like]

Mike Cain Yeah, well I'd like to see you two as conjoined butt-twins but God didn't grant me that request so it's unlikely I'll be letting you ride me like a dolphin any time soon. *Posted Sunday 1st July at 22:03* [Comment . Like]

Victoria Zeng You do know canned food comes in colours other than red, right? There's peas, corn, beans, beetroot, carrot; basically you can get everything in a can. I even saw a place that sold farts in a can. You can't eat those though. *Posted Sunday 1st July at 22:43* [Comment . Like]

Madeline Cain Fashion Star I hadn't even thought about canned goods other than spaghetti and tuna. You can blame Tim for that, when he was saving for his home sound system that was what he ate to save money. The idea must have burrowed in my brain. I could make myself a whole meal for under five dollars! All colours of the rainbow. *Posted Sunday 1st July at 23:00* [Comment . Like]

Tim Gleeve Will you be throwing a gay pride party for that? *Posted Sunday 1st July at 23:01* [Comment . Like]

Richard Arnoou Because regular bowel movements are always a plus ? *Posted Sunday 1st July at 23:13* [Comment . Like]

Jarrah Annelli So is prestige. Sorella's intership sounds awesome. I'll totally help you out, though I'd never go near it myself. You think the socialite mothers are a box of cats, wait until you have to corral male models – they're like strippers, you have to pay them to keep their clothes on. So no need to jealously guard your plans ? Great thing is you'll be able to see Sorella at work at Fashion Week and get a feel for her style. I hear a year working for Sorella can give you your pick of any fashion job in Europe. So you could come and join us in London! *Posted Sunday 1st July at 23:19* [Comment . Like]

Richard Arnoou I love my job, I wouldn't trade rockers for Barbie's no matter what you paid me. But Jarrah's right, Sorella is a veteran and super well connected. If you're in with her, you're in with the best. You could get some awesome grungy jean shots at the Garden. The lighting guy would totally help us organise something after the show. It would be like having your own epic studio. *Posted Sunday 1st July at 23:24* [Comment . Like]

Madeline Cain Fashion Star Yes to all the above! You guys are legends! *Posted Sunday 1st July at 23:25* [Comment . Like]

Kevin Doherty Babe, I saw you tagged me and the answer is yes, I will be your rock-hard abs model. Mould me as you wish ? Didn't get the chance to read it all, but this intern thing sounds sweet as, so tots do it. Look at me, I dreamed big and got my own kickass show. You can too! Hey, reckon you could include the team in some of your photos? The boys need some shots for their CV's. Know you'd do the job proud. *Posted Sunday 1st July at 23:30* [Comment . Like]

Madeline Cain Fashion Star Excellent! Fingers crossed I can get some sexy clothes to match my subject. I suppose I could do some shots for the guys, should probably give sports photography a go as part of my experimentations. *Posted Sunday 1st July at 23:33* [Comment . Like]

Kevin Doherty Ace. Say hi to your Dad for me, was cool hearing him talk about that Australian Football thing when he called the other day. We had a sick chat about how they bounce that spazzed out ball while you were being a lizard hunter. Where did you find the reptile? *Posted Sunday 1st July at 23:40* [Comment . Like]

Madeline Cain Fashion Star He was imitating the fire hose this time. Thanks heaps for keeping my dad entertained while I caught the slippery sucker. The payphone on the landing is a bit dodgy so sorry if you have trouble understanding his accent. *Posted Sunday 1st July at 23:43* [Comment . Like]

Nadine Cain It was delightful talking to someone with a Yankee accent. I hope you don't give up your football for all this Hollywood, TV hoopla, keeping up the cardio and muscle tone is essential for someone on the camera. I hear it adds twenty pounds… Maddie, I'm so proud of your instincts! You got those quick reflexes from me. You said sport would never pay off but all those cricket sessions turned out to be a good idea, didn't they? *Posted Sunday 1st July at 23:48* [Comment . Like]

Madeline Cain Fashion Star Who are you and what have you done with my Mother? Where's the freak out, the demanding I lock myself in my room and never, never, never leave my house again? Wait, I never played cricket with you! *Posted Sunday 1st July at 23:50* [Comment . Like]

Nadine Cain I thought you would have recognised your Dad, Pookie. *Posted Sunday 1st July at 23:51* [Comment . Like]

Madeline Cain Fashion Star So it was you calling Kevin 'delightful'? *Posted Sunday 1st July at 23:51* [Comment . Like]

Nadine Cain What, a man can't have a delightful

conversation with his daughter's boyfriend? *Posted Sunday 1st July at 23:52* [Comment . Like]

Madeline Cain Fashion Star Come on, admit it, you were trying to pretend to be Mum. *Posted Sunday 1st July at 23:53* [Comment . Like]

Nadine Cain Caught me red handed. Lol. *Posted Sunday 1st July at 23:53* [Comment . Like]

Madeline Cain Fashion Star I CAN'T BELIEVE YOU JUST LOL-ED! *Posted Sunday 1st July at 23:54* [Comment . Like]

Nadine Cain I'm up with the new lingo. But I just had to tell you how proud I was of your killer arm. Or should I say anti-killer arm. *Posted Sunday 1st July at 23:55* [Comment . Like]

Madeline Cain Fashion Star How I've missed your Dad jokes. Truthfully, it scared the shitkittens out of me. Mind getting Mum to rant at me on the phone rather than Facebook? *Posted Sunday 1st July at 23:55* [Comment . Like]

Nadine Cain Happy to appease the home sickness one Dad joke at a time. Sure. I can do that. Love you. P.S. It would have scared the shitkittens out of me too. *Posted Sunday 1st July at 23:56* [Comment . Like]

Kevin Doherty You too Mr C! Pookie? *Posted Sunday 1st July at 23:56* [Comment . Like]

Madeline Cain Fashion Star Don't you *dare* explain Dad! *Posted Sunday 1st July at 23:56* [Comment . Like]

Nadine Cain Fine, Mum's the word. But let's just say that while her teenage years may not have warranted a 5 second perv by a mobster, her adult self deserves at least a fifteen minute conversation. *Posted Sunday 1st July at 23:57* [Comment . Like]

Madeline Cain Fashion Star That's why I only set up a Facebook account for Mum. *Posted Sunday 1st July at 23:57* [Comment . Like]

Kevin Doherty At least a 30 minute conversation, Mr C. *Posted Sunday 1st July at 23:58* [Comment . Like]

Mike Cain Must resist hysterical projectile-laugh-vomit. *Posted Sunday 1st July at 00:00* [Comment . Like]

Cain Michaels Madeline, you cannot keep me way from this! Fashion and beautiful people are my dream. *Posted Monday 2nd July at 10:24* [Comment . Like]

Madeline Cain Fashion Star Bring it, Cain. Bring it. *Posted Monday 2nd July at 13:25* [Comment . Like]

Cain Michaels Unicorn farts live in your head? *Posted Monday 2nd July at 13:31* [Comment . Like]

Madeline Cain Fashion Star I hate you so bad right now. *Posted Monday 2nd July at 13:33* [Comment . Like]

Kathy Bloomingdale Would like to go back to bed now, preferably minus two little white dogs. *Posted Tuesday 3rd July at 20:20* [Comment . Like]

Madeline Cain Fashion Star Where did the dogs come from? *Posted Tuesday 3rd July at 20:33* [Comment . Like]

Kathy Bloomingdale Rescued from the side of the road by

Mum. Apparently they were lizards in a previous life, I can't convince them that places other than my lap and under the covers exist. If they could, they would attach themselves to each leg like koalas. *Posted Tuesday 3rd July at 20:38* [Comment . Like]

Diana Lynal Cute! *Posted Tuesday 3rd July at 22:10* [Comment . Like]

Kathy Bloomingdale Hardly. It's like having two fluffy ghosts as companions. *Posted Tuesday 3rd July at 22:16* [Comment . Like]

Cliff Wheeland Happy Fourth of July everybody! *Posted Wednesday 4th July at 09:45* [Comment . Like]

Cain Michael Happy Fourth of July, bitches! *Posted Wednesday 4th July at 09:57* [Comment . Like]

Kim Enuik Happy Independence Day! *Posted Wednesday 4th July at 11:18* [Comment . Like]

Victoria Zeng Happy red, blue and white fireworks day! *Posted Wednesday 4th July at 12:00* [Comment . Like]

Richard Arnoou Happy Day of Independence! Let's sign a Constitution! *Posted Wednesday 4th July at 12:36* [Comment . Like]

Kevin Doherty Happy 4th of July! *Posted Wednesday 4th July at 17:04* [Comment . Like]

Madeline Cain Fashion Star So apparently the Fourth of July is a big deal. I just thought it was a date. *Posted Wednesday 4th July at 18:29* [Comment . Like]

Kim Enuik Are you kidding? Even when we lived in the middle of nowhere we still took a day off for picnics and fireworks, if we could get our hands on them. The independence of a nation as big as this is going to equal one heck of a celebration. *Posted Wednesday 4th July at 18:42* [Comment . Like]

Madeline Cain Fashion Star Celebration? Central Park was one giant hazard zone! Thousands of people trying to play every sport ever invented at the same time. I almost coped a Frisbee in the boob, you almost got a football in the head. *Posted Wednesday 4th July at 18:48* [Comment . Like]

Kim Enuik Only because Kevin's football team used the picnic blanket as a try line. I told you it was a bad idea. *Posted Wednesday 4th July at 18:50* [Comment . Like]

Madeline Cain Fashion Star I wouldn't have had a chance to see him otherwise. The best we've managed is fleeting meet ups in the hall in which I've met Kevin the Knight In Shining Armour, Kevin the Hillbilly, Kevin the Priest, Kevin the Wizard, Kevin the Magician, Kevin the Explosion Engineer, and Kevin the FBI Agent. Other than that I think we've managed to catch an episode of Friends on the couch where he wormed his way into my heart with a specially bought pint of chocolate chip cookie dough ice-cream. At least I got to see him in sunlight so I know he's not a vampire. *Posted Wednesday 4th July at 18:54* [Comment . Like]

Kim Enuik Ah, then you missed the day I was bailed up by Kevin the Vampire, Kevin the Racetrack Announcer and Kevin the Time Travelling Soldier. *Posted Wednesday 4th July at 18:56* [Comment . Like]

Cliff Wheeland Seriously, what's his deal? *Posted Wednesday 4th July at 18:58* [Comment . Like]

Madeline Cain Fashion Star What do you mean? He's a method actor and he's the host of a massive show. You write every day, always taking notes in that ratty notebook of yours.

How is this different? *Posted Wednesday 4th July at 19:05* [Comment . Like]

Kim Enuik From what I can tell Kevin's testing reactions. It's a bit of a guessing game wondering who's going to greet you on the landing in the morning. Thankfully, today it was just regular football Kevin and his goon squad. *Posted Wednesday 4th July at 19:15* [Comment . Like]

Madeline Cain Fashion Star It *was* good to spend a day with real-Kevin. Staying out for the fireworks was amazing too. *Posted Wednesday 4th July at 19:20* [Comment . Like]

Cain Michaels Bet you don't have a light show as awesome as that in Kangaroo Land. Aren't you like, still owned by a Queen or something. *Posted Wednesday 4th July at 19:23* [Comment . Like]

Madeline Cain Fashion Star Cain, you haven't lived until you've seen an Australia Day. We celebrate our uniting of states with style. BBQ's on the beach, beach cricket, tennis, more beach, Aussie flags as capes, dunny races ('dunny' also known as an outdoor toilet), pavlova, and fireworks. Yes, we may hold onto our Queen (what can I say, we like the ol' bat), but we know how to party like a nation – on a beach, with an Esky. *Posted Wednesday 4th July at 19:35* [Comment . Like]

Mike Cain Here's the problem I face: [(4x^2-26)divided by 5)] times[4x^2) divided by(6-3x)]divided by [(x^2+4x) divided by 6]. Any ideas about the answer? *Posted Thursday 5th July at 16:20* [Comment . Like]

Jamiee Anderson Rum. Rum is the answer. *Posted Thursday 5th July at 16:43* [Comment . Like]

Tim Gleeve Bugger the answer, get rid of the problem. Hiring an assassin worked a treat for your sister. *Posted Thursday 5th July at 16:54* [Comment . Like]

Madeline Cain Fashion Star Turn the numbers into fruit and create fruit salad. Present to tutor as bribe. *Posted Thursday 5th July at 17:40* [Comment . Like]

Mike Cain She's already fruity enough. Don't you think if I could bribe this vindictive excuse for a human being I would have done so already? *Posted Thursday 5th July at 17:49* [Comment . Like]

Madeline Cain Fashion Star This is the watermelon teacher isn't it? *Posted Thursday 5th July at 17:50* [Comment . Like]

Mike Cain Maybe. *Posted Thursday 5th July at 17:53* [Comment . Like]

Madeline Cain Fashion Star You've dug your own grave with that one. *Posted Thursday 5th July at 17:54* [Comment . Like]

Lulu Tanaki Beanie: "When you watch Titanic backwards, it's a movie about a magic boat that saves lives…" *Posted Friday 6th July at 07:50* [Comment . Like]

Ray Star Oh how cute! So I suppose that means the Little Mermaid is a story about a girl who becomes a mermaid and a princess! *Posted Friday 6th July at 12:11* [Comment . Like]

Madeline Cain Fashion Star When you watch Psycho backwards, it's a tale about a guy with magic healing hands… *Posted Friday 6th July at 18:15* [Comment . Like]

Tim Gleeve If you watch Phone Booth backwards it's still about a man who spends an hour and a half in a phone booth. Ten points for consistency. It's like the palindrome of movies. *Posted Friday 6th July at 19:01* [Comment . Like]

Tim Gleeve OH! If you watch Texas Chainsaw Massacre it's about a guy who puts people back together with a chainsaw. *Posted Friday 6th July at 19:05* [Comment . Like]

Jade Annelli You're in a Horror Movie with the eight people in your friend box on your profile page. In order from top left (no cheating, Facebook knows exactly what it's doing):

- Decides the creepy house is safe – **Madeline Cain Fashion Star**
- Screams like a girl – **Cain Michaels**
- The one who trips while trying to escape – **Jarrah Annelli**
- The first to disappear – **Victoria Zeng**
- Murdered while saving you – **Richard Arnoou**
- Survives by faking death – **Josh Annelli**
- Has a solid plan for survival everyone ignores – **Kim Enuik**
- Is really the killer – **Cliff Wheeland**

Posted Saturday 7th July at 10:15 [Comment . Like]

You and **five other people** like this.

Josh Annelli It would be Maddie that got us into that mess. How is she so darn convincing? *Posted Saturday 7th July at 10:24* [Comment . Like]

Jarrah Annelli Not so much convincing as curious. She sees an open door and has to enter, it comes from her pizza delivery training. As a result we have to follow her to make sure the stories she tells us are actually true. *Posted Saturday 7th July at 10:37* [Comment . Like]

Madeline Cain Fashion Star I have witnesses to all my stories! At least I don't forsake you all to the killer by faking my own death. *Posted Saturday 7th July at 10:42* [Comment . Like]

Josh Annelli Hey, it's a dog eat serial killer world and I'll do what I have to, to survive, even if it means leaving a sister behind when she trips... *Posted Saturday 7th July at 10:54* [Comment . Like]

Jarrah Annelli Knew it, it was probably you who kicked me in the womb and gave me those funky cranial bruises. Doctors had no explanation, until now... *Posted Saturday 7th July at 10:58* [Comment . Like]

Cain Michaels Hey! How come I'm the screaming girl? *Posted Saturday 7th July at 11:12* [Comment . Like]

Jade Annelli Facebook always knows the right people for the job. *Posted Saturday 7th July at 11:17* [Comment . Like]

Madeline Cain Fashion Star I seem to recall a very hysterical noise being made when you first encountered Duncan... *Posted Saturday 7th July at 11:19* [Comment . Like]

Victoria Zeng At least you're not the first one to be murdered. By a crime writer no less. *Posted Saturday 7th July at 11:22* [Comment . Like]

Kim Enuik Always knew crime writers were secretly the world's best professional killers. They know such ingenious methods, in such great detail, there's no way they haven't 'dabbled' in the 'profession.' If no one listens to me on this then no wonder my survival advice is ignored. After living with my parents in every jungle on the south continent you'd have to hope I had a solid survival plan for all occasions. *Posted Saturday 7th July at 11:30* [Comment . Like]

Victoria Zeng Do you have one for zombie apocalypse? *Posted Saturday 7th July at 11:33* [Comment . Like]

Kim Enuik Um, I suppose so. *Posted Saturday 7th July at 11:34* [Comment . Like]

Victoria Zeng Doesn't fill me with confidence. No wonder no one listened to your plan. *Posted Saturday 7th July at 11:38* [Comment . Like]

Cliff Wheeland Like a magician, a writer never reveals his secrets or his sources. We just look for gullible subjects. *Posted Saturday 7th July at 11:50* [Comment . Like]

Kim Enuik A magician would be the best serial killer, or more to the point, messing with a magician's tricks and having them unknowingly skewer people with real knives while the real mastermind gets away would be a great serial killer. It's the perfect framed murder. *Posted Saturday 7th July at 11:53* [Comment . Like]

Madeline Cain Fashion Star Ok, where's the option of a friend developing Stockholm syndrome and helping the killer hunt the rest of us down? I vote Kim be moved to that character. *Posted Saturday 7th July at 11:56* [Comment . Like]

Jade Annelli Agreed. Cliff is the perfect killer. I'd be keeping my eye on those two. May Duncan protect you. *Posted Saturday 7th July at 11:59* [Comment . Like]

Richard Arnoou I would protect you, but I'm sorry to say I've already died a gory death protecting Jade via a ninja star made of ball point pens. *Posted Saturday 7th July at 12:06* [Comment . Like]

Kim Enuik Maybe serial killer Cliff will fill his pen with the blood of his victims and use it as ink to write his next master piece and sign books. *Posted Saturday 7th July at 12:10* [Comment . Like]

Madeline Cain Fashion Star Stop giving the serial killer ideas! Maybe you're the *real* killer. *Posted Saturday 7th July at 12:11* [Comment . Like]

Cliff Wheeland And the plot thickens... mwahahahaha! *Posted Saturday 7th July at 12:15* [Comment . Like]

Mike Cain joined the group **I Try Not To Laugh At My Own Jokes, But We All know I'm Hilarious.** [Like . Join]

Madeline Cain Fashion Star We all know you're funny, in the head... *Posted Saturday 7th July at 14:14* [Comment . Like]

Cliff Wheeland Has decided to write a book, something about a ring, swords and short people... "A Guide To Medieval Themed Weddings For Cats." *Posted Sunday 8th July at 17:00* [Comment . Like]

Kathy Bloomingdale Or perhaps "A Cat's Guide To Medieval Themed Weddings For The Vertically Challenged." *Posted Sunday 8th July at 17:30* [Comment . Like]

Cliff Wheeland Yes! Change the specification to ring, sword and beast! A Guide To Training Circus Lions. *Posted Sunday 8th July at 17:35* [Comment . Like]

Madeline Cain Fashion Star A Guide to Gladiator Tournaments For Dwarves. *Posted Sunday 8th July at 17:47* [Comment . Like]

Kathy Bloomingdale A Guide To Medieval Cage Fighting For Children. *Posted Sunday 8th July at 17:50* [Comment . Like]

Cliff Wheeland A Guide To Medieval Wedding Halloween Costumes For Minors. *Posted Sunday 8th July at 17:56* [Comment . Like]

Kathy Bloomingdale ?? *Posted Sunday 8th July at 17:58* [Comment . Like]

Cliff Wheeland You're right, that sounded funnier in my head. *Posted Sunday 8th July at 17:58* [Comment . Like]

Kevin Doherty The pilot episode goes live tonight! Will you choose The Job, Or The Money?? *Posted Monday 9th July at 11:28* [Comment . Like]

Madeline Cain Fashion Star Wow, that was some first episode… *Posted Monday 9th July at 19:46* [Comment . Like]

Kevin Doherty It was, wasn't it!? The executives were afraid it would be too confronting but I think everyone in there got the jest, even that sour faced CEO! *Posted Monday 9th July at 19:47* [Comment . Like]

Madeline Cain Fashion Star How did those patrons feel about walking the plank out a three story window? *Posted Monday 9th July at 19:50* [Comment . Like]

Kevin Doherty This was our first show, out biggest test, so a lot of the 'diners' were our extras. In the later shows we'll only be planting one person. I'll let you guess which were real members of the public! *Posted Monday 9th July at 19:55* [Comment . Like]

Madeline Cain Fashion Star Hm, the ones dressed as pirates? *Posted Monday 9th July at 19:57* [Comment . Like]

Kevin Doherty No, no, they were helping us 'take over the ship'. You get it? *Posted Monday 9th July at 19:59* [Comment . Like]

Madeline Cain Fashion Star Oh, I get it, I was just… Never mind. How exactly did you get permission to put a two story-high pool on the sidewalk? *Posted Monday 9th July at 20:02* [Comment . Like]

Kevin Doherty Ah, that was the most ingenious part, we just backed it in on a truck, already filled so no one would suspect. *Posted Monday 9th July at 20:02* [Comment . Like]

Kim Enuik Was that real rum you were forcing that poor

waiter to drink? *Posted Monday 9th July at 20:10* [Comment . Like]

Kevin Doherty Would a real pirate drink anything other than real rum? *Posted Monday 9th July at 20:12* [Comment . Like]

Kim Enuik I suppose not. *Posted Monday 9th July at 20:12* [Comment . Like]

Kevin Doherty Exactly! You can't call it *Your Job or The Money* if there's no risk of getting fired. People are expecting real life comedy, none of this fake scenario stuff. *Posted Monday 9th July at 20:14* [Comment . Like]

Cliff Wheeland There is nothing artificial at all... very realistic... *Posted Monday 9th July at 21:35* [Comment . Like]

Kevin Doherty Thank you! And funny right? *Posted Monday 9th July at 21:36* [Comment . Like]

Madeline Cain Fashion Star The look on the CEO's face when you mutinied and took his patrons hostage is one for TV history books. Shocked does not begin to describe his expression when you asked if he'd prefer a hook on his right or left hand. The parrot got the expression right, "Ark! Abandon Ship!" *Posted Monday 9th July at 21:40* [Comment . Like]

Kevin Doherty Heck yes! Thanks for holding my hand through the show. I know I analysed it a million times with you after it finished but I just get so excited you know? *Posted Monday 9th July at 21:41* [Comment . Like]

Madeline Cain Fashion Star Congrats on your first TV spot hon. May the ratings follow you like a foul mouthed pirate parrot. *Posted Monday 9th July at 21:42* [Comment . Like]

Kevin Doherty Took inspiration from your umbrella for that one. *Posted Monday 9th July at 21:43* [Comment . Like]

Mike Cain Yes! Laani's birthed a pirate version! My creative genius has crossed oceans! My teenage dream, to spawn an American sitcom has been realised. Do I get royalties on this? *Posted Monday 9th July at 22:17* [Comment . Like]

Madeline Cain Fashion Star Unfortunately brother dear, you do not have the monopoly on abusive companions of an inanimate or bestial variety. *Posted Monday 9th July at 22:26* [Comment . Like]

Kevin Doherty I did the voice for Pirate Polly too ? I do as many voices on the show as I can, apparently it not only saves money, but makes use of all my talents. *Posted Monday 9th July at 22:27* [Comment . Like]

So How Did It Really Go?.....[New Message]

[Back to messages. Mark as unread . Report spam . Delete]

Between **Kathy Bloomingdale, 2 others** and **You.**

Kathy Bloomingdale 10 July 2012 at 09:00 [Report]

Seriously, you can tell me. How was it really?

Tim Gleeve 10 July 2012 at 09:30 [Report]

Gonna give it to you straight; I'm not sure what that was.

Kim Enuik 10 July 2012 at 09:32 [Report]

Don't think they knew either.

Madeline Cain Fashion Star 10 July 2012 at 09:38

It wasn't that bad! How would you know anyway, Tim?

Tim Gleeve 10 July 2012 at 09:40 [Report]

I can get Netflix. How hard do you think it is for me to see your imaginary boyfriend's show?

Madeline Cain Fashion Star 10 July 2012 at 09:42

He's not imaginary! The whole of America can see him.

Tim Gleeve 10 July 2012 at 09:43 [Report]

You haven't been on a first date with him. That screams imaginary boyfriend to me.

Madeline Cain Fashion Star 10 July 2012 at 09:48

We've made out heaps of times! And swap texts every day.

Kim Enuik 10 July 2012 at 09:50 [Report]

She always comes home with this stupid grin on her face and spends five minutes in the doorway sucking his face off. Have you ever tried to keep a chameleon who loves freedom distracted for five minutes? It's like herding the Invisible Man.

Tim Gleeve 10 July 2012 at 09:52 [Report]

Texting and sucking face is called a booty call.

Kathy Bloomingdale 10 July 2012 at 09:52 [Report]

Hang on, you told me nothing had happened yet! Why haven't I heard any of this?

Madeline Cain Fashion Star 10 July 2012 at 09:53

It's not the sort of thing you throw around Facebook. Geez, I'm not an exhibitionist.

Kim Enuik 10 July 2012 at 09:53 [Report]

I beg to differ.

Madeline Cain Fashion Star 10 July 2012 at 09:54

Don't hate me because your soul mate is a lizard. People who post updates about their intimate lives make me gag. It's no one else's business.

Kathy Bloomingdale 10 July 2012 at 09:56 [Report]

Except mine. Are his abs as real as you thought they were? Does his touch give you goose bumps?

Madeline Cain Fashion Star 10 July 2012 at 09:58

Not now Kathy, there are men in this conversation.

Kim Enuik 10 July 2012 at 09:58 [Report]

Ugh! Build a bridge of romance books and get over it. So, getting back on topic, it was horrible.

Kathy Bloomingdale 10 July 2012 at 09:59 [Report]

What I understand is Kevin got some people to mutiny and then took something over and made people walk the plank out of a three story window?

Kim Enuik 10 July 2012 at 10:04 [Report]

The premise was awesome but the execution was in your face, kind of like Borat's mankini. Basically, a young waiter in this third floor restaurant has put his name in for Kevin's show, and for want of a better word, he's a dick. So Kevin, picking one of a dozen personalities he's perfected on Maddie and I in the past month, shows up as a pirate. The costume department, in my mind, should be shot. They took Jonny Depp's costume from Pirates Of The Caribbean and made it gayer.

Madeline Cain Fashion Star 10 July 2012 at 10:05

Say 'more flamboyant' Kim, it sounds better.

Kim Enuik 10 July 2012 at 10:07 [Report]

Whatever it was, he looked like a camp Aladdin. Kevin might be an actor, but he's also a footballer and one thing he can't do, is gay. Or funny, apparently.

Tim Gleeve 10 July 2012 at 10:09 [Report]

They probably had a photo of the contestant because they got the right guy straight away. The bloke must have hated his job. After Kevin set the whole mutiny scene into motion the waiter vaulted the counter, grabbed Kevin's rum bottle and took the biggest swig of courage I've ever seen. He then proceeded, with much gusto, to lead several dozen pirates into the kitchen to tie up the boss and the head chef.

Kevin and the cast of thousands insisted on including 'Arrrrr' in every sentence and in some places just replaced entire words with 'Arrrr'. It was like watching Maddie's pirate English Facebook page come to life.

Madeline Cain Fashion Star 10 July 2012 at 10:20

Kevin had a fake parrot on his shoulder that, like Laani, was particularly abusive towards heavily weighted individuals, dwarves, IQ and humans as a race.

Tim Gleeve 10 July 2012 at 10:21 [Report]

The parrot was the only thing that even partially redeemed the end of the show. "Walk the plank, we need a better gene pool," was my favourite.

Kim Enuik 10 July 2012 at 10:24 [Report]

Or, "This is how I teach my children to fly. Don't know why you're all so crap."

Madeline Cain Fashion Star 10 July 2012 at 10:28

Imagine this, Kathy: You're having a nice dinner and then a mob of pirates (with questionable sexuality) come roaring in, whisk away your waiting staff to a holding pen in the corner and proceed to 'loot' the shop, cash register and then give one very unstable and highly vindictive young man his own pirate patch and sword. It was a modern Atila the Hun in the making.

Tim Gleeve 10 July 2012 at 10:34 [Report]

I think the looting of the cash register was the point the manager started to cry, the big, bald pumpkin.

Kim Enuik 10 July 2012 at 10:35 [Report]

What was hilarious started going downhill from there.

Tim Gleeve 10 July 2012 at 10:38 [Report]

Gary the waiter started herding staff and customers off the plank, pushing them out the window with various kicks, pokes and calls of 'Arr' and 'Avast!'. It kind of became the story of one guy's revenge on the people he works with. Like Revenge of the Nerds but for psychopaths.

Kim Enuik 10 July 2012 at 10:42 [Report]

Pretty sure he's fired.

Tim Gleeve 10 July 2012 at 10:44 [Report]

Problem was, the parrot got all the best lines which made Kevin look like B-grade reality TV. Even though the parrot *was* Kevin, well, his voice.

Kathy Bloomingdale 10 July 2012 at 10:45 [Report]

Is it going past the pilot stage?

Madeline Cain Fashion Star 10 July 2012 at 10:48

Of course it is. Why do you think Wipeout is still airing? Anything involving pushing people out a two story window into a four metre high blow-up pool is going to be a hit. Also, people like seeing other people wacked with sticks. It's like the middle ages over here.

Tim Gleeve 10 July 2012 at 10:49 [Report]

I've already started seeing parrot memes taking off, but mainly these involve insulting the show or contestant.

Kim Enuik 10 July 2012 at 10:49 [Report]

Not the fame I think Kevin was going for.

Kathy Bloomingdale 10 July 2012 at 10:50 [Report]

Is he insulted?

Madeline Cain Fashion Star 10 July 2012 at 10:50

He doesn't know about the memes, but when he found out it was being picked up for a whole season he went out to party. Of course I got the pleasure of declining the party to deliver pizza. Yay… *Transforms into the Hulk and starts stomping on pizza ordering public*.

Kathy Bloomingdale 10 July 2012 at 10:51 [Report]

Are any of you going to show him the memes?

Madeline Cain Fashion Star 10 July 2012 at 10:52

Are you insane? I want to continue having a boyfriend. If I do that I might *never* get a first date.

Tim Gleeve 10 July 2012 at 10:53 [Report]

Need you ask? I'm spreading the memes as widely as possible, in as many languages as possible. Thank you Google Translate!

Kathy Bloomingdale 10 July 2012 at 10:54 [Report]

I reserve my judgement until I see the YouTube clips.

Tim Gleeve 10 July 2012 at 10:56 [Report]

Ah landlubber, ye of little faith. I won't offer to re-watch it with you, I may be tempted to punch that jumped up waiter in the testies and then I'd have a hole in my TV.

Kevin Doherty Look, I get it, I'm hot, but please stop staring. *Posted Thursday 12th July at 12:12* [Comment . Like]

> **Joe 'Touchdown' Patterson** Some chicks just can't get it out of their head that yeah, you're famous, but that doesn't mean you want their eyes on your junk all the time. *Posted Thursday 12th July at 14:00* [Comment . Like]
>
> **Kevin Doherty** It's super weird, it's like they're expecting me to walk around in costume all the time. I was hoping it would be more people asking for autographs and less people just staring, you know? *Posted Thursday 12th July at 16:09* [Comment . Like]
>
> **Madeline Cain Fashion Star** Maybe, they've all signed up for your show and think you're there for them and they finally have to decide if they're going to give their boss the finger! *Posted Thursday 12th July at 18:30* [Comment . Like]
>
> **Kevin Doherty** Man, I never thought of that. Thanks babe! Now I'm just gonna mess with their heads and wink at them. *Posted Thursday 12th July at 19:19* [Comment . Like]

Claire Holderness "Damn it Jim, I'm a duck, not a food processor." #MyDucksNameIsBones #HeIsOneThousandPercentDoneWithYourShit #FoodProcessorInsanity *Posted Friday 13th July at 18:00* [Comment . Like]

You and **Wyate Yosime** like this.

Claire Holderness Lasagne experiments are more tiring than anticipated. #TheMoreYouKnow #FoodProcessorInsanity *Posted Friday 13th July at 20:00* [Comment . Like]

Wyate Yosime Tell me about it yo. Making food from scratch is the bomb but sucks when you eat it in ten minutes and it took three hours study time to make. *Posted Friday 13th July at 20:45* [Comment . Like]

Madeline Cain Fashion Star I hope to do my own food experimentation shortly. Come on bank account! *Posted Friday 13th July at 20:50* [Comment . Like]

Claire Holderness #NotGivingIn #WillTriumph #BonesWillDefendMyHonour *Posted Friday 13th July at 20:55* [Comment . Like]

Jarrah Annelli Being inside Jade's room today has been an eye-opening experience. How come I don't have a brain that insists on organization of clothes by colour and type rather than freshly washed and last worn in High School? *Posted Monday 16th July at 09:43* [Comment . Like]

Madeline Cain Fashion Star Jade, your obsessive compulsiveness is weirding me out. *Posted Monday 16th July at 18:00* [Comment . Like]

Josh Annelli She's always been like that. If she lived at your house, all your food cans would be ordered first by expiration date and second by colour. *Posted Monday 16th July at 18:10* [Comment . Like]

Jade Annelli Don't hate me 'cause you ain't me. You all just wish you had me to Super Nanny your house. *Posted Monday 16th July at 19:25* [Comment . Like]

Mike Cain Intergalactic Spacemonkeys! *Posted Tuesday 17th July at 17:48* [Comment . Like]

Madeline Cain Fashion Star Have you been sending radio signals into space again? Or are you imagining your latest experiment? *Posted Tuesday 17th July at 17:56* [Comment . Like]

Mike Cain Merely imagining grander futures for my pets, dear sister. *Posted Tuesday 17th July at 18:10* [Comment . Like]

Madeline Cain Fashion Star If Mum has let you get a pet monkey, then I too am a monkey and we live on the planet of the apes. *Posted Tuesday 17th July at 18:29* [Comment . Like]

Madeline Cain Fashion Star I got paid! Woohoo! #ProbablyCookedTooMuch #ProbablyDontCare #YouCantTellMeWhatToDo *Posted Thursday 18th July at 13:29* [Comment . Like]

Claire Holderness Go Maddie #ImSoProudOfYou #HashtagORama #ConvertedToTheDarkSide *Posted Thursday 18th July at 14:22* [Comment . Like]

Kim Enuik Does this mean we'll no longer have enough tins to survive the apocalypse? *Posted Thursday 18th July at 14:30* [Comment . Like]

Madeline Cain Fashion Star No, it means we'll have no freezer space as I'm not letting this go to waste and you're not eating it! *Posted Thursday 18th July at 14:31* [Comment . Like]

Kim Enuik When have I stolen any before? *Posted Thursday 18th July at 14:32* [Comment . Like]

Madeline Cain Fashion Star Just setting the ground rules for Duncan. *Posted Thursday 18th July at 14:33* [Comment . Like]

Nadine Cain Congratulations baby! How was the first gig?
Posted Thursday 18th July at 15:42 [Comment . Like]

Madeline Cain Fashion Star Let's just say it was interesting…
Posted Thursday 18th July at 15:48 [Comment . Like]

P-Day

NOTES > My Notes [Write a note]

By **Madeline Cain P-hotographer.** Thursday, 18th July 2012 at 16:36.

I'm not quite sure what P-Day is supposed to achieve or why a school would want to run it on photo day. When I say 'school' it's really more of a day-care centre for kids whose parents are too stingy for summer school but too invested in their morning kickboxing/Botox sessions.

All I know for sure is, children are crazy. Nuts. Bonkers. And more than a little racist.

I'm not sure if they're born with it, or if baby food is laced with crazy pills, but they're all types of weird and have the energy of a small planet. Being a child high on life is probably the reason why I must now have afternoon naps. I used half a life's worth of energy in the first twelve years.

These masters of mayhem must make the parents also slightly crazy, it's the only way to explain my first encounter of the day. This woman was a prime I-use-day-care-to-go-shopping candidate. She wore an immaculate skirt suit in varying shades of pink, platinum blond locks, and a rock on her ring finger big enough to topple a twelve year old. Looking like everything I never wanted to be (a: a bimbo and b: in pink), she sashayed down the street, lead in hand, walking the world's cutest dog as I helped Josh haul boxes and lights from his hire car.

Flashes of fluffy white and black had me turn and say, "What a gorgeous dog, can I pat it?"

Next thing I know my pat has peeled off its scalp, like a horror movie, to reveal the curly locks of a young boy. On a leash. Dressed as a panda. Being walked by his mother.

"That's my son!" She looked like I'd just force fed her a Vegemite sandwich.

The boy looked up, all fours on the ground. "I'm a panda."

"God, I'm so sorry! I didn't get a proper – " I hadn't even finished my sentence before she stalked past me.

The kid said, "Your voice is weird." Turning his head, he then bit my finger.

"Sweet baby cheeses!" I shouted, wrenching my finger from the toothy Chinese finger trap.

I kid you not, this next bit 100% happened. The mother turned around and tapped her son on the nose like a dog. "No Rowan. No bitting."

"But I'm being a panda."

"I know baby, but pandas only bite animals, not people. Even if they look like more of a dog than you."

What?! Excuse me lady, but I wasn't the woman who had her child on a leash! Yes, kids are curlier than a pig's tail when it comes to speaking like a sane person, but they are *not* animals. If you're going to treat him like a dog and allow him to walk on all fours attached to a bloody *leash*, I, my next door neighbour, the homeless man across the road and every other human being is going to make that first leap to DOG. You can say he was a 'panda' until you're blue in the face, I've never seen a panda being taken for a morning walk.

Josh shook his head. "Gee, you sure know how to start off on the wrong foot."

Thanks Josh. You were a ton of anti-help topped with useless cream.

This boy and his mother were one of the illustrious families that attend the school we were about to enter. That should give you an idea of the level of insanity we had to deal with on my first 'real' photography gig.

Proudly proclaiming establishment before the First World War, the main building looked like it had been transplanted straight from the grounds of Oxford University. A three story building of long arched hallways and cathedral like windows, lofty columns and grey sandstone bricks, it looked like the wings had been appended in a rather haphazard fashion that only old buildings trying to keep up with the times had. Inside the entrance hall hard wood floors were hidden under thick patterned rugs in a vain effort to protect them from the variety of toys that littered the floor like a primary coloured night sky.

Children are the perfect white noise generator, using their lungs as bellows for a sound which can only be described as chaos.

When Josh told me the day was themed I couldn't bring myself to go pirate, so I figured 'photographer' would do. Josh, on the other hand, borrowed Kevin's costume, and *still* came away with three phone numbers.

Everything you can think of starting with P was represented in that room. We had pirates, painters, punks, princesses, polar bears, professors, prisoner (complete with black shoe polish on the face – see, racist), President (again with the shoe polish and racism), perfect (yep, that happened), policeman (with the most epic mo I have ever seen on a man let alone a child), Pink (singer), pink (colour), pilot, a pride of lions, Pokemon and a park ranger dressed like a Canadian Mountie. Oh, and a kid who was dressed like a French 'Poet' and wrote like a Trucker.

A short woman with a mass of curly brown hair the same chestnut as the wooden panelling on the walls, moved out from behind an oak desk and bustled towards us, dodging kids like they were balls.

"Joshua, what a pleasure!" Even though Josh is a stocky man of average height, she still had to raise to tippy toes to kiss both his cheeks.

"Hello again Miriam. I'd like to introduce you to my fellow photographer and assistant, Madeline Cain. She's from Australia."

"Ooh! An assistant, my you're moving up in the world aren't you, an assistant at your age," she cooed, slapping his arm lightly. It was like her gaze was magnetically fixed to his face.

Josh gave his trademark broad grin and turned his back to her to place his cases at my feet. He rolled his eyes and mouthed 'sorry'. I shrugged, knowing he'd done it because saying 'classmate' might indicate he wasn't a professional photographer.

Easy smile back, he turned towards Miriam again and she almost swooned. I was seeing the moves of a middle-aged-ladies' man in action and it was just as inexplicable now as it was when his sisters were teasing him. At least he had the sense to put on a t-shirt under the pirate vest, otherwise we'd have a Lynx ad on our hands. For those of you not aware, Lynx, is a male deodorant and according to TV ad execs, all a man has to do is spray it on and he's crash tackled by about fifty women in a supermarket isle wanting some of that sweet, sweet man odour.

"This wasn't quite what I was expecting from our initial meeting," he said as a 'police man' was divested of his gun at plastic sword point. "Are the kids having their solo photos in costume too?"

The woman's face fell. "Do you think it's too much? We've had such a hard time getting enrolments recently I thought if we could prove this is a *fun* place to be, we wouldn't have to close down. Oh God, it was wishful thinking, wasn't it?" she wailed.

Josh patted the older women's shoulder. Oh Josh, you rogue you. "No, not at all. We'll do our best to get you some great shots."

Putting down my shoulder bag, I blurted, "I can help with that."

Miriam looked at me in surprise, clearly she'd forgotten I was there in the midst of her Josh daydreams. I bent over the bag and started laying out the clothing that had me convinced yesterday that Dom was as crazy as the little people running around my legs.

Earlier the previous day, a man with a thick New York accent, buzzed my apartment dressed in a sharp black suit and crisp white shirt like a groom.

"The Boss sent these," he whisper-spoke, looking from side to side before shoving a massive box into my arms. "There's high demand in Europe for these and they're about to explode in the US. The kids can keep them, but make sure they tell anyone who asks, they're from Animal Designs. Got it?"

The man wasn't handsome but had a certain chiselled charisma about him that had me tongue tied. He stared at me until I realised he expected a verbal response. "Got it."

I'd opened the box to find the onesies I now laid at Miriam's feet. Looking around I realised Dom wasn't crazy, I just hadn't understood a kid's idea of fashion. These would fit in like a dinosaur at a Wiggle's concert. Each onesie was a different size and animal, some real, some from mythology, all utterly adorable.

"I've got another project I'm shooting for a fashion studio. I need some models for these *fun* and *funky* onesies. I know they're not all within the P-Day theme but my fashion shots would be great for a brochure to show to new prospective clients. Couple that with the photos we'll be taking for the current parents to take home and show their friends, and I think you'll have all the bases covered. I just need permission from the parents to use the kids."

I couldn't bring myself to look up, my mouth prattling too fast for my brain to apply the brakes. Yes, I stretched the truth a little, but I was living in empty wallet lane, all bets are off when you're wandering in that dodgy part of town. I finally looked up from my arranging to Miriam bouncing up and down with a smile so wide it looked like it would crack her cheeks.

Unable to help herself she clapped her hands. "What an amazing idea! You get set up for the regular shoot and I'll sort out permissions. Would there be a fee?"

Again my mouth jumped in before my brain. "Look, if we can get the kids to do it for free I'm sure I could convince my boss to allow you non-exclusive rights to the photos for a flat fee of five hundred dollars, *and* the kids can keep the Animal Designs suits. If the parents insist on payment that will unfortunately increase the cost for you."

I instantly regretted opening my big mouth and asking for payment, imagining scenes where Miriam demanded to know 'who is your boss', and 'why is your designer not pay for models'. I was already getting paid, I could have done it for free. But then I reminded myself to stand strong. I'd baulked at being bribed for a million dollars and ended up eating the colour red for two months. That changes a person from 'I just love photography' to hustling a school teacher for proper payment. I'd lost a pretend fortune and gained some perspective.

"They're expensive clothes and Madeline does some great stuff. Given that you need more students, I'd say an extra brochure is a perfect addition," said Josh, nonchalant as he rummaged through boxes, unpacking equipment.

Josh, I'd like to say you're a champ, and at that moment I would have put my underpants on the outside of my jeans and declared myself saviour of New York, fighting crime in your name if you'd asked me to.

Miriam eyed off the six onesies muttering, "Kyle, Jackie, Sophia, Michael, Storm and Lauren." Her hand rose and fell as though gauging height and size. Miriam looked me in the eye and said, "You leave it to me." She strode off towards her desk and phone.

Josh winked. "You're learning. Nice opportunity spotting. It's how I got my first gig taking photos of puppies graduating from puppy school. Now to mould these photos into an assignment in two weeks."

I groaned.

"Don't sweat it; fitting the brief will be easy. A little birdy told me it's 'Urban Jungle'."

"How would you know?"

"I'm in with the older ladies." Of course, May… "I'll start setting up chairs and rises in the library; you find a broom to clear the dust."

He hauled some planks under each arm and headed off across the carpet, passing through a door way at the far end and disappearing to the right. Miriam was chatting away on the phone so I cast around for other teachers, spotting two slightly harried women surrounded by a circle of children. I approached one, a redhead in a bright blue dress, in discussion with a pirate with a stuffed parrot in his hand; one of two dozen pirates scattered around the room.

"Excuse the interruption, but I was wondering where I might find a broom?"

"I know!" shrieked the pirate. Not waiting for a response he took off, legs motoring furiously.

"Miss! Miss! Miss!" A little princess tugged the bottom of the teacher's dress.

"Excuse me," she sighed. "Yes Mya, what is it?"

"Robert said he keeps his wee in the cupboard. Why does he keep wee in there?"

It's hard to believe people went to university to prepare for a Q&A like that.

"A Wii is a video game," she started to explain.

"Miss, miss!" The pirate was back. Proudly, chest puffed up, he thrust out a purple, plastic broom with straw bristles. "Here you are. Is this for sweeping the floor or are you going somewhere?"

I've never seen a more earnest face on someone who just asked me if I was a witch. Because of course a broom has two options for usage in the mind of a seven year old boy. I'm hoping the assumption was made because I was a woman who would look good in a pointy hat, not because I looked like a wart ridden hag who dresses like a bat.

Tugging the broom from his hand, I asked, "Don't you have class or something?"

"It's holiday time and we get recess *all* day, and sometimes we do arts and crafts. I glued my fingers to my eyebrows. See?" He craned his head back like a Pez dispenser and lo and behold half his left eyebrow was missing. No wonder the teachers looked shell shocked.

"Alright Kyle, move along please, our very important guest has things to do," said Miriam, swooping in to shoo away the boy. She was breathless and beaming. I figured being upgraded from 'assistant' to 'important guest' meant the calls had gone well. "It's done. They've all said yes! It took a bit of persuading, but when I looked up Animal Designs on the Google machine and told them each onesie was worth three hundred dollars, they agreed quick enough."

Three hundred dollars?? I'd been carrying around eighteen hundred dollars' worth of clothing for midgets in my bag! And had just given it all away to children who glued their fingers to their face in exchange for five hundred dollars. That'll teach me to not use my own Google machine before opening my mouth.

"I'll get the trolley for you so you can move the rest of your equipment to the library. That's where you'll be taking the photos. Brilliant idea right? Fun *and* learning in the one photo!" She bustled away, very much like one of her pupils, a bundle of unstoppable energy.

We managed to cram all the gear on the trolley and made our way through the impressively high vaulted hall to the library. If you've ever seen the Facebook page, 'Bookshelf Porn', ever salivated over the floor to ceiling books of Beauty and the Beast, the mahogany shelves, the rich piled rug, the massive windows set with window seats, then this room would have been your wet dream. Well, if it was minus a hundred and fifty kids wearing P-themed costumes.

While I slowly spun feeling like Belle, Josh was explaining to

Miriam. "It's best to only have twenty children in here at once during individual photos; otherwise the kids get self-conscious."

"I'm the king of the world!" shouted one kid.

Uh huh, soooo self-conscious. But as soon as we started taking shots, I realised the limit was less about the kids and more about making sure we weren't subjected to more than one crazy conversation at a time.

"I like bacon, do you like bacon?" asked the first kid to sit in front of a pretty set of book spines. I'd asked Miriam for someone who could sit still while I set up the lights and got the world's biggest bacon fan – a four foot tall boy dressed as a punk with his hair spiked in a ridge above his head.

"Sure mate, bacon's fine," I replied, shuffling the light box forward (a tall stand with a cube of white material that diffuses light).

"It's *amazing*. Bacon's chewy, bacon's crunchy! I will eat bacon today, tonight, tomorrow, next year..." He gazed off into the middle distance as though he'd seen Valhalla for bacon lovers.

I upped the exposure on the light to compensated for the dark of the library and swooped in to turn the boy to a 'pleasing angle' as Josh had shown me.

Three metres away Josh was doing the same thing for another little boy who said, "I want to be like you when I grow up, but with more hair."

I smothered a bark of laughter. Josh is by no means bald, but he's thinning a bit on the crown.

"Is that so mate? Cause I want to be like *you* when I'm older, except with more teeth."

It became apparent as we tried to cycle quickly through kids, that they were in some kind of unconscious competition to be the most bizarre human on the planet. In fact, Josh and I started rating them on our newly invented Bizarro Scale where zero was Future Accountant and ten was The Cause Of World War Three. An example of the rated conversations are included below for anthropologic study:

Miss Clueless = *4*

Me: Christmas will be here before you know it. Want to smile for Santa?

Kid: [Concerned] But, I haven't gotten a present for Mrs M yet.

Me: What did you get her last year?

Kid: Chocolates. It was bo-o-ring! I wanted to get her a toy.

Me: Nice, adults like toys. Where from?

Kid: From the adult toy store down the street.

Me: *Smile for Santa!*

The Five Year Old Widow = 5

Kid: My husband died.

Me: I beg your pardon?

Kid: My husband died. Choked on a toenail.

Me: Your husband? Do you mean your Dad? Have you lost your Dad? Was he…giving your Mum a foot massage?

Kid: No, my *husband*. But it's ok, I got a new one.

Me: Okay… good to know you're moving on.

Miss And-Then = 7

Kid: [Competing for the world record of number of words said in ten seconds] And-then-I-ate-a-bug-and-it-was-squishy-and-then-I-threw-up-and-my-Mommy-had-a-friend-over-and-they-threw-up-and-then-my-Barbie-ate-the-spew.

Me: I'm feeling nauseous myself.

Kid: And-then-the-Barry's-rolled-in-the-spew-and-Daddy-came-home-and-then-Mommy's-friend-was-pushed-into-a-window-so-I-went-onto-the-balcony-and-then-I-buried-my-sister-in-

Me: [Faintly] Who's Barry?

Kid: My-dog-and-my-brother-and-Mommy's-friend-they're-all-Barry-but-they-all-ignore-me-so-I-kicked-them-all-in-the-naughty-spot.

Mr Logic = 8

Me: Can we put that lantern down?

Kid: It's not a lantern. It's a bug catcher.

Me: Oh, are you catching butterflies?

Kid: No. I'm catching ladybugs… [He looks around furtively, then whispers] and leprechauns.

Me: I'm sorry did you say leprechauns? As in gold at the end of the rainbow?

Kid: [Silence]

Me: You know, leprechauns aren't really bugs, I mean, most stories say they're little people.

Kid: [Agitated, he climbs off the seat swinging the lantern like a lasso] They can't be people.

Me: [Tries to herd boy back to seat] Why can't they be people, mate?

Kid: Because... because... they can't be *people,* because... [whispers] because people don't have green parts on them.

Me: Fair call.

Kid: Why won't my lady bug walk straight?

There were so many wriggly bums, twitching heads, lost attention spans and stopping mid-sentence that you'd be forgiven for thinking you were dealing with speed addicts who had dementia. At one point an adorable princess, the bane of my existence, couldn't sit still for long enough to take a non-blurry photo, and I entertained the possibility that Josh had put a pea under the seat cushion to prove her royalty. That made me think of the 'wee' in the cupboard and I couldn't control my sudden chuckle.

After a moment of surprise the girl joined me and my internal photographic instinct kicked in snapping the best shot of the morning. I realised my crazed laughter was a secret weapon. It made grumpy kids smile, angry kids become confused (which looks more photogenic), wiggly kids sit still to laugh and the other kids in line all arrive at the chair attentive and focused on my every move, trying to figure out what the previous kids were laughing about. Which of course, was nothing.

I'd finally found my groove and the kids were all merging into one amorphous mass in my head. I fear I may have lost a little bit of sanity the more speed we gained. There was almost no need to apply the Bizzaro Scale anymore; the kids didn't have time for their crazy to manifest before the flash went off.

That was until we met the Mr Bubbles and Mr Panda tag team. Collectively they are a seventeen on the Scale, a blow it up, organise an alien invasion kind of home run. They waited until the whole school picture for their Bizzaro Scale audition, when all two hundred children had to join together in one second of co-ordinated merriment.

I'm not quite sure where Josh got his energy from (he probably never grew up, like a ginger Peter Pan) but he moved like a machine setting up the tiered stands. Then row by row we allowed certifiably insane miniature humans to bounce, dance and climb on those foot wide platforms.

"Fit them!" I declared triumphantly as the last plastic surgeon (good one Mum and Dad) stood in the bottom row.

But Miriam was shaking her head, counting and recounting. "Where's Ian? Everyone, where's Ian? He's dressed like a pumpkin."

"He's in the pooper!"

A kid fell off each end of the top tier as a wave of laughter crashed upon us and near made me deaf.

Unable to hear each other over the noise, Josh mimed the universal sign for searching for a wayward trouble maker and returned three minutes later with a young boy, the front of his balloon like costume soaking wet, his hair spiked up with water. My noise wrinkled at the strong smell of hand wash and toilet cleaner.

"What happened? How are we going to hide this?" Miriam looked as though someone had punched her in the stomach.

Frankly, it wouldn't have mattered if the stain was rainbow coloured with sparkles, there was enough going on in the photo without someone wondering about the discoloured pumpkin.

"I found him playing," Josh said.

Hands on hips, Miriam put on her stern teacher voice. "The washroom is not a water park, young man. Sinks are for washing hands only-"

Josh held up a hand to stop her. "Wait, there's more. Ian was blowing bubbles. In the toilet bowl. Repeatedly."

"I'm sorry, did you say *in* the toilet bowl. As in, put his face in the water and…" I couldn't finish.

"Expelled air in a violent manner, yes." Josh nodded, lips pursed. The sparkle in his eye (yes, they god damn sparkled!) said he was less angry and more just managing to keep it together.

"The bubbles are bigger the deeper I go," said Ian, head rolling from one face to the other, gauging just how naughty he'd been and just how awesome that now made him.

That's when phase two began. Mr Panda leant forward and bit a 'polar bear' in the first tier. As the polar bear head butted Mr Panda into the back row, the voice of that Barbie of a mother replayed in my head, *Animals only bite animals, not people.* Stupid woman. Children were too literal for that kind of inaccurate phrasing.

It was a domino effect, the polar bear flailed knocking a policeman into a small planet. A long, drawn out shriek pierced the air. Children bailed off the edge of the platform if they could, but the rest fell forward towards a poor young man, five at the most, dressed like a present.

I found myself moving against the tide of scattering children. It was a run by, if I'd been on a horse I would have hoisted his square little body up behind me on the saddle. As it was I swung in, grasped the cardboard armpit hole and hauled the little building block away from the descending tower of P.

When we cleared the melee the young boy plopped on his arse and stared at me, blinking.

"You alright?" Blink, blink. "If you're ok I'm going to fish the rest of your classmates out of their epic game of stacks-on." Blink, blink. "Alright then, nice rescuing you, Batman style. If only I had a cape, hey? I could be P-girl."

"What?"

"You're right, bad choice of superhero name."

In the thick of the fray Josh was grabbing the closest piece of material, lifting it into the air with its attached body, dusting each kid down and then providing this very scientific doctoral advice:

"Where does it hurt?"

Child points to body part.

"Put a tissue on it. There's a box next to my camera. Off you go."

I'd never known the vast array of medicinal purposes a tissue could cover, which in this instance included curing bruises, cuts, grazes, sore thumbs and unspecified boo-boos. Within five minutes we had a sea of children happily pressing white squares to a variety of body parts and one wiggling panda under Josh's muscled arm.

"Rowan, that was unacceptable," said Miriam, pointing a finger sternly at his face and almost losing it to gnashing teeth.

"I've got this," I said. Quick as a flash I rapped him on the nose and said, "No Rowan, no bitting. You're not a panda, you're a child."

"But Mom-"

"Is wrong, and you know better. Now behave or we'll chain you up like the animal you're pretending to be. And we'll feed you dog biscuits which are made from cat fur, ox butt and chicken blood. You don't want that, do you?"

His eyes were massive as Josh set him down.

"Now sit, and stay until we call you."

He nodded.

I'm pleased to say with Mr Panda delegated to the front row that the full class shot, with fidgets, poked tongues and all, only took five minutes to get right. I've never seen a group of kids stand with such military precision and I'm certain this time they all had their exit strategy planned out.

While Miriam organised the crowd into irregular lines for an arts and crafts session in another room, I convinced six young children in onesies to build human pyramids, and growl at the camera. When Miriam was particularly inattentive I also urged the kid in the monkey onesie to clamber up a book shelf for a particularly endearing shot of a monkey child reading a book.

The session was cut short by home time and a sudden influx of parents. Josh had done most of the pack down and I was helping him load the final piece of equipment onto the trolley when I felt a tug on my dress.

It was the 'present' I had rescued, shuffling from foot to foot. He thrust a note into my hand not lifting his eyes from his toes. With more than a little trepidation I opened it to find the following:

Wil u go out wit me?

☐ *No* ☐ *Yes*

Why is it the most romantic gesture I've ever received is from a boy who only comes up to my thighs? How is it that the romance in this novelty sized man gets squashed out of boys over eighteen? Does testosterone not only lower your voice but destroy your best chance of getting laid? Do all men go through some traumatic event that ruins them for life? Maybe romance goes out the window when you start playing with yourself.

I gave him my biggest smile. "Mate, this is so sweet, but you don't want to go out with someone like me. I'm too old."

"I don't care," he told his toes. "You're much nicer than the girls here. They're sticky and wear pink. Pink's disgusting." I nod at his words, wanting to be encouraging while letting him down gently. "I wanted to ask if you would marry me but I don't know how to spell 'marry'."

"Pink isn't all bad, I wear it sometimes and not all girls your age are sticky. I'm sure the girls here would line up to marry you."

"My dad said you need a woman with experience. The girls here, they think cooties is sex."

Speechless. I'm not exactly sure what it was about me that screamed, *experienced enough to know the difference between cooties and sex,* but I'm pretty sure that's not the message I want to send five year olds.

I licked my lips (not in a creepy way, more in a 'what have I walked into' way) and said, "Just to confirm, just so *I'm* not mistaking… sex for cooties, what do you think sex is?"

"Sex is when you take your clothes off…"

Check, step one.

"And you feel each other's skin…"

I suppose that's one way to phrase it, check step two.

"And you get kisses all the time."

Yep, still step two. But there was no more forth coming, he just stood there grinning at me. "And," I prompted, uncertain I wanted him to go further but far too curious to stop.

"And you have to be married."

I blinked.

"Yep, clothes, skin, kisses, marriage, you got sex figured out buddy," said Josh, face red from suppressed laughter. He casually draped an arm across my shoulders. "Sorry to disappoint you little dude, but I'm already going out with Maddie. So she's gonna have to tick the 'no' box, but there's a girl out there who wants kisses from you, I promise."

"Sean!" A lady appeared in the doorway to the library.

The kid, Sean, took back the paper I offered, his expression crestfallen. "Aw man. This blows," he said ,with the air of someone repeating words he doesn't know the meaning of.

We watched him in stunned silence as he wandered out to his Mum.

"Well, that was interesting," said Josh, removing his hand from my shoulder.

I shook my head. "I don't think I'll ever be ready for children."

I went to grab the trolley but Josh brushed me off. "Don't worry about it. Tomorrow, you'll feel like you've been hit by a bus. Go home."

He's right, oh so painfully right. I'm pretty sure kids steal a part of your soul. I don't think I've ever done that much work in seven hours *ever.* At least with pizza delivery you get alone time on the scooter. There are aches on top of my aches. I've barely moved from the couch since yesterday. I think Duncan thought I was dead; he kept licking me in the ear as though checking my temperature via ear canal.

The money we made on the job doesn't, proportionally, seem worth a day in a mental asylum. Thanks for the hospitality and opportunity Josh, truly, but you're as mad as the rest of them and are welcome to working those Mums solo.

[Comment . Like . Share]

Derek Chan and **74 others** like this.

Josh Annelli What the? You called me a middle-aged-ladies-man! I'm twenty one! *Posted Thursday 18th July at 17:04* [Comment . Like]

Madeline Cain P-hotographer That wasn't what I meant!

What I meant was you are a ladies' man for middle-aged woman. They're putty in your fingertips, your baby face charms them into imagining they're younger and... Gah, I think I'm making this worse. What I mean to say is you're young, they're middle aged. At least with me around you had more time to charm the ladies pirate style. *Posted Thursday 18th July at 17:17* [Comment . Like]

Josh Annelli I'll forgive you as long as you confirm these facts: 1) I am twenty one; 2) I'm a hottie and that 'bald spot' is a result of hat hair, nothing more and; 3) I, like Sean, like the older women and that's a sign of respect not creepiness! I understand where he was coming from, older women are mature, experienced, witty, a little desperate, and are way less sticky than women your own age. *Posted Thursday 18th July at 17:24* [Comment . Like]

Madeline Cain P-hotographer Agreed on all basic facts with the disclaimer that I don't pick up women so cannot confirm or deny any female specific benefits. *Posted Thursday 18th July at 17:25* [Comment . Like]

Josh Annelli Fair 'nuff. It was really nice having someone along to help out. That hour you were making the little 'animals' pose for fake fashion photos I would have normally spent trying to finish the shoot. I get RSI in my finger from that final hour. But this time I got to clean the equipment of unidentifiable sticky substances, back-up the photographs onto my hard drive, and do it all at a leisurely pace while having some delightful conversations with early arrived single-Mums. *Posted Thursday 18th July at 17:30* [Comment . Like]

Madeline Cain P-hotographer Holy donut, did I spend an hour on those photos? I can't believe the kids didn't chuck a tantrum. If we made that first kid sit on the chair for an hour he would have imploded from lack of bacon. *Posted Thursday 18th July at 17:33* [Comment . Like]

Josh Annelli You made the posing fun! You made it playtime where they were encouraged to do things Miriam would have pulled them over hot coals for. Too bad you don't want to keep doing it, we made a good team. The extra time I was able to take means the photos are better and more likely to sell. *Posted Thursday 18th July at 17:38* [Comment . Like]

Madeline Cain P-hotographer I'm not sure I believe you when you say we went at a 'slow' pace. I'm pretty sure I've developed arthritis. Sorry bud, I'm too young to take 'old days' after every job. *Posted Thursday 18th July at 17:41* [Comment . Like]

Josh Annelli Old days? *Posted Thursday 18th July at 17:41* [Comment . Like]

Madeline Cain P-hotographer Yeah, where you can't lever yourself up from the couch and you hold off weeing until the last moment because you just don't want to bend your joints. Having 'old days' when you're nineteen invites old age sooner. And I want to keep that arthritic, saggy breast visage at a hundred foot squint for a least another eight decades. *Posted Thursday 18th July at 17:43* [Comment . Like]

Josh Annelli Eh, you get used to it. How do you think I toned these muscles? *Posted Thursday 18th July at 17:43* [Comment . Like]

Jade Annelli You go to the gym every day. Don't pretend. *Posted Thursday 18th July at 17:44* [Comment . Like]

Josh Annelli You don't get this tone from a one hour work out. You get it from fishing costumed children out of a human pyramid. *Posted Thursday 18th July at 17:45* [Comment . Like]

Madeline Cain P-hotographer I understand your appeal to middle-aged women now! You manhandle their children, while showing off the guns. It's Kevin's guns that get me every time. *Posted Thursday 18th July at 17:48* [Comment . Like]

Kim Enuik Just to clarify, we're talking about upper arm muscles, right? You didn't just become a supporter for the National Gun Lobby? *Posted Thursday 18th July at 17:50* [Comment . Like]

Madeline Cain P-hotographer Of course not! What a stupid thing to do, allow any person a weapon when ninety-nine percent of people don't make reasoned decisions under pressure. That's just a recipe for craziness. Australia had a massacre in the nineties and that was enough for us to realise more of us are bonkers than we let on in public. *Posted Thursday 18th July at 17:54* [Comment . Like]

Kim Enuik Good, I thought the children may have broken you. *Posted Thursday 18th July at 17:54* [Comment . Like]

Madeline Cain P-hotographer Nope, and they'll never get the chance. Sorry Josh. But thank you for taking me out of poverty central and back into the realm of making ends meet. *Posted Thursday 18th July at 17:55* [Comment . Like]

Josh Annelli Pleasure. Don't forget, we're not done yet, we have a viewing at school tomorrow so we can convince parents these are the best photos ever taken of their kids and they should gloat to all the relatives by buying multiple copies. That's where the real money is made, the initial bundle was just the money paid by the school to have copies. Bring your game face. *Posted Thursday 18th July at 17:58* [Comment . Like]

Lulu Tanaki That kid was spot on about those leprechauns. Crafty little buggers, all this hording and hanging out near rainbows, probably more of a dragon than a human. Wow, it sounds like you got five years with my Beanie packed into one day, poor you. One of my most memorable days was when Beanie turned two and we left her in the bath for a minute (tops). When we came back there was poo in the bath! This had *never* happened before.

I said, "What is poo doing in the bath?"

To which she replied, "Floating." *Posted Thursday 18th July at 17:50* [Comment . Like]

> **Madeline Cain P-hotographer** That would have gotten a seven on the Bizzaro Scale. *Posted Thursday 18th July at 18:01* [Comment . Like]
>
> **Lulu Tanaki** I had it easier than my hubbie's Mum, he and his brothers used to pee in empty chip packets and leave them for each other to find. *Posted Thursday 18th July at 18:03* [Comment . Like]
>
> **Ray Star** My Mr D would have gotten a seven too! When we were travelling through Tasmania, all the constant moving around and being sick made him contrary. We were at a pub trying to order dinner. He kept saying he didn't want anything, and because we were in public we had to board the patience train even though we wanted to get off at 'stop being a little shit' station. Eventually he decided he would have calamari.
>
> Now, we always insist you use manners like please and thank you. So when Mr D said, "I want calamari." We breathed a sigh of relief and automatically asked, "What's the magic word?"
>
> His response?
>
> Abracadabra. *Posted Thursday 18th July at 18:05* [Comment . Like]
>
> **Lulu Tanaki** Kids! Where would we be without them! *Posted Thursday 18th July at 18:05* [Comment . Like]
>
> **Ray Star** I was a terror when I was a kid. My friend and I used

little pen knives to cut bamboos stalks and sharpen them into little spears. How there was no death, dismemberment or loss of eyes I shall never know! *Posted Thursday 18th July at 18:07* [Comment . Like]

Madeline Cain P-hotographer I've a very serious question for you guys: how do you discipline kids when every stupid thing they do makes you want to wet your pants from laughing? *Posted Thursday 18th July at 18:10* [Comment . Like]

Lulu Tanaki Over the years I've cultivated a great stunned rabbit look. It allows me to move my facial muscles in an upward direction, satisfying my smile impulse without actually breaking into a grin. *Posted Thursday 18th July at 18:12* [Comment . Like]

Ray Star I laugh really hard and then tell them they're grounded. *Posted Thursday 18th July at 18:15* [Comment . Like]

Madeline Cain P-hotographer The thing that got to me was how they're all twitchy, looking left and right like they're following ten tennis matches at once. I started to develop a complex. "Oh God, I'm totally the most boring person on the planet, aren't I? They can't even be bothered to finish their responses. Quick! Say something interesting." *Posted Thursday 18th July at 18:19* [Comment . Like]

Lulu Tanaki They're like crows; they see something shiny and they want to touch it. Don't take it personal. *Posted Thursday 18th July at 18:21* [Comment . Like]

Nadine Cain Honey, I can't wait until you have kids, I'm just going to laugh and laugh and laugh, particularly if they are as wilful as you were. If you met your child self in that room I can guarantee you would have won the bizarre human competition. You call your brother an evil genius but you were the original. I remember the time you and Mike were in the cubby house in the back yard with Kathy; you would have been about five. Then a hail storm came through. The next thing I know Mike is pounding on the door with his little fists, ice-cream container on his head demanding to be let in. You and Kathy had had a hankering for ice cream and weren't stupid enough to go out in the storm yourself, but you were persuasive enough to convince your brother to don the container as a helmet and get them for you. *Posted Thursday 18th July at 18:10* [Comment . Like]

Jarrah Annelli Maddie, you didn't!? *Posted Thursday 18th July at 18:20* [Comment . Like]

Madeline Cain P-hotographer Hey now, this is *not* a forum for your embarrassing stories. *Posted Thursday 18th July at 18:23* [Comment . Like]

Mike Cain What about the time you and I were on a see-saw going up and down, and you just *had* to see if you could break this particular rock in half? All except it rebounded off the ground and into my face. Three stiches and thirteen years later and I still have a wonky eyebrow. Girls say it's charming; I suppose I have Harry Potter to thank for that. Otherwise my prospects would be ruined. Ruined I tell you! *Posted Thursday 18th July at 18:30* [Comment . Like]

Madeline Cain P-hotographer Oh, so you want to go there? You want to 'play dirty'? Well then, everybody here may like to know a little story about a young boy who cleared a playground because he decided to have a poop as he went down the slide, leaving a nice, thick, brown trail for the other kids. *Posted Thursday 18th July at 18:31* [Comment . Like]

Mike Cain You always go to the God damn poo story! Get some new material! *Posted Thursday 18th July at 18:31* [Comment . Like]

Madeline Cain P-hotographer Why get new material when

the old works so well? *Posted Thursday 18th July at 18:31* [Comment . Like]

Nadine Cain Ok children, don't make me break up a fight on the internet. You were both very wilful children, you both did a plethora of fun things I'm saving up for your twenty-first birthday parties, to which all of your Facebook buddies are invited. I never fed you baby food (I preferred to make my own) so I can't claim the presence of crazy pills, but I did lace your food or drink with spirits sometimes. *Posted Thursday 18th July at 18:35* [Comment . Like]

Madeline Cain P-hotographer What? *Posted Thursday 18th July at 18:35* [Comment . Like]

Mike Cain You got me drunk before I could even walk? *Posted Thursday 18th July at 18:35* [Comment . Like]

Nadine Cain It was only the tiniest amount, I wasn't trying to make you alcoholics. But sometimes a mother needs her sleep and that was how we did it in those days. These days they say it prohibits mental growth, but you two turned out alright. Young children are very resilient. *Posted Thursday 18th July at 18:37* [Comment . Like]

Tim Gleeve I like bacon, do you like bacon? Of course you do, everyone likes bacon. Whether it's crispy bacon, salty bacon, smoked bacon, soft bacon, Christmas ham bacon, turkey bacon, American style bacon, maple bacon, chocolate covered bacon, back bacon, cottage bacon, jowl bacon, slab bacon, side bacon, streaky bacon, middle bacon, hock, gammon, collar, picnic, on toast, on waffles, on its own, bacon is a tasty meat all should partake in and rejoice. Except Jews. You'll go to hell for that. Sorry. Our God doesn't care as much because he probably eats bacon too. *Posted Thursday 18th July at 18:50* [Comment . Like]

Madeline Cain P-hotographer You and that kid are soul mates. *Posted Thursday 18th July at 18:51* [Comment . Like]

Tim Gleeve What can I say, bacon gets my juices flowing. I'd like to point out you were incorrect in your assumption that every P-related thing was represented in your costume frenzy. Where were the pancakes, the pinecones, the plants, and the penguins? More importantly, where was Pacman? What's wrong with these kids that there's not a single Pacman among them? *Posted Thursday 18th July at 18:53* [Comment . Like]

Kathy Bloomingdale There was no Polly Anna! No Pippy-Long-Stockings. *Posted Thursday 18th July at 18:54* [Comment . Like]

Tim Gleeve Also, there were no paedophiles. There should have been at least one kid with a handle bar moustache going around slapping peoples' butts. *Posted Thursday 18th July at 18:54* [Comment . Like]

Madeline Cain P-hotographer Dude, no! That's not cool; you can't joke about that shit. *Posted Thursday 18th July at 18:55* [Comment . Like]

Tim Gleeve You're right, sorry. Did anyone at least go as a pansy? In costume form it would probably look like a boy wearing a dress and making limp hand movements. *Posted Thursday 18th July at 18:55* [Comment . Like]

Madeline Cain P-hotographer Sorry, we only had the flower kind of pansy. I can see why you don't have children. Pretty sure you couldn't romance a girl for long enough. If you ever, I don't know, adopt, please dress your child as Pacman. *Posted Thursday 18th July at 18:57* [Comment . Like]

Tim Gleeve Incidentally, the traumatic experience that sucks all romance out of boys is accidentally seeing your mother walking naked through the house when she thinks you're away for the night. *Posted Thursday 18th July at 18:58* [Comment . Like]

Victoria Zeng How do you write poetry like a trucker? *Posted Thursday 18th July at 18:51* [Comment . Like]

Cain Michaels Roses are red, violets are blue, my poems stink, like Mike's poo poo? *Posted Thursday 18th July at 18:54* [Comment . Like]

Mike Cain I hit a Kangaroo last night, now it is road kill, that little critter was in the way, of my run to the mill. *Posted Thursday 18th July at 18:57* [Comment . Like]

Tim Gleeve Roses are red, bacon is red, something something something, bacon. *Posted Thursday 18th July at 19:00* [Comment . Like]

Kathy Bloomingdale Dom came through, that's amazing! I thought for sure it was one of those 'in the moment' promises. Reckon I could pull off a photo shoot? I wouldn't mind me some of that. It's a shame your first fashion models weren't the fizziest cans in the six pack. Next time, promise them copies of the photos. That way the super expensive brands won't be represented by people who glue their fingers to their face. By the way, what the hell is a 'whisper-spoke'? *Posted Thursday 18th July at 19:14* [Comment . Like]

Madeline Cain P-hotographer I know right! It makes me uneasy that random people are going to be appearing at my door though. What if there's more than one person out to kill Dom and they're pissed I stopped the first attempt? Should probably send him an email about sending only one messenger so I know who to open the door to... It kind of feels like I have a patron, who would also take a bullet for me. It's bizarre. And to answer your question a whisper-spoke is half way between a whisper and speaking. *Posted Thursday 18th July at 19:16* [Comment . Like]

Kathy Bloomingdale That's not a thing. The closest thing to what you described is a 'stage whisper'. *Posted Thursday 18th July at 19:16* [Comment . Like]

Jason I'Anson Good on you for asking for money for your work, a big step forward! I hope it's the course that has given you the confidence. I remember working with kids, it was like taking a visit to topsy-turvy world. Good to see you're making a move for Sorella's internship. I was surprised you were interested. If I'd known I would have told you all sooner. Sorella has a wealth of knowledge, so there's no doubt she could teach you a lot. See you on the 30th for our first lesson back! I know it was a short break but there's a lot we need to fit into a one-year course. *Posted Thursday 18th July at 19:22* [Comment . Like]

Madeline Cain P-hotographer Thanks for your support, Jason! I heard about the internship and thought it was a great way to learn from another of my favourite photographers. I've never had a photography preference so am making sure I have a full range of experience before the year is over. See you on the 30th! *Posted Thursday 18th July at 19:28* [Comment . Like]

Mike Cain Fake it until you make it, baby. *Posted Thursday 18th July at 19:29* [Comment . Like]

Virginia Low How inhuman, walking a child like a dog! No living thing should be subjected to a leash, it's cruel. That mother should be reported to child services. *Posted Thursday 18th July at 19:33* [Comment . Like]

Madeline Cain P-hotographer It's silly sure, but it's not considered reportable, I mean the leash isn't around the neck or the mouth, it's like a harness. *Posted Thursday 18th July at 19:40* [Comment . Like]

Lulu Tanaki Sometimes I wish I had a leash for Beanie. While I would tell myself it was for her safety, I would know it was really because I was too lazy to run after her. *Posted Thursday 18th July at 19:41* [Comment . Like]

Mike Cain No surprise the young pirate called you a witch. You say your cackle was used as a secret weapon, I say it was your witchy-ness showing through. Then there was this talk of feeding young children dog biscuits made from cat fur, ox butt and chicken blood. Classic witchy behaviour. The kid was probably psychic, sniffing out your inner nature before you even knew yourself. You can't stop the transformation now, the children have unlocked it and your inner witch will not be silenced! *Posted Thursday 18th July at 19:46* [Comment . Like]

Madeline Cain P-hotographer If she won't be silenced then perhaps she can tell me how to cast a hex on an annoying little brother. *Posted Thursday 18th July at 19:50* [Comment . Like]

Mike Cain What could you hex me with? A 'descending tower of Pee'? Turning my Wii in the cupboard into actual wee? Come on P-girl, do your worst. *Posted Thursday 18th July at 19:52* [Comment . Like]

Tim Gleeve P-girl, not your finest brain fart. *Posted Thursday 18th July at 19:52* [Comment . Like]

Madeline Cain P-hotographer I hex you both to be hairless and for every woman you touch to suddenly love someone else! *Posted Thursday 18th July at 19:53* [Comment . Like]

Richard Arnoou Bet it took them ages to figure out a tissue was a Kleenex. *Posted Thursday 18th July at 19:58* [Comment . Like]

Madeline Cain P-hotographer Not as long as you might think. They may be as crazy as a Picasso, but they're use to people throwing words at them and working out what that means. *Posted Thursday 18th July at 20:00* [Comment . Like]

Jade Annelli What was with the girl who told you her husband died? *Posted Thursday 18th July at 20:02* [Comment . Like]

Madeline Cain P-hotographer Haven't got a clue. I asked Miriam and she said her Mum and Dad had been happily married for as long as she's been kicking around earth. They've never been in a previous divorce; no one has died in the making of her story. I'd say she picked it up from somewhere else and says it to people because of their reaction. *Posted Thursday 18th July at 20:04* [Comment . Like]

Kim Enuik I'm staying the hell away from the one who kicks all the male characters in her story in the 'naughty spot'. She would have been my pick for the Bizarro Award. Though the kid blowing bubbles in the toilet made me gag. *Posted Thursday 18th July at 20:06* [Comment . Like]

Josh Annelli Try being the one to find him. Young boys usually find enjoyment by peeing up the walls or in the sink or throwing toilet paper rolls around the room. But sticking your face in the hole reserved for your bottom end? *Posted Thursday 18th July at 20:10* [Comment . Like]

Cain Michaels Pretty sure this kid is going to get pink eye. That'll teach him. *Posted Thursday 18th July at 20:12* [Comment . Like]

Tim Pirate Parrott -> Madeline Cain P-hotographer Arr! Just a shame the sun isn't yet o'er the yardarm! Need me rum ration! *Posted Thursday 19th July at 10:07* [Comment . Like]

Madeline Cain P-hotographer Thought you said you weren't going to watch it again? *Posted Thursday 19th July at 12:34* [Comment . Like]

Tim Pirate Parrott There are better things to do than re-watching reality TV. No, I'm just passing on a Pirate Parrott meme from a certain show we both know and are confused by. *Posted Thursday 19th July at 13:47* [Comment . Like]

Madeline Cain P-hotographer Don't you drag me into this or so help me I'll start making memes about your unfortunate sexual and bug collecting hobbies. I know more people than you do here. *Posted Thursday 19th July at 14:26* [Comment . Like]

Kathy Bloomingdale Apparently I wore my shirt inside out ALL day. *Posted Saturday 21st July at 19:23* [Comment . Like]

Tim Pirate Parrot Is that Gangnam style? *Posted Saturday 21st July at 19:48* [Comment . Like]

Madeline Cain P-hotographer What does it say about your dress sense that you can't tell when something is reversed? *Posted Saturday 21st July at 19:55* [Comment . Like]

Kathy Bloomingdale Dress sense has nothing to do with it. It means I need to start sewing tags onto the clothes I make. Who knew that's what the subconscious dresser looks for to determine you're not walking around like a retard. *Posted Saturday 21st July at 20:13* [Comment . Like]

Jarrah Annelli I tried to tell my boss her shirt was inside out and she got a bit shirty ? She told me ragged seams was the style. Which would have been fine if the tag wasn't hanging out the back… *Posted Saturday 21st July at 20:18* [Comment . Like]

Madeline Cain P-hotographer Did you say, "Cool. I think it's great marketing to let everyone know the size and brand you're wearing, in case they want to buy one." *Posted Saturday 21st July at 20:23* [Comment . Like]

Jarrah Annelli Should have. *Shrug*. Instead I just yelled in my head, "Fine. You look like a hobo if you want." *Posted Saturday 21st July at 20:25* [Comment . Like]

Diana Lynal That's supposed to be good luck. Did anything amazing happen? *Posted Saturday 21st July at 20:48* [Comment . Like]

Kathy Bloomingdale Not unless you count a bird pooping on your head as also lucky. In which case, I should buy a lottery ticket. *Posted Saturday 21st July at 20:51* [Comment . Like]

Jade Annelli I once wore a dress backward at a convention. Moderated a fan-fic panel on stage and everything. *Posted Saturday 21st July at 20:57* [Comment . Like]

Tim Pirate Parrot I feel like we would be good friends, Jade. *Posted Saturday 21st July at 20:59* [Comment . Like]

Madeline Cain P-hotographer I feel like I would never introduce you in real life. *Posted Saturday 21st July at 21:00* [Comment . Like]

Harry Lee We built this city! We built this city on the wrong, damn road! *Posted Sunday 22nd July at 09:31* [Comment . Like]

Tim Gleeve I think you'll find it's 'rock and roll' mate. *Posted Sunday 22nd July at 16:11* [Comment . Like]

Tim Pirate Parrot <3 <3 <3 <3 Copy this and put it in your status if you know anyone, or have heard of anyone, who knows someone. If you don't know someone, than it's even more important that you copy this. We need to spread the message… and the hearts. For f#%&s sake, don't forget the hearts! <3 <3 <3 <3 *Posted Tuesday 24th July at 12:35* [Comment . Like]

Mike Cain Word. *Posted Tuesday 24th July at 16:33* [Comment . Like]

Madeline Cain P-hotographer You two should have been brothers. *Posted Tuesday 24th July at 17:14* [Comment . Like]

Tim Pirate Parrot I could deal with that. *Posted Tuesday 24th July at 17:20* [Comment . Like]

Mike Cain Hypothetical High Five... *Posted Tuesday 24th July at 17:35* [Comment . Like]

Madeline Cain P-hotographer -> Jarrah Annelli and **Jade Annelli** I know half naked men isn't really 'our' thing. But I felt something was missing from your wall today...you're welcome ? *Posted Thursday 26th July at 11:24* [Comment . Like]

Jarrah Annelli You know just how to sustain us on our long flight back to New York ? *Posted Thursday 26th July at 13:06* [Comment . Like]

Jade Annelli I can tell you that isn't Photoshopped, I've seen enough to know ? *Posted Thursday 26th July at 13:07* [Comment . Like]

Derek Chan Excuse me Mr. Pringle, but I can't get my hand inside your tin of goodness... *Posted Friday 27th July at 13:49* [Comment . Like]

You and **5 others** like this.

Ray Star Yesterday, Mr D made his first ever snowman at our holiday cabin in New Zealand. He said the balls were too heavy to stack vertically. The result? A drunken, passed out snowman. The look on the next door neighbour's face was priceless. *Posted Sunday 29th July at 14:12* [Comment . Like]

> **Madeline Cain P-hotographer** THAT's what I'm going to do in Central Park when Christmas comes. A whole field of them! Who's with me? *Posted Sunday 29th July at 16:58* [Comment . Like]

> **Josh Annelli** Done! *Posted Sunday 29th July at 17:30* [Comment . Like]

Lulu Tanaki Oh dear. I love my Beanie, but when the pre-schoolers have a 'jam' session in music it sounds like a really bad Hari Krishna band. *Posted Monday 30th July at 10:24* [Comment . Like]

> **You** and **Ray Star** like this.

Josh Annelli -> Madeline Cain P-hotographer Phew! *Wipes heavy sweat from his brow*. See, told you the assignment fit. Good to have class again! *Posted Monday 30th July at 17:52* [Comment . Like]

> **Kim Enuik** Ooooh, what was it? *Posted Monday 30th July at 18:10* [Comment . Like]

> **Josh Annelli** 'Urban Jungle'. Basically, Jason wanted us to 'create art out of order', taking something 'rigid and conformed' and showing its 'wild side'. If you have the ability to create atmosphere in a sterile, uniform environment, you're on your way to a collar full of gold stars. Or should I say a onsie full of gold stars. *Posted Monday 30th July at 18:24* [Comment . Like]

> **Madeline Cain P-hotographer** I think he was going for an architectural angle here. But instead of getting buildings, Jason's getting children in pyjamas. *Posted Monday 30th July at 18:39* [Comment . Like]

> **Tim Gleeve** Kind of like Bananas in Pyjama's but less yellow. *Posted Monday 30th July at 20:15* [Comment . Like]

Madeline Cain P-hotographer And slightly less edible. *Posted Monday 30th July at 20:22* [Comment . Like]

Tim Gleeve What sort of a potential mother are you, advocating the consumption of childhood icons?? *Posted Monday 30th July at 20:27* [Comment . Like]

Madeline Cain P-hotographer Pass the iceberg lettuce, I'm having a party! *Posted Thursday 2nd August at 10:24* [Comment . Like]

Kathy Bloomingdale Why? *Posted Thursday 2nd August at 14:10* [Comment . Like]

Madeline Cain P-hotographer Because we finally have a date locked in! *Posted Thursday 2nd August at 17:19* [Comment . Like]

Kathy Bloomingdale Thank GOD! Go pop that date cherry. *Posted Thursday 2nd August at 18:00* [Comment . Like]

Madeline Cain P-hotographer Seriously, Kathy, you need to go on more dates… *Posted Thursday 2nd August at 20:40* [Comment . Like]

The Most Understanding Man In The World.....[New Message]

[Back to messages. Mark as unread . Report spam . Delete]

Between **Kathy Bloomingdale, 2 others** and **You.**

Madeline Cain Date Destroyer 6 August 2012 at 01:05

I don't understand why I was so nervous… I should have been zen like Bruce Lee, but instead I was like a grandmother who found herself in crotch-less panties. As popping date cherries go, that was one hell of a bang.

Kathy Bloomindale 6 August 2012 at 01:10 [Report]

Can it be any worse than face planting in his crotch and turning his uniforms pink? It doesn't get much worse than remaking a football team into a fairy tea party.

Jade Annelli 6 August 2012 at 01:12 [Report]

She's right, put it in perspective, how much worse is it than the Flamingo League?

Madeline Cain Date Destroyer 6 August 2012 at 01:13

Let's call it a sliding scale. As Kevin's embarrassment decreases, mine reaches infinity and beyond. Really, I should never have given myself the whole day to get ready.

Jarrah Annelli 6 August 2012 at 01:15 [Report]

Oh no, *never* give yourself more than forty minutes prep time. Or before you know it your floor-drobe is out of control and you're buried neck deep in your roommate's knickers.

Early prep was your first mistake. You don't mind if we analyse this date of yours do you? It's how Jade and I refine our game plan. You make mistakes so we can avoid them.

Madeline Cain Date Destroyer 6 August 2012 at 01:16

You'll find some great what *not* to do's in this story. There was no reason to be worked up, but there I was dancing around like I had ants, bees and leprechauns (proved to be a 'bug' in last month's FB note) in my pants. I was dressed and ready at 1pm for a 6pm date.

I couldn't stand the thought of battling my insecurities for five hours. So I did the only thing I could think of; I took some of Kim's Valium.

Kathy Bloomingdale 6 August 2012 at 01:16 [Report]

I'm sorry, I could have sworn you just told us you opened someone's *unknown prescription medication and took one of the pills*. I clearly had wax in my eyeballs. Could you please repeat?

Jarrah Annelli 6 August 2012 at 01:17 [Report]

No wait, let me guess! It wasn't Valium, was it? Was this 'Death at a Funeral' Madeline style? I can see Kim as an uppers rather than a downers man. What did the pill make you do? Hallucinate? Build a blanket fort? Strip to your underwear and go running down the halls screaming, 'The Asians are coming!'

Madeline Cain Date Destroyer 6 August 2012 at 01:17

What? No. It was definitely Valium. I passed out on the couch. But it wasn't a, 'I'm tired' pass out or a, 'I drank too much' pass out. It was a, 'miss the apocalypse' pass out.

Jade Annelli 6 August 2012 at 01:17 [Report]

This is the most boring embarrassment story ever. So basically, you drooled through your meal, maybe fell asleep on your spaghetti? Is that what happened?

Madeline Cain Date Destroyer 6 August 2012 at 01:25

I wish. That scenario is like puppies and rainbows.

No, Duncan happened. I take Valium, lose five hours of my life to a drug induced coma and then wake up to a knock, only to find Duncan using my face as a jungle gym. Let me reiterate: I was so out of it I *didn't even notice a chameleon on my face!*

A rough, wet tongue slapped me on the forehead. "Hola!"

I did the appropriate hair raising shriek and leapt to my feet divesting myself of lizard. Disorientation doesn't begin to describe my state of mind.

Kevin called in his best cowboy impersonation, "Is everything okay there pretty lady? You need me to kill some varmints for you?"

Meanwhile, I've yelled at Duncan, "Does my face look like a bed to you?!"

I stumbled to the kitchen to collect my hand bag only to find El Whappo had gotten into the dark coco again, powder strewn across the counter. The clock on the wall said 6:30 *you-don't-have-time-to-clean-me-up* pm. No wonder Kevin thought something was wrong, I was half an hour late for our first date.

So I raced to the front door and dove through, slamming it shut behind me to foil Lizard Houdini's escape. Kevin, forced to the opposite wall as I barrelled out of my apartment, stared at me, stunned.

"I'm so sorry I'm late, I had lizard troubles," I gushed, all the calming properties of the Valium flushed out of my system by the adrenaline fuelled wake up call. "You said we had a booking for six forty-five right? I'll grab us a cab. It's so great to see you, man you smell nice."

Eyes wide, he nodded slowly.

I kept telling myself to *just shut up and stop babbling*, but when have I ever listened to myself? "Let's do this, cowboy!"

"Um, ok," he said, hesitating slightly before following my power walk to the elevator.

In trying to get my brain in order I'll admit, some things were working double speed at the expense of more important functions, like lucidity. Slurring may also have occurred as I tried to figure out how my mouth worked after five hours of intense relaxation.

Hitting the elevator button, I gave him my best sexy grin. Back then I still thought I could normalise things. He had the most peculiar expression on his face. It was like he'd something to ask but wasn't quite sure how to begin. He didn't even try one of his endless parades of characters on me, the cowboy seemingly left for dead. I stupidly took it as a feather in my cap.

Look at that, muscle man Kevin is made nervous by little old me.

The elevator door opened and expelled the thickly bearded medical student who lived down the hall. Normally a quiet fellow who mumbles 'hello' to his feet, he looked at us and said, "What's with the mo?"

It was awkward for a second but he didn't bother to stare us down; shrugging, he walking off.

We stepped into the elevator and I turned to my clean shaven boyfriend. "What was that about?"

To which he responded, with words I never thought to hear from his mouth, "You have a Hitler-stache. You know I'm Jewish, right?"

Jarrah Annelli 6 August 2012 at 01:25 [Report]

You had a WHAT?

Madeline Cain Date Destroyer 6 August 2012 at 01:26

That's not all. Not only did I have a Hitler moustache, I also had a monobrow *and* a goatee.

Kathy Bloomingdale 6 August 2012 at 01:26 [Report]

How could you possibly have – oh wait, this new facial hair of yours wouldn't happen to have a bitter, chocolaty taste would it?

Madeline Cain Date Destroyer 6 August 2012 at 01:27

Give the lady a super hero cape, she figured it out.

Jarrah Annelli 6 August 2012 at 01:27 [Report]

I don't understand, how could you spend all that time getting ready for a date and not look in a mirror? Did you binge eat in your sleep?

Kathy Bloomingdale 6 August 2012 at 01:27 [Report]

It was Duncan. He made himself a finger painting in the kitchen with coco and thought he'd share the love with his favourite coma patient.

Jade Annelli 6 August 2012 at 01:28 [Report]

You're joking!? That's some strategic finger painting for a reptile.

Madeline Cain Date Destroyer 6 August 2012 at 01:28

Yes indeedy, I was a combination of Freda, Hitler and Keith Urban. It was like Movember had come early and wanted to decorate my face from all angles. May rotten cucumbers drag you to the depths of hell Kim and Duncan! It's like they tag teamed my imminent demise.

Kathy Bloomingdale 6 August 2012 at 01:29 [Report]

Come on, that's a bit dramatic. I'm sure Duncan doesn't even know what a Jew is, let alone how to purposely offend one.

Madeline Cain Date Destroyer 6 August 2012 at 01:29

I CAME OUT ON A FIRST DATE WITH A JEW IN A HITLER-STACHE!

Jade Annelli 6 August 2012 at 01:29 [Report]

It's like Duncan *wants* Kevin to dump you so he can have you all to himself again. He seems like a jealous creature, bad at sharing his humans.

Kathy Bloomingdale 6 August 2012 at 01:30 [Report]

You're right; this kind of trumps the pink uniforms incident. So what did he do? He didn't cry again did he?

Madeline Cain Date Destroyer 6 August 2012 at 01:34

You'd think a moustache of such historical importance would have ended our relationship by the ground floor, but no, Kevin is the most understanding human on the planet. There aren't many men who'd give you a second shot after that.

"I'm so sorry! Duncan crawled on my face while I was sitting on the couch and I didn't realise. I'm gonna kill that lizard!"

Not the best choice of words, considering.

I couldn't look at Kevin. All I could do was listen to the sound of walls rushing by.

Then, to my relief, cowboy Kevin manifested. "Damn critters, getting into things they're not supposed to!"

I never thought I'd be glad to hear him enter multiple-personality land.

Not only did he take my explanation at face value, but he dirtied his handkerchief cleaning the mess from my face.

Jarrah Annelli 6 August 2012 at 01:35 [Report]

Holy toast! I wasn't expecting that from a narcissistic method actor. Sorry, I know he's your boyfriend but sitting through fifteen minutes of his method acting made me feel like I'd taken crazy pills. I understand the purpose is to immerse yourself in character, but I don't think Kevin understands that cycling through a character a minute is not immersive, it's schizophrenic. This has redeemed him a little in my eyes, that was champion of him.

So, crisis over?

Madeline Cain Date Destroyer 6 August 2012 at 01:38

Oh young smurf, it was just the beginning, we hadn't even sat down to masticate our food yet. The next incident happened at the restaurant. I've never been to one quite like it. For example, you get no choices as it's a set menu for the night. If you had a 'delicate constitution', also known by its less wanky term, 'allergies', you could then, and only then, get the chef to make slight changes to the ingredients.

This was a *fancy* place with chandeliers, lace edged table cloths, tableware polished to a mirror, fresh flowers on each table and cloth napkins that waiters placed on your lap when you sat down. It came as a relief, being such a fancy place meant that Kevin would just have to be Kevin, right? Turns out it doesn't matter how fancy a place is, the acting *always* comes first.

"Howdy partner," Kevin hailed the host. "Got a booking for me and this pretty little filly. Give us a seat away from the in-ji-ans will ya?"

Now, I don't know how you'd feel sitting opposite a man acting like a cowboy, but I felt I'd already used my embarrassment tolerance for the night. But how to broach the subject of acting normal when I'd recently emerged from my apartment as Freitler Urban?

So I did the only thing I could think of, started fiddling with the lace table cloth and asked him very loudly to explain how Iron Grid works. Then promptly tuned out.

Jarrah Annelli 6 August 2012 at 01:39 [Report]

I think the term you are looking for is Grid Iron, though American Football would have sufficed.

Madeline Cain Date Destroyer 6 August 2012 at 01:39

Oh, I know now. Kevin took it as a sign that I knew next to nothing and would relish the chance to know *everything*. Every rule, every play, and apparently, he thought it best explained as a cowboy. So not only had I put myself into a conversation I'd avoided since meeting him, but he STILL talked like a cowboy. Which meant I just fiddled with that stupid table cloth more while fretting how I was going to ask him to stop. There's wanting your boyfriend to like you, and smother you with kisses, and then there's cowboys.

Kathy Bloomingdale 6 August 2012 at 01:40 [Report]

You keep saying, 'So I did the only thing I could think of.' It makes me nervous, I keep thinking FBI cells. Stop it. Did you ask him to stop?

Madeline Cain Date Destroyer 6 August 2012 at 01:50

When he started talking about 'tight ends' – whatever they are – I decided it was time to channel Kathy.

"Are you ok?" I asked cutting off his Wild West drawl. "Why are you trying out your characters on me? I'm mean, you do them *soooo* well, but I thought this was about getting to know each other. Do you reckon we could just have a date with Madeline and everyday Kevin? Please?"

He flushed, looking at his hands and I instantly felt like the heartless bitch who told him to stop doing what he loves.

"You really think I'm good? Because they don't." He jerked his head towards the other patrons.

"Of course! What do you mean they don't think you're good?"

"The ratings aren't good. I mean, they're fine, if you want to be a B grade show, but they're not the viral ratings I need to make it, you know? Everyone keeps talking about that stupid parrot and it was only in one episode. We've done four other shows since then!" He buried his face in his hands. "I thought maybe I needed to practise more, you know?"

My heart went out to him, he was a great actor, it was just his comedy that needed refining. But how to build him up without making him feel worse? My thoughts were interrupted by the waiter who passed steaming bowls of pea green soup to each of us. The fragrant garlic fumes made my mouth water.

"How long would you like your steak tartar seared, Sir? Mademoiselle?"

Kevin wouldn't look up so I shrugged and said, "Can we have it medium?"

"Medium?" He repeated as though he'd swallowed a fly.

"That's what I said," I confirmed when he didn't immediately leave. Frowning, he shrugged and walked away.

I sighed, taking Kevin's hand and leaving the soup untouched (even though my stomach was trying to climb outside my mouth it was so hungry. Does Valium give you the munchies?). "If it's one thing you do really well it's pretending to be someone else. But maybe slap stick humour isn't the answer, I mean people made memes of the parrot because the lines were witty, not because it fell off your shoulder drunk. Why not play up the fish out of water humour?"

"What do you mean?"

"Well, how would a person who's not from New York react? How would a cowboy act, an alien act? Take it from me, all the trouble I get into is because I'm in a place I don't quite understand, assuming things work like they do at home and that's where the comedy comes from. Think Crocodile Dundee."

I now had Kevin's undivided attention. "That was a great movie."

"I suppose… a bit culturally inaccurate but it's the right idea. Use real life to inspire you. The fish out of water thing works for heaps of things. A couple of weeks ago I went to take photos of kids. I've never been around kids in my life! I actually mistook one for a dog. And that lead to all kinds of crazy."

Kevin let out a great barking laugh, making me jump. "A dog? That's amazing." His shoulders relaxed and it was as though I'd released some hidden pressure valve. "I'm so glad I said something! No one else listened, but you just made me feel a ton better. Shapelle never did that."

Then to my delight Kevin stands up, arms wide and inviting.

You could almost hear my cheeks creaking I was smiling so wide. I was *better* than his previous girlfriend, I *listened.* I bounced up and flung my arms wide, only to feel a tug on my wrist. The sound of smashing glasses and plates assaulted us and suddenly I was covered in green spots and surrounded by broken bowl shards.

Kathy Bloomingdale 6 August 2012 at 01:51 [Report]

That's a magic trick gone wrong.

Jade Annelli 6 August 2012 at 01:51 [Report]

What, did you 'accidentally' pulled the table cloth from the table, or something? Who did you piss off in a past life?

Madeline Cain Date Destroyer 6 August 2012 at 01:52

Yeah, magic trick was totally where I was going with that, Kathy. Basically, the lace got caught on my bracelet while I was fiddling with it. It was hard to miss with the table cloth hanging from my wrist and all. But that wasn't the end, oh no, we were well on our way to the third and final act.

Jarrah Annelli 6 August 2012 at 01:52

Uh-oh…

Madeline Cain Date Destroyer 6 August 2012 at 01:57

As you'd expect from such a spectacular display of clumsiness, a commotion came from the two white doors to the kitchen. They burst open and out stormed a rotund man, red faced, with a chef's hat quivering on his fat head. He roared, "Where is Medium!?"

Our waiter points at us and our pea green polka dot explosion. The chef zeroed in, moving faster than any fat man I've ever seen, until we stood chin to bald patch.

"Medium! MEDIUM!" he shrieked at my throat. "This is steak tartar YOU IDIOT WOMAN! You may have one second, two second, three second MAXIMUM! But we do not MEDIUM!" He marched to another table, reached down and grabbed a handful of meat. On his return he thrust the chunk in my face, blood oozing from between his fingers. "This is PERFECTO! PERFECTO TARTAR!"

"You ordered the steak tartar medium?" muttered Kevin, licking the soup off the corners of his mouth. "How did I miss that?"

"Doesn't it come in medium?" I replied, horror freezing me in place. "But it's steak."

The chef's eyes bulged, his face almost purple. "It is RAW STEAK you daughter of a motherless goat! You plague of a prophet! You… You… NINNY!"

"You feed *people* raw meat?" asked my traitor of a mouth.

If you've ever wanted to see someone go insane before your eyes, find yourself a French chef and order your raw rump medium.

Jarrah Annelli 6 August 2012 at 01:58 [Report]

You must have been at 'Amour', the chef is infamous for his rants on food 'fit for royalty'. He has a reputation for smearing food on customer's faces if they sass him. Did you get a face of raw meat?

Jade Annelli 6 August 2012 at 01:58 [Report]

I once had a friend who knew the chef's reputation, so he and his fiancé conducted a little experiment. They ate the first two courses in full and half the desert (which I was assured was divine) and then sent the other half back as 'unpalatable'. They endured a ten minute rant on the making of marzipan and their 'dubious' parentage before being ejected from the restaurant, full, happy and with a pocket full of money to spend on the rest of their anniversary.

Madeline Cain Date Destroyer 6 August 2012 at 02:00

I didn't get a face full of steak, thank God! However, he did eat a chunk of one steak then throw it to the ground only to grab another and another, yelling, "PERFECTO!" after each blood filled bite.

It took two renditions of open mouthed chewing of raw, bloody meat to turn me off all steak for life. There were about ten steaks on the floor before one of the patrons identified himself as a health inspector.

Kathy Bloomingdale 6 August 2012 at 02:01 [Report]

Oh my god, I saw a video of this! They showed it on the news. A chef running around a ballroom being chased by a guy in a suit, up ending tables and then being tripped up by one of his own waiters. You started that? How could you not know what steak tartar was? Tim insists on eating it every time we go out.

Madeline Cain date Destroyer 6 August 2012 at 02:01

What? Not when I've been around him he hasn't. Since when have you been going out?

Kathy Bloomingdale 6 August 2012 at 02:02 [Report]

Don't be silly, not going out going out, just 'we are now grown-ups who can make our own plans' going out. Actually, now I think about it, that might have been only a recent fad of his...

But you *actually* turned someone insane. On a first date. With a boy who looks like he's come from a superhero comic.

Madeline Cain Date Destroyer 6 August 2012 at 02:04

I would have been buggered anyway, they had soufflé for dessert and I would have asked if the eggs were free range or caged. You know how I feel about caging chickens for eggs. They can't even walk! It's barbaric!

Anyway, that's not the point, the point is I gave Kevin three valid reasons to back the hell away from the date destroyer and creator of maniacs. Hitler-stache, failed magic trick and melt down of a Frenchman. Frankly, I wouldn't even date me.

Jade Annelli 6 August 2012 at 02:04 [Report]

Maybe your best match is someone with no shame, they'd just enjoy the ride.

Madeline Cain Date Destroyer 6 August 2012 at 02:07

Gee, thanks for the vote of confidence.

Kevin was following the chase like a tennis match when I said, "I understand if you want to call it quits. I'm a disaster."

He lifted a finger to suck off a splash of green and said, "This joint is too fancy for me anyway. Wanna get some pizza?"

All I could do was stare at him.

"What? Have I got some in my hair?" he asked, combing his hands through his locks worriedly. "You got a mirror or something?"

"You don't want to run for the hills?" I asked hazarding a step closer.

"Are you kidding? I have this great skit idea that's going to be perfect for the show! Wouldn't have happened without this. Looks like you're my muse babe. So, pizza?"

I don't care that his method acting drives me nuts, or that he doesn't get my jokes, or he isn't around as much as I would like, or that he's into sport when I'd rather watch grass grow.

He survived a full blown 'Madeline Cain' event and didn't run. If someone that hot can still say, I want to be around you, I still want to kiss you even though that moustache haunts my dreams, then he's a keeper.

Jade Annelli 6 August 2012 at 02:08 [Report]

I really don't think we can make a game plan out of this, Jarrah. Not because there aren't lessons to be learnt, but because it's not possible for more than one human being to be that unlucky. If we were writing one of those quirky books that lists how to survive a sand storm, how to survive the sinking of your boat, how to survive an earthquake etc, then we would probably include you as an example of how to survive the date from your worst nightmares.

Kathy Bloomingdale 6 August 2012 at 02:09 [Report]

His lack of reaction does worry me a bit. Sure he's not a tad thick?

Jarrah Annelli 6 August 2012 at 02:11 [Report]

Kevin is way more switched on than some of the guys I've dated, Kathy. I once went out with a guy who reached for a copy of Apuleisus' The Golden Ass at the same time I did in a book store. I assumed he was interested in classical literature and therefore cultured. Turned out he thought it was about bottoms.

Kathy Bloomingdale 6 August 2012 at 02:12 [Report]

Hmm, Kevin *is* looking a lot brighter :p Well Mad, when life gets you down and you've given all you can give, just think, "Yes this may have been the date from hell, but at least I'm not a dead body on Mount Everest."

Madeline Cain Date Destroyer 6 August 2012 at 02:13

There's a cheery life lesson. Thank you? This year in New York has made me realise what I need is someone who doesn't laugh at my embarrassing moments. Maybe it's because he's thick, but Kevin doesn't pay me out, and I like that. Not like Cliff pissing himself after the DVD incident.

Kathy Bloomingdale 6 August 2012 at 02:14 [Report]

Whatever makes you happy, love. Let's hope being a muse doesn't require you to continue on your path of bizarre and inventive destruction.

Madeline Cain Date Destroyer 6 August 2012 at 02:15

Oh please God make is so, or at least put me out of my misery in a freak gasoline fight accident. Don't know if I could bare having the weirdness that is my life acted out on TV!

Kathy Bloomingdale 6 August 2012 at 02:14 [Report]

Ah Zoolander, an appropriate line for every occasion.

Kyle Trayba Sun is shining, the coffee is hot and I'm rocking it out with no pants! Man, I love having a back yard with a fence! *Posted Tuesday 7th August at 08:04* [Comment . Like]

> **Tim Gleeve** TMI man, TMI. *Posted Tuesday 7th August at 13:23* [Comment . Like]

Madeline Cain Date Destroyer likes the band **The Wombats** [Like]

Kathy Bloomingdale -> Madeline Cain Date Destroyer So… I found your replacement! She's from my politics tutorial, speaks as much randomness as you, loves a debate and she makes you one of my more mature aged friends (yes, I'm calling you old). You thought you were irreplaceable. *Posted Thursday 9th August at 18:16* [Comment . Like]

> **Madeline Cain Date Destroyer** Bet she's a poor facsimile of my awesomeness. Can she induce a Frenchman into destroying his own restaurant? *Posted Thursday 9th August at 19:20* [Comment . Like]

> **Kathy Bloomingdale** No, she can't, she has replaced the *old* Maddie, the one who didn't invite the twilight zone in every time she looked at something cross-eyed. *Posted Thursday 9th August at 19:28* [Comment . Like]

> **Madeline Cain Date Destroyer** If I'm old what does that make you? *Posted Thursday 9th August at 19:33* [Comment . Like]

> **Kathy Bloomingdale** Vintage, Maddie, it makes me vintage. Everybody likes vintage. *Posted Thursday 9th August at 19:50* [Comment . Like]

> **Madeline Cain Date Destroyer** Sure, it's kind of musty and is brought out for bad taste parties. *Posted Thursday 9th August at 19:52* [Comment . Like]

Tim Gleeve Damon straight you are. *Posted Thursday 9th August at 21:12* [Comment . Like]

Tim Gleeve Wait! *Damn straight not Damon. Rtf phone? *Posted Thursday 9th August at 21:12* [Comment . Like]

Tim Gleeve Are you kidding me?! *Wtf not rtf. Argh!!!!!! *Posted Thursday 9th August at 21:13* [Comment . Like]

Kathy Bloomingdale If you're old and I'm vintage, what does that make Mr Spak-attack? *Posted Thursday 9th August at 22:00* [Comment . Like]

Madeline Cain Date Destroyer A grandpa, he doesn't get the new-fangled gadgets. Also needs a little 'jump' to charge it up for the ladies, if you know what I mean… *Posted Thursday 9th August at 22:14* [Comment . Like]

Kim Enuik likes the page **Embarrassing Night Club Photos** [Like]

Madeline Cain Date Destroyer Yes! With a bit of ingenuity and duct tape, I've managed to build an impenetrable goodie fortress for my latest care package from Mum! Let's see you riddle that you invisible terror! *Posted Saturday 11th August at 10:31* [Comment . Like]

Jade Annelli Yay you! Ah, this reminds me of the time I lived with a vampire and kept a secret string of garlic hidden behind my door… And she kept her filthy dishes in the cupboard in her room. Good times. *Posted Saturday 11th August at 12:25* [Comment . Like]

Jarrah Annelli We banished her with the aid of a fearsome poodle who had a lusty laugh, and magic ability to light the dark! *Posted Saturday 11th August at 12:35* [Comment . Like]

Josh Annelli Too bad she shacked up with the werewolf next door, now we have little Varwolf babies pooping on our lawn and bitting our cats. *Posted Saturday 11th August at 12:47* [Comment . Like]

Madeline Cain Date Destroyer Okay… either you guys have been constructing some weird SIMS world or I should avoid living in London… *Posted Saturday 11th August at 17:10* [Comment . Like]

Kathy Bloomingdale Insomnia, we've got to stop meeting like this… Sleep is getting very suspicious. *Posted Sunday 12th August at 02:39* [Comment . Like]

Madeline Cain Date Destroyer Your body clock is preparing for your trip to NYC in a month. I sent it a secret coded transmission when we last spoke on Skype. *Posted Sunday 12th August at 08:52* [Comment . Like]

Kathy Bloomingdale Are you responsible for these hot flushes too? Because that makes you a bad friend. I told you, I refuse to cook pancakes on my face. Pay the gas bill already and stop folding my body into your September plans! *Posted Sunday 12th August at 10:50* [Comment . Like]

Madeline Cain Date Destroyer Sorry, it was a one way transmission. Can't take it back. So do you like blueberry or chocolate chip? *Posted Sunday 12th August at 11:08* [Comment . Like]

Wyate Yosime Very confused about which person to speak in, but… have ninja bread men. *Posted Tuesday 14th August at 16:44* [Comment . Like]

Harry Lee Is that code for you burnt your gingerbread? *Posted Tuesday 14th August at 17:22* [Comment . Like]

Wyate Yosime No, they are 'ninja bread men'. From biscuit cut-outs. *Posted Tuesday 14th August at 18:00* [Comment . Like]

> **Tim Gleeve** Apparently the biscuits disappear fast. *Posted Tuesday 14th August at 18:32* [Comment . Like]

Kate Nikles liked the page **Now That's Funny Shit** and 20 other pages. [Like]

Cliff Wheeland How I love O'Week, where I can test all my theories on the excitable and intoxicated! *Posted Friday 17th August at 17:00* [Comment . Like]

> **Kim Enuik** You're finally back from your cabin in the woods! Does Maddie know? *Posted Friday 17th August at 20:16* [Comment . Like]

> **Madeline Cain Granny-Wear** I think I know too much *wink wink*. *Posted Friday 17th August at 00:03* [Comment . Like]

Madeline Cain Granny-Wear liked the page **There's Always That One Person Who Catches You Doing Something Weird.** [Like]

> **Madeline Cain Granny-Wear** I dedicate this to you Cliff. *Posted Saturday 18th August at 10:30* [Comment . Like]

> **Cliff Wheeland** This is part of my kiss-and-make-up deal isn't it? *Posted Saturday 18th August at 10:45* [Comment . Like]

> **Madeline Cain Granny-Wear** Still waiting for you to wow me double D. *Posted Saturday 18th August at 10:46* [Comment . Like]

In Which I Realised Other People Are Weird Too.....[New Message]

[Back to messages. Mark as unread . Report spam . Delete]

Between **Kathy Bloomingdale, Tim Gleeve** and **You.**

Madeline Cain Granny-Wear 18 August 2012 at 11:01

Finally! Cliff has returned from whatever Planet Strange he's been inhabiting and acknowledged he's been a jackass. Admittedly he didn't have a choice when I caught him like that. It's great to know I'm not the only one in the running for the Nobel Prize of Weird Shit.

Kathy Bloomingdale 18 August 2012 at 11:04 [Report]

You're going to have to be a little more specific. Why was Cliff being a jackass? What exactly did you catch him doing?

Tim Gleeve 18 August 2012 at 11:06 [Report]

I feel like we're entering some sort of fruity sex story. Well, that's the vibe I'm getting from your Facebook name. Is it a fruity sex story? Please say yes.

Madeline Cain Granny-Wear 18 August 2012 at 11:06

Kath, Cliff has been ignoring me ever since June! He might be all over your Facebook profile like a bad smell but mine has suddenly became radioactive.

Also, the answer to that question will never be yes, Tim. I will not encourage fetishes from you. However, if you asked me does Cliff look good in a bra, the answer would be yes.

Tim Gleeve 18 August 2012 at 11:07 [Report]

As always, this is going in a direction I didn't anticipate.

Kathy Bloomingdale 18 August 2012 at 11:08 [Report]

Right... You're worrying me here. Did the Little Y's somehow brain wash you with promises of book discussions which turned a little 'fruiter' as Tim would say?

Madeline Cain Granny-Wear 18 August 2012 at 11:08

Let's stop with the speculation and start with the facts. I found a dead body in the elevator.

Tim Gleeve 18 August 2012 at 11:09 [Report]

And Jennifer Lawrence is my lover. Hey, if you just stepped onto the set of a movie why can't I?

Madeline Cain Granny-Wear 18 August 2012 at 11:09

In your dreams. As you may have guessed I got in the elevator before I actually noticed it, because, as always, I was playing with my camera.

Kathy Bloomingdale 18 August 2012 at 11:10 [Report]

What!? How are you feeling? Oh my god, were we right? Is Dom a mobster and you're embroiled in a gang war?? I don't know what I'd do if I came that close to a corpse! Did the doors actually closed on you and... it?

Madeline Cain Granny-Wear 18 August 2012 at 11:10

The elevator broke down with me inside.

Kathy Bloomingdale 18 August 2012 at 11:11 [Report]

Fine. I get it. Haha very funny. What, does America have some weird second April Fool's day each year? Keep this up and one day you're going to be in so much trouble but no one is going to listen. Can we get to the real story of how Cliff admitted he was a jackass so I can do my assignment?

Madeline Cain Granny-Wear 18 August 2012 at 11:21

You're my best friends, would I lie about something like this? This is all true, and none of it is my fault! It's all on Cliff. Let me don my crime writer hat for a moment, shall I?

A young woman walks down the corridor. Only dim lights illuminate the scuffed carpet. There's an eerie silence broken only by a monotonous beep drumming out a rhythm. It's late, past chameleon bedtime, and she's off to practise taking photos of lights in the dark. She has a mission to capture the essence of rock and roll in a single frame and has only a few short days to practise her steady hand. She is consumed by settings and levels.

The elevator doors are conveniently open, an unusual occurrence but welcome as this metal box is known to take five minutes to arrive on the fifth floor. But something is wrong, they aren't closing behind her when she presses 'G'. The young woman, stunning and intelligent, tears herself away from her buttons and dials and notices two things: the beeping is all around her; and the reason for the beeping is a black bag against the elevator door, keeping it from its mission to close and convey.

The artist reaches out a dainty hand to shift the bag into the hall so she can be on her way. But it is immovable, as though filled with dumbbells, doorbells, sleigh bells, any kind of bell really. She places her camera down next to a hand and kneels shoving the bag with all her might. It moves an inch, then two, then out into the hall. She lets go of the bag and finally wonders why there would be a hand on the elevator floor.

Slowly she turns, almost wishing Halloween had come early and it was just her mind playing tricks to stop her getting fat on candy. But alas that hand, more bone white than her own, was most definitely present and attached to someone face down with blood clotting across their bare back.

She shrieks like a banshee when she realises the thing is not breathing. She staggers to her feet only to slip, landing on her back, winded and gasping next to the body. She lays in a pool of blood, the doors closing, when someone dives through the gap, leaping over her in a blur. The lift groans as a man lands with a heavy thud, moving down a floor, maybe more, before it stops with a jerk, a loud noise drowning out everything else. The lights go out and red emergency lights flicker on.

A voice, oddly familiar, shouts over a high pitched shriek, "It's not ready! It's not what you think!"

It's only when she hitches a breath and the noise stops that she realises the shriek was hers at her operatic, survival mode best.

"Better." The man, hard to see in the emergency lighting, stands and she grasps her camera, ready to turn her tool of art into a can of whoop-ass.

Then, as suddenly as they disappeared, the bright white lights come back on, blinding her. She struggles to sit, to get in some firm position to swing from, when the man says, "Shit, Madeline."

She opens her eyes to a stunned African American man who she knows as Cliff. He is standing in his boxers, his heavily muscled chest bare except for a large, fluoro pink bra.

Kathy Bloomingdale 18 August 2012 at 11:22 [Report]

Cliff, your neighbour, who wears preppy vests and tailored black jackets, sits in front of a computer all day, is wandering around the halls at night, ripped and in womens' lingerie? You realise you are not just asking me to sip vodka with a bit of lime here; you're asking me to scull the whole bottle. Because that's what I'd need to hallucinate this scenario.

Tim Gleeve 18 August 2012 at 11:22 [Report]

What is it with you and pink? Pink uniforms, pink weapon bags, pink man bras? It's like a plague that turns real life into a stage musical.

Madeline Cain Granny-Wear 18 August 2012 at 11:29

It's the weirdest stage musical I've ever seen, with too much comedy and not much singing. You won't needed vodka to visualise, in fact, you may see it at some point as I am holding my photographs at ransom. That's right, black mail for real this time!

If I were to describe that bra kindly, I would call it a granny bra, because cups that size were only meant for boobs that have headed south for the winter. Cliff may have had the most defined pecks I'd seen for a while (and that includes Kevin's) but even his muscle couldn't fill in the voluminous fabric of that bra.

I was caught on the boarder of surprise and hysterical laughing and could only manage to choke out, "You're back, how long have you been back?"

"Three days... Look, I can explain everything!" He waved his hands to encompass the prone body and blood spatter on the walls. "Really, it's not what you think. Just, please, let me get us out of here first."

I almost flung my camera at him. Three days? Three bloody days he'd been home and he hadn't bothered to walk the five feet to my door and knock! No, 'Hey Madeline, sorry I've been out of touch, but a bear ate my phone and all those messages on other peoples' walls were typed by his stomach lining'? Here we were in a broken elevator, where he couldn't escape, and *now* he wanted to explain?

The urge to point and laugh warred with the urge to tell him how much of asshole he'd been and we weren't fixing this elevator until he damn well explained why. It sounds weak, I know, but unless he'd actually turned serial killer, I'd just about forgive him anything. Kim had tried to fill the fun-times-with-Cliff gap, but he had Den work and Kevin was always away, and I'd had so much extra time on my hands when I lost my delivery hours… not having a best mate around was hard! I mean, you guys are on Facebook but you're not *here.*

So I decided revenge was the best compromise between anger and delight at his predicament. "We aren't going anywhere buddy," I said, sliding myself between him and the emergency speaker. "As you said, you have some explaining to do. What do you want to explain first? The dead body, or the bra?"

I've never seen anyone move as fast as Cliff did when he whipped up his hands to clutch at the bra cups, fingers splayed, his hands scrunching a little as though testing it was really there. It was so undignified I almost lost my load then and there. But I bit my lip and forced back the giggles. *God damn it Madeline you are ANGRY at him, don't let his mess distract you from your goal.*

"Shiza!" He whipped his hands behind his back, fumbling at whatever hook held it on. His arms flailed like a demented short-armed demi-god.

I let him squirm for a bit, cursing, as I casually wrapped my hands around my camera. "Or perhaps you want to explain why you haven't been talking to me? And why I shouldn't take this photo of you and post it on Facebook right now?"

I pressed the shutter button, the flash freezing him in place.

Tim Gleeve 18 August 2012 at 11:30 [Report]

Oooh, you're evil. I like it. My mission in life is complete, I have created a monster and it is GLORIOUS!

Kathy Bloomingdale 18 August 2012 at 11:30 [Report]

Not sure how I feel about black mailing friends via Facebook photos.

The number of shots you have of Tim and I in many an unflattering light is enough to see us start our own Amish cult. Because living somewhere without internet is the only way we could escape the horror of our own stupidity.

Tim Gleeve 18 August 2012 at 11:31 [Report]

Stupidity at doing said undesirable activities, or stupidity at letting Maddie chronicle them? By the way, you're not invited to my twenty-first, Maddie.

Kathy Bloomingdale 18 August 2012 at 11:31 [Report]

Both. I'm still confused about why Cliff was playing with a body (real? Not real?) in an elevator.

Madeline Cain Granny-Wear 18 August 2012 at 11:39

You guys have nothing to worry about. I'd never *post* them. Just threaten too. You should know that. But Cliff has no such safety net of knowledge.

He looked like he'd swallowed a pinecone. He lowered his chicken dance wings and held out a hand in what he clearly thought was a placating gesture but actually made him look like he was about to do ballet. "Ok, let's not get ahead of ourselves."

I nodded at his décolleté. "Don't think pink's your colour, but the frills match you perfectly. You filling that with socks or are you planning implants a la Pamela Anderson?"

"It's not mine, it's supposed to be hers!" he blurted.

"So you've stolen a dead woman's bra? Bras are a dime a dozen, you don't have to kill for them. Although maybe you do for that one. I don't think anyone would want to be seen in public buying it."

"I'm not a pervert! It's an experiment!"

"In killing people?"

"Yes in killing people."

I leant back with my arms crossed, trying not to smirk.

Realising what he'd said, he cried, "No! I mean in *pretending* to kill people! Not actually killing people. Why would I actually kill people?"

"I don't know, you tell me. Probably comes from the same place that said *let's try on this pretty little number*."

He growled and bending double flipped the body over like she weight nothing, which she probably didn't judging by the waxy face with fake features painted on. "She's a mannequin! I'm testing a scene in my latest book, it's set in a dorm building during O-Week. I want to see how people would react when they found a murder scene. Specifically, how they would react when they stumble home from whatever illegal underage party they'd just been to. I'd just finished the blood and still needed to set up the spy cam when, well, you know…" He squeaked, failing his hands, clearly an imitation of my epic scream.

"Do you always set up murder scenes looking like Frank N. Furter from Rocky Horror?"

Tim Gleeve 18 August 2012 at 11:43 [Report]

Please tell me he wasn't wearing fishnets too?? There are lines a man just does *not* cross, experimentation or not. Does he have no boundaries?

Madeline Cain Granny-Wear 18 August 2012 at 11:49

No fishnets but I'm sure he'd look good in those too.

He pulled at the fabric in frustration. "Look, could you get this off?"

"I'm assuming you put it there, I think it's best you remove it. I don't want to get in the way of your transvestite fun-times."

"I'm not… look, the killer in my book goes into the elevator with his victims, all women, and kills them. Then he stops the elevator on a floor, puts on a wig and changes into their clothes before going back down and strolling out of the building. He looks like the woman he just killed in all the security cameras and gets away. *He's* the cross dresser, not me!"

"Why are you the one wearing the bra?"

"I had to test how long it took him to change into her clothes, didn't I? Because he would have to consider that when choosing his victims."

"How's that working out for you?"

He threw his hands up in the air. "Come on, Madeline! Give me a break."

Uhuh, yeah right, not when I was on a roll.

"So you give Kevin all this shit for method acting then you turn around and do the same thing."

"I'm not pretending I'm someone else! Running around like I've got the world's most intense multiple personality disorder. I'm just testing a theory."

"By traumatising some poor innocent fresher into thinking someone slipped inside their secure building and left a girl dead and naked in her elevator?" I paused for a minute looking between the plastic woman and Cliff's bra, finally considering the flaws in his scene. "Why would the killer take her underwear anyway? Clearly the killer is worried about the time it takes to get away, so it doesn't make sense to go that far, even if he has a fetish for his victim's clothing. A bra is super fiddly, as you well know." I wiggled my eyebrows at him.

Cliff reached up to scratch his chin, studying his ruined crime scene. "You think? It did take me like, five minutes to get this on." He snapped a strap then winced. Picking at the fabric he said, "Would you wear this?"

“Beg your pardon?” I crossed my arms. “Did you just ask me what underwear I wear?”

“No! I mean, kind of…” he scrubbed a hand across the short curly stubble on his head. “I’m just… curious… do you choose your underwear in the morning thinking about whether you would want to be found dead in it?”

Kathy Bloomingdale 18 August 2012 at 11:50 [Report]

What?! That has to be the most horribly morbid thing a person could think of in the morning. You’d spend your day being a human Eeyore. May as well live in a hut made of sticks.

Tim Gleeve 18 August 2012 at 11:51 [Report]

Way to put a dampener on things. Though he does have a point. What if I get run over by a grandma in one of those old-people scooters and a hot paramedic has to strip off my pants to save my legs and I’m wearing undies with skid marks? I’ve been choosing outfits all wrong.

Madeline Cain Granny-Wear 18 August 2012 at 11:56

It scares me how alike you and Cliff are, Tim. But hey, if that’s what it takes to get you out of your Star Wars pyjamas every day then more power to you. My reaction was closer to Kathy’s.

“What?!”

“Come on, surely you have an ‘if I was hit by a bus’ plan. I know it’s morbid, but as a guy I make sure my underwear is skid mark free. Just in case. If I was a girl the first thing I’d be doing is making sure I’m wearing my first-date underwear every day.”

I pulled my shirt collar out, chin to chest, to check out my own gear. Serviceable, but kind of boring to be found dead in if I’m honest. “I never did before but you’ve made me paranoid now. I mean, who has those kind of thoughts?”

He shrugged, contorting his arms behind his back again. "Crime writers. These things are impossible to get off. You're right, a killer like that wouldn't waste his time."

"One thing I can tell you is no sane young woman would wear that Granny bra. It's an insult to the eye. I feel like I've got a fire brand in the eyeball looking at that. Of course, if I was making a 'if I get hit by a bus' plan I'd be making sure I was on good terms with all my mates."

Cliff sighed. Bra still firmly attached, he lowered his arms, shoulders slumped. "I'm sorry Maddie, I was going through some… stuff."

"You're going to have to do better than *stuff*."

"It's best if I don't." He looked me straight in the eyes, gaze steady. "But I can tell you I'm over it. It's done. I didn't know how to apologise. I was just looking for something to break the ice."

Plucking the straining fabric, I said, "Reckon this about does it. You could break a ship out of an ice plateau with this."

Laughter welled up and I tried to muffle giggles behind a hand, but it was so hard and the uncomfortable look on his face was so *satisfying*! It was the most perfect moment of *Schadenfreude* I'd ever experienced and it was glorious!

I snorted, startling him, and as the lols kept coming Cliff finally relaxed and joined me in a hysterical laughing competition. Which freaked the shit out of the guy on the other end of the elevator emergency speaker. I must have pressed the button with the corner of my camera as I bent over clutching my stomach.

Kathy Bloomingdale. 18 August 2012 at 11:51 [Report]

Manic laughter coming from your emergency line at midnight is probably going to give you nightmares of the clown kind. So, did you let him off the hook?

Tim Gleeve 18 August 2012 at 11:53 [Report]

I don't get it, when you girls are all like 'We had lady problems' you expect that we don't pry any further. If we do it's like Godzilla manifests before our eyes. So we respect your inner monster because frankly we don't want the shit kicked out of us. But as soon as men say 'I was going through some things that I don't want to talk about, but it's over now and you don't have to worry,' which frankly is a much longer and clearer explanation, women are all like, that's not good enough and Godzilla comes out again and terrorises us until we confess. Then we're stomped on for giving an answer we knew they didn't want to hear in the first place. Where's the trust I ask you? THE TRUST.

Of course Madeline didn't let him off the hook, with her pictures she could have Cliff on a kiddy leash eating from a dog bowl for the rest of his life.

Madeline Cain Granny-Wear 18 August 2012 at 11:59

That's a highly unfair assessment Tim, we say lady problems as a consideration to men, because the majority of lady problems involve blood and/or some form of emotion. It would make your emotionally retardant head explode in a burst of rainbow confetti. But you're right, I couldn't let him off the hook that easy.

After explaining our need for an elevator service provider (and omitting our pretend murder scene) I applied the pressure. "I thought we were friends, friends talk to each other, especially when they're going through 'stuff'." I did air quotation marks. "Unless… you're not gay are you?"

"No!" he cried, "Not that that's a bad thing, but no, I'm most definitely not. It was 'stuff', but not of that magnitude. Well, to anyone but me. I just had to get over myself."

"I do that all the time, I'm so over myself I'm under myself." He gave me a strange look. Sigh, sometimes I wish American's got Australian sarcasm. "If you're not bating for Team Pole, and you won't tell me what 'stuff' had you acting like a young boy avoiding cooties, then I'm afraid you are going to have to prove to me how sorry you are."

He looked at me wearily. "What kind of proof are we talking about?"

I got off another two shots with my camera. Cliff flinched with each click. "I'm talking epic kiss and make-up here compadre. An 'I'm sorry' gesture so big that I'll know it as soon as I see it. I shall hold off on revenge until then, but any funny business and your pretty D cups are going front and centre on my profile page."

"I promise you'll have your proof before Christmas. Just as I promise I won't tackle you for that camera if you remove this god awful anaconda from my chest before the repair men opens those doors."

"We have an accord sir." I gave my finger a little twirl.

Cliff spun and with barely a touch I had his bra undone. The End.

Tim Gleeve 18 August 2012 at 12:00 [Report]

That's not a phrase you hear often. Yet somehow I feel this is not the last time you will utter it.

Kathy Bloomingdale 18 August 2012 at 12:01 [Report]

I fear Tim is less likely to explode into confetti and more likely to explode into frankfurts and donuts, because food drives his emotions. Tim, you have the emotional sensitivity of a murder weapon. While your big gesture would involve letting a lady have her pick of Star Trek episodes, Cliff's is probably going to involve sleigh rides and big romantic meetings on top of the Empire State Building.

Madeline Cain Granny-Wear 18 August 2012 at 12:02 [Report]

Have you been watching Sleepless in Seattle again? You need to stop watching those romcom New York movies, they merely provide your brain with delusions. I wasn't demanding a romantic gesture; I was demanding a 'I'm sorry coolest person in the world' gesture. Frankly, I had something greater than love to provide motivation, I had black mail.

Kathy Bloomingdale 18 August 2012 at 12:03 [Report]

You don't know what's going on in that boy's head if testing crime scenes and speed cross dressing is acceptable. All I'm saying is, it's New York, you're a hottie, and you've seen him in his underwear. Big romantic gestures have started with weirder things.

Tim Gleeve 18 August 2012 at 12:03 [Report]

I set you free young awesome-stine to wreak havoc on New York, and then, the world!

Madeline Cain Granny-Wear 18 August 2012 at 12:04 [Report]

A) Thanks; B) Kevin; C) Proving ones sorry-ness, not love and; D) call me a monster again and I may go back on my no posting of the knife-bread-toaster incident.

Tim Gleeve 18 August 2012 at 12:04 [Report]

See, Godzilla.

Madeline Cain Granny-Wear likes the page **I Check Behind The Shower Curtain For Murderers When I Go Into The Bathroom.** [Like]

> **Madeline Cain Granny-Wear** Or elevator. Anything with a door really. Makes my apartment block an OCD hell. *Posted Sunday 19th August at 10:46* [Comment . Like]

Tim Gleeve Kicking down all those doors CIS style must really hurt your knee. *Posted Sunday 19th August at 12:15* [Comment . Like]

Madeline Cain Granny-Wear As long as no one kills me for my Granny bra, I'm good. *Posted Sunday 19th August at 13:50* [Comment . Like]

Cliff Wheeland likes the page **Those "We Shall Never Speak Of This Again" Moments** [Like]

Madeline Cain Granny-Wear likes the page **The Awkwardness Of Standing In An Elevator With Strangers.** [Like]

Cliff Wheeland Strangers? *Posted Sunday 19th August at 16:00* [Comment . Like]

Cliff Wheeland Oh I get it, I've been the stranger, yada yada. I'm working on the Proof, ok? Just don't test Stranger Danger protocols on me before you see it. *Posted Sunday 19th August at 17:02* [Comment . Like]

Madeline Cain Granny-Wear I am a lily floating on a calm ocean… *Posted Sunday 19th August at 17:22* [Comment . Like]

Claire Holderness Things I learnt at the museum today: Maggie Thatcher brought the lols; the history of button making is boring; sometimes you need sunglasses inside; and, Woolworths doesn't appear to have Maple Bacon. *Posted Monday20th August at 10:46* [Comment . Like]

Madeline Cain Granny-Wear They felt it important to include the lack of Maple Bacon in the exhibit? *Posted Monday20th August at 08:21* [Comment . Like]

Claire Holderness No, that was just my after museum craving. *Posted Monday20th August at 17:43* [Comment . Like]

Madeline Cain Granny-Wear How Canadian of you. *Posted Monday20th August at 19:17* [Comment . Like]

Victoria Zeng I heartily endorse this event and/or product. *Posted Tuesday 21st August at 11:53* [Comment . Like]

Madeline Cain Granny-Wear Do you really, or is that just in your event contract? 'I must sell my soul to product placement and in return shall receive the boss's grandmother as payment.' *Posted Tuesday 21st August at 11:58* [Comment . Like]

Cain Michaels What *are* you on about, Aussie? *Posted Tuesday 21st August at 12:20* [Comment . Like]

Madeline Cain Granny-Wear You know the saying, 'He was so crooked he sold his grandmother for five dollars'? *Posted Tuesday 21st August at 12:37* [Comment . Like]

Richard Arnoou You're making Victoria sound like a reverse Rumplestiltskin. 'I will turn all your photographs into gold for the price of your first born grandmother.' *Posted Tuesday 21st August at 12:39* [Comment . Like]

Victoria Zeng I heartily endorse this event and/or product. ? *Posted Tuesday 21st August at 12:43* [Comment . Like]

Cliff Wheeland I was climbing out of a cab in Times Square, when an old man asked me, "Excuse me, are you here for the International Astronauts Conference?" For a second I contemplated saying, "Yes, I'm the Keynote Speaker," and just seeing where the night took me. Then, after an awkwardly long silence I came to my senses and said, "No… sorry." I'm not sure why I apologised… *Posted Wednesday 22nd August at 18:30* [Comment . Like]

You and **three others** like this.

Madeline Cain Granny-Wear Were you wearing your alfoil/

tin hat again? *Posted Wednesday 22nd August at 18:40* [Comment . Like]

Cliff Wheeland What? Suddenly I'm costume guy?? What the hell is alfoil? Sounds like an aeroplane part. *Posted Wednesday 22nd August at 18:45* [Comment . Like]

Madeline Cain Granny-Wear If the bra fits… Aluminium foil. *Posted Wednesday 22nd August at 18:48* [Comment . Like]

Josh Annelli Aussies, can't be bothered calling anything by its full name. *Posted Wednesday 22nd August at 19:00* [Comment . Like]

Madeline Cain Granny-Wear *Shrugs* soz. *Posted Wednesday 22nd August at 19:06* [Comment . Like]

Kim Enuik I wish you said yes, it would have made for an interesting status update. Wasn't your radar for awesome background material going crazy? If not, then I don't know how you can call yourself a writer. *Posted Wednesday 22nd August at 19:11* [Comment . Like]

Kathy Bloomingdale 'Are you the moon police?' *Posted Wednesday 22nd August at 19:20* [Comment . Like]

Josh Annelli You might be interested to know that that was, in fact, a fake astronaut's conference you were invited to. One of Kevin's latest creations on prime time. Did you know his show had been moved to prime time? It was surprisingly pant-splitting. *Posted Wednesday 22nd August at 19:24* [Comment . Like]

Madeline Cain Granny-Wear I believe the term you are looking for is side-splitting. And really? I haven't been able to watch it the past couple of weeks because of pizza runs. *Posted Wednesday 22nd August at 19:27* [Comment . Like]

Josh Annelli No, I can assure you I was being scrupulously accurate in my word choice. *Posted Wednesday 22nd August at 19:30* [Comment . Like]

Tim Gleeve That's awkward. Nearly as awkward as the time we got pulled over by the quarantine inspector and my mind went blank. *Posted Wednesday 22nd August at 19:39* [Comment . Like]

Kathy Bloomingdale You mean when you suddenly went mute. Don't forget the moustache… *Posted Wednesday 22nd August at 19:48* [Comment . Like]

Tim Gleeve Yes, it was a dirty moustache… *Posted Wednesday 22nd August at 19:51* [Comment . Like]

Cliff Wheeland That makes me feel slightly better about telling the truth. Being caught out as a liar on TV is most definitely not on my list of top ten pastimes. *Posted Wednesday 22nd August at 20:04* [Comment . Like]

Josh Annelli You can imagine that Kevin came as an alien to that party. I'm being literal here, Maddie, I know how spec you tots like me to be, lols. *Posted Wednesday 22nd August at 20:14* [Comment . Like]

Jamiee Anderson Jay Z = freaking amazing. U2 up next… As Mike would say, happy in the pants! *Posted Thursday 23rd August at 04:10* [Comment . Like]

Mike Cain I would never be happy in the pants for Jay Z young grasshopper, but his wife is more than welcome to join me at my pants party. *Posted Thursday 23rd August at 08:30* [Comment . Like]

Madeline Cain Granny-Wear Have fun! I'm getting ready for my own concert extravaganza this week! But I get to go back stage. And Mike, it's a wonder you have friends at all. *Posted Thursday 23rd August at 12:21* [Comment . Like]

Mike Cain I just realized immature spells I'm mature. *Posted Friday 24th August at 07:09* [Comment . Like]

Madeline Cain Granny-Wear So mature you put blue Gatorade in a Windex bottle last week and drank that shit in public. More specifically, at your athletics day. Just before a race. Is there no length you won't go to, to avoid doing sport? *Posted Friday 24th August at 14:33* [Comment . Like]

Mike Cain When sport is involved no stunt is too dangerous, too crude, or too low brow. I've already got next year planned out thanks to Nurse Brown, the sultry minx. She knows, that I know, that she knows, that I know. Now all sorts of fake maladies are at my command! *Posted Friday 24th August at 16:40* [Comment . Like]

Madeline Cain Granny-Wear Here is a demonstration of the average IQ of our pizza ordering customers: "Do you ride kangaroos in Australia?" Thing is, they're not even kidding.

What I wanted to say was, "No, do you ride fat people in America?"

What I actually said was, "No, they're not as cute and fuzzy as they appear. They'll kick your front bum through your back bum."

Posted Friday 24th August at 17:00 [Comment . Like]

Kim Enuik Ooh, touché. *Posted Friday 24th August at 17:16* [Comment . Like]

Madeline Cain Granny-Wear This from the guy who'll fight a duel to the death if someone dares call his chameleon Mexican or Spanish. *Posted Friday 24th August at 18:00* [Comment . Like]

Cliff Wheelands Just imagine it! Delivering pizzas on your very own American. Travelling interstate, around Central Park, to your local coffee store, all on the back of your very own American. Talk about building a country on the backs of your countrymen. *Posted Friday 24th August at 18:42* [Comment . Like]

Richard Arnoou One Direction Duct Tape – the weirdest example of band branding I have ever seen. Yet something must be working at a hundred and fifty thousand dollars in royalties a quarter. The depth of teenage obsession is disturbing. *Posted Friday 24th August at 20:07* [Comment . Like]

Josh Annelli Does their slogan happen to be: 1D duct tape – turning teenage girls into handymen across America? My guess is a Dad thought this one up. *Posted Friday 24th August at 21:32* [Comment . Like]

Madeline Cain Granny-Wear Forget the slogan, the product reviews are *amazing.* My favourite is, "This was a thirteenth birthday present and fell into the category of 'anything' 1D". Mothers, you've got to choose your words carefully with them. This is second best only to, "It came when they said it would, and as soon as I got it, I started using it. I recommend it." I recommend this product because I could use it as soon as I got it folks. That's all you can ask from a product, right? Right? *Posted Friday 24th August at 21:35* [Comment . Like]

Jade Annelli This one sounds like my yoga teacher, "My daughter love this group to death and she love to make things out of duct tape." It disturbs me that duct tape is no longer duct tape and has now become a legitimate art medium… "I love the creative opportunities." Seriously? I mean, who loves making things out of duct tape? Fixing things yes, but making *what* exactly? *Posted Friday 24th August at 21:40* [Comment . Like]

Jarrah Annelli According to this happy customer, "I didn't know 1D duct tape existed. I bought it and let me tell you, it did *not* disappoint." My query is, in what way could duct tape disappoint? Because there is only one way in which it could *ever* disappoint and that is by not sticking. It's like saying, "I bought this sharp implement to cut things in two. It did not disappoint." No, that's because cutting things is its function god damn it! *Posted Friday 24th August at 21:44* [Comment . Like]

Victoria Zeng Then there were the people leaving reviews for 'duck' tape. I assume this is mighty handy when kidnapping ducks. *Posted Friday 24th August at 21:46* [Comment . Like]

Cain Michaels We should really get in on the action, pull together a business proposal. One Direction eye drops, One Direction hedge trimmers, One Direction tractors, heck, let's go for One Direction gyms and nip this obesity problem in the butt. *Posted Friday 24th August at 22:13* [Comment . Like]

Madeline Cain Granny-Wear And for young men we'd have what? *Posted Friday 24th August at 22:24* [Comment . Like]

Cain Michaels Beyonce gyms. Duh. *Posted Friday 24th August at 22:33* [Comment . Like]

Bring A Chameleon To Work Day

NOTES > My Notes [Write a note]

By **Madeline Cain Riot Photographer.** Saturday, 25th August 2012 at 04:40.

Duncan has made me bipolar, in that I both hate and love him and have no doubt all this seesawing is going to filter into my health.

Kim called Duncan a hero. "He exposed the truth and helped hide your part in the escapade."

Yeah Kim? Well Duncan almost caused a riot in an enclosed space and then Richard and I had to use a *literal trail of breadcrumbs* to lure him back into my backpack. He's Denis the Menace reincarnate, he's all the Home Alone movies rolled into one, he's a weapons engineer who's found a case of C4 he's got to get rid of. Can't we put him in a cage? Why don't you ever get Duncan shaped surprises at your university lectures or The Den?

Even without Duncan to mess things up spectacularly, I'm not sure how Richard does it. I've decided he can keep his concert photography. Those people are too highly strung for me. I thought 'diva' only applied to female performers but I was wrong. It also applies to bands of fully grown men with tats. From the sounds of it, this behaviour is normal. Frankly, I'd rather play with a can of snakes. No wonder you have trouble getting out words (sorry Richard, but you know this high stress job isn't helping). My bizarre brand of life is just too volatile when mixed with people of their special sort of entitlement.

In a nutshell, my night of concert photography went like this: I met the band (they were dickheads, sorry Kim); and with the help of Duncan, I managed to destroy their reputation in under five seconds.

It started with the little bundle of chaos stowing away in my camera backpack. Richard met me at the stage door of Madison Square

Garden when I arrived. I'm not going to sugar coat it, the back stage is as ugly as a baboon's bottom. It's about as far removed from a garden as I am from a Victoria's Secret model. There's no garden, just slabs of concrete and stadium seating. A massive round building ten stories high, it takes up an entire city block and perches on top of Penn Station below. The immense ugliness is put in greater contrast by the elegant, many columned post office across the road, one of the biggest in the US.

The home to NYC basketball and hockey, its massive arena on occasion gets converted into a concert hall. Only bands with gigantic crowds get the big stage, the rest play at a 'little' side stage which still takes fifteen hundred people. Lost in Transfusion was a band that demanded the big arena.

You'd think having the world's most famous bands performing there would mean the backstage corridors would be like the sumptuous halls of The Plaza. You'd think that, but you'd be wrong. After entering the plain metal stage door we made our way along the most uninspiring corridor I'd ever walked down, and I live in student housing.

Walls were made of large besser bricks painted white, and the floors were lino. The ceiling was the only thing that varied: square patterned ceilings (of office blocks everywhere) in the corridors; and exposed pipes and air ducts in the soaring space behind stage. Shots of famous bands and shows performed at the Garden hung on the walls at regular intervals.

"You r-r-ready to r-rock?" Richard asked. "O-one of those p-p-photos is g-going to b-be mine s-some day. M-maybe yours t-too."

I examined a classic black and white shot of Elvis, arms flung out wide. "That would be amazing. I think I'm ready to rock. That is, if hard core rockers wear earplugs."

Richard grinned, his beard twitching like a living creature, and said –

Hold on. Before I go any further in this story. You all know Richard has what the dictionary calls, 'Speech with spasmodic repetitions or prolonging of sounds,' right? You don't need me to annoy you with dashed letters that make it seem like my laptop keys are stuck, right? So I'm going to ask you to take out your little inner stutterer, dust them off, and read his lines in that voice instead of me typing it.

Now we've got that sorted... Richard grinned, his beard twitching like a living creature and said, "You've been reading about the perils of working at gigs?"

"I prefer to not have a vacuum cleaner in my head at the end of the show is all. It would make giving directions to the models afterwards a bit challenging. By the way, did you manage to convince them? The hot ones that work here?"

He shrugged, leading me into the bowels of back stage. "No convincing needed, they practically draped themselves over me when I asked them. They all go to FIT, the Fashion Institute of Technology a couple of blocks south. Anything that gets them on the stage rather than sweeping the crap off the floor in front is a step up. You may now be their god. Just no human sacrifice, ok?"

Spending time with Richard makes you jumpy. 'Twitchy' is still as good a nickname as ever for him with his head constantly moving from side to side, and eyes roving as though he'd miss something if he didn't look at everything at once. His finger continually tapped the shutter button, ready to snap a shot within a split second. It was like the nervous energy of New York had gathered together to form a person. By the time we peered out at the teaming crowd grooving to the first support act, I was so keyed up it was as though I'd drunk several energy drinks. With double shots of zing.

Though we'd only been hired to shoot Lost in Transfusion, I dumped my backpack at my feet and fished around for my camera, keen to get a feel for the good angles. I hoisted the camera to my chest with a grunt looking for a good vantage point.

Gee, I thought, *must have been a while since I used this body and lens combo; feel like I'm holding a small bowling ball.* Who needs the gym when you've got a camera that can knock out small children?

It was the *absence* of movement that attracted my attention, Richard halting in mid twitch to suddenly zero in on my chest.

"Eyes up here buddy." I lifted a hand to point two fingers at my eyeballs.

Richard shhh-ed me, finger to his lips, his attention on my breasts unwavering. Now, while Richard may have a paedophile beard, he is not a pervert.

"What, is my camera showing its knickers or something?" I looked down and froze, instantly spotting what Richard had suspected but couldn't see. If you'd seen that shimmer enough times, you'd pick it up instantly too.

Just my luck, at that moment my hand spasmed and Duncan shifted, exposing himself to Richard.

"Duncan!"

The next thing I knew all the wind was knocked out of me as Richard reached out in a manic lunge, missed Duncan by a mile (his superhero genes transferring him from the camera to the top of my head in the blink of an eye) and instead tackled me to the hard concrete floor.

"No, nonono," groaned Richard, clearly remembering the first time he met my mini-stowaway.

Make no mistake, Richard is a hefty man and his beard was so thick it coated my face in a hair mask. I wheezed, hands above my head holding my camera out of harm's way. Richard swung his hands around like propellers as he squashed the remaining air out of my lungs. If I had breath, I'd tell him Duncan was too fast for the helicopter manoeuvre.

Somehow, though all of this, we'd missed the first support band coming off stage. It was only when someone cleared their throat that we realised the second support band was looming over us on the cusp of indecision, trying to decide if this was some bizarre make-out session, or an attack by the wolf man.

"Break a leg," said Richard, polite as you please. I gave them a weak smile and a thumbs up.

They nodded, hovered a little, then decided it was best to do what they came for and ran onto the stage.

"Hola!" croaked the reptilian, right next to my ear.

Before I could grasp him, the bugger was off. I gasped. "Can't breathe. Get off hephalump!"

Thus began the Great Search, creeping around like a couple of

Ghostbusters backstage, whispering Duncan's name in our most seductive 'I'm going to give you love not strangulation' voices. There was no limit to where or how high he could be. However, I knew he liked to: a) be in the action; b) view things from a vantage point and; c) play games. Unfortunately, this situation probably fell under all three.

"This guy is ripping it up on the drums," said Richard as we searched some curtains in the wings. "Totally changed up the beat of the song."

"Aww, shitkittens." On a hunch, I looked out at the drum set.

It was a classic, 'likes to be in the action,' Duncan interference manoeuvre. While the audience and his band mates would have seen it as the theatrical facial and drum performance of the year, I knew the frantic 'what is that' face was because of a speeding chameleon playing a game of 'hit me if you can' across the drum set. Later, I read a review of the band which praised the 'out of this world drum solo'. Now that poor drummer is going to have to learn how to do it on purpose.

The drummer lost control of one stick and then the other, hitting the sound guy off stage straight in the face knocking him off his chair. The speeding blur had disappeared and I knew Duncan had 'left the building'.

"Catch him if he comes this way," I ordered Richard, "I'll take the other side. And make sure the sound guy doesn't have a drum stick for a nose."

In the game of Duncan catching, you've got to run, so I sprinted like an Olympian toward the far side of the stage. If you've worked back stage before you'd know the first rule (other than whispers only) is don't run. Odds are you'll trip on something and end up with a face like a pug dog, whether it be cords, or stray drum sticks that have launched the sound guy off his chair.

For a moment it felt like I was on drum-stick roller skates. I'd always sucked at roller skates, about as graceful as Kermit the Frog doing ballet. My arm swept across the top of some equipment, knocking CDs and cords to the ground in an effort to stop. I saved myself in the end by slamming into a wall ala George of the Jungle.

The crowd was going off in the arena as the support act dashed off stage to check whether or not the sound guy lived. They trampled across the knickknacks I'd scattered across the floor and heaved the stunned technician to his feet. Not wanting to add clean-up duty to the poor guy's list of things to deal with, I collected the CDs and cords, arranging them neatly on top of the black box which was some sort of control system.

Try as I might I could not find Duncan and it was coming closer and closer to when we needed to be on the floor making sure our settings were right.

"We've got to go, Maddie." Richard pulled me away from my latest search.

My knees ached from scuttling across the floor looking for low hiding places. "But what if he causes another –"

"Can't worry about it. These guys will be so hyped up they'll probably brush him off without noticing."

"Wait," I pleaded, "Let me lay a food trap. Maybe food will excite him more than causing the concert to implode."

Finding my backpack abandoned on the side of the stage, I retrieved my last 'luxury' food, a ham and salad sandwich and a chocolate chip muffin. It was to be tins of spaghetti again after this until I got paid for that night's gig. Moving to an out of the way corner, I put my paper wrapped clothing bundle off to one side and removed the rest of my photographic equipment (flash, lens etc), slotting it into pouches on the belt I'd strapped around my waist. Folding back the lip of the backpack, I stuffed the ham and salad filling into my mouth and crumbled the bread and muffin (after one desperate bite) in a two meter trail leading into my backpack....

Nadine Cain

Today **[Clear Chat history]**

I think your father taught Michael how to pick locks.

Doesn't surprise me, I always thought he was the secret puppet master behind Mike's schemes.

Mike Cain

Today **[Clear Chat history]**

There is no way they can pin this on me.

Is that a boast or an indignant claim of innocence?

I plead the fifth.

I'm serious! This could get him into real trouble.

Allowing porn access to adolescents is only considered minor trouble now?

Madeline, you're not helping.

But apparently Dad is ;-) Ha!

Mum?

Ok, sorry I antagonised you, really. Seriously, tell me why Mike knowing how to pick locks is a problem. Other than, you know, the probability he'll turn to organised crime to fund his evil genius addiction.

This the third time the school has called us about your brother.

What did they say he did?

They didn't *exactly* say he did it… They just strongly hinted their suspicions.

Their suspicions of WHAT?!

No need to internet shout at me young lady.

You and Mike are a bad as each other at getting to the point. I think you enjoy the drama.

I could do without half the drama your brother brings into our life. When he finally leaves home, I'm throwing a week long party.

…They hinted that…

They think your brother broke into the Principal's office.

You can't plead the fifth, you're Australian.

All I'll say is, if it wasn't me, then it was someone of equal intelligence and wit.

Ah, Neil pretending to be you.

Particularly when he's pretending to be you. Pray tell, what is it Neil couldn't pull off and you apparently had zero red hands in.

The Principal was asking for it, allowing any old rot into her assembly speeches. I'm convinced she's a robot.

I'm guessing you decided to test that theory like a Ron Burgundy teleprompter?

No, that's too easy. Besides, it's already been done (All hail Anchorman!). I'm not a copycat.

Ha! Screen-shotting for blackmail purposes!

Just imagining myself in the shoes of the criminal, my dear sister. I, of course, meant the perpetrator is not a copycat.

Save me your pleas of innocence. Instead, use your clearly gifted storytelling skills in explaining why you risked getting expelled. Did you draw moustaches on the photos of her kids? Steal answers to the Year 12 exams and sell them at a premium?

Shit! Really? Hey, how come every time Mike's in trouble he's 'my brother' and not 'your son'? I didn't make him this way. By the sounds of things it was all Dad. Why do you think Dad's involved anyway?

Because your father was a locksmith once upon a time, and I was assured most fervently that the Principal's door is locked every time she leaves the room.

Seriously? How did I not know this? Oh my god, can Dad break into safes too? Have we missed a grand opportunity to start our own Robin Hood band of merry men?

You never were one to pay attention to your father's stories of the old days, darling. That's beside the point. The point is, someone added fake achievement awards to yesterday's assembly and that has your brother's signature all over it.

His signature is being a smart arse. But so is the signature of every adolescent male under the age of 25. How can they be so sure it's him?

It was fairly simple to extrapolate after he won the 'Most Likely To Succeed' award.

But they don't have the proof?

It doesn't matter if they don't have the proof. *We* know.

Look Mum, now's not the time to be diplomatic. Let him have it. But also be cool and don't rat him out to the Principal. Because you're right, if this wasn't him I'll eat my left shoe.

Oh I'll be cool alright. It's technology lockdown time for that mutated gene.

No to all but filing those babies away for later… Let's just say someone took advantage of the Principle's inattentive personality for maximum public laughs.

Ah, hence the assembly reference. The only thing I can recall the Principal doing at those things, other than boring the whole school with her speeches, was giving out the achievement awards.

And today's awards were particularly spectacular.

Of course they were. What, did you grant Neil the 'Most Likely To Be A 40 Year Old Virgin' award?

Nothing so crude. No, these awards included such classics as: 'Fanciest Horse Drawing' and; 'Most Likely To Get A Tattoo Of A Butterfly'.

Snort! Principal Slater never was the fizziest can in the six pack.

I think the point she got suspicious was when she announced the award for, 'Most Likely To Morph Into A Rainbow Trout'.

You sure it wasn't at the point you were declared, 'Most Likely To Succeed'? Because we all know that's a belly full of laughs.

The perp knows who's King in this school. Either way, they can't prove anything with the other decoy awards thrown into the mix. I overheard them call at least six potential suspects in to be interrogated.

In addition to yourself. Well, if I were you, I'd morph into a rainbow trout and swim up river from Mum for a while. She's pissed and she's headed your way.

Love it when you talk science Mama Bear.

Roger that. Mike Out.

Try to suppress the idiot inside. Or don't. I'm still gunning for pictures of you limping through boot camp.

Can't tame this dragon. Soz.

...Richard and I looked at each other, crossed our fingers, then made our way through the wings and out into the roar of the crowd, the racket surrounding us like liquid. It gave a new meaning to surround sound. Though the ear plugs dulled the clamour, it gave me the feeling I was swimming under an ocean of noise.

The vibe from the crowd was intense. Chantings of 'Lost In Transfusion' bounced around the arena like a pinball. It was like the floor and walls were made of people, not concrete and seating, just a slopping sea of human on three sides joining in a mosh pit at ground level. Harsh yellow spotlights lit the crowd who were doing some epic Kermit the Frog wavy-arms, limbs flailing even though it was only the roadies on stage testing equipment. The roof sloped down like a funnel, with a host of black screens hanging from the point; score boards for the various sporting games played here.

Richard, I, and half a dozen security guards had access to a one and a half metre strip of floor between the stage and barricade that kept back the juiced up crowd. The air already smelt of spilt beer and sweat and the air conditioning did nothing to shift the humidity that had built. The stage, highly polished, was at chest height allowing us a good arm rest to get steady shots in the low light.

The arena went black and the show was on!

I'm the sort of person who will have favourite songs of which I know neither the band name or the song. While I'd sworn to Kim I didn't know who Lost in Transfusion were, I realised these songs were ones I'd listened to every day this year, blasted out of every second shop I'd walked past. I had been inducted into the Lost in Transfusion fan club just by walking the streets. As such it was really hard NOT to let my inner groove-monster gyrate like a Mr Bean dance party.

But we had a job to do and I was intent on filling up sixteen gig of memory card. I'm pretty sure I had the lead singer, a crowd pleaser in black leather with a moustache that could rival Freddie Mercury, in every hue on the colour scale. Blasting power ballads in blue, singing his fury at politics in red, and rocking out in purple, green, and orange. Richard and I communicated like SAS troops, hand signals our language as we moved from side to side, then split off into the wings to take dramatic shots of the band in front of a devoted crowd. Then we made our way back to the front of the stage.

We were maybe an hour in when the band struck up their most well-known song, 'Blowing Out Bad Atmosphere'.

It was then that everything exploded.

The lead singer leant into the chorus, mouth wide. "Because I'm blooooowing, out, ba-" and while his mouth kept going his voice did not.

But it was not his voice cracking. Oh no, it was the sound system blasting, "Ba-ba-ba-ba-ba-ba-ba-ba-ba-ba," through the speakers like a demented electronic sheep while his mouth continued miming the word 'atmosphere'.

Cheers faded, the band faltered and the demented sheep noise filled the proverbial awkward silence.

A hand grabbed me by the elbow, jerking me along the stage towards the wings. "Holy shit, Ziggy was lip syncing. We've got to get the hell out of this no man's land before the bombs start falling," said Richard.

"Bombs?" I asked as a plastic bottle whizzed by my side, exploding against the edge of the stage.

It was the first of a hail of refuse as pandemonium ensued, the adoration of the crowd being rework and twisted into that of a mob with fire brands and pitchforks. Richard didn't have to tell me twice, we pounded up the steps to the wings. Curtains moved across the stage as the band members abandoned their instruments for the safety of backstage.

An announcer's voice came across the sound system. "Ladies and gentlemen. Due to technical difficulties in the *final* act of this event, we regret to inform you that the event has reached an early conclusion. Please exit via the doors in an orderly fashion. Our apologies for the inconvenience. Have a pleasant evening."

We entered the wings in time to see Ziggy have a complete melt down. For those with delicate ears, I shall replace some of his more fruitier language with the word 'cupcake'.

Stabbing at a button on the black box I'd run into earlier, Ziggy shouted, "What the cupcake?! Cupcake mother cupcake, you piece of cupcake! You're mother cupcaking professionals? Cupcake you are! Cupcake, cupcake, cupcake, cupcake, CUPCAKE!"

The box spit out a disk which he snapped up and flipped over. "This has been scratched to the cupcake, it looks like a cupcaking slasher film. Which cupcake did this? I'm gonna chew his cupcaking head off."

The sound guy was terrified, his face white except for a livid red mark across the forehead and over his right eye from the drum stick earlier. "There was an accident before. People everywhere!" He waved his hand vaguely at the puffy line on his face. "Anyone could have… I just put it in…I *told* you an MP3 file-"

He didn't get to finish as Ziggy reached over and performed the most vicious nipple-cripple I'd ever seen. It was like he was turning oven dials. A high pitched squeak followed the sound technician to the floor for the second time that night.

"Do I look like I've got cupcaking time to play around with computers? You get what you're given and you don't cupcake it up."

My nipples twitched in sympathy. But you know what? I was glad it had been him semi-conscious on the floor an hour ago. Because that meant I was the only person who knew a panicked photographer looking for her housemate's chameleon was at the root of all lip synching mayhem.

"We need to get you guys out of here," said a nervous assistant. "It's not safe."

She was right, the boo-ing frenzy in the arena had picked up momentum.

"Not until whatever cupcaker who did this pays for it," spat Ziggy.

The assistant shot a pleading look at the rest of us.

"CCTV," said Richard suddenly. "They'll have footage of backstage recorded. I'm sure the Garden will be able to pass it onto your manager once you're safely out of harm's way."

My heart stopped. I almost slapped Richard upside the head. He didn't know, but still, was he insane!? Letting a crazy, probably pill popping rocker called *Ziggy* know who ruined his career?

"Cupcake that. We're going to security NOW." He stalked off in the direction of the green rooms, his band mates following like lemmings.

I let fly some expletives of my own. "Richard, what the cupcake did you do that for?"

He popped out his earplugs. "Management wouldn't have given him the recording; I was just trying to move them out. I thought a combination of the crowd sounding like they were going to turn him into a voodoo doll, and the promise of revenge would convince him to leave. The sooner management can make an announcement that the band has left by helicopter, the less trouble security will get into. At least the band are moving in the direction of the elevators."

"We've got to stop Ziggy from seeing it!" I felt sick to my stomach, the sound guy's moans making the rolling in my gullet worse.

"Why-"

"Because it was me you daft Jesus look-a-like! I slipped on a drum stick and knocked the lip synching CD over!"

I took off after Ziggy, Richard keeping pace, his beard flapping like a flag. "Why, didn't, you, nudge, me? I, wouldn't, have, said, anything!"

"I didn't know I'd etched a line graph in a lip synching CD! If I'd thought it was going to result in a riot, be assured I would have bloody said something!"

"Shitshitshitshitshit," chanted Richard as we skidded round the corner. "Where's Duncan when you need a distraction?"

But we were WAY too late. I skidded into the room ahead of Richard to see a grainy black and white video of the sound guy getting brained and flying like a sack of rice off his stool. I held my breath, knowing what was coming next, yet somehow unable to move away from danger. All five members of the band focused on the tiny screen before them, about the size of a notebook, their gazes seeming to combine into one ray of rage directed at the screen. They were going to tear me apart.

Any minute, any minute now I was going to…A black smudge appeared on the image, like a little four fingered hand which was then joined by another. A wedge with a massive pinhole eye popped into view, the eye shifting slowly as though taking in the little security room packed with people. Ziggy jerked back with a hiss. Then, like a veil being moved from left to right, Duncan, the saver of my skin, slithered across the field of view, blocking the picture completely.

"What the cupcake was that?" asked Ziggy.

Richard plucked the back of my shirt and slowly drew me out of the room. "We don't need to hear how that conversation plays out. Besides, your face is way too honest and I'm afraid you're going to say something stupid. Let's see how that food trap worked."

Shell-shocked, I let him lead me down the horribly dated corridors to my backpack which housed a few crumbs and one bloated chameleon making crazy eyes at me. Unable to decide if I wanted to strangle or kiss him, I left Richard to zip him up and collapsed against a wall.

I was exhausted, and I still had to direct a fashion shoot before we hightailed it out of there. I reached for the bundle wrapped in brown paper and twine I'd set next to my backpack and pulled it into my lap.

I hadn't opened Dom's latest 'package' yet as it arrived only an hour before I was due at the gig. Still not sure what our relationship was, I'd emailed him telling him about the gig and how I'd managed to nab the stage for as long as it took the cleaning crew to pick up the refuse of the crowd (two-three hours apparently). I'd awkwardly talked about my idea to set up the shoot as a rock concert and sent it off before I lost my nerve.

Thank god my vaguely stalker-ish email came off as intended. He arrived at my doorstep personally, wearing a navy blue high-necked vest over a dusty blue shirt. "Sorry it took a while darl-face. I had to pull some strings but lucky Jonny and Carlo owe me a favour, if you know what I mean."

He winked, glancing from side to side. "I changed their lives forever, they own me big time, get what I'm saying?"

No. I did not get what he meant, nor did I know what he was saying, but I thought it best just to nod like I did, because only that seemed to make him happy and I was still uncertain if I should worry about him being unhappy.

"I'm pretty good at the whole, right connections thing if you get where I'm sliding, kid. When you're with me, you're taken care of. If anyone gives you any trouble, you just send them to me."

Crap,what does this guy DO for a living? How many people owe him favours? For what??

"Now get some sexy ladies into those threads and don't let them sneak away with any. They may look grungy but one piece costs more than a box full of my more standard shipments." Treated to a parting wink I stood, overwhelmed, as he swaggered his short man swagger down the street, whistling like a cartoon character trying to prove his innocence.

While we waited for Lost in Transfusion to exit via the roof, and disgruntled patrons to leave, I unwrapped the bundle and used Richard as a clothes rack, draping across his legs lacy corsets, full bodied skirts (ruffled and short at the front, long at the back), black and white striped pants, shear bras and short Sergeant Pepper jackets that just reached the lower rib cage. It took a bit of rearranging on the floor to figure out that the first two and the last three were separate outfits. It seemed my 'band' for the shoot was going to be a cross between steam punk and the Beatles.

The fashion shoot was the only thing that went right that whole night. The FIT girls turned up with their hair already styled, and make-up as dramatic as the clothing. *And* they were drop dead gorgeous. If I don't see half of them at fashion week, I'll eat one of my shoes. They took to their assigned instruments as though they had been born making noise for the camera. The sound guy, bless his battered body, even put on the Lost in Transfusion lip synching CD to get everyone into the mood.

In fact, this self-appointed fashion portfolio gig has been the only one where something hasn't gone horribly pear shaped. Do I understand fashion yet? No. But you know what? It's the only thing in my life that's going right and it feels amazing to be a normal person who doesn't attract oddities like Lady GaGa attracts costumes.

It must be what I'm meant to do. If it wasn't surely Duncan would have escaped and blown a fuse switch or something.

[Comment . Like . Share]

Kyle Traybna and **77 others** like this.

Kim Enuik No you may NOT put Duncan in a cage. He's a free spirit! And a hero. He never acted like himself when he listened to Lost in Transfusion, somehow he knew. He was determined to get to the bottom of it while protecting his befuddled side-kick. Duncan stands for justice, and music lovers, why would you want to tame such a noble creature? *Posted Saturday 25th August at 10:25* [Comment . Like]

> **Madeline Cain Lipsyncher** I've got two words for you buddy, 'Riot Police'. Because that's who we almost had to call. Next time he can be a free spirit inside YOUR backpack. Then you can deal with the mob. Wouldn't be surprised if they had Taser guns next time round. *Posted Saturday 25th August at 12:08* [Comment . Like]
>
> **Victoria Zeng** Sounds to me like Duncan stands for muffins. Maddie left with the last one, he followed. *Posted Saturday 25th August at 12:17* [Comment . Like]
>
> **Jade Annelli** I love it when real life turns into a fairy tale. A trail of bread crumbs makes it so Hansel and Gretel. *Posted Saturday 25th August at 12:26* [Comment . Like]
>
> **Cliff Wheeland** Indeed. Did you have a miniature house made of gingerbread? Are you planning to fatten him up and eat him when dinner has become one spaghetti tin too much? *Posted Saturday 25th August at 12:37* [Comment . Like]
>
> **Madeline Cain Lipsyncher** What a waste of perfectly good gingerbread! By the way Kim, you owe me a muffin for getting

your 'free spirit' home in one piece. *Posted Saturday 25th August at 12:44* [Comment . Like]

Cliff Wheeland Should know better than to lunge for Duncan, Richard. He needs gentle coaxing and the promise of a good scratch. *Posted Saturday 25th August at 12:52* [Comment . Like]

Richard Arnoou If I ever have to deal with that lizard demon again I won't shirk at sacrificing a gingerbread house. Then I'll eat him myself. *Posted Saturday 25th August at 12:55* [Comment . Like]

Josh Annelli Official word on the street is the lead singer had a throat condition but didn't want to disappoint fans. *Posted Saturday 25th August at 14:40* [Comment . Like]

Richard Arnoou I heard him yell at the technician and I can tell you, his throat was fine. *Posted Saturday 25th August at 14:45* [Comment . Like]

Madeline Cain Lipsyncher I agree. If Ziggy had a throat condition, I'm a cactus. *Posted Saturday 25th August at 14:48* [Comment . Like]

Kathy Bloomingdale I can't believe you exposed them as frauds! It's amazing you didn't get trampled or end up with a garbage bag for hair. Forget photography, you should be a journalist. Hope you got photos of the moment when everyone realised they'd just been listening to the band play along with a CD. Might as well start your tabloid photography stint with a riot. *Posted Saturday 25th August at 14:51* [Comment . Like]

Madeline Cain Lipsyncher Can't sell those photos Kathy, every photo taken during the concert belongs to the Garden because we are 'employees', not freelancers. The band buys exclusive rights to all the photos. If I tried to on-sell not only would it be double dipping, but I would get a reputation for making the client look bad. I thought it would make it awkward to complete the assignment for this month, but it turned out my fashion shots fitted the criteria perfectly. This assignment focused on mixing genres. *Posted Saturday 25th August at 14:58* [Comment . Like]

Josh Annelli You've got a triple whammy there, not only are you mixing a literary genre with music, but steampunk with the Beatles, *and* your mixing concert photography with fashion photography. I knew you'd get the hang of this. *Posted Saturday 25th August at 14:59* [Comment . Like]

Cain Michaels I've been on the receiving end of a nipple cripple, it's soul destroying. *Posted Saturday 25th August at 15:05* [Comment . Like]

Richard Arnoou Yet you're still here, soulless. Must be why you're a photographer, you're hoping to steal enough souls with your camera to make you a new one. *Posted Saturday 25th August at 15:07* [Comment . Like]

Cain Michaels At least my beard doesn't provide a functioning ecosystem for a bug village. *Posted Saturday 25th August at 15:12* [Comment . Like]

Richard Arnoou You took some mega awesome shots Mad, if you just chilled out (and stopped smuggling amphibians) you'd fit in easy. Sure, concert photography isn't for everyone, you get some arseholes, but when you're chill like me, nothing gets under your skin. I'm there for the music, can't play for shit, but I can shoot a good still and that allows me to be near what I love without people bleeding out the ears. *Posted Saturday 25th August at 15:20* [Comment . Like]

Madeline Cain Lipsyncher Nothing gets under your skin, hey? Except Cain. *Posted Saturday 25th August at 15:22* [Comment . Like]

Richard Arnoou That boy would get under anyone's skin.

That's why we're bros, I figure together, with my positive and his negative, we create neutral. *Posted Saturday 25th August at 15:26* [Comment . Like]

Kevin Doherty The uninspired backstage is the bane of all show business, every backstage is like that. Babe, these notes of yours are *amazing* source material. I mean, getting someone to pretend to be someone else by lip synching is hilarious. We've got a couple of PA's for celebrities who've put their hands up for the show and this could be dynamite! You just keep scoring the muse tries for me. I'm going through all your old notes now. I'm free every night this week, we should hang. *Posted Saturday 25th August at 16:02* [Comment . Like]

Madeline Cain Lipsyncher You're going back through *all* of them? I'm glad this helped spark ideas, just make sure no one knows your girlfriend is such a klutz, ok? I'd prefer people to be laughing with me rather than at me. *Posted Saturday 25th August at 16:21* [Comment . Like]

Kevin Doherty Don't sweat it baby doll, I make them think it was all me ? *Posted Saturday 25th August at 16:22* [Comment . Like]

Madeline Cain Lipsyncher Great? *Posted Saturday 25th August at 16:23* [Comment . Like]

Nadine Cain What a packed two months! First you're fighting crime and now you're exposing shonky showmen. What will you think of next? I thank you for your use of the word cupcake rather than swear words. Takes me back to the days when your father and I had to get used to not swearing because you picked up words as soon as we said them. We couldn't have you waltzing around playschool using words like a lumberjack. We used 'sugar' and 'frankfurt' as substitutes. For example: Where the sugar is the frankfurt dog? Or: What the frankfurt? *Posted Saturday 25th August at 17:00* [Comment . Like]

Mike Cain Other words you could use: What the duck? What the maxi pad? What the thong? What the wagtail? What the pants? Or perhaps replace them with lesser swear words: what the damn? What the boob? What the butt hole? *Posted Saturday 25th August at 17:14* [Comment . Like]

Nadine Cain Enough, Michael. Honey, Dom's a bit of an odd character, what's with all the winking? Is he seducing you? Did you tell him you were taken? You shouldn't go stringing boys along, even if they're giving you expensive clothes. *Posted Saturday 25th August at 17:22* [Comment . Like]

Madeline Cain Lipsyncher No mum, he's not sleazy just a little overconfident. And you know me better than that; I would never string anyone along. I'm not sure if 'anyone gives you trouble' applies to someone specific or just the world in general. Because I've got a lizard who needs a talking to. *Posted Saturday 25th August at 17:31* [Comment . Like]

Jarrah Annelli I'm telling you, mobster. *Posted Saturday 25th August at 17:47* [Comment . Like]

Tim Gleeve I think there's something in commercialising the sound of a demented electronic sheep. You could take over the world with a craze like that. *Posted Saturday 25th August at 17:59* [Comment . Like]

Mike Cain The remix is already on YouTube, baby. Pulling in the advertising dollars. *Posted Saturday 25th August at 17:59* [Comment . Like]

Cliff Wheeland Finding a job you can do without causing an international incident is something that should be applauded. Congratulations on your normality. *Posted Saturday 25th August at 21:17* [Comment . Like]

Kathy Bloomingdale It won't last long, it never does. I'm looking forward to finally meeting you in person, Cliff. *Posted Saturday 25th August at 21:48* [Comment . Like]

Cliff Wheeland And I you, sweet friend of Madeline. *Posted Saturday 25th August at 21:55* [Comment . Like]

Madeline Cain Lipsyncher Since when have you guys been so buddy buddy? *Posted Saturday 25th August at 22:27* [Comment . Like]

Mike Cain likes the page **DO NOT TRY THIS AT HOME – Dude, We Have To Try This…** [Like]

Harry Lee Why can't math be like a Gaga song? (Ra)2 (Ah)3 + Ro (Ma + Mama) + (Ga)2 + Ooo(La)2 = Bad Romance. *Posted Monday 27th August at 14:10* [Comment . Like]

Tim Gleeve Didn't pick you for a Gaga fan. Maybe you should keep that level of obsession to yourself… *Posted Monday 27th August at 19:12* [Comment . Like]

Madeline Cain Lipsyncher likes the page **My Best Friend Would Be My Only Friend If People Knew How Weird We Were In Private** [Like]

Cliff Wheeland Like that time we were watching Babe and you said, "I love you future bacon"? *Posted Thursday 30th August at 12:36* [Comment . Like]

Madeline Cain Lipsyncher Yet we are still friends. *Posted Thursday 30th August at 12:56* [Comment . Like]

Madeline Cain Lipsyncher –> Kathy Bloomingdale I just had the weirdest night with Kevin. We were chatting, and I said something funny and he pulls out a tape recorder and insists I say it again. But I couldn't remember exactly what I said and *apparently* said it wrong the second time. "No, say it how you said it the first time." This happened both nights I went over. That's odd, isn't it? I'm not just being picky? *Posted Sunday 2nd September at 22:00* [Comment . Like]

Kathy Bloomingdale A tape recorder? As in a real life, makes a swish noise when you fast forward tape recorder? Did he switch careers while I was packing? Is he a journalist now? Not that I'm quite clear on why you would be worthy of recording. *Posted Sunday 2nd September at 22:09* [Comment . Like]

Madeline Cain Lipsyncher I'm pretty sure those don't exist outside eighties movies. No, it was a digital Dictaphone. I kid you not it was in his pocket. Like a writer's notebook for actors. I spoke some off the cuff comment and he whipped it out all ninja like and then the next thing I know I'm looking down the mesh of a microphone. It happened twice on the first night and six times the next. He was intense, I mean *really* intense, watching my mouth like I was about to puke up Emmy Awards. Half the stuff I said was garbage and I could never exactly remember it. Now I'm so paranoid I won't be able to say things back correctly that I find myself repeating sentences. Out loud. I'm like my own echo. *Posted Sunday 2nd September at 22:17* [Comment . Like]

Kathy Bloomingdale I know he says you're his muse, but that's a little weird. Don't hate me for this, but I'm not sure half the stuff that comes out of your mouth is television worthy. I mean you're funny, but in a slap stick, Charlie Chaplin kind of way. *Posted Sunday 2nd September at 22:20* [Comment . Like]

Madeline Cain Lipsyncher Hold on a minute while I pull that knife out of my back… Just because I'm not your muse doesn't mean I'm not a lyrical genius. Though I do wonder if Kevin isn't grasping at straws, particularly because the sentence he thought so recordable went something along the lines of, "A lot of shit is going to happen when pigs learn to fly." *Posted Sunday 2nd September at 22:24* [Comment . Like]

Kathy Bloomingdale Not up there with the comic greats, but not as Dad-joke as I feared. Are you ok with your life being broadcast as laughable to a whole nation? *Posted Sunday 2nd September at 22:26* [Comment . Like]

Madeline Cain Lipsyncher What are you on about? He's just looking for a catch phrase. *Posted Sunday 2nd September at 22:29* [Comment . Like]

Kathy Bloomingdale Then you haven't seen the most recent episodes of 'Your Job or The Money'? *Posted Sunday 2nd September at 22:30* [Comment . Like]

Madeline Cain Lipsyncher No… I've been working pizza delivery the nights it's been on. Why? *Posted Sunday 2nd September at 22:30* [Comment . Like]

Kathy Bloomingdale Because the show has some interesting parallels with your Facebook notes. Let's go with a recent example. Take your first date shenanigans which ended in a health inspector chasing a vampire chef with blood dripping from his mouth. Now compare it to a YJOTM show of a similar theme. Kevin poses as a health inspector and enters a chain restaurant (who shall remain nameless). He demands the contestant show that the floors are clean enough to literally eat off. Of course he comes in rush hour and of course he does it in front of the other patrons. He then demands that the employee serve the guests on the floor as well. When the manager protests, fake inspector Kevin says the contestant employee is the whistle blower and has proven his claims. Then we watch as the manager snaps and chases the waiter around a crowded restaurant. Hilarious. The shortened clip on YouTube has 1.5 million hits. *Posted Sunday 2nd September at 22:35* [Comment . Like]

Madeline Cain Lipsyncher So what? Kevin draws his funnies from real life. I do the same thing. It doesn't mention me, or have me ordering cooked steak tartar, or insulting Jews across the world with edible facial hair. He's altered it to fit the show. It's weird he thinks I'm some sort of inspiration-money-tree though. Maybe that's why he's gone from barely seeing me to texting me nearly *every* day wanting to catch up. It's awesome, (especially on the sucking face side of things) but I'm finally busy with stuff other than pizza delivery and I want to take advantage. *Posted Sunday 2nd September at 22:40* [Comment . Like]

Kathy Bloomingdale Correction, he's drawing his funnies from YOUR real life. How else do you explain the strangers I've seen walking around Adelaide wearing t-shirts saying, "Her penis is a gun!" Because that little tag line features in episode nine of YJOTM. *Posted Sunday 2nd September at 22:41* [Comment . Like]

Madeline Cain Lipsyncher WHAT! *Posted Sunday 2nd September at 22:42* [Comment . Like]

Kathy Bloomingdale Yep, one of their contestants was a bouncer. You can guess what scenario was played out. *Posted Sunday 2nd September at 22:42* [Comment . Like]

Madeline Cain Lipsyncher I've caught up. This is insane. It's like seeing my life in some weird, parallel, game show universe. There's an online t-shirt store dedicated to phrases I thought about for all of thirty seconds. *There is an online store dedicated to game show me!! Posted Monday 3rd September at 08:00* [Comment . Like]

Kathy Bloomingdale Now you understand the Dictaphone. Are you sure you're still ok being the muse? *Posted Monday 3rd September at 22:47* [Comment . Like]

Madeline Cain Lipsyncher I don't know. I guess? It's not like my life is exactly replicated, but there's enough to make me feel a little bit weird about it. I mean, he's not tapping me for material on every date. We make out, I get chocolates and flowers all the time. *Posted Monday 3rd September at 22:50* [Comment . Like]

Kathy Bloomingdale He's not Indian giving gifts from set is he? *Posted Monday 3rd September at 22:51* [Comment . Like]

Madeline Cain Lipsyncher No way, he's not like that. Kevin is a stratosphere above my last boyfriend. He kissed like fish and smelt like a turtle. I think the only thing he ever gave me was a cold. *Posted Monday 3rd September at 22:53* [Comment . Like]

Kathy Bloomingdale Anything is better than your last one. Well, maybe suggest to Kevin that you're not too keen on the Dictaphone. If he's so keen on remembering what you said, he can write it down like a normal person. Not record it like a gag reel. *Posted Sunday 2nd September at 22:55* [Comment . Like]

Madeline Cain Lipsyncher I think I might. Thanks Kath. Can't believe I'm going to see you soon! Then you can meet Kevin for yourself. *Posted Monday 3rd September at 22:57* [Comment . Like]

Kathy Bloomingdale Should be a hoot. *Posted Monday 3rd September at 22:58* [Comment . Like]

Virginia Lowe It's ocean week! Let's think about those lesser known of the oceanic kingdom who are forgotten in the excitement of whales and dolphins. Forgetting for the moment that confining nature's creatures to tanks is cruel, if you had an aquarium, would you fill it with sea horses or barnacles? *Posted Wednesday 5th September at 08:30* [Comment . Like]

Madeline Cain Lipsyncher Sea horse. *Posted Wednesday 5th September at 15:21* [Comment . Like]

Virginia Low Why? What is it about these majestic creatures that you find so fascinating? *Posted Wednesday 5th September at 17:10* [Comment . Like]

Tim Gleeve Seriously, you're asking us to pick between something that is exotic and looks like an skeleton horse and a creature that does nothing? What kind of idiot would be like, 'Let's make a super fun aquarium and fill it with barnacles'? *Posted Wednesday 5th September at 18:02* [Comment . Like]

Madeline Cain Lipsyncher I was just going for what I thought would be easier to feed… *Posted Wednesday 5th September at 20:33* [Comment . Like]

Tim Gleeve Excited to finally be a full-time employee! I believe I can now access cheap public transport and a discount at Sizzler. *Posted Saturday 8th September at 14:15* [Comment . Like]

Madeline Cain Lipsyncher Cheese toast for everyone! *Posted Saturday 8th September at 19:42* [Comment . Like]

Kathy Bloomingdale Congrats. Now you get to work big boy hours. *Posted Saturday 8th September at 20:00* [Comment . Like]

Madeline Cain Lipsyncher I wonder how many times you can tell people to turn it off and on again in a day? *Posted Saturday 8th September at 20:31* [Comment . Like]

Tim Gleeve Oh God, what have I signed up for?! *Posted Saturday 8th September at 21:50* [Comment . Like]

Madeline Cain Lipsyncher Sick as a dog. Feel like there are midgets in my head with hammers. *Posted Tuesday 11th September at 10:11* [Comment . Like]

Jade Annelli Get better! Have Kim make a teapot of lemon and honey. That always helps me. *Posted Tuesday 11th September at 11:00* [Comment . Like]

Cliff Wheeland Eating a whole clove of garlic raw is a winner. Even colds dislike garlic breath. *Posted Tuesday 11th September at 11:38* [Comment . Like]

Tim Gleeve I'll give your midgets a bit of advice. There aren't any diamonds in there. Move on. *Posted Tuesday 11th September at 13:19* [Comment . Like]

Madeline Cain Lipsyncher I'm sorry what was that? *Spits in Tim's cup*. *Posted Tuesday 11th September at 15:00* [Comment . Like]

Derek Chan Now begins the part of the week where I drink bourbon and pretend to be Batman, which I guess puts me somewhere on the spectrum between Bruce Wayne and Tony Stark. *Posted Wednesday 12th September at 20:53* [Comment . Like]

Tim Gleeve If I was going to do a DC/Marvel mash up, Iron Bat would be the first character I'd draw up. *Posted Wednesday 12th September at 21:47* [Comment . Like]

Mike Cain I've put a lot of thought into it, and I just don't think being an adult is gonna work for me. *Posted Friday 14th September at 15:26* [Comment . Like]

Madeline Cain Lipsyncher I don't like where this is going. *Posted Friday 14th September at 17:00* [Comment . Like]

Hello Fashion Week, Meet My Minions

NOTES > My Notes [Write a note]

By **Madeline Cain Rent-A-Minion** Saturday, 15th September 2012 at 16:40

Laani the umbrella has unintentionally become an activist for women's health, which is interesting considering her normal tirade of fat jokes. I should probably be thankful, otherwise we'd have a set of models taking the next step to becoming walking skeletons. As it is Laani not only started a cat fight between two fashion giants, but has pushed one of them into pretending he was 'making a statement' that he'll now have to honour for the rest of his career. Since Laani's horrifying debut on Broadway, she has gone from strength to strength in the shit-storm department.

It's only after Fashion Week that I've realised I've somehow collected minions of chaos with my bizarre Midas touch. With my left hand I introduce abusive accessories, and with my right hand amphibians that speak like a broken Spanish record. Combine my minions with fashion and you get trends that should never grace the world stage.

To be fair, if it weren't for the 'Duncan Incident' that struck from afar the first day, and the 'Laani Incident' that occurred the final day, it would have been a perfect week learning from our guest lecturer, and my second favourite idol, Sorella Fontain. Amazeballs doesn't even begin to cover the experience.

The main shows were held in Damrosch Park at the Lincoln Centre for Performing Arts in massive tents that backed onto each other. The backstage is chaos, normally divided into two tiny tent areas. In the hair and make-up area two rows of mirrors line either side of the crowded space with bright lights riming each mirror like a cliché Hollywood dressing room. Teams of make-up artists applied make-up like an elaborate face painting while a separate horde of hairdressers teased hair into towers. There we took photos of the crews, the models prepping, before and afters and, on more than one occasion, a model cracking the shits in a spectacular performance that would put a toddler's tantrum to shame.

The second room backed onto the end of the runway and was crowded with designers, stylists, dressers, models, clothes racks and steaming machines. In a show of exhibitionism, the models get changed between racks before posing for a photograph with their designer and striding on stage in heels that could double as weapons.

Half the clothes I wanted to spirit away to my wardrobe and the other half I wanted to bury in a deep sea trench where no one would ever find them. One show and collection would be stunning, the next looked like the designer ate a big bowl full of crazy for breakfast before sitting down at the sewing machine.

Over the week I got to work a show a day with a different task each time, building on my fashion portfolio with the world's best designers and models. It was a relief not to have to negotiate clothing with a certain dubious son of an Italian pizza maker. The tasks varied from photographic essays of backstage prep to sitting at the end of the runway and photographing the walking mannequins as they sashayed along it. Professional models are so dull, their personalities couldn't fight their way out of a paper bag.

They were basically walking coat hangers. I don't understand why designers want models showcasing their work with next to no facial expression. They all looked like: a) they were about to vampire stake someone in the chest with their heel or; b) their brain had been wiped and was being rented as vacant space. It doesn't send the most appealing 'buy me' vibe.

Every task was performed under the guidance of Sorella, who had halved her personal work load for the week so she could spend mornings preparing us for our afternoon jobs. Throughout the week I got the most tantalising hint of what a full year internship with her would be like. This was the woman I was destined to work with.

The first morning I wasted no time in letting Sorella know I was gunning for her internship. She was easy to find, flaming hair in a smooth bun, neatly pressed dress pants and a shimmering scoop-neck black top that looked classy while allowing her the free-ranging movement she needed to get the best photographic angles.

Fingers tangled like a nervous school girl, I said, "Good morning Sorella, you may not remember me from Jason's ball, but I just wanted to say I'm very excited to be learning from you."

"That's kind," she said absently, her vibrant green eyes flickering up before returning to her run sheet. "Ah yes, the undecided, photographer. I remember."

"Not so undecided now, I've been doing a lot of thinking and defining of my goals and have decided my passion lies in fashion. I'm currently building a portfolio for submission to your internship program."

That made her look up. "Is that so…"

"Madeline," I jumped in.

"Madeline." She looked me up and down. Suddenly my bright rainbow skirt and wrinkled, black shirt seemed ill considered. "Well, if you have the passion we can work on the fashion. You may regret telling me that."

My heart spluttered. "R-really?"

She pursed her lips. "Yes, I'll have to give you more attention, be a bit pickier. Throw you in more deep-ends than the others."

I managed to hide a sigh. Perfect, that was exactly what I was aiming for. Better to know what she was like to work with now rather than finding out later I'd rather tango with a dragon. "It's what I'm here for. You'll find I'm great at doggy paddle."

Maybe you guys can explain why these sorts of comments continue to spurt from my mouth around people I want to impress, it's like I contract verbal diarrhoea every time I see them.

Sorella stared at me for a moment. "Right, each to their own… Perhaps you can start by gathering together your cohort for me."

I dashed off before my mouth found further ways to make her doubt her judgement. It turned out all I had to do was listen and watch. Sorella was a calm island among the turbulent tide of show preparation. She was a professional in every sense of the word and ran her little pocket of Fashion Week with military precision. People *listened* to her, asking her advice on every element of styling, and she managed all this while supervising seven wide-eyed photography students.

If she aimed to hire an assistant who could not only chronicle but *create* fashion trends than there was no doubt I was her girl. My influence on the fashion world came in two parts. One destined to grace the catwalk in 2013, the other destined to induce show rivalry and sabotage for decades to come.

Though it has me telling events in reverse order, I feel the more dramatic affair on the final day has to be told first. After fairly stellar weather, the morning had dawned dark with the grey sky like a ceiling above our heads. Naturally, I wished to protect my expensive electronic equipment and brought Laani in case the clouds cashed in on their promise between home and the subway. Only on that leg of my journey was I willing to brave my inanimate, cackling protector; there was no way I'd open her near those Fashion Week tents. I'd take a cab from the station to the festival if I had to. And no, I haven't been able to disable the more… disagreeable parts of her yet. She's like Fort Knox, booby trapped with electronic zaps so no one can approach her without losing facial hair. It turned out I shouldn't have bothered bringing her. Because the only place it rained was *inside.*

So, I make it safely to the festival without the need to subject my fellow New Yorkers to a cranky umbrella. So far so good. As I had done for the previous days I'd been there, I left my extra gear, including Laani, in a corner next to the divide between hair & make-up, and the dressing room.

We met with Sorella and the designer who showed us beautiful red creations of silk and lace. The models looked like tall candle flames with their shoes representing the candle stick, for every model wore high heeled, cream coloured gumboots.

"It makes more sense when you see them with the umbrellas. We're going for an oriental Singing In the Rain," said the designer, Casey.

This announcement should have raised alarm bells and preventative measures. I blame my complacency on summer, during which Laani has been in the corner of my wardrobe while the subways and walkways turned into a smelter. It was enough time to allow the memory of Laani's tirades to dim, until I could almost convince myself the comments Mike recorded were merely funny and not embarrassing, riot inducing insults that were likely to see me wedgied, wet-Willie, then punched. Laani had merely contracted an uncomfortable condition that I would get Mike to reverse after I shredded his comic books in front of him while playing the Spice Girls album I had in my bedroom. Hopefully the psychological trauma would dissuade him from trying such a hair brained scheme again.

Boy, was I a dumbass.

Instead of imagining versions of Singing In the Rain where Gene Kelly gets mobbed by cast members, I was contemplating how I could make the 'rain' blur while keeping the models crisp in my photos. Somehow I'd gotten it into my head that the 'rain' would be gold dust or streamers. Oh past me, how naive you were.

When we broke our designer briefing Victoria had been delegated to take photos of the setup, Josh of the designer and his creations and myself of the runway. The other four were in different tents covering other shows. Jarrah had kindly swapped positions with me after I discovered Shapelle, AKA Kevin's bat-shit crazy ex, was headlining the show I was originally assigned to cover.

As I went to join the photographers from fashion magazines across the globe, I had no premonitions of impending doom. Great Richard's beard, I was in the middle of the front row of New York Fashion Week! There were five rows of chairs on either side of the runway; important fashion and famous people sat in the first row with each row decreasing in celebrity to general public in the back row.

Nibbling on some raisins I surveyed the front row and almost choked on a couple. There was Dom, as proud as you please in the front row about half way down. He looked like the cat who swallowed not one, but a whole flock of canaries. As though feeling the weight of my gaze he looked over and winked. I didn't have any time to ponder the appearance of my mysterious benefactor as the lights dimmed and music began blaring from the speakers in the ceiling, signalling the first wafer thin model.

She twirled something straight and red in her hand like a baton, before stabbing it forward and snapping open a red ruffled umbrella, swinging it onto her shoulder with a flourish. Her hand sensually stroked the intricately carved handle as she pouted a geisha white face and full red lips.

"Son of a motherless bagpipe, this can't be happening to me!" My cry was lost in a round of polite applause as the model, face a blank as a blackboard, slowly twirled Laani in her grip. Suddenly it seemed the photographers jostling either side of me were too close, the atmosphere too claustrophobic. The model moved further away as I resisted the urge to scatter photographers and launch myself onto the runway.

Visions of tackling the model around the knees flitted through my head before a brief image of me snapping her in half at her tiny waist dissuaded me from such actions. I stamped hard on the panic. Other models walked down the catwalk with their own red umbrellas and I saw how Laani had somehow found her way into the mix. No two umbrellas were the same and all were intricate and vivid.

It's okay Madeline, we're inside, control yourself!

Surely Mike couldn't have recorded *that* many sayings, I thought.

Stupido. I should learn never to underestimate my brother's obsessions. World hunger would be solved if he put in one percent of the effort he used to create Laani the Terror of Manhattan.

There were more outfits than models which meant Laani made recurring appearances that saw me flinch every time the model flicked her too hard. But the umbrella held her silence and slowly I relaxed. It seemed there was nothing I could do, so the best thing was to stop panicking and do my job.

The costume changes were finally at an end and the models filed along the runway to a standing ovation from the crowd. The sour faced model with Laani stood two from the end.

"I wonder what the surprise is going to be this year," whispered a dark skinned photographer on my right to another. He shrugged.

"Surprise? What do you mean?" It felt as though a stone had landed in my stomach.

"Casey Cole is known for his… dramatics," whispered the man as the designer strolled down the runway waving. "It makes his shows popular. He's also known for making big announcements. Two years ago he tripled the price of his clothes to cover moving the manufacturing from China to the US. It saw the label explode. They did a cabaret number in stars and stripes that year."

"That's... tame," I replied. It didn't sound too moisture inducing.

Casey stood at the end of the runway beaming and raised his hands for quiet. "As you may have guessed I've something special to announce. But first the front row should reach under their seats and retrieve their special end-of-show-wear and put it on."

No longer did my stomach feel like it had a stone, it felt like someone had unloaded a dump truck of gravel down my gullet. The front row was shrugging on coats of transparent red plastic. Then a low electronic growling filled the air followed by a 'boom' of thunder.

I watched in horror as a row of sprinklers, unnoticed until now, burst, spraying across the runway and Casey's upturned face. There was a beat or two where he raised his hands in a Jesus pose, free from abuse, and I dared to hope. But Mike's handiwork appeared like a fart in a shower.

"I've Seen More Meat On A Chicken Than You. You Look Like You're Getting Ready For A Trip To Ethiopia."

It was like Casey was hosting a confusion competition. The models stared out, their dance steps forgotten, and the crowd stared *in* knowing after a look left and right that it wasn't the person next to them

"Hey Stick Figure, The Earth's Full, Go Home. Your Mama Is So Skinny I Could Thread Her Through A Needle."

It took Casey at least half a dozen insults to realise they were coming from his rank of models.

"You're So Skinny, When You Turn Sideways You Disappear. You Do Realise There's A Point Where Thin Is Too Thin Right?"

By this time the model holding Laani had finally figured out where the crotchety grandma voice was coming from and started looking around the top of Laani with a slightly manic look. "Very funny Casey, haha. Now how do you turn this thing off?"

She pointed Laani at in the direction of a heavily made-up woman with a dress in a shock of fluoro colours. "Who Picked Out Your Clothing? A Blind Person Who Hates You?"

The crowd was starting to titter. They liked a good show as much as the next person but this was a bit much. Hear that Mike? Even twelve sentences is TOO MUCH.

"Did you do this?" one model asks and looks like she's going to start a rumble on the runway.

"I did not!" cried Laani's minder. She put a hand on her hip, glaring at Casey. "Was this because I told you this was my last show? Are you punishing me?"

Casey made a cutting motion at the tech guy, who cut the rain, but of course it didn't stop Laani, who would keep yelling abuse as long as she was wet. Casey's eyes were wide and it was clear he was still trying to find the culprit in the crowd. His eyes narrowed when they sighted Dom and his employee.

Before I could even fathom the meaning of the look the model demanded, "Well, is it?"

Casey stilled as he latched onto what she was saying, like he'd suddenly found a lifeline. "Yes Kate, that's exactly right." Now he was grinning like a serial killer.

"At Least I Don't Look Like A Skeleton. No, I'm Wrong. You Look Like An Umbrella. Stop Stealing My Look!"

Shrieking, the woman dumped Laani on the ground (and into a pooling puddle of water – oh God!) and splashed off in a fury. That's when I started elbowing photographers out of the way with all the skill of a drunken martial arts instructor.

"Ladies and gentlemen!" cried Casey. "I know you were expecting Singing In The Rain, but that was merely a decoy to the real announcement."

Unfortunately I was still six metres away from Laani the riot starter.

"I Bet You All Shop For Your Clothes At Baby Gap."

Dom looked like he was watching a game of cricket that had just been high jacked by blue aliens in Borat bikinis.

Casey was practically yelling over Laani at this point. "As of next year's show, I will only be using size four models or greater in my shows. The reign of the skeletons at Casey Cole shows is at an end.

Only healthy bodies will be modelling my new range of accessories! Accessories for real women!"

Ah, there is was, the announcement that Laani had hijacked, finally worked into his message.

"Red Makes You Look Like A HB Pencil!"

A scattered applause began, becoming more firm when Laani yelled, "You Realise Thin Has Turned You Into The Invisible Woman, Right?"

I finally reached the puddle, the soap box where Laani vulgarly defended the body image of women, and snatched her into my arms, only half successful in muffling her parting words.

"You Look Like A Prey-mantis. Haven't You Eaten Enough Husbands Yet?"

Hair draped over my face to hide my identity, I dashed toward backstage as Laani ran out of skinny jokes and just went for insulting.

"People Like You Are The Reason I Eat!"

The last thing I saw before I got the hell out of there was a half-hearted dance, Casey backing slowly down the runway and Dom whispering to a man beside him who I recognised as the man who delivered my first bundle of clothes.

I burst through a cloth door and out into the patchy sunshine, Laani yelling insults at my chest. Thankfully the area was empty as the other shows were in full swing. I popped Laani open again and gave her an expert twist, water flying everywhere, her voice getting softer with each turn. Then pulling out a handkerchief I wiped any moisture off the crowning point.

Laani whispered one final, "...And Really Bad Eggs," before falling silent.

I hid her under the flooring of the tent on the left edge and went in search of the umbrella that *should* have been used in the show instead of Laani. I wanted to have one in my hand in case Casey recognised me as the person who spirited away his unexpected show stopper. I didn't want him to think I was the saboteur.

Entering the tent, I realised it was much too late to do anything as calm as hand Casey an umbrella and tell him how impressed I was he'd become an advocate for women's body issues. Backstage was pure mayhem.

I ducked as a stick thin model with a waist no thicker than my pinkie threw a chair over the top of my head. It was like the Anchorman fight scene, but instead of news crews it was models running around with still hot hair straighteners, wrestling brunettes and clothing tug of wars.

"You OWE me these clothes since you put me out of a job!" yelled one bean pole redhead.

Don't quote me on this but I'm pretty sure someone was running around with cream pies and slamming them in people's faces. Either that or someone was trying to fill models mouths with whipped cream.

I'm sure the scene was something out of Mike's wildest dreams, the ones he had when kids at school called him a square and he'd imagine parties in the future where models would fight for his attention. Well Mike, congratulations, you got models fighting over one of your infamous devices and as deliciously sweet karma would dictate, you were half a world away. Why do you boys get off on this fantasy? It's as inexplicable as edible boat races or extreme ironing (they're a thing, look them up). I think you should know, models are nasty and they *don't* respect the face.

They're ferrets set loose, pixies intent on destruction and way too insecure. I saw more than one hoeing down on a chocolate bar. I don't think they were mentally prepared for the barrage of skinny insults flung their way. Are you done with your little social experiment now, Mike? If you continue the Universe is only going to gift me with more of your fantasies, and frankly, I've seen enough.

Loudest of all in the melee was Casey, in the middle of the madness, being restrained by a burly security guard as he yelled full into the face of none other than Dom's henchman.

"Your patron ruined my show, Gabriel! He saw an opportunity to show me up and he took it. Look what happened! Now I have to design clothes that look good on curves! I don't know how to do that! I treat every person who wears my clothes like a man!"

"So basically, your ideal clientele are cross-dressers?" drawled

Dom's man, his New York accent so thick I was instantly transported to the 1920's.

Casey's face went fuchsia. "My ideal clientele are ones with money! The only reason I do women's fashion is women buy more crap. I hate clothes! When I finally make the jump to accessories your boss and his 'network' feel threatened so they conspire to ruin me! RUIN ME!"

The security guy had Casey around the chest with his arms awkwardly in the air as he wiggled like some sort of demented caterpillar.

Keeping his chiselled features cool, Gabriel brushed at imaginary fluff on his midnight black jacket. When Casey hung gracelessly puffing, Gabriel stepped forward and calmly patted Casey's face, which purpled with rage. "My… *patron*… doesn't have time for stupid games. If he was… displeased, he doesn't need some *prop* to get the message across." He gave a nod.

The security guard locked an arm in a sleeper hold around Casey's neck. On closer inspection I realised though he was wearing a dark suit like other guards at the festival, he wasn't wearing a security badge.

"I'm sure you understand what that means." Gabriel nodded at the guard who gently placed a dazed Casey into a sitting position on the ground. "I'd look closer to home if I were you. But until then, I'd keep a tight lid on rumours, for your own reputation, understand. We all want your newest line to go well…"

Casey nodded, not looking up.

Gabriel gave a tight smile of satisfaction. Followed by his lackey guard he dodged his way out through the epic model war.

"Size four is the new fat!" wailed Casey as he broke into sobs.

"Don't be ridiculous." Sorella entered the room and hauled the short man to his feet. "Design for normal people and they'll come to you. You're marketing budget will halve. Whoever did this did you a favour. That talking umbrella has created a wave, a trend you need to ride."

I dived in to help her steady him. "Yeah, turn it around on those smart arse activists," I said.

Casey rubbed a hand across his nose and streaming eyes. "You think it was feminists?"

Sorella and I looked at each other and shrugged. "Sure. Probably nerdy feminists, who don't have any fashion sense and like to torture their sisters with their social stupidity. Who still live with their mother and have really bad BO."

Sorella's patted his shoulder. "Let's take this as an opportunity to turn these saboteurs into customers. Who knows, maybe people will get a taste for accessories who talk to them and you'll be the instigator of a trend."

Let me just say, it has already spawned a range of Furby like toys who shout for people to shut up when noise gets too loud. I'm not sure that's the sort of legacy Casey wanted to leave. Mike on the other hand… I dread to think of someone purposefully making voice boxes for umbrellas. It's a trend that should die with Laani (and *will* die with her Mike, or so help me God I'll make you watch reruns of Sabrina The Teenage Witch until you explode). But I wouldn't mind a necklace that told me how pretty I looked… A girl needs a boost every now and then, you know?

At least if this comes back to bite me on the arse that I can honestly claim Mike ruined my life. Which in turn gives me license to ruin his. Publically. All across the Internet.

It looked like I'd walked unscathed from fashion week, with only a mental image of the model slumber party gone wrong to haunt me. But then came the second 'incident'.

In chronological order it was really the first 'incident' of the week, I just hadn't realised it happened until after Fashion Week had packed up and I set out to develop my assignment photos. Thanks heaps Kim for involving me and my career in your lizard love affair.

To give context, our challenge for this assignment was to experiment with double exposures giving an art house feel to the normally bland backgrounds of the catwalk.

"The thing I love about having students to puppeteer, is they can try out my little thought experiments," said Sorella on the first morning as we clustered outside in the shade of a tent. "When clients hire me they want a specific look, a technique I'm known for and frankly I'm too booked to be able to experiment. But doing the same old, no matter how in demand, is dangerous. You need to be at the forefront of your field or some young star…" Her mouth twitched as she surveyed us. "…Will sweep in and rip the carpet from beneath your feet. So to balance demand with development of new techniques, I have interns road test my light bulb moments. See what might work and what looks like it was taken by a five year old child on red cordial. This gives you an advantage over other photography students who still discuss basics like rule of thirds."

"Aren't you worried some upstart intern might use their experience to take business off you with your own idea?" asked Josh.

"As a client, would you take the woman with the reputation and twenty years of experience, or the young, inexperienced ginger who worked under her that one time?"

Josh shrugged off the barb with an easy grin. "I always bet on the ginger, but then again, if I had a several million dollar budget and a flame haired beauty, I'd probably go the Pro."

She raised a perfectly manicured eyebrow. "It's good work that will get you through this assignment, not taking me to Cougar Town. Fashion is wearable art and while the primary purpose of fashion photography is to not detract from the clothing but to display it, I wish to move my techniques towards storytelling, making the shot a work of art in and of itself. Something people not only want to wear but hang on the wall. So for this assignment you will be double exposing your shots. You'll work with film as all my experiments are in film first. Get clear shots of runway models and then re-expose the film to a landscape or background that not only creates a mood, but a story. You'll have to keep a note of which shot belongs to which outfit so you can get a complimentary background. Take a second shot with your digital to help keep track. You'll take your runway shots for the assignment today so you don't have to carry around two cameras for the week."

Cain's hand shot up like a school boy begging for approval. "So, do we get to set the mood of the pieces? I'm good at mood." That was less of a wink, Cain, and more of a disturbing facial twitch you should get seen to.

"Absolutely not! It's never about your vision. You're working for the designer. They're very specific on the mood and look they want to evoke. Each of you will attend the meetings I have with the designers where they'll detail exactly what they're trying to convey. It will be your responsibility the week after to match a landscape to this overall vision."

It all sounds easy enough right? No ghouls hiding around the corner waiting to dak the unweary photographer, no hidden trap doors that drop you into a Pit Of Doom. I had it all figured out, my show in the afternoon was full of shinning metallics with fan like material in gold, silver and bronze. I was going classy like Ron Burgandy, keeping with the 1920's vibe and using the inside of the Empire State Building, The Plaza and Penn Station for my secondary shots. But my grand plans were foiled by one lizard and his besotted lover.

Sorry, I mean owner.

I arrived at the Empire State Building today only to find my remaining-shots counter reading zero. It was odd. I distinctly remembered rewinding the film back to the original shot using a film bag not ten days ago, making sure the tail of the film hadn't disappeared into the canister. With film I couldn't just check it in the foyer, it was lit up like a Christmas Tree on fire. It's every photographer's worst nightmare to find the camera mechanics are broken and you've opened the film compartment to film still stretched across the lens. So rather than potentially end up with pictures that represented a whiteboard, I raced back to the dark room at college to use the film bag *yet again* to check the film wasn't stuck. All my hand found was a smooth film canister with the film safely stored inside.

So I did the only thing I could think of, I developed the film.

Ok, I'll admit I was going to cheat. I'd put on my evil mastermind hat and primed the bullshit-o-metre. I'd taken the same photographs frame for frame with my digital camera and knew at a pinch I could work a little digital fakery. The only ones who'd know the difference were Jason and Sorella and surely I'd be able to explain when I figured out what the second lot of exposures were. I just hoped I hadn't somehow sleep-walk-photographed over my assignment. Who knew what my unconscious mind liked to shoot?

When I finally viewed the dripping prints I almost performed the world's first spontaneous transport to my housemate's bedroom to slap him upside the head. Kim, what were you doing? Practising for a Christmas card? Preparing this camouflaging fiend for a modelling career? Selling him on eBay? It looked like they were having a picnic in the forest followed by a date at the zoo. Kim had snapped more photos of Duncan than a paedophile at a Wiggle's concert. It was obsession at psychiatric levels. You need help.

Duncan featured in Every. Single. Picture. He appeared on the heads of sour faced models who looked like they'd just smelled a particularly stinky brand of cheese, he draped himself over the shoulders of expensive golden jackets, and his beady eye looked out from the boob of several models. It was like I'd unintentionally captured the Jungle Book on the runway, all forest and trees behind, but instead of Tarzan there was a scrawny chameleon in a Where's Wally parody (Where's Waldo to you American's). It looked like the show was some sort of chameleon print frenzy. I couldn't show that to our 'client', experiment or not.

It is more than likely those photographs would never have seen the light of day if Jason hadn't walked in attracted by my donkey like squeaks of alarm.

"Something tells me the experiment went awry," he said with a crooked grin. "You've been having an interesting run of it this week."

"And now I've retrospectively stuffed up another show. Well, Duncan has."

Jason shook his head now red and black in the dark room light. "There's no way that majestic creature could do anything other than add to a show."

I snorted, visions of flying drumsticks and lipsynching rockers filling my head. "If by add, you mean chaos, then yes."

He peered at a fairly tame shot dripping from a drying line. Duncan was forming a kind of belt around the non-existent waist of a model. "The mood asked for by the designer was…"

"Classy. 1920's glamour and poise."

"And you accidentally used the camera to take nature shots?"

"My housemate availed himself of the opportunity to use one of my cameras for his obsessive compulsive habits." I winced as Jason examined one shot where Duncan appeared to be dancing on a model's shoulder.

Jason chuckled. "The look on Daniella's face when she sees these is going to be amazing."

"You're going to make me use them?"

Jason looked at me like I'd just asked him to ride a double butted llama down the yellow brick road. "I can't *make* you do anything. But why would you want to show her something else? These are great."

My mouth opened and shut a couple of times. "You're serious? But I completely, well accidentally, ignored the brief."

"They're cute. It brings the design back to Daniella's roots. Frankly, she's been taking her design a little too seriously lately. This will remind her of what made her designs so popular in the first place."

"But I didn't do it on purpose," I stressed. "What if I'd done it with Calvin Klein underwear models or something? We'd have chameleon crutch pants."

"Thank you for that mental image, does it come with mental soap and a mental scrubbing brush? You always learn from your mistakes and from now on you'll make sure you lock up your equipment. Which you should do anyway considering the number of robberies in this city. The trick is to make the mistake look like it was calculated. You always try that before admitting to a stuff up."

"You mean pretend I created the chameleon road show on purpose?"

"Normally you catch on quicker than this Madeline. I've made worse mistakes." He gazed into the middle distance with a smile on his face. "I once did a shoot with the incorrect white balance and made every person look like an Oompa Loompa. That was before digital photography so it was a much harder problem to correct."

I hissed and just stopped myself from patting him on the arm. "That's a hard one to pretend you did on purpose."

He shrugged. "It took a bit of creative thinking. It was only because all the clothes were black that it worked. I sold the 'concept' to the designer by saying he could use the slogan, *No matter your colour, you look good in black.* He loved it. Made me do the prints in blue and green too. Daniella will love this. You watch, by next season chameleon prints will be a trend."

Which, somehow, I think was your plan all along Kim.

[Comment . Like . Share]

Ray Star and **80 others** like this.

Mike Cain The fate of the world shall turn on my whims! Fashion week is only the beginning. All ye humans bow down to me in awe. You are my slaves! *Posted Saturday 15th September at 16:57* [Comment . Like]

> **Madeline Cain Rent-A-Minion** What did I tell you, a jackass, and a deluded one at that. *Posted Saturday 15th September at 17:01* [Comment . Like]
>
> **Kathy Bloomingdale** How could you underestimate your brother's obsessions?? This is the kid who waited on the roof of your house for eighteen hours to prove Santa Claus existed. And took your Dad's only ladder with him so no one could follow him. Your Mum had to convince her old military buddies to airlift your Dad up there in a Santa suit at *4am* and explain to Mike that the times had changed and he now uses black hawk helicopters for his present runs. This is the boy who obsessively stuck together pages of your diary after you shredded them and then mailed them to your latest love interest. Yes, he may be into computer games now, yes he may do role play and actually *has* friends, this does not mean he's too busy to obsess over something that will cause him endless hours of amusement. I think it's time to retire Laani until a cease fire agreement can be reached. *Posted Saturday 15th September at 17:15* [Comment . Like]
>
> **Tim Gleeve** It takes dedication to do the job and booby trap it so no one can *undo* it. That's guerrilla warfare tactics, and

let's face it, all sibling rivalries involve guerrilla warfare. You better step up your game. *Posted Saturday 15th September at 17:20* [Comment . Like]

Madeline Cain Rent-A-Minion I do *not* negotiate with sixteen year old terrorists who live with their mother! Laani will *not* be retired, she will be fixed, or the memes now littering Buzzfeed with Mike's baby picture will only be the start of my online campaign to ruin him. *Posted Saturday 15th September at 17:24* [Comment . Like]

Mike Cain Hey now, what's all this talk about 'ruining' me on the Internet? Not only did I make the dreams of the men in that tent come true (you're welcome gents) but I also convinced a sizest pig at umbrella point to advocate for more big butts (again gents, you're welcome). Being an advocate for men while championing women takes genius. *Posted Saturday 15th September at 17:29* [Comment . Like]

Madeline Cain Rent-A-Minion It's not championing women's rights if it's by accident. *Posted Saturday 15th September at 17:35* [Comment . Like]

Cliff Wheeland I don't think it was by accident. Laani always seems to pull out the most appropriate dig for any moment: all the racist jokes around me; all the Indian jokes around taxi drivers; all the midget jokes around children (or actual midgets). I think she knows exactly what she's saying, when and to whom. I think Mike has created an artificial intelligence. *Posted Saturday 15th September at 17:52* [Comment . Like]

Kathy Bloomingdale Why men find women fighting women so titillating I'll never know. *Posted Saturday 15th September at 17:55* [Comment . Like]

Tim Gleeve Mmmmm, titillating.... *Posted Saturday 15th September at 17:57* [Comment . Like]

Madeline Cain Rent-A-Minion I doubt the men in that tent had dreams of being held up at scissor point or being threatened with curling irons. Or having models scream at them, "What do you people want?? I'm not a human weight yoyo, just tell me what you want!" Half the men would have slit the tent with a knife just to get out of that crazy house. *Posted Saturday 15th September at 18:04* [Comment . Like]

Tim Gleeve They were probably the gay ones. *Posted Saturday 15th September at 18:14* [Comment . Like]

Madeline Cain Rent-A-Minion Oi! None of those sentiments on my Facebook notes thank you. You may not have meant it as a slur but it is, and there have been enough insults this week. Kapeesh? *Posted Saturday 15th September at 18:20* [Comment . Like]

Tim Gleeve Looks like someone else is championing rights. Fine. I'll just go make my own meme using Mike's baby-has-to-go-potty picture. *Posted Saturday 15th September at 18:28* [Comment . Like]

Mike Cain Awww Mad, you used the potty face picture?! And put it in a 'Where are they now' post with my current face?! All I did was add a bit of social commentary to your life and you reciprocate with personal shit. That hurts. *Posted Saturday 15th September at 18:37* [Comment . Like]

Tim Gleeve That prey-mantis comment was a kicker. That would have really hit home if Maddie's chest didn't spoil the fun. *Posted Saturday 15th September at 18:40* [Comment . Like]

Madeline Cain Rent-A-Minion That's it! You Mike, will send me dismantlement instructions or baby Mike's Rocky Horror Picture Show photo is going to make it to Buzzfeed. Tim, you have been banned until some undetermined future date from my private message sessions. You'll regret that when you're the only person who doesn't know what I'm doing about Dom and his 'network'. *Posted Saturday 15th September at 18:45* [Comment . Like]

Mike Cain Fine, I'll send you your precious instructions. It's boring when I can't see any of this supposed chaos anyway. But you'll never fully erase Laani, for the original files are hidden where you will never find them. Mwahahahaha! *Posted Saturday 15th September at 18:52* [Comment . Like]

Tim Gleeve Wait! What do you mean? What have you done with Dom? Did you confront him? Did he confess? What did he confess *too? Posted Saturday 15th September at 18:58* [Comment . Like]

Madeline Cain Rent-A-Minion You'll never know. Repent oh sinner-against-Madeline and maybe you'll be folded once again into the bosom of my confidence. *Posted Saturday 15th September at 19:05* [Comment . Like]

Cliff Wheeland I seem to have missed the original Dom post but am still ready to jump aboard the whole Dom's-a-little-weird wagon. Do you think he's gone from visiting your house with 'thank you' gifts to stalking? *Posted Saturday 15th September at 19:06* [Comment . Like]

Kathy Bloomingdale But the show designer knew him, in fact knew him well enough to accuse him of sabotage. Though still not clear on why he was there. *Posted Saturday 15th September at 19:10* [Comment . Like]

Cliff Wheeland Well he's not a designer, only a 'patron' which means he's the one with the monetary backing. *Posted Saturday 15th September at 19:16* [Comment . Like]

Tim Gleeve An investor if you will. The shadow behind the shady side of fashion. *Posted Saturday 15th September at 19:24* [Comment . Like]

Madeline Cain Rent-A-Minion Nice try, Tim. Leave it guys, I'll private message you about it. I have some thoughts… *Posted Saturday 15th September at 19:25* [Comment . Like]

Tim Gleeve Come on, I'm sorry! *Posted Saturday 15th September at 19:26* [Comment . Like]

Madeline Cain Rent-A-Minion Prove it, Judas. *Posted Saturday 15th September at 19:27* [Comment . Like]

Jarrah Annelli There is a running theme in this note: when in doubt, say you did something on purpose. I like that. Thank you Casey, Jason and Maddie for your lessons on getting away with the mistakes life springs on you. *Posted Saturday 15th September at 20:03* [Comment . Like]

Richard Arnoou Teasing hair into a tower sounds like one of those mistakes you try to hide under the 'art' banner. I think half the clothes were stuff ups at the sewing machine. It's why all the fashion induced a 50/50 impulse to steal or burn. *Posted Saturday 15th September at 20:07* [Comment . Like]

Josh Annelli Cheating on your assignment? Sneaky Madeline (Not that I wouldn't have tried the exact same thing). *Posted Saturday 15th September at 20:12* [Comment . Like]

Madeline Cain Rent-A-Minion I think we can all agree, Jason is a genius. *Posted Saturday 15th September at 20:14* [Comment . Like]

Richard Arnoou Don't know if I could keep a straight face while telling a client I *meant* to make their models look like Oompa Loompas. *Posted Saturday 15th September at 20:18* [Comment . Like]

Jade Annelli The lengths we go to, to appear professional. I enjoyed the lengths you went to, to convince Casey you weren't the saboteur even though you clearly were. *Posted Saturday 15th September at 20:30* [Comment . Like]

Madeline Cain Rent-A-Minion Inadvertently! It's not like I broke into his studio, saw umbrellas and said, "You beauty! I'm gonna have me some fun tomorrow." Some overzealous stylist obviously spotted Laani's good looks. You can then thank the weather for her presence. I'm not some weather woman who can tell if it's going to rain by squeezing her breasts. *Posted Saturday 15th September at 20:43* [Comment . Like]

Kathy Bloomingdale I think I'll have to be a calming influence on you when I'm in New York (next week!). Whatever it is that's making this a regular occurrence might be countered by a presence from your old, normal life. In saying that, I'm a little disappointed you didn't tackle a model off the runway. *Posted Saturday 15th September at 21:17* [Comment . Like]

Cliff Wheeland Agreed. Maybe you should've gone to Shapelle's show, that way she would have dived off stage to tackle *you*. That's about as amusing an image as the thought of taking photos while sleep walking. I bet they'd be blurry photos of toes and used Tim Tam packets. Then a couple of Kim sleeping face down with a cigarette in his mouth. Speaking of Kim, he's off to visit his parents soon. Maddie's on chameleon sitting duty. *Posted Saturday 15th September at 21:34* [Comment . Like]

Madeline Cain Rent-A-Minion Kathy I'm so excited to see you!! Even if *shudder* I am responsible for one rather excitable lizard. I tell you what, how about you two do the model tackling and I sit around and laugh at you? *Posted Saturday 15th September at 21:40* [Comment . Like]

Kathy Bloomingdale I'm sure we can work something out,

can't we Cliff *wink*. *Posted Saturday 15th September at 21:56* [Comment . Like]

Cliff Wheeland You betcha pretty lady. *Posted Saturday 15th September at 21:57* [Comment . Like]

Mike Cain Weird. *Posted Saturday 15th September at 21:59* [Comment . Like]

Cain Michaels A glimpse of the future as Sorella's intern? I think not! *Posted Sunday 16th September at 10:15* [Comment . Like]

Madeline Cain Rent-A-Minion No use denying the inevitable. She liked me. I'm cute. I'm a female in a male dominated industry kicking arse! *Posted Sunday 16th September at 10:52* [Comment . Like]

Cain Michaels 'My passion lies in fashion'? Are you sure? Not in bad poetry? *Posted Sunday 16th September at 11:12* [Comment . Like]

Madeline Cain Rent-A-Minion Like to see you do better under the pressure of those laser eyes. Oh wait, you didn't, you just fawned like a little school boy. *Posted Sunday 16th September at 11:14* [Comment . Like]

Cain Michaels We'll see who comes out on top in the assignment. Those who follow the brief or those who lend their cameras to the 'I Heart Chameleons' club. *Posted Sunday 16th September at 11:17* [Comment . Like]

Madeline Cain Rent-A-Minion Nothing is a mistake, everything is an opportunity! *Posted Sunday 16th September at 11:19* [Comment . Like]

Mike Cain 'If you have the passion, we can work on the

fashion'. Ouch. But accurate. *Posted Sunday 16th September at 11:22* [Comment . Like]

Cain Michaels No one asked you 'brother'. If that is your real name. I'm thinking it's really 'man with a death wish'. *Posted Sunday 16th September at 11:25* [Comment . Like]

Madeline Cain Rent-A-Minion I think I'm swapping the two of you out. Cain is now my brother preference. *Posted Sunday 16th September at 11:28* [Comment . Like]

Cain Michaels Aww, thanks! Still gonna kick your ass for the internship though. *P.S.* I need to change our photography date from November to like, two weeks from now, the special French lady we're photographing needed her shoot sooner… *Posted Sunday 16th September at 11:41* [Comment . Like]

Madeline Cain Rent-A-Minion Bring it. *P.S.* Fine. But Kathy's got to tag along, I'm not leaving my best friend behind when she's only here for twelve days. *Posted Sunday 16th September at 11:49* [Comment . Like]

Kevin Doherty Babe this is amazing! The stories write themselves around you! *Posted Sunday 16th September at 12:00* [Comment . Like]

Madeline Cain Rent-A-Minion I'd prefer I was plain Jane who didn't have quite so many heart attack moments … *Posted Sunday 16th September at 12:24* [Comment . Like]

Kevin Doherty But if this stuff didn't happen you wouldn't be my muse. *Posted Sunday 16th September at 12:27* [Comment . Like]

Madeline Cain Rent-A-Minion Well in that case I better hope that the craziness keeps coming then. Would suck if I was just a plain ol' girlfriend, hey? *Posted Sunday 16th September at 12:30* [Comment . Like]

Kevin Doherty Definitely! Don't want my muse disappearing when I've only just found her. So, hangout? I've got a ton of Japanese game shows I wanna catch up on. And I've got a couple of new characters I want to try on you! *Posted Sunday 16th September at 12:33* [Comment . Like]

Madeline Cain Rent-A-Minion Wow, that sounds like awesome fun, but I'm afraid I've only got time to come to that football match of yours to take photos. Otherwise, I've picked up some shifts at Giovanni's so I can have ten days off when Kathy's here. *Posted Sunday 16th September at 12:37* [Comment . Like]

Kevin Doherty Who's Kathy? *Posted Sunday 16th September at 12:42* [Comment . Like]

Cliff Wheeland Madeline's best friend and partner in crime from Australia. She's the one you'll have to impress to get the tick of approval. *Posted Sunday 16th September at 12:46* [Comment . Like]

Kevin Doherty Ah, better walk around with my shirt off for the next week then, hey babe? *Wink*. *Posted Sunday 16th September at 12:50* [Comment . Like]

Cliff Wheeland I said 'tick of approval' not seduce. *Posted Sunday 16th September at 12:54* [Comment . Like]

Madeline Cain Rent-A-Minion I'll never say no to shirtless Kevin ? But please be careful how recognisable your 'source material' for the show is, ok? *Posted Sunday 16th September at 12:55* [Comment . Like]

Kevin Doherty You betcha babe. *Posted Sunday 16th September at 13:00* [Comment . Like]

Nadine Cain Oh darling backstage sounds so glamorous! What a star studded life you lead! Do you think maybe one day you could get your father and I into one of them? Not in the front row obviously but it would be a hoot! Maybe this Sorella person could organise it. Speaking of which, what's this internship? It doesn't mean you're going to be away for longer does it? This woman seems knowledgeable but also a bit crabby, what with the 'ginger' comment. You don't want those sorts of manners rubbing off on you. *Posted Sunday 16th September at 15:17* [Comment . Like]

> **Madeline Cain Rent-A-Minion** If I get this internship it's more than possible I can get you into Fashion Week. Sorella's not rude, she just has a dry sense of humour. The internship is for fashion photography. I told Dad about it on the phone months ago. *Posted Sunday 16th September at 15:47* [Comment . Like]
>
> **Nadine Cain** You know your father forgets to pass things on. Best if you tell me all the details direct. Including how much longer that would mean you're away... *Posted Sunday 16th September at 16:00* [Comment . Like]
>
> **Madeline Cain Rent-A-Minion** Maybe we should talk about this on the phone... *Posted Sunday 16th September at 16:10* [Comment . Like]
>
> **Nadine Cain** How long, Madeline? *Posted Sunday 16th September at 16:14* [Comment . Like]
>
> **Madeline Cain Rent-A-Minion** Definitely on the phone. *Posted Sunday 16th September at 16:19* [Comment . Like]

Kim Enuik I don't take kindly to Duncan being called a Minion of Chaos. But I will take ownership of chameleon prints. If I knew the front end from the ass end of a sewing machine I'd have been on that boat years ago. *Posted Sunday 16th September at 16:32* [Comment . Like]

Madeline Cain Rent-A-Minion I don't take kindly to you borrowing my equipment without asking. Maybe you can tell me exactly why you felt you needed to take that many photos of Duncan? FYI, if you want a copy the photos also include stick thin women who look like they're going to murder your precious pet. *Posted Sunday 16th September at 16:37* [Comment . Like]

Kim Enuik How am I supposed to know the difference between a film and digital camera? Duncan deserves halls of photos dedicated to his glory. *Posted Sunday 16th September at 16:39* [Comment . Like]

Madeline Cain Rent-A-Minion Not being able to see the photo on a screen is the giveaway on that one. And halls of his photos would be very boring. He only has one look. *Posted Sunday 16th September at 16:43* [Comment . Like]

Kim Enuik One look?! I'll give you one look! *Posted Sunday 16th September at 16:44* [Comment . Like]

Madeline Cain Rent-A-Minion Are you responsible for the chameleon pictures now clogging my desktop? How did you get past the password? *Posted Sunday 16th September at 16:48* [Comment . Like]

Kim Enuik DUNCAN SEES ALL! *Posted Sunday 16th September at 16:50* [Comment . Like]

Madeline Cain Rent-A-Minion liked the page **I Didn't Trip. I Was Testing Gravity. It Still Works.** [Like]

Cliff Wheeland likes the page **"Let's Eat Grandma," or "Let's eat, Grandma." Punctuation Saves Lives.** [Like]

Kathy Bloomingdale -> Cliff Wheeland So, there are problems at the ranch. Not that our subject knows it herself yet. Well, enough to split from the 'golden egg'. But we're close. Now Operation Man Up is complete I think all we need is to give our subject a jealous push in the right direction (your gym time has been noted by the subject, though I don't think the best time to reveal your guns was while wearing ladies underwear...). *Posted Sunday 16th September at 20:00* [Comment . Like]

> **Cliff Wheeland** That definitely *wasn't* the planned reveal of gym time efforts. I was aiming for a run-around-shirtless-in-the-park and casual 'I'm back'. Urgh! It's like I'm catching her chaos disease. *Posted Sunday 16th September at 20:30* [Comment . Like]
>
> **Kathy Bloomingdale** You mean the subject's disease. *Posted Sunday 16th September at 20:37* [Comment . Like]
>
> **Cliff Wheeland** Ok, that psychology talk is weird. Can't we give... the subject, a code name? So I feel like I'm talking about a person and not a lab experiment? Let's go for 'douche-face' rather than 'golden egg' and 'the wombat'. *Posted Sunday 16th September at 20:40* [Comment . Like]
>
> **Kathy Bloomingdale** Come on, as if that isn't half obvious even to douche-face. So is kangaroo, gumtree, emu and any other Australian thing you can think of. Let's go for something generic, like 'the park'. *Posted Sunday 16th September at 20:42* [Comment . Like]
>
> **Cliff Wheeland** Fine. You have no sense of artistic irony. So, it's been weird between them? I've been avoiding talking to or commenting on douche-face, just like you suggested. Though I figured douche-face was going to bugger up with a smart park

like our park eventually. I just hope you aren't charmed when you get here. *Posted Sunday 16th September at 20:47* [Comment . Like]

Kathy Bloomingdale I'm not one to be swayed by a pretty face if it's all douche underneath. The park's previous admirers have been rather odd looking so I think all the glitter dazzled her. *Posted Sunday 16th September at 20:48* [Comment . Like]

Cliff Wheeland The thing is, he's genuinely nice, but it's the narcissism and thick head that make the douche. Just be prepared. Even I feel like an arse with Operation win-back-the-park. *Posted Sunday 16th September at 20:49* [Comment . Like]

Kathy Bloomingdale Guys like that always land on their feet. So, we're still going ahead with making the park jealous? *Posted Sunday 16th September at 20:49* [Comment . Like]

Cliff Wheeland And operation making-the-park-realise-she-doesn't-like-other-women-being-with-black-ice-cream. *Posted Sunday 16th September at 20:52* [Comment . Like]

Kathy Bloomingdale What? Black ice cream? *Posted Sunday 16th September at 20:52* [Comment . Like]

Cliff Wheeland Ice cream is delicious, don't knock the code name. Look, I know I don't know you well but thank you, for everything. Just don't fall in love with the charms that are flung your way, that could be awkward. I'm not looking to start a New York City Twilight tribute. *Posted Sunday 16th September at 20:54* [Comment . Like]

Kathy Bloomingdale Not that you aren't lovely, and I'm sure, very charming (and now ripped) in person, but I've got my heart set on an obnoxious geek at home. If I don't get flowers when I come in, I'm going to doubt your wooing skills. *Posted Sunday 16th September at 21:01* [Comment . Like]

Cliff Wheeland Not only will you get flowers, but I've hired a car so I can fetch you at the airport. *Posted Sunday 16th September at 21:02* [Comment . Like]

Kathy Bloomingdale Anyone else guessed who you are yet? *Posted Sunday 16th September at 21:02* [Comment . Like]

Cliff Wheeland Not yet. After the previous flop I'm kind of glad. *Posted Sunday 16th September at 21:03* [Comment . Like]

Kathy Bloomingdale But you're going to tell the park? *Posted Sunday 16th September at 21:03* [Comment . Like]

Cliff Wheeland For sure! It's part of my grand, 'I'm sorry for being a jackass' gesture. That and getting her another paid gig. *Posted Sunday 16th September at 21:03* [Comment . Like]

Kathy Bloomingdale Ooh! You'll have to tell me all about the grand gesture and gig when I'm there! I'm off in two days. Kind of panicking about the flight. I've never been that far before. *Posted Sunday 16th September at 21:05* [Comment . Like]

Cliff Wheeland You'll be fine. See you soon! And really, thanks. *Posted Sunday 16th September at 21:06* [Comment . Like]

Mike Cain Liking your own status is like high-fiving yourself. *Posted Monday 17th September at 07:23* [Comment . Like]

Mike Cain likes this.

Madeline Cain Rent-A-Minion In the face. Also known as inviting others to punch you. *Posted Monday 17th September at 08:40* [Comment . Like]

Mike Cain That's called a facepalm, and that is what I'm doing right now because of how un-cool you are. *Posted Monday 17th September at 08:49* [Comment . Like]

Madeline Cain Rent-A-Minion At least I have friends to high-five with. *Posted Monday 17th September at 08:51* [Comment . Like]

Mike Cain That's not the... you don't... GRRRRR! *Facepalm*. *Posted Monday 17th September at 08:59* [Comment . Like]

Derek Chan This is pants. *Posted Monday 17th September at 09:10* [Comment . Like]

Kathy Bloomingdale -> Madeline Cain Rent-A-Minion I had a dream last night that I was in France and I was Facebook chatting you and you were in Italy, and we were all like, "We're so close! We should hang!" Then I passed out on the table for no good reason. I think the salt and pepper was spiked. *Posted Monday 17th September at 13:20* [Comment . Like]

Madeline Cain Rent-A-Minion Did you think I managed to spike it from a distance via social media? Good to know you're already on holidays in your head... *Posted Monday 17th September at 14:01* [Comment . Like]

The Problem With Dom…..[New Message]

[Back to messages. Mark as unread . Report spam . Delete]

Between **Kathy Bloomingdale, Two Others** and **You.**

Madeline Cain Rent-A-Minion 17th September 2012 at 14:15

So it appears the reason I have been living in my own happy little Madeline world with zero regard for the bizarrities of Dom, is because I thought I was safely being watched by the FBI. In hindsight, that might have been a little conceited. Once that security blanket was set alight I found myself finally listening to that part of my mind I had gagged and drawn moustaches on three months ago.

The problem with Dom is this: I feel sorry for him. Under all that try-hard personality there is something there that is charming and good hearted. Generous with tips and life owing favours. But at the same time there's never a straight answer when you ask him what he does, he wears a small house deposit in suits, he *gives* me a small fortune in clothing, is a 'patron' for fashion designers (whatever the hell *that* means) and his little 'network' put an irate designer in a sleeper hold.

Him feeling like he 'owes' me only complicates things. Because, I think you guys were right.

I just reported Dom as a suspected mobster to the FBI. It wasn't the plan when I got up in the morning, it just happened, and frankly, I feel like a dick.

What if he's just an average Joe? Or what if he *is* a mobster and I have to testify? Then I'll be living in a safe house for the rest of my life in midtown America, where rednecks say *y'all* and shoot anything that has too much hair.

Either way, I'm an asshole or wanted. Neither makes me particularly comfortable.

Kathy Bloomingdale 17 September 2012 at 14:23 [Report]

Finally! Thought I'd have to start the surveillance myself. You realise the more presents you get the deeper you're drawn in? Like serial killers with lollypops.

You like seeing the good in people, Maddie; it's admirable but rather impractical. I'm surprised you came to your senses so quickly. At the same time… is it wise to dob him in? I'd prefer you didn't become the target of your own gun wielding cross-dresser.

Cliff Wheeland 17 September 2012 at 14:25 [Report]

Duh. Sure the expensive clothes and his 'networks' are an indicator, but I think you're missing the major 'mobster vibe' contributor. He was wanted by a HITMAN. No one orders a hit on someone else unless they're in an action movie, or they're a nasty piece of work who has shit other nasty pieces of work want. Having one owe you their life is more dangerous than letting them get shot in the first place. So, did you go to headquarters or just hit up the guys across the road?

Kim Enuik 17 September 2012 at 14:27 [Report]

You've got enough shots of women wearing clothes to fill a portfolio ten times over. You don't need any more. Break the connection, say no to mob money

Madeline Cain Rent-A-Minion 17 September 2012 at 14:28

How did you know there were people watching our apartment!? Why didn't you *tell* me?

Cliff Wheeland 17 September 2012 at 14:30 [Report]

They're not hard to spot with their black suits and ear pieces. The café across the road is their morning meeting spot. Probably put a tail on you every Monday and Wednesday to make sure you're the klutz photographer from Kangarooland you claim to be.

Kim Enuik 17 September 2012 at 14:31 [Report]

I'd say they use you as an excuse to drink coffee at The Bean, that shit is the best stuff in NYC. They probably don't even bother to tail you any more, they just file fake reports about your spy-o-grapher capabilities so they can get more of that sweet, sweet liquid drug.

Cliff Wheeland 17 September 2012 at 14:32 [Report]

I take it you were surprised they were there?

Madeline Cain Rent-A-Minion 17 September 2012 at 14:32

Surprised? I literally ran into Penguin 2 before I realised. Some shitty spy-o-grapher I turned out to be in real life.

Cliff Wheeland 17 September 2012 at 14:33 [Report]

We all have our delusions of grandeur.

Madeline Cain Rent-A-Minion 17 September 2012 at 14:34

You can talk! I wasn't planning on reporting Dom, but all the weird coincidences were rolling around my head, and well, the agents might as well be useful, right?

Cliff Wheeland 17 September 2012 at 14:34 [Report]

There are many things I'd call the FBI, but useful is probably number one-hundred on that list.

Madeline Cain Rent-A-Minion 17 September 2012 at 14:40

I bet 'vague' is somewhere at the top. So I was doing my usual mad dash to class when a man in a suit stepped onto the path in front of me and I slammed into his mountain of a back. It took a moment of furious ineffective mopping of his shirt with my hands before I recognised his long nosed and square jawed features

"Penguin… I mean Agent Brown. What are you doing here?"

You've never seen a man look so uncomfortable. It may have been because I was still pawing at his coffee chest with sticky hands, but more likely he's not use to doing a stake out where the subject recognises and nicknames the operatives.

"Ms Cain," came a melodic voice as a plain woman stepped out onto the sidewalk. "What a surprise."

"Ms Smith?" I asked hesitantly. I never quite knew what she looked like, even after I'd followed her for an entire day in April. Probably why she was one of their best agents.

She stood there with a small smile, neither confirming nor denying her name. I looked from one overly innocent face to one that looked like he'd been caught stealing cookies from the jar.

"Are you keeping tabs on me?"

"We don't follow nationals from other countries," said Mr Brown.

"Ahuh…"

"The CIA do."

"Whoop, there it is. Which one of you would be CIA then?"

Agent Brown's face instantly changing from white to fuchsia. He was probably one of their worst Agents.

"You're wearing your enigmatic face," I prodded.

"This is my normal face."

"Then your 'normal' face looks like it suffers middle distance syndrome."

"What's that?"

"You know, looking into the distance all pensive when really, you're thinking about the sausage you ate last night." Agent Smith's eyes widened slightly and I ran over the sentence again in my head. Now it was my turn to look like a tomato. "Sorry…that came out wrong."

"What do you want, Ms Cain?" he asked gruffly.

Which, let's face it, was a very odd question to ask when they were the ones standing outside *my* apartment.

Cliff Wheeland 17 September 2012 at 14:43 [Report]

I know! You want good photos, less FBI tails and more trips to Broadway. Oh, and more money so you don't have to eat your way through a spaghetti fort.

Kathy Bloomingdale 17 September 2012 at 14:43 [Report]

I hope you didn't sass the FBI with, 'I want a pony,' or ,'all I want for Christmas is my two front teeth'.

Kim Enuik 17 September 2012 at 14:44 [Report]

"I want information!" That's what I'd have said. Sounds all action movie that way.

Madeline Cain Rent-A-Minion 17 September 2012 at 14:50

Kathy knows me well. I went for two front teeth; then, "You're the ones following me. Clearly you think I know something."

"And what do you know?" asked Agent Brown, his professional face back on.

"That I'm not worth a morning coffee stake out, not unless you enjoy watching someone make a fool out of themselves on a regular basis."

This is where your prediction came true, Kim: "It's worth the coffee though," said Agent Smith with an average grin. I immediately forgot what her expression looked like as soon as it was gone. "Sorry to disappoint. We *may* have monitored you previously, but now we're here for the caffeine."

"That's the lamest cover story I've ever heard."

Agent Smith sighed. "The truth is more boring than the movie. Feel free to speculate, we've got to get back to work."

It was then I realised I'd assumed the FBI *had* been watching me these past months. Because the panic I felt when I learnt they'd been doing no such thing made me feel like I was about to puke jackhammers. This was NOT on. Not when I was dealing with a potential mobster. Feeling sorry for Dom wasn't going to stop bullets.

I reached out and snatched Agent Brown's sleeve. "Wait! So you haven't seen Dom the mobster come over?"

Agent Brown pulled his arm from my grip with a dismissive wave of his arm. "We've got enough tip offs without you entertaining us with fake ones."

"I'm serious! I saved him from being shot by a cross-dressing gunwoman a couple of weeks ago." Agent Brown snorted but I powered on. "Now I keep getting all these ridiculously expensive presents and I saw a guy who works for him put someone in a sleeper hold."

The two agents looked at each other, eyebrows raised. Then Agent Smith gave a tiny nod. "Alright, I think we can spare ten minutes to hear about this supposed mobster."

Who knew I'd been keeping the suspicion all bottled up because I thought the FBI was already watching?

Kathy Bloomingdale 17 September 2012 at 14:51 [Report]

Hopefully they don't think you're a spoilt child looking for attention. What made you think you're special enough to still be watched anyway? I mean, you *are* special and lovely and watchable, but just not in an FBI sense.

Madeline Cain Rent-A-Minion 17 September 2012 at 14:53

Nice save. Did you suddenly remember you were going to be staying at my house in two days?

I don't know. I just had it in my head that they would already know Dom and as such had started watching me again after the whole penis-gun incident. And because of the previous spy-o-grapher thing. I don't think they quite bought Jason's story.

Cliff Wheeland 17 September 2012 at 14:53 [Report]

It's tempting to think the FBI are all powerful but they just want you to think that. The only reason they're on half the cases they are is because people tip them off.

Kim Enuik 17 September 2012 at 14:54 [Report]

I thought you were a bit blasé about the whole 'Dom might be a mobster' thing. Normally you overreact more. Kinda like you did when you realised they weren't watching you.

Kathy Bloomingdale 17 September 2012 at 14:54 [Report]

I don't shirk from the hard questions. It's why I'm your best friend.

Madeline Cain Rent-A-Minion 17 September 2012 at 14:55

Do you want someone to look after Duncan or not while you're away, Kim?

Kim Enuik 17 September 2012 at 14:55 [Report]

How come Kathy can ask the hard questions and I can't?

Madeline Cain Rent-A-Minion 17 September 2012 at 14:55

Because they weren't questions and you haven't know me since I had braces and wrote about school boy crushes in my diary.

Cliff Wheeland 17 September 2012 at 14:56 [Report]

Enough bickering children. What did the Agents say?

Madeline Cain Rent-A-Minion 17 September 2012 at 14:57

Just that they'd keep an eye on him. And not to go into any dark alleys. But I think that was standard advice rather than case specific.

Cliff Wheeland 17 September 2012 at 14:57 [Report]

So not to avoid him like a baboon with a hangover?

Madeline Cain Rent-A-Minion 17 September 2012 at 14:57

No. They said to keep contacting him like normal. They said the more I can make him visible, the more they can link up where he goes and who he visits.

Cliff Wheeland 17 September 2012 at 14:58 [Report]

Just as long as they've got a tail on you to keep you safe.

Madeline Cain Rent-A-Minion 17 September 2012 at 14:58

Yep. I got my very own armed shadow in Agent Brown. Like a ninja, but with coffee.

Kathy Bloomingdale 17 September 2012 at 14:58 [Report]

Bet he was thrilled.

Madeline Cain Rent-A-Minion 17 September 2012 at 14:59

Why wouldn't he be? I'm the most entertaining person in NYC to follow according to Kevin.

Cliff Wheeland 17 September 2012 at 14:59 [Report]

Good thing he's not an FBI agent, he'd be making his own sound effects as he followed you down the street.

Madeline Cain Rent-A-Minion 17 September 2012 at 15:00

Yeah, apparently method acting still hasn't gotten old for him. At least he's stopped recording me with the Dictaphone. But now he goes to the toilet nearly every five minutes when I'm over. It's like one bad habit is replaced with another, weirder one.

Don't get me wrong, it's the most attentive relationship I've ever been in. I don't think I've been so thoroughly listened to in all my life. Or had quite so many hallway speed dates. With the number of flowers and chocolates I've gotten I could open up my own store (though I wish he'd stop giving me copies of game shows). But I just get the feeling that whatever he's doing in the toilet isn't peeing.

Cliff Wheeland 17 September 2012 at 15:04 [Report]

I'd prefer not to imagine what else he's doing, thank you. Does he talk about anything other than acting and football yet?

Madeline Cain Rent-A-Minion 17 September 2012 at 15:06

Of course he does! I mean, our physical connection is stronger at the moment, sure, he makes me all tingly, but the conversation will morph. Eventually.

Kim Enuik 17 September 2012 at 15:06 [Report]

Give me boobs and conversation is not required.

Madeline Cain Rent-A-Minion 17 September 2012 at 15:07

Constructive as always, Kim.

Kathy Bloomingdale 17 September 2012 at 15:09 [Report]

Getting back to the topic, does this mean I get followed by the FBI when I'm there too? Because that sounds kinda awesome.

Madeline Cain Rent-A-Minion 17 September 2012 at 15:10

So NOW who's the one who has cards on herself? Bet you're planning to do something suspicious just so you can play pick-the-agent.

Kathy Bloomingdale 17 September 2012 at 15:13 [Report]

Of course I'd play pick-the-agent. It would be the most exciting thing that's happened to me all year! I don't want to get you into trouble mind, I just want to run a little social experiment. How many lady outings does it take to drive an FBI agent crazy? Particularly if you take to calling him Brownie. God, I can't *wait* to try brownies. Maybe with Brownie.

Cliff Wheeland 17 September 2012 at 15:14 [Report]

It's going to be *fun* hanging with you Kathy. When Maddie gets waylaid as Kevin's acting practise I'll be more than happy to take you out on the town. I know all the romantic spots to eat brownies.

Madeline Cain Rent-A-Minion 17 September 2012 at 15:14

Hey now, no one is going ANYWHERE without me. Think of Kathy and I as Siamese twins for the duration of the visit. Anything you do to her you have to do to me!

Cliff Wheeland 17 September 2012 at 15:15 [Report]

With pleasure ?

Madeline Cain Rent-A-Minion 17 September 2012 at 15:17

I am NOT your social experiment, Mr Wheeland!

Agent Brown is probably going to hate me for the next two weeks; he'll be visiting all the tourist attractions without the fun of actually going in *and* he's going to see a lot of girl talk, frivolity, dancing, laughing, and selfies. Basically, we'll have him wearing pink by the end of this. I'll show him what happens when the FBI has enough nerve to stop following me!

Kathy Bloomingdale 17 September 2012 at 15:17 [Report]

Bring on the experiments! See you soon!

Cliff Wheeland 17 September 2012 at 15:18 [Report]

What? First you're annoyed because you think they're watching you, then you freak out because they aren't, and now you're punishing them following you again by trying to drive them crazy?

Madeline Cain Rent-A-Minion 17 September 2012 at 15:18

Just roll with it. I do.

Bye lovely!

Cliff Wheeland 17 September 2012 at 15:19 [Report]

Women are weird.

Kim Enuik 17 September 2012 at 15:19 [Report]

Or as Sheldon from Big Bang says, "Bitches be crazy."

Kim Enuik 17 September 2012 at 15:25 [Report]

Ok, I just heard you slam out of the bedroom. I'm sorry Maddie. Please don't punish Duncan for my run away fingers. He loves you.

Cliff Wheeland 17 September 2012 at 15:27 [Report]

A little too much.

Kim Enuik 17 September 2012 at 15:27 [Report]

Be my backup Cliff?

Cliff Wheeland 17 September 2012 at 15:28 [Report]

That bundle of insanity ain't living with me. Be a good boy and make up with the crazy lady.

Derek Chan likes the page **Drunk People Taking Care Of Drunker People** [Like]

> **Derek Chan** Dear Liver, you are a trooper. Thanks again man. D-dog. *Posted Monday 17th September at 23:00* [Comment . Like]

> **Tim Gleeve** Well done! D IS for dog. *Posted Monday 17th September at 23:30* [Comment . Like]

Kate Nikle joined the groups **Irish Dancing Out Of An Awkward Situation** and **I'm Pretty Sure You're Not A Car. Get An Actual Photo For Your Profile Pic.** [Join . Like]

Tim Gleeve -> Kathy Bloomingdale I will gladly babysit your fish, so just let me know... *Posted Tuesday 18th September at 09:03* [Comment . Like]

> **Kathy Bloomingdale** As long as you promise to keep your pants on. I don't want my fish traumatised every three seconds. *Posted Tuesday 18th September at 09:08* [Comment . Like]

Tim Gleeve So no mirror in the water to see if it fights itself then? *Posted Tuesday 18th September at 09:10* [Comment . Like]

Mike Cain I don't understand, why do we need algebra? Finding X is only useful if you're a pirate. *Posted Tuesday 18th September at 12:11* [Comment . Like]

Jamie Anderson Why is all the rum gone!? *Posted Tuesday 18th September at 12:26* [Comment . Like]

Mike Cain Bet maths would be more interesting on rum. *Posted Tuesday 18th September at 12:40* [Comment . Like]

Madeline Cain Rent-A-Minion I hope you didn't draw a pirate map around your x's. *Posted Tuesday 18th September at 13:00* [Comment . Like]

Mike Cain Maybe I did, maybe I didn't. Maybe I showed up to class with an eye patch. You'll never know… *Posted Tuesday 18th September at 13:50* [Comment . Like]

Jack Fox Man I am itchy down there, what gives? *Posted Tuesday 18th September at 14:05* [Comment . Like]

Madeline Cain Rent-A-Minion TMI man. *Posted Tuesday 18th September at 14:07* [Comment . Like]

Tim Gleeve In kindergarten we called it cooties, in the real world we call it STDs. *Posted Tuesday 18th September at 14:11* [Comment . Like]

Alexa McMarshal Babe, I told you not to shave down there, hair growth makes things itchy. Besides, I love your hair! *Posted Tuesday 18th September at 14:14* [Comment . Like]

Cliff Wheeland Dear Mr Undercover Police Man, I like the five extra antennas on your van… *Posted Tuesday 18th September at 14:58* [Comment . Like]

You and **3 others** like this.

Madeline Cain Butt Photographer Apparently sports photography is not my forte. I kept missing photos of the players in Kevin's team and instead got pictures of their butts. Touch down? *Posted Tuesday 18th September at 16:24* [Comment . Like]

Jarrah Annelli I'd say you've captured the most important part of football for all women. You should be their marketing director. I can see another calendar forming. By the way, how did that fake tan turn out? Did you look like a babe on the field taking the photos? *Posted Tuesday 18th September at 16:41* [Comment . Like]

Kevin Doherty Yes! Another calendar. That's a brilliant idea! We can call it League of Butts. *Posted Tuesday 18th September at 16:46* [Comment . Like]

Madeline Cain Butt Photographer Bahaha! Yes! It would get your team back in the media, which really, is what they wanted, not boring portraits in the locker room. *Posted Tuesday 18th September at 16:54* [Comment . Like]

Kathy Bloomingdale You got a fake tan? Whatever for? *Posted Tuesday 18th September at 16:59* [Comment . Like]

Kevin Doherty Genius babe! You make me look so good. What would I do without you? *Posted Tuesday 18th September at 17:00* [Comment . Like]

Josh Annelli Ah, applying Jason's principle to unplanned photos. I like it. Kind of glad you suck. I was starting to think you could do no wrong. It's a bit emasculating. Now I know you're as normal as the rest of us. *Posted Tuesday 18th September at 17:09* [Comment . Like]

Jade Annelli You got to go into the locker room?! Where's the love? What happened to sharing the experience with your girlfriends? *Posted Tuesday 18th September at 17:14* [Comment . Like]

Madeline Cain Butt Photographer Shhh. Don't give away our photographic secrets! And don't judge me, Kathy. I'm as white as a yeti and it's the middle of summer. Somehow sunbaking in Central Park seems wrong, probably because there's nowhere to swim. I might look good, Jarrah, but looking after Duncan is hell. He keeps licking me! I'm lying there, minding my own business on the couch and the next thing I know I have a tongue stuck to my cheek. *Posted Tuesday 18th September at 17:21* [Comment . Like]

Cliff Wheeland That's strange, even for Duncan. *Posted Tuesday 18th September at 17:23* [Comment . Like]

Kim Enuik Bahaha! You don't happen to have black pores from the fake tan by any chance? *Posted Tuesday 18th September at 17:30* [Comment . Like]

Madeline Cain Butt Photographer Yes... Why? Aren't you supposed to be in the middle of the stone ages right now? You know, jungle and zero phone reception? *Posted Tuesday 18th September at 17:31* [Comment . Like]

Kim Enuik He thinks you're covered in insects! That's why he keeps stalking you like a tasty buffet. I'm in the airport waiting for a transfer. Last internet for the trip so have to get my civilization fill. *Posted Tuesday 18th September at 17:32* [Comment . Like]

Madeline Cain Butt Photographer Crap! This tan is going to be like this for ages! Last thing I need is a chameleon feeling me up with his tongue every time I sit down. *Posted Tuesday 18th September at 17:34* [Comment . Like]

Cliff Wheeland Could probably make a calendar of that too. *Posted Tuesday 18th September at 17:35* [Comment . Like]

Mike Cain Kathy, you MUST get the photos for this calendar. *Posted Tuesday 18th September at 17:43* [Comment . Like]

Kevin Doherty I can take Duncan for a couple of days babe, until your tan settles. You do look sexy and it's the least I can do for putting together another calendar for the boys. Besides, the critter likes me. *Posted Tuesday 18th September at 17:57* [Comment . Like]

Madeline Cain Butt Photographer Yes please! You're a life saver. At this rate, he'll wash the tan off with his tongue. He just licked me in the eye. It's the weirdest feel up I've ever had. *Posted Tuesday 18th September at 18:04* [Comment . Like]

Kathy Bloomingdale I think I'm shaking so hard I'm losing teeth. God, I hate flying. Being in the air is ok, but take-off and landing just make me want to projectile vomit. Probably shouldn't have mentioned that to the guy next to me, he looks green now. But it's best to warn your fellow neighbour about the possibility right? So they're prepared. *Posted Wednesday 19th September at 11:30* [Comment . Like]

Kathy Bloomingdale Holy crap, why are we still on the tarmac?? "There's been a slight delay while the engineers make their final engine checks." That is NOT a comforting announcement Mr Pilot Man. You think it is but you're *wrong.* Why wasn't it all ready before you *loaded your passengers?! Posted Wednesday 19th September at 11:35* [Comment . Like]

Kathy Bloomingdale Great, the latest announcement was even worse: "Running the final checks of the landing gear, we'll be on our way shortly." What. The. Hell? What if they get it wrong? What if we can't land? *Posted Wednesday 19th September at 11:41* [Comment . Like]

Tim Gleeve One way or another, Kathy, they all land. *Posted Wednesday 19th September at 11:42* [Comment . Like]

Kathy Bloomingdale That was NOT the reassurance I was after. Any chance you're in the pilot seat of my plane? If you are I WILL stab you with this pair of tweezers I got through security. *Posted Wednesday 19th September at 11:44* [Comment . Like]

Tim Gleeve Less worrying about my piloting skills (which are awesome thanks to all those hours on Xbox 360) and more about whether the guy next to you is going to duct tape your mouth shut to stem the flow of gut juice. *Posted Wednesday 19th September at 11:54* [Comment . Like]

Madeline Cain Butt Photographer Damn it Duncan, I am NOT AN ICECREAM!! *Posted Wednesday 19th September at 16:31* [Comment . Like]

Tim Gleeve Where is Kim? Surely he has a few tricks up his sleeve. *Posted Wednesday 19th September at 16:48* [Comment . Like]

Cliff Wheeland Kim's probably being forced to eat bugs by his parents while they measure nutritional value. He won't be back from the Amazon for another five days. What I want to know is, where's a hidden camera when I need one? What do you say, **Kevin**? *Posted Wednesday 19th September at 17:14* [Comment . Like]

Kevin Doherty I don't know man, that's a little creepy. *Posted Wednesday 19th September at 18:12* [Comment . Like]

Cliff Wheeland That, was a joke. *Posted Wednesday 19th September at 19:20* [Comment . Like]

Kathy Bloomingdale OH MY GOD I'M IN ANOTHER

COUNTRY!! This is soooo weird, all those accents. If only I didn't have such a headache. One more flight to go... *Posted Wednesday 19th September at 23:45* [Comment . Like]

> **Tim Gleeve** That's what you get for leaving a soldier behind! You didn't even try to fit me in your suitcase. I'm bendy! *Posted Thursday 20th September at 01:15* [Comment . Like]

Madeline Cain Butt Photographer Wow, did I look like that much of a zombie when I arrived? It's like the international planes are disgorging a plague. *Posted Thursday 20th September at 08:19* [Comment . Like]

> **Cliff Wheeland** You kind of looked like a red nosed Noddy character when you arrived, being January and all. *Posted Thursday 20th September at 08:22* [Comment . Like]

> **Madeline Cain Butt Photographer** I'm standing right next to you! Try using your mouth. *Posted Thursday 20th September at 08:23* [Comment . Like]

> **Cliff Wheeland** I'm a writer, we only use our mouths for reading work to the masses. *Posted Thursday 20th September at 08:23* [Comment . Like]

Kathy Bloomingdale Time Square is AMAZING!! *Posted Thursday 20th September at 13:19* [Comment . Like]

> **Nadine Cain** I take it you have a SIM card for your phone darling, within a day of arriving too. How wonderful for your mother! Don't forget to give her your new phone number. It makes me wonder why it seemed to take Madeline a whole week after her arrival to achieve the same... *Posted Thursday 20th September at 13:20* [Comment . Like]

> **Madeline Cain Tour Guide** Because I had to figure out how it worked on my own. Kathy's got a local to show her the ropes.

Will call soon, promise! *Posted Thursday 20th September at 13:22* [Comment . Like]

Madeline Cain Tour Guide Wow, Kathy's been staring at the Naked Cowboy for like, a minute. Any longer and he'll be playing suggestive western songs in our direction. *Posted Thursday 20th September at 13:30* [Comment . Like]

Kathy Bloomingdale I had a bagel! How did I not know about cream cheese before now?? *Posted Friday 21st September at 09:15* [Comment . Like]

Kathy Bloomingdale Wow, the view from the top of the Empire State is so much prettier at night than during the day! *Posted Saturday 22nd September at 20:37* [Comment . Like]

Madeline Cain Tour Guide I can't believe Kathy made me go up the Empire State twice. Thanks ever so much Cliff for reminding her of Sleepless in Seattle. I owe you a karate throw off the top. We could have done a Broadway show instead! *Posted Saturday 22nd September at 20:37* [Comment . Like]

Cliff Wheeland If you don't go up twice, you're sucking in the tour guide department. *Posted Saturday 22nd September at 21:00* [Comment . Like]

Kathy Bloomingdale Sad face, we can't take Duncan with us on our carriage ride in Central Park. Apparently he's been banned for life. *Posted Sunday 23rd September at 11:52* [Comment . Like]

Tim Gleeve Do you think? How am I the one who remembers the chaos he caused? I think that clearly shows I should be there rather than you. *Posted Sunday 23rd September at 11:55* [Comment . Like]

Kathy Bloomingdale The horse would be perfectly safe; Duncan is too busy cleaning Maddie with his tongue. He's quite convinced she's an hors d'oeuvres platter. *Posted Sunday 23rd September at 11:58* [Comment . Like]

Kathy Bloomindale The Statue of Liberty is massive! And so green (what a weird choice of colour…). I now understand why Maddie had to buy one of those little green crowns. It's like a rite of passage. *Posted Monday 24th September at 14:00* [Comment . Like]

Madeline Cain Tour Guide If a photograph is supposed to steal a piece of your soul, then Kathy has about two thousand stolen souls in her backpack. In fact, if the Statue of Liberty had a soul, Kathy would now have the soul of American Independence in her backpack. I'm snap happy like any other tourist, but there are only so many photos you need of other tourists and green statues. *Posted Monday 24th September at 14:50* [Comment . Like]

Kathy Bloomingdale We shopped today, and I think we only managed to cover 1% of them. They should just call New York the Island Mall. *Posted Tuesday 25th September at 17:22* [Comment . Like]

Madeline Cain Tour Guide There is nothing worse than going shopping and weighing up whether you are willing not to eat for a night so you can wear a new dress. Maybe I should make a diet book and fill it with shopping plans rather than meal plans. It will curb both shopping addiction *and* obesity. *Posted Tuesday 25th September at 17:41* [Comment . Like]

Richard Arnoou liked the page **Stroking My Beard While Pondering The Mysteries Of The Universe** [Like]

The Hypnotist And The Dog Whisperer

NOTES > My Notes [Write a note]

By **Madeline Cain Barking Mad** Monday, 1st October 2012 at 08:00

When Cain brought up Lifestyle Photography, he made it seem like a glamorous and dignified portrait session in the oak panelled library of some uppity society mansion on 5th Avenue. I was promised class, and the chance to sticky beak through someone's extravagant house under the pretence of scouting locations. 'Kathy will like that,' I told myself, 'a real New York experience no other tourist can claim.'

But instead of testing leather lounges, ogling chandeliers and taking a sneaky sip from the crystal whiskey decanter in the Den, we got saliva, hearing loss and a game of Simon Says with the elderly.

Next time Cain says, 'Our subject is a special French Lady,' I'm going to run for the hills. Madam Gemma Claire lived on the upper east side of Manhattan, the type of area you lived in if you had dog food bags full of money.

"Her house is magnificent, I would sell my mother's family into slavery to own half of her front parlour," Cain said as he drew us further into Central Park.

"Wish half your slave family was carrying this circus tent," muttered Kathy, blowing at a stray curl that insisted on being eaten.

"Sure you didn't just meet a hobo with a French accent who claimed they lived in Belvedere Castle?" I grunted as the suspiciously burden free Cain pranced ahead.

He fluttered his fingers at me over his shoulder. "The thing you need to learn about Lifestyle my dear trainees, is how to find the most interesting aspect of your subject and photograph that aspect in its natural element. Let it bloom like a flower and bask in the rays of passion."

"I'll train my knee, to kick you in the balls," said Kathy. (When did you get so violent oh friend of mine?)

"So you're telling me that in among the New York smoke stacks, lives a genuine, no imitation, dog whisperer? Not a walker, or a trainer, but a whisperer who can make a dog dance a waltz, do a summersault and then eat some white boy's absurdly large camera? What are you planning to capture with that monstrosity by the way? Wildebeests?"

More likely this woman sewed dog treats into the hems of her dress so they'd behave.

"I've already seen Central Park guys," said Kathy pointedly, "You sure we couldn't retire after her training class to her stunning townhouse you've been prattling on about for forty minutes?"

"She wants the action shot ladies! The action shot of her unique and utterly bonkers ability," Cain declared, flashing his own manic grin. "Ah, here we are."

So rather than being served by a butler, Kathy and I found ourselves sticky with sweat, and weighed down with enough equipment to fell an elephant, on the edge of one of Central Park's many water bodies, Turtle Pond. A field of baseball pitches was behind us and across the little lake was Belvedere Castle in all its fake, medieval glory.

When Cain first suggested moving our appointment forward I almost said no. Then I realised how idiotic that was; I needed to capitalise on the normality that had descended on my life since Kathy arrived in New York. I'd never had a smoother run of security lines, helpful waiters, or embarrassment free outings as I've had when showing Kathy my adopted home. All I wanted was to undertake just one type of photography that didn't involve chameleons or umbrellas or any type of mentally unstable person. I needed to ride that wave before it reached the beach of fickle fortunes and dashed me against the rocks of chaos.

I'd have recognised our peril from half a continent away if Cain had elaborated this 'special' French lady had a habit of talking to dogs as though they were well educated Harvard graduates. When I did find out I was already cocooned in my safety blanket, I thought I was invincible with Kathy there, any crazy dog lady could be overcome by the sheer weight of our normality.

In a smallish area of grass by the lake, cordoned off by orange cones, was a petite woman in black slacks and loose shirt making kissy faces at a Chihuahua in her arms. She must have been wearing some cyclone proof make-up because her face was still immaculate after being vigorously licked. Her blue eyes alighted on us and her red mouth parted to reveal tiny pearl like teeth. I could hear Kathy sigh in envy at her milky white and freckle free skin. Yes, I've known Kathy so long I can categorise her sighs.

"'Ello," said Gemma in a heavily accented English that all French people seemed to have. The type of accent that could be fashioned into a weapon aimed to weaken the knees and make you fall into lust harder than Tim at a Comic Con convention. That accent was sex to the ears, a sensual sound that stroked your brain and turned it into mush. Even Cain, gayer than a flower garland, was not entirely immune. "Welcome to my school. You must be the photography, no? I am Gemma Claire, an zis…" She turned to the pooch, nuzzling her mouth into that licking machine. "Zis is Monique, my darling."

A large clatter behind me indicated Kathy had lost her load, no doubt trying to hide the same grimace I could feel tugging at my own lips. I would have dunked my head in a vat of anti-bacterial gel by the second lick.

"Please, come," Gemma said.

It seemed her accent was capable of turning even me into an obedient puppy as I found myself following her into the area marked out by the cones without any conscious thought.

"I want ze shot of ze lake an' ze furry darlings an' mwah," she said, her butt swaying from side to side as she walked, like a bobble head doll that moved from the hips.

"Of course, Madam," said Cain, spreading his hands wide. "It's your shoot. I'm thinking several different poses. With your legs folded beneath you, lying on the ground with your face in your hands, and several standing with a couple of doggy tricks I think. All aimed to look flattering of course." He rocked on his heels, clearly in his element.

Looking horrified Gemma shook her head. "Oh no, no. Zis will not do! I do not want robotic photos, I want in the action shots, yes? You understand? They must see I am not, how do you say?" She tapped a finger to her chin.

"A charlatan," murmured Kathy.

"Off her rocker," I replied out the corner of my mouth.

"A con woman!" she said, snapping her fingers. "There are too many fakes. They must see I am real dog talker, yes?"

Cain stilled, watching the woman wearily. No doubt his strong and rather flamboyant personality flattered and bent most society women to his 'expertise'.

"They're like dolls," he had said to me once. "Pretty dolls that turn as I ask and play as they're told. It's fabulous. They all want to prove they're not homophobic and I take advantage of that. Pure, no holds barred, head butt to the face, advantage."

"Sooooo," said present day Cain, moving a hand to one hip. "What would an in action shot look like? Am I setting up high, middle or low?"

"About dog height is best," she said, setting Monique down at her feet. "Zis is a beginner class for older dogs. Ones who have never lived in ze city an' must learn to behave like city dogs. Zis is where the magic happens."

Cain cast a desperate look over the very tall tripods and light stands. "At dog height you said? Are we going to be moving around?"

"Yes! Everywhere, in the action," Gemma insisted, clapping her hands together and raising her voice. "Collect in a line! Time to start."

Looking down at his pristine white pants and barely suppressing a pout, Cain said, "Well then, better do it by hand."

Kathy tapped me on the shoulder as I lowered my haphazard bundle of stands and light boxes to the ground. I turned to see her eyebrows up near her hair line as she pointed to a dog circling itself in a frenzy trying to capture its tail in its snapping jaws. Next to it what looked like a miniature pony with teeth (AKA a Great Dane) had wrapped its owner up in its lead leaving them a mummy from the waist down.

"No Dane! Bad Dane!" said the owner, weakly swatting at the dog.

"Original naming," Kathy snorted.

I surveyed a dozen dogs and their humans. Because clearly those dogs owned their 'owners' arses. None were behaving in a sane manner. Dog logic seemed to go like this:

Want to do the thing Doing the thing Turns out bad Do the thing Turns out bad Keep doing it until works.

A methodology proven to be dodgy by a dog who tried to eat not one, not two, but three bees as it was wrestled into line.

"I'm gonna need a drink before this," said Kathy, making for my bag tangled in various stands.

"I've only got the soft stuff," I replied, "And grab me some almonds, I need the energy." I observed a small fluffball head butt a Dalmatian then power hump an elderly man on the leg before charging off. "A LOT of energy."

"Here." A packet was thrust into my hand by Kathy. "We're going to get a show, I can feel it. Another classic Madeline Cain moment and I'm going to be here in person. I should have brought popcorn." Kathy took an enthusiastic swig from her bottle of Dr Pepper, a disgusting drink she'd taken a liking to.

"Don't you *dare* jinx me." I palmed a handful of almonds from the packet. "I've been having the most amazing week of normality I've had this year. I've never enjoyed being so average in my life. Don't you dare take that away from me."

Kathy shrugged. "When you've got a feeling you've got a feeling. And I've got a feeling I'll feature heavily in your next post."

Oh Kathy, little did you realise you had just roundly jinxed yourself.

Cain clicked his fingers impatiently and it took me a moment to realise it was my attention he was trying to gain. "Madeline, you like being horizontal, you can do the low shots."

"Said the man who got so drunk he used the hallway outside my apartment as his own personal nap stop," I shot back. I flicked several almonds into my mouth as I unzipped my bag with one slippery hand and lowered my camera strap over my neck. Though the greenery took some of the heat out of the day, being in direct sunlight still made for a sweat soaked Madeline.

Cain poked out his tongue and made further clicking motions at Kathy. "You, friend of Madeline, you need to be a clown."

"I beg your pardon?! If we're going to start calling each other names then you're a-"

"He means you have to make the dogs look this way," I cut in. "Like portrait photographers have someone who makes funny faces at babies to make them look and smile at the camera."

"Oh, right," said Kathy, her shoulders loosening, face flushed.

"Don' worry, ze men like ze wild hair, no? An' ze dogs cannot say no to you when you have some of zis." Gemma walked to a bag the size of a flour sack with a droopy eared dog on the front, and scooped up something inside. With the clack of dried wood she poured a pile of dog kibble into Kathy's hands. "My own recipe. Zey cannot resist!"

"Sit," said Kathy jokingly to Monique.

The little dog reversed mid stride, slapping her butt to the ground and looked from Kathy to her hands and back again.

"Huh." She dropped several pieces of kibble onto her right hand and held it out to Monique who politely scooped up each piece with her tongue.

By this time all the dogs were in a rough semblance of a line. Well, when they weren't fidgeting, turning circles, scratching or wiggling like they were filled with worms. We appeared to have an audience that glorious morning. The elderly man who'd just been flash humped by a walking teddy bear had been joined by about a dozen other old folks in various stages of osteoporosis, from Hunchback of Notredame severity to doubling as their own table top. All were dazedly contemplating the line of twitching dogs.

Gemma, oblivious to the crowd strode forward, dropping to her knees before the massive Great Dane, Dane. "First I will connect with ze puppies before we move on to learning how to build your own connection."

Placing a hand on either side of the dog's head she pressed her nose to its snout. She started to huff in a most peculiar manner. The dog froze, as though her gaze had made him forget how moving worked. In my peripherals I could see the elderly cheer squad taking huge gulps of air and blowing them out in apparent imitation of Gemma, while a middle aged woman with a shock of curly salt and pepper hair, their carer, watched on with a small smile and a sharp eye.

Really, I should have sensed the omens then: dog whisperer, a crowd of Nanas and Pops not all there in the head. But as we know, picking up on the signs is not my forte. If it was, I wouldn't have reams of Facebook notes dedicated to my daily visits to Struggletown.

"Look," I said to Kathy, pointing at the carer then dropping another couple of almonds in my mouth. "That's you in fifty years, Madam Clown." I danced out of her reach as she swiped at me with her spare hand. Laughing, I tilted my head back dropping the last of the almonds in my mouth and headed for my designated horizontal position.

"Mmmm, that's crunchy," mumbled Kathy behind me.

It was only when I was down on one knee that the shrieking started.

"Oh My GOD!" The sound of hacking filled the air like a cat with a fist sized fur ball.

I turned to see Kathy bend over, hands on knees, spitting for all she was worth, her intermittent shrieking causing instant chaos among the furry ranks.

"Kathy, what the hell?"

Understanding was further hindered by the miniature poodle that decided if the human got to make noise, it did too.

Kathy stumbled towards me, waving a closed fist. She wheezed, "Dog food. I just ate dog food. Oh God I can still taste it! You and your God damned almonds!" She continued to stagger to a water cooler that had been set up by the lakeside.

Then like a slap across the face her words registered and I collapsed into a giggling mess. I love surprises, I surprise myself quite regularly, but nothing is more delightful than a surprise that doesn't involve you.

I had, dear friends, unconsciously achieved the level of Master Hypnotist. After watching me flick almonds into my mouth for over five minutes, you too, would have followed suit in a moment of inattention. Like Kathy did with her handful of almond sized objects...

What kept me incapacitated with laughter was that Kathy's first thought had not been, "This tastes funny." But, "This is a bit crunchy."

Finally, someone else pulled into my web of misadventure! Imagine what thoughts I could implant into the brains of all you mere mortals if I used my hypnotist powers for evil. Eating dog food would only be the beginning of my reign!

But the fun didn't end there.

Gemma, determined to prove her dog whispering stripes had crawled to the howling poodle and staring it straight in the eye, commanded, "No." To absolutely no effect. If anything, the pitch of the bark was now at permanent hearing damage levels. Undeterred, Gemma started barking back to the poodle, a deep throated sound that alternated between short and sharp, and long and booming.

The poodle matched the woman bark for bark, like a howling symphony conducted by someone with a dog biscuit for a baton. A stray bark joined the composition, and another, and another. The dogs moved in unison, their heads turning towards me and cocking to the left in synchronous motion, ears pricked, all fidgeting momentarily forgotten.

"None of that," snapped a woman.

For the barks were not coming from the dogs, they were coming from the group of elderly men and women, baying and howling and barking like they had absorbed the thoughts of the silent dogs in line and were in some canine-mind-control trance.

"Stop this nonsense!" demanded their carer as she tried covering mouths and eyes, snapping fingers and clapping her hands under their noses. But they were fixated, and like their childhood selves of old, they were having way too much fun.

Then various members of the grey-haired choir started shuffling into the training area and everything exploded into a chaotic mess.

It was like a grey hound race that started in a dozen directions. Dogs burst forth from their hodge-podge line with (or without) their owners staggering behind them. Dane dragged his human across the ground behind him at high speed, the owner screaming some truly inspirational swear words yet somehow unable to delegate enough brain power to convince her hands to let go of the lead.

Several dogs seemed to assume some sort of choir was forming and, paring up with their favourite batty grandparent, threw their barks into a deafening sound track for this scene of mayhem.

A chocolate lab was dashing around digging holes to China (or potentially building traps for unweary humans to turn an ankle in), a Collie's chief concern seemed to be treating sticks as violently as possible, and a German Sheppard embarked on a game of 'turn objects into pieces of objects' and within minutes had an impressive pile of t-shirt material and pieces of picnic basket strewn around him. Another dog seemed to be playing the 'running into knees as fast as possible with a stick in the mouth' game as owner after owner suddenly disappeared from my line of sight like a clichéd horror film.

Cain looked like he'd stepped into his worst nightmare. I'm sure those watching outside the training area thought we were the first step towards a rabid apocalypse and only those innocent orange cones were containing the mayhem. Outside the cones was where I certainly retreated. It was such a delight to find myself on the outside of the chaos that, I admit, I got a bit carried away with my commentary:

"Dance Cain, dance!" I shrieked as a Dalmatian planted its dirty paws on Cain's tailored shirt.

"He's getting away!"

"Dive! Tackle! Loudest bark wins!"

"Drag him by the tail! Lick him on the knee!"

"The kibble is there! Attack!"

On the far side of the human-dog circus, Kathy was finally straightening having decided all particles of kibble were flushed from her mouth. If she'd just stayed still, bent over in a nauseous huddle, she may have been spared the attention of Dane, but it was not to be. The dog was on a beeline as Kathy reorientated herself and unfortunately, she didn't interpret my frantic hand waving as the warning it was. Probably because I was grinning like a maniac.

She waved back weakly, then her eyes widened. She only had time enough to mouth a surprised, 'Oh,' before Dane sped through her legs, and collected her on his back, charging into Turtle Pond.

I would describe the moment as priceless. I wouldn't trade that for a room full of pandas, or a life time supply of chocolate from Mr Wonka himself. Her skinny white ankles kicked out, her curly hair whipped forward, and the buck from Dane as he jumped into the water sent her sailing like a graceless rag doll into the air. She hit the lake in an epic bomb dive that Mike would have been proud of.

Shaking so hard I could barely hold my camera still, I captured a dozen shots of Kathy exploding back up into the air, gasping, water level with her chest, and hair mashed to her head streaming dirty pond water. Like some sort of demented scarecrow from the deep, she stuck her arms out awkwardly to the sides and waded to the edge of the lake to haul herself out.

The absence of the psychotic Dane, now happily paddling, appeared to have calmed the atmosphere in the training area. Which is what made the next instant more of a surprise.

In a fit of what I think was desperation, Gemma Clair stopped barking, darted forward, and began licking the face and ears of the poodle. The poodle's barks, like a toy dog running out of battery, slowly faded until it sat in stunned silence as this woman painted its face with her saliva. It made my tongue itch just watching.

Identifying this moment as one she probably wanted on camera, I hazarded a step into the cone circle, then two. When I was certain I wasn't about to be humped or knocked over like a bowling pin, I knelt down and started snapping away.

It took another half minute for the elderly trouble makers to realise the barking had stopped and to then start licking anything that moved: dogs, each other, their poor carer who was on the phone in tears. One grandma got a solid lick in the eye from a fellow grandpa which she followed up by sticking her tongue in his ear. It appeared I had now entered a twilight zone in which everybody turned to the person/canine next to them and had a good taste.

"I just can't control them! I don't know what to do; they're licking dogs, Garry. Dogs! And pedestrians," said the hysterical carer into her phone. "For Christ sake, Garry! I *told* you, you need more than one person on the Alzheimer patients."

It may disappoint you to know, as it did me, that this was where things started to return to normality.

The dogs, as though they had come to some secret understanding, began casually converging on Gemma, sitting in a neat circle around her and the poodle like they had meant to do it all along... they just had to attend to some mayhem before they got there. The dog owners were huddled in a dazed group not unlike the Alzheimer's patients who had calmed down and were now only occasionally licking the person beside them.

And I, Queen of Chaos, come out of the event completely unscathed and with an immense sense of pride. Because no matter what else goes pear-shaped this year I can proudly say, I have *never* eaten dog food. That honour is reserved for you, Kathy, forevermore.

[Comment . Like . Share]

Tim Gleeve and **81 others** like this.

Kathy Bloomingdale This was NOT the post I had imagined in the park. I was expecting Madeline to be bitten on the bum by a dog, or lovingly attacked by Monique's tongue. Instead I have the dubious honour of being the woman who ate dog food and turned the park into an insane asylum. If your crazy luck has somehow transferred itself to me and shit like this goes down when I'm back in Australia, we are no longer friends. *Posted Monday 1st October at 09:05* [Comment . Like]

> **Cliff Wheeland** Truthfully, I thought the reason Mad brought Kathy along was because she wanted to prove she wasn't making all these stories up. Now I see she was hoping someone else would take the brunt of her superpower. *Posted Monday 1st October at 09:09* [Comment . Like]
>
> **Kathy Bloomingdale** I fully believe she hasn't made a single one of these Facebook Notes up. In fact, I think she *down* plays the events. Some of the crazier stuff I saw is not described in this tale, mainly because if it was, it would haunt your dreams. *Posted Monday 1st October at 09:13* [Comment . Like]
>
> **Cain Michaels** To all of you who have yet to host Madeline on a photographic outing I testify that the events in this here

Facebook Note are the whole truth and nothing but the truth so help me God. I warn you to gird your loins, hire riot gear, lock your children out of harm's way, and may God have mercy on your expensive designer clothes. *Posted Monday 1st October at 09:19* [Comment . Like]

Madeline Cain Barking Mad Hey, you can clearly see I had *nothing* to do with this escapade. Well, except the commentary. That, I take full responsibility for. *Posted Monday 1st October at 09:22* [Comment . Like]

Josh Annelli Bet that commentary involved a lot more swearing than you transcribed. *Posted Monday 1st October at 09:31* [Comment . Like]

Cain Michaels I'm sorry, who was eating almonds in front of their friend holding a handful of kibble? If I wasn't able to charge the replacement of my clothes to Madam, there would have been a double homicide. I promise you. *Posted Monday 1st October at 09:37* [Comment . Like]

Cliff Wheeland Oh God, I'm next on the photography gig list. Excuse me while I ask the newspaper if they cover the cost of riot gear... *Posted Monday 1st October at 09:41* [Comment . Like]

Kevin Doherty Pure gold baby! I'm surprised baseballs didn't figure in there somewhere, you were close enough to the grounds. Actually, that's an awesome add for a skit, right?! Your friend sounds as much of a muse as you, I can feel the ideas flowing already. Let's all go out to dinner, my treat ? *Posted Monday 1st October at 09:45* [Comment . Like]

Madeline Cain Barking Mad You don't want to do a skit with dogs, trust me. You can't control them, they're children with teeth. Dinosaurs with fur. Adding baseballs to the mix would just be asking for trouble. Kathy's got a pretty tight schedule of things she wants to do, I don't know if we could fit in a dinner... *Posted Monday 1st October at 09:47* [Comment . Like]

Kathy Bloomingdale Not a muse, just caught in the cross-fire between Madeline and sanity. That sounds like fun! Don't be a party pooper, Maddie, you're the one with the schedule, not me. I'd like a chance to chat rather than just say hello in the hallway. I don't want to be a third wheel though... *Posted Monday 1st October at 09:50* [Comment . Like]

Cliff Wheeland Let's double date it! I'll come too, then we'll be four. *Posted Monday 1st October at 09:53* [Comment . Like]

Kathy Bloomingdale Done! *Posted Monday 1st October at 09:53* [Comment . Like]

Madeline Cain Barking Mad Oh well, you're all so enthusiastic, how can I say no to that? Sure, thanks Kevin. Though Cliff, turning up with the wrong colour roses at the airport does not make Kathy your insta-girlfriend (though they're my favourite colour, and Kathy is staying with me, so win for me!). You've got to be actually dating to make that a double date. *Posted Monday 1st October at 09:55* [Comment . Like]

Cliff Wheeland That could be arranged... *Posted Monday 1st October at 09:58* [Comment . Like]

Madeline Cain Barking Mad None of that! Make your kissy faces at someone other than my best friend. *Posted Monday 1st October at 09:58* [Comment . Like]

Kevin Doherty But not at me dude. Haha! *Posted Monday 1st October at 09:59* [Comment . Like]

Mike Cain I had an epic game of Simon Says once, only it didn't involve licking. *Posted Monday 1st October at 12:15* [Comment . Like]

Madeline Cain Barking Mad Oh I remember, it involved broken bones and the banning of a blossoming friendship by both sets of parents. Only you could turn something so innocent into something that fits the descriptor, 'epic'. Well, you and a group of addled grandparents. I have visions of you at eighty doing wheelchair races down the corridors of the old folks' home. You'd be a menace people could no longer threaten with boot camp. *Posted Monday 1st October at 18:00* [Comment . Like]

Kathy Bloomingdale But could probably poison with custard. *Posted Monday 1st October at 18:07* [Comment . Like]

Mike Cain I always knew you were into dog food, Kathy. You can tell by how shinny your arm hair is... Can't wait to be a dirty old man. Those buggers get away with so much mischief, and mischief is my natural state. Bet you every one of those grandpa's knew exactly what they were doing, they just wanted to see how far they could go before they broke their carer. I understand their experimental methods perfectly. *Posted Monday 1st October at 18:14* [Comment . Like]

Kathy Bloomingdale Just as I know you are into custard, and that old folks' homes are very easy to walk into with hidden vials in your handbag. Just saying. *Posted Monday 1st October at 18:18* [Comment . Like]

Nadine Cain This takes me back to the days when *my* grandmother (your great grandmother) went into her home, they use to play Simon Says quite regularly. And bingo. Poor Grandma, she was quite batty near the end. Kind of like your dog whisperer. Can you imagine spending your days licking and talking to dogs? No sane person would go down that path so she must have been off her rocker quite early in life. Parents probably did drugs. Are you sure you should be exposing poor Kathy to these people? Speaking of Kathy, are you enjoying it over there love? Is my baby eating well? Is she exercising? Being safe? Does that boyfriend of hers treat her nicely? You'd tell me if Madeline was keeping things from me, wouldn't you love? *Posted Monday 1st October at 18:22* [Comment . Like]

Madeline Cain Barking Mad Mum! Stop it, I haven't all of the sudden turned into a deviant. Yes, my client was certifiably mad, but not everyone is doing drugs, you always say that. If we lived in your imaginary worry world, half the population would be doing drugs. Stop trying to guilt my friends into giving you information. I know this is coming from love, but your love is its own special brand of crazy. Just relax, and don't follow your grandma down the same life path to Bingo. *Posted Monday 1st October at 18:29* [Comment . Like]

Kathy Bloomingdale It's been swell, Mrs Cain, you would love it over here, Maddie is a regular local now and knows all the great spots. She only gets into trouble she can get out of (and post about), and she makes sure she's surrounded by great friends and a chameleon guard dog. You have no reason to worry, nothing hidden here (except the occasional tin can in the back of the cupboard). *Posted Monday 1st October at 18:36* [Comment . Like]

Nadine Cain I wouldn't be a good mother if I didn't ask the questions, sweetheart. I'm glad you're both having such a wonderful time. Try to keep your culinary explorations to human food though. *Posted Monday 1st October at 18:43* [Comment . Like]

Virginia Lowe There needs to be a campaign against New York dog owners. It's cruel to lock dogs in apartments, particularly a Great Dane! They need space to be healthy. I strongly urge you to take up the cause, Madeline. *Posted Monday 1st October at 18:50* [Comment . Like]

Madeline Cain Barking Mad I wish I could, Vee, but I'm a bit snowed under right now, no time to hand out flyers about this terrible issue. Maybe when I have my photography internship and don't have to do deliveries. But I'll be sure to mention it to dog owners if the opportunity arises. *Posted Monday 1st October at 18:55* [Comment . Like]

Tim Gleeve Make sure Cliff has got you that riot gear beforehand. *Posted Monday 1st October at 18:58* [Comment . Like]

Virginia Lowe Free speech doesn't require riot gear, jackass. *Posted Monday 1st October at 18:59* [Comment . Like]

Tim Gleeve I believe what you experienced was a Normality Transfer. Good news is, the transfer is probably temporary, bad news is the likelihood of Maddie giving up her hard won normality is minus infinity. That's a lot of zeros. *Posted Monday 1st October at 19:27* [Comment . Like]

Kathy Bloomingdale That's encouraging. Did you know your head is full of a lot of zeros? *Posted Monday 1st October at 19:30* [Comment . Like]

Tim Gleeve The Normality Transfer seems to have also transferred some of Madeline's sarcasm, though I'm not sure where the violent tendencies have come from. *Posted Monday 1st October at 19:38* [Comment . Like]

Madeline Cain Barking Mad Kathy's always had some closet violence, it comes from her repressed Catholic side. *Posted Monday 1st October at 19:39* [Comment . Like]

Richard Arnoou Cain isn't keen on doing action shots? Figures. *Posted Monday 1st October at 19:46* [Comment . Like]

Cain Michaels Not all of us have a magic carpet for a beard. *Posted Monday 1st October at 19:49* [Comment . Like]

Richard Arnoou If your dad hasn't got a beard, you've got two moms. *Posted Monday 1st October at 19:49* [Comment . Like]

Victoria Zeng Does Gemma's accent and the dog kissing cancel each other out? So that rather than feeling totally in lust, or totally grossed out, you just feel like eating a sandwich? *Posted Monday 1st October at 19:55* [Comment . Like]

Jade Annelli My grandmother use to do that with her dog, until one day it bit her on the tongue. I was drinking coke at the time and it squirted out my nose. Maybe if she had an accent they would have cancelled each other out and my nasal passages would have been safe. *Posted Monday 1st October at 19:57* [Comment . Like]

Madeline Cain Barking Mad No, the accent was definitely stronger. Even though I wanted to throw up in my mouth, I couldn't help but follow her. *Posted Monday 1st October at 20:11* [Comment . Like]

Jarrah Annelli The whole species is insane. They're like children but with fur. *Posted Monday 1st October at 20:14* [Comment . Like]

Josh Annelli If only I'd managed to teach our family dog that the word, 'No,' didn't mean: a) we're being sound buddies and you should join in; b) just bark quieter; c) continue to poke me in the groin with your paws; d) that's a nice hole you've got there, keep digging; e) please, pretend you have no legs when we attempt to leave the dog park; or e) don't stop doing what you're doing until I say, 'No,' at least fifty more times. *Posted Monday 1st October at 20:18* [Comment . Like]

Madeline Cain Barking Mad We once put a cone on our dog's head so he couldn't dig holes. He looked like a dog shaped satellite, but at least we no longer found worms on our carpet. *Posted Monday 1st October at 20:20* [Comment . Like]

Richard Arnoou The big question is, is she a real dog whisperer? *Posted Monday 1st October at 20:21* [Comment . Like]

Madeline Cain Barking Mad If you mean, do the dogs understand what she is mind-beaming them? I'm gonna go with no. I think she startles them into behaving with the licking. And she probably puts doggy drugs in her kibble. Kathy was speaking a little funny after she ate some… *Posted Monday 1st October at 20:23* [Comment . Like]

Victoria Zeng It's like Jason's latest World In Motion assignment was made for you… *Posted Monday 1st October at 20:27* [Comment . Like]

Cliff Wheeland Explain. Kim needs to know Maddie's got this in the bag so Duncan can relax. *Posted Monday 1st October at 20:28* [Comment . Like]

Madeline Cain Barking Mad Photography is a static medium, so Jason wanted us to convey a sense of motion in a scene. He says it's essential to capturing emotion. I say it's essential to capturing you best friend's epic melt down at the hands of dogs on a kibble version of Speed. *Posted Monday 1st October at 20:36* [Comment . Like]

Mike Cain joined the page **Changing The Word 'Wand' To 'Willy' In Harry Potter Quotes.** [Like]

Kathy Bloomingdale Wow, Japanese tourists take photos of the most pointless things. *Posted Tuesday 2nd October at 15:14* [Comment . Like]

Madeline Cain Barking Mad Ok, so we're at the Metropolitan Museum of Art and Kathy is taking photos of the weirdest things, aka

Japanese tourists taking photos of weird things. I feel she's being a bit hypocritical here... *Posted Tuesday 2nd October at 15:17* [Comment . Like]

Victoria Zeng I just read that 1 in 5 people are Chinese. I have five people in my family, so taking this to the logical conclusion, one person in my family has to be Asian. So, mum, dad, Craig or Ho-Min-Chu. I think it's Craig x_x *Posted Tuesday 2nd October at 21:12* [Comment . Like]

> **Josh Annelli** Dude, either you need your eyes checked, or your real family is dispersed across states... *Posted Tuesday 2nd October at 21:21* [Comment . Like]

Kathy Bloomingdale I've always wanted to get into a Cab and say, "Follow that car!" Dream accomplished. *Posted Tuesday 2nd October at 22:13* [Comment . Like]

Madeline Cain Barking Mad Epic facepalm. Why do I have such weird friends? Kathy to Cab Driver: "Follow that car!" Cab Driver to Kathy: "Am I really following that car or are you just saying that? Have you got money?" Kathy to Cab Driver: "Follow that car!" You do know we could have fit in one Cab don't you, Kathy? *Posted Tuesday 2nd October at 22:14* [Comment . Like]

Don't Want To Leave.....[New Message]

[Back to messages. Mark as unread . Report spam . Delete]

Between **Kathy Bloomingdale** and **You.**

Kathy Bloomindale 3rd October 2012 at 18:42 [Report]

My plane has been delayed by like, a billion hours. Ugghhh! I need something to do to stop myself shaking so much. What's with the delays? It better not be the engines, or I'm going to tell the engineers where they can shove that plane.

Instead, I choose to focus on bugging you and holding onto my first trip to the US with an iron grip. I wish I was staying, this trip has been amazing, even with the grandpa-dog kerfuffle. Wouldn't mind getting to know Cliff a bit more either. You never mentioned he was a hunk. Though I think I'd keep the double dates to a minimum...

Madeline Cain Barking Mad 3rd October 2012 at 18:48

Could you stop that? It weirds me out, my two separate lives coming together like that.

Oh no! Am I turning into one of those possessive friends who always sees people separately so they never do things without me??

Kathy Bloomingdale 3rd October 2012 at 18:50 [Report]

Woah, I said I wanted to get to know him more, not that I wanted to have his babies. It was just a throwaway thought, I like your friends.

Madeline Cain Barking Mad 3rd October 2012 at 18:52

Right, sorry, it's just I thought you meant seriously as in, like, *date* seriously. You know, I've never seen Cliff try to woo anyone but during this visit, there was all this wooing directed at you.

Kathy Bloomingdale 3rd October 2012 at 18:53 [Report]

He was probably trying to prove he could play nice with your friends, all part of his make-it-up-to-Maddie pact. That's a pretty strong reaction you've got for someone you claim is only a friend.

Madeline Cain Barking Mad 3rd October 2012 at 18:53

Maybe it would be a time thing, you know, getting use to you being in this little compartmentalised section of my life.

Kathy Bloomingdale 3rd October 2012 at 18:53 [Report]

Or a trouble with Kevin thing.

Madeline Cain Barking Mad 3rd October 2012 at 18:55

I know, it was embarrassing and I'm so sorry about that. I've never noticed before how much Kevin hijacks every conversation to talk about us. When did that even start happening? He's fine on his own with me. Having every topic anyone uttered suddenly turned into a story about him or me was just the weirdest, 'You're on display' vibe I've ever had.

Kathy Bloomingdale 3rd October 2012 at 18:56 [Report]

It's sweet he seems so proud of you but I'm not sure how narcissists keep it up. Have you guys gone out with other people before? Or at least with people who aren't part of the wider world of Kevin? That's probably why you didn't notice it until we went for our double date.

Madeline Cain Barking Mad 3rd October 2012 at 18:56

It was NOT a double date. It was a 'getting to know you' gesture which turned into a getting to know you and Cliff. It was a meeting of friends.

Kathy Bloomingdale 3rd October 2012 at 18:57 [Report]

Or getting know you and Kevin...It felt like a date. Cliff was such a gentleman.

Madeline Cain Barking Mad 3rd October 2012 at 18:57

That he was... Why does this weird me out??

Kathy Bloomingdale 3rd October 2012 at 18:59 [Report]

I may have been misreading the signs, but it seemed he was wooing you a bit in your first couple of months, maybe it's something to do with that.

He *has* been on his best behaviour since the elevator, though. Maybe you should relent a little, give him more of a chance. You used to do a lot of stuff together.

Madeline Cain Barking Mad 3rd October 2012 at 18:59

I miss the fun we had. Maybe I should. Cliff did get me my next photography gig after all. But I want you to know, I'm not trying to pussy block your romantic interests, I just want to make up with old friends.

Kathy Bloomingdale 3rd October 2012 at 19:00 [Report]

Hey, spend all the time with Cliff you want, you're the one who lives here, not me. Besides, you knew him first.

Madeline Cain Barking Mad 3rd October 2012 at 19:00

Yeah I did! First dibs!

Kathy Bloomingdale 3rd October 2012 at 19:04 [Report]

Like I said, I'm just holding onto New York for grim death, I've probably developed a romantic interest in the Statue of Liberty as well. I *really* don't want to go ? I'll be heading back to jetlag, exams, *Mum,* and hanging out with Tim and not you. *And* I'll be replacing New York with Adelaide, bleg! The sacrifices I make.

Also, I don't know what pussy blocking is, but I assume it's like cock blocking, so I beg you, please don't ever use that phrase again.

Madeline Cain Barking Mad 3rd October 2012 at 19:06

Sorry, it's not something I do often so I wasn't sure of the correct term. Clam Jam maybe? Clitorferance? Beaver Impeder?

Kathy Bloomingdale 3rd October 2012 at 19:06 [Report]

Stop! Just stop! I'm reading this on a public airport computer for crying out loud!

Madeline Cain Barking Mad 3rd October 2012 at 19:08

Soz. No offense, because I love you to death, but I know what you mean. I don't want to go home. I'm dreading the thought of leaving New York in December, I'm just not ready to go back to Australia. I love Mum and Dad, and I suppose I could be convinced not to strangle Mike for an hour or two, but being here is exciting! I get to do what I love, and there is way more opportunity. If I came home I'd probably have to move to Sydney or Melbourne to find work. Then I'd be away from NYC, away from Cliff and my friends here *and* away from you.

Kathy Bloomingdale 3rd October 2012 at 19:09 [Report]

And your boyfriend.

Madeline Cain Barking Mad 3rd October 2012 at 19:11

Yes, Kevin too, of course. It's why I've got to make sure I don't f-up this internship thing, it comes with a Green Card. I know you guys think I'm mad to do this last exchange with Dom, but I'm just so desperate to make this internship a reality! Otherwise, as soon as college ends I've got to stop work and leave the country in ninety days. Before you suggest it, I'm not marrying anyone just so I can stay! That way ends in babies and I am *so* not ready to go there.

Kathy Bloomingdale 3rd October 2012 at 19:13 [Report]

Yeah, no. Ah! Finally! My flight's been called. Oh shit, my flight's been called :S

Madeline Cain Barking Mad 3rd October 2012 at 19:14

You'll be fine, stop being a stress nut. I'm going to miss you!!

Kathy Bloomingdale 3rd October 2012 at 19:14

Me to! Be good, give the boy a chance, and remember, you're fabulous! They want to keep you, not deport you.

Jamie Anderson liked the page **On A Scale Of 1 To Osama Bin Ladin, How Good Was My Hiding Spot?** [Like]

Kathy Bloomingdale My gay-dar doesn't seem to function properly in Europe. *Posted Thursday 4th October at 05:19* [Comment . Like]

> **Tim Gleeve** My gay-dar doesn't function anywhere. I assume everyone is gay. *Posted Thursday 4th October at 07:40* [Comment . Like]
>
> **Madeline Cain Barking Mad** Why are you in Europe? *Posted Thursday 4th October at 07:53* [Comment . Like]

Kathy Bloomingdale Ask my travel agent, apparently Singapore is also on a giant list of stops to get home. Something about buying an around the world ticket, and being on a plane until I die. *Posted Thursday 4th October at 08:10* [Comment . Like]

Madeline Cain Barking Mad Well, at least you'll get over your fear of flying. *Posted Thursday 4th October at 08:14* [Comment . Like]

Kathy Bloomingdale Are you kidding? I'm so drunk I don't know whether it's the air, sea or ground rocking beneath me. And I'm staying this way until I can be certain no-one else is going to force me on a plane. *Posted Thursday 4th October at 08:16* [Comment . Like]

Wyate Yosim Some people should not be in the food business:

"Can I have a Coke?"

"Is Pepsi okay?"

"I don't know, is Monopoly money okay?"

Posted Monday 8th October at 16:10 [Comment . Like]

Harry Lee Clearly, your waiter was never a teenage boy. *Posted Monday 8th October at 19:25* [Comment . Like]

Tim Gleeve I asked for water the other day and the wanker brought me some sparkling shit. Do I look like a man who has little girl bubbles in my water? Do I?? *Posted Monday 8th October at 20:57* [Comment . Like]

Alex McMarshal Remember, whenever you feel worthless, you were once the quickest sperm. *Posted Friday 12th October at 11:43* [Comment . Like]

Jack Fox Yeah I was, baby! *Posted Friday 12th October at 12:13* [Comment . Like]

Kyle Traybna Woah! The phrase 'ipod!' is the same upside down! *Posted Tuesday 16th October at 14:47* [Comment . Like]

Kathy Bloomingdale !dogi? I think you mean upside down and mirrored there buddy. *Posted Tuesday 16th October at 20:00* [Comment . Like]

Kathy Bloomingdale Y'all welcome for this epic weather. I had a huge suitcase and so I thought I'd bring back some sunshine. *Posted Tuesday 23rd October at 13:15* [Comment . Like]

Tim Gleeve If that's the present you brought me from your trip, I'm going to cover you in molten metal and make my own Hans Solo statue. *Posted Tuesday 23rd October at 13:50* [Comment . Like]

Kim Enuik This is a city God damn it! Not the bloody Amazon. Stop. Raining. *Posted Saturday 27th October at 16:24* [Comment . Like]

Cliff Wheeland Welcome to New York in October my friend. *Posted Saturday 27th October at 17:40* [Comment . Like]

Kate Nickles likes the pages **Dear Mathematics, Stop Making Me Find Your X. He's Not Coming Back** and **Saying Random Numbers When Someone Is Counting To Make Them Stuff Up.** [Like]

Madeline Cain Barking Mad Turns out playing in the subway sewers, eating pizza and practising karate will not make me an honorary ninja turtle. Now I just smell like shit. *Posted Wednesday 31st October at 23:00* [Comment . Like]

Mike Cain What the hell have you been doing? *Posted Wednesday 31st October at 23:30* [Comment . Like]

DECK

Halloween & Subway Zombies

NOTES > My Notes [Write a note]

By **Madeline Cain Queen of the Night** Thursday, 1st November 2012 at 09:52

You North Americans are mental. This obsession with turning pumpkin, not into dinner, but into artwork is bizarre. Pumpkin is *not* a sweet, or a platform for Italian style carvings of Obama or toothless ghouls. It is a vegetable! You eat it, with meat and other vegetables. It's *not* a giant orange balloon on steroids. Also, putting candles inside your food is a waste of food. Just saying.

Then there's this whole obsession with fancy dress. I'm fairly certain All Hallows Eve is about honouring ancestors and keeping the Dead dead, not about dressing up as sexy versions of your favourite cartoon character. This Halloween I've seen too many Playboy bunnies (of *all* sizes) to ever get the image out of my head. They're burnt into my brain like an adult version of Beatrix Potter's books.

The obsession with Vampires and Zombie's is also a little overboard. Are you trying to give people heart attacks? What is the appeal of congregating so you can pretend to be dead?? The dirty undead at that, because clearly anything that involves one-bite-and-you're-a-monster means you're carrying some sort of pathogen. America, why do you insist on bring my irrational fears and nightmares to life? I'm certain I wasn't the only child to almost strangle myself with blankets because they were wrapped so around my throat for fang protection.

If I'd known Cliff's newspaper job meant being in the dark depths of the subway system on Halloween, I probably would've told him to shove it. I blame my Dom-anxiety for not probing into the subject matter of our "assignment".

Why did I have Dom-anxiety? Because Halloween was the day I released Dom from his well-intentioned, possibly criminally related life-debt. Or tried to. Our conversation went something like this:

Me: (Brightly) Heeeeyyyyy Dom, good to see you.

Dom: You too sugar. I've got a special delivery for my lil' lifesaver (wink wink).

Me: (Takes small, brown paper package with a manly grunt) Wow, this is heavy. You shouldn't ha-

Dom: Nonsense! I've barely paid back ten percent of my debt!

Me: (Faintly) Only ten percent. Wow. Look, about that-

Dom: I would've said five percent but this package is my best yet and worth at least another five percent; guess how many suits are in that?

Me: (Looks at package the size of three thick books) Uh, two?

Dom: Ten. Ten! Revolutionary technology has made this foldable, wrinkle free, and sexy Armani style tux possible! It's going to put a lot of old families out of business. They'd *kill* for that technology if they knew about it.

Me: Riggghhhtt. (Tries for a quick look at the coffee shop across the road) And you made this to-die-for clothing line?

Dom: Not me! Marchetti owes me a favour. I'm just getting it into the right hands, if you know what I mean.

Me: Uhhhhhhh.

Dom: Are you ok?

Me: Wha-what do you mean?

Dom: There's something wrong with your eye. It keeps scrunching up.

Me: (Stops ineffective winking at Agent across the road) Oh that, yeah, light sensitivity, I just woke up.

Dom: (Looks at watch, eyebrows raised) Well, nice to see you again, Sugar. Until next month-

Me: No!

Dom: Sorry?

Me: I mean, no need. I've got all the fashion shots I need to build my portfolio. This is my last shoot. Sooooo I guess this is goodbye. So glad you're alive. This has been nice.

Dom: Oh no no no little bambina. I'm not going anywhere until I'm satisfied I've given you everything within my power to give.

Me: That's really not necessary. I've got all the things I need right now-

Dom: Ah, you can't know that! Life throws curve balls. Who knows, one day you might need one of your competing fashion photographers out of the picture and I'm sure I could arrange that too (wink wink).

Me: (Speechless)

Dom: You can't get rid of me that easy. I pay my debts. I'll be checking in on you, Madeline. You'll be looked after, don't worry. Anything you need; all you have to do is ask.

With a cheerful wave his well-dressed, stunted body swaggered off down the sidewalk. To my relief, as Dom approached the corner of the block, one drably dressed individual casually got up from their table outside The Bean and strolled after him while his coffee mate gave a brief thumbs up in my direction. You can imagine how I may have been too preoccupied that afternoon to think about the less pressing parts of my life like what I was taking pictures of for a mere newspaper.

It wasn't until I was standing in the elevator at 5pm with a casually dressed Cliff in a black parker and shorts showing off muscular legs (sans his normal tailored jacket), that I thought to ask where the hell we were headed.

"I know I said loose clothing, but I kind of meant stuff you can get dirty in," said Cliff, taking in my new jeans, sparkly gold top, red jacket and bulging backpack full of camera gear and wrinkle free suits.

"Why? Where are we going?"

"To meet my source." Cliff strode out of the elevator, lino squeaking under his shoes. "He's an anonymous urban adventurer who knows a hidden subway station and a kind of off limits art gallery in the tunnels nearby."

I dashed after him, just catching the front door as it began to swing shut. "I'm sorry; did you say we are going to follow someone who won't tell you his name into subway tunnels? On Halloween?"

Cliff shrugged with a broad grin, turning south. "I've named him, Max."

"Oh giving him a name makes following a stranger in the dark a *hundred* times better."

"Did he mention you'll be blindfolded too?" drawled a male voice from the shadows of a nearby doorway.

'Max' was a tall, gangly guy in a dark hoody, freckles peppering his face like spray paint. True to his word, once we reached the vicinity of City Hall in lower Manhattan he blindfolded us and lead us down some pungent alleyways, probably for shits and giggles. If you asked Cliff, he seemed to think the purpose of that putrid walk was to confuse our sense of direction. The blindfolds were to stop us from knowing the entry to this secret subway station. Because of course, what we were doing was highly illegal. Either Max thought we were going to take over his business or we were going to get him arrested. The expedition was fairly dangerous given the station, though abandoned by people, was not abandoned by the trains, which still used the station to turn around.

The smells didn't get any better as darkness filled in the light at the edges of my blindfold. If anything, they just got wetter, the scent of damp and mould overwhelming. I gripped a handful of Max's jacket as my feet stumbled against the wet ground and set up an echo like a thousand slugs hitting the pavement at once. The hot air of the underground in Autumn draped itself around me like a cloak, stifling and overly familiar.

"What I'm about to show you has only been witnessed by Metro workers and urban explorers who prowl the tunnel system at night." Max's whisper echoed and amplified in the space.

"The station or the street art?" asked Cliff.

"Both." We ran into Max as he paused. The sound of rusted hinges being forced to work scrapped through the air.

The oppressive heat lessened, the atmosphere dryer in this new space. The echo changed subtly, and took on a more cavernous feel, wet slapping replaced by the tap of shoes against tile. The sound of a door closing and a switch flicking followed.

I jumped as Max's voice came right next to my ear. "I'll show you the station first."

He whipped off our blindfolds.

My eyes shouted abuse at me as they adjusted to the brighter light. We stood in a medium sized antechamber decorated with tall arches lined in glossy green and tan tiles and brass fixtures with ancient flickering light bulbs. Where the arches met at the roof apex was a beautiful blue skylight with diamond shaped patterns letting in the fading glow of the October day. One arch opened on to what appeared to be a platform. This was confirmed a moment later when background rumbling became a full throated roar and a subway car, then another, screeched its way past.

"That'll be the Six train," shouted Max over the high pitched assault on our ears. "In the past they made you get off at the Brooklyn Bridge stop before it made the turn. But now you're allowed to stay on it while it turns around, though you can't get off." The final car moved out of sight and the piercing sounds faded. "Come on, let's see the station proper, this room is just a taster."

We stepped out of the archway, onto the platform, and into one of the most beautiful buildings I'd seen since moving to New York, there, in the deep belly of the subway system. The train tracks were a little over four metres away. Tiles on the wall claimed it to be 'City Hall' station. The tiled walls vaulted in elegant arches above us and four-limbed electric chandeliers made of brass hung at intervals from the ceiling. Every line in the architecture was curved, not a straight line to be seen and that included the track which arced away into the darkness. By far the most fabulous feature of this forgotten place was the skylights in the ceiling.

I fumbled for my camera in the depths of my backpack.

"The station was opened in 1904," said Max, shuffling down the platform with his hands in his pockets. "It was to be the crowning glory of the New York Subway system. This was where all the plaques and shit were going to go, to commemorate the city's success in building such a massive underground network."

I swung up my camera and attempted to capture as much of the curve of the station as I could before the twilight left us and the skylights dimmed. Though they were slightly grimy, the skylights still provided a band of sky blue glass that added a dream like element to the photos. They ran across the entire curve of the station, but calling them a skylight was doing them an injustice, for they had all the elegance of stain glass windows you see in churches. Iron circles and semi-circles, curve-edged diamonds and flower petals patterned the glass and cast whirling shadows across the platform. It was hard to believe we were underground but if you looked closely through the glass you could see side walk grates protecting the station from the world above.

Slowly, I followed the boys who were already half way along the platform, taking about a hundred shots for every step.

Max's voice drifted back in snatches. "- Closed in 1945... No not the war...It closed because new, longer cars were purchased to match passenger demand... but the station's tracks are severely curved...makes a dangerous gap between train doors and the platform... too unsafe..."

"Oi! Maddie!" Cliff's voice jerked me out of my snap happy dream. "I think we're good for station photos. Anymore and you'll melt your shutter."

"Just one more!" I spun and took several shots in the other direction.

"One more my arse," he replied. "Come on!"

I looked up from my lens and baulked. Both boys had jumped from the platform to the tracks, flashlights in hand. "What the hell are you doing? There are still trains here!"

"The Underbelly Project has turned some of the surrounding tunnels into a kind of off-limits art gallery," said Cliff

"Well whoop-dee-do for them. Whoever the hell they are. Now get off those tracks before a train hits you in the face."

"They're a group of street artists," Max supplied, "There are over a hundred murals by graffiti artists, including some of the greats like PAC and Workhorse." From the enthusiasm in his voice I could tell this was why he'd really agreed to be our tour guide, not for the beautiful station that was our entry point.

"Come on, it's a spooky art exhibition. Perfect for Halloween. Besides, Max has been here hundreds of times, he knows how this works."

I groaned, how was I buying into this insanity? Carefully I sat on the edge of the soot streaked platform in my brand new jeans and dropped onto the dirty track. "There are at least two doors at the end of this platform, you're telling me we couldn't have taken a less dangerous route?"

"The only way to reach it is through here," said Max.

Cliff waited until I reached him and his flashlight before setting off. It was only thirty metres down the track until we turned into a tunnel devoid of train tracks. I breathed a sigh, and felt my shoulders loosening. But it wasn't long before I was once again wound up as tight as a rusted spring.

In stark contrast to the City Hall platform, these walls and square arches were made of ugly, grey concrete. The space was a combination of cement cavern with half-finished platforms and track beds, hidden rooms and tight concrete enclosed alleys. As we wound our way into this labyrinth I became hopelessly lost. We were probably under Liberty Island for all I could tell. If I was claustrophobic, I would have been buggered. As it was, I was scared shitless, like a diver wearing a swimsuit of steaks in shark infested waters. We had flashlights but they barely cut into the inky blackness. The air was hot, humid and thick with the rail dust we kicked up with every step. The ceilings leaked fluid from God knew where and we had to be careful not to fall down any of the dozens of random, bottomless holes in the ground.

We rounded a corner and Cliff flicked his light at one of the walls. A burst of colour flared. "Wow!" He ran the beam along the rest of the wall to reveal a massive tunnel wall littered with art.

Stairs led from the lower level to the unfinished platforms and walls which were covered with brightly painted caricatures, abstract paintings, a cartoon of a walking house, surrealist pieces, giant rats, portraits and spray painted pieces that declared, 'We Own The Night.'

"Thank God I bought a tripod," I whispered, the atmosphere and secrecy of the place already getting to me. "This will be perfect for Jason's shadow assignment."

"We're four stories underground. Over the course of a year almost one hundred street artists came down here and each had one night to paint what they wanted," said Max, leading us deeper into this maze of artwork that crawled along the walls and over archways, equal parts creepy and breath taking.

"I have the perfect piece to take your first photo." Max grinned, leading us under a low hanging doorway, turning into yet another disused platform.

The flashlights illuminated a brightly coloured word.

I hazarded a guess. "Zon? Con? I don't get—" then I looked down and flipped the hell out like Kathy on doggy treats.

My scream echoed through the space as I tripped over my feet and tripod to get away, slamming into Cliff who held me fast, his flashlight making crazy patterns on the ceiling. Max, was laughing so hard he bent double. Blessedly, neither flashlight illuminated the wall as I tried to gain control.

"It's not real," Max wheezed, tears of mirth tracking down his face. "It's a sculpture."

"Christ! Warn a girl! I shoot people for a living. You won't be missed." I shoved myself away from Cliff who'd also started shaking with laughter.

Snatching Max's flashlight from his unresisting hand, I lit up the figure that crouched at the base of the spray painted word. Dressed in jeans and a black hoody, you would be forgiven for initially thinking it was a homeless man, that is until you saw its contorted monster face.

"Thanks guys, you're making my first Halloween soooo special. Now let's take some photos and get the hell out of here before I 'accidentally' punch someone in the gonads."

So I set up my tripod at our favourite (and not so favourite) pieces, exposing for several seconds while the boys played the light of their torches across each art piece. All my senses were heightened in this black void, and so was my active imagination. The occasional dull roar of a train echoed in the distance and somewhere nearby, pipes clanked and the earth groaned.

"Seriously, Madeline, stop jumping at every sound. You'll make the photos blurry if you don't pull it together," whispered Cliff, making me jump yet again.

"Your fault. You didn't prepare me, I'm like an under done steak."

"Best Halloween experience ever though, right?"

"Haven't got much to compare it to—"

"Turn your torches out, someone's coming," Max hissed.

"Haha, you're funny. I get it, scaring the Australian is a right laugh—"

"We're not supposed to be here, turn the stupid thing off!"

Then suddenly it was oppressive black night all around, and the sounds of groans, pipes and more groans. *Bugger this*, I thought, *this is the last straw*. What the hell did this Max guy think I was? A guineapig?

I was *not* a scare experiment. Enough of being the only person without a flashlight, it was Cliff's idea, he *owed* me his.

I stuck out a hand towards Cliff and struck something soft. Cliff left out a muffled squeak and as he doubled over I snatched the torch from his hand.

"I know you're not going to believe me," I whispered, "But that *was* an accidental gonads punch. But you know what? I'm not a bit sorry. I have a *very* active imagination, and right now it's telling me that every time I turn the light off, that bloody statue is coming to life and stalking me."

Cliff's face creased in bewilderment and behind me Max let out a hiss. "*What the-*"

I held up my hand, forestalling them. "I know it's irrational but that bloody possessed dummy movie Kevin made me watch yesterday is firmly rooted in my head. Can we just go? Let's do the normal Halloween thing and dress up like Dracula and scare kids into leaving their candy behind, ok? Thank you for turning on a flashlight, Max."

There was a loud groan right by my head and a hand pawed at my shoulder. "Christ sake, real mature! Why don't you-" I whirled around and the words died on my tongue.

A zombie stared back at me. No, make that a sea of zombies stared back at me, crowded into the space behind a small archway in the wall. Candles, torches and phones were gripped in dirty outstretched hands and lit up pallid green skin, blood streaked faces and wide, blackened mouths. It was their lights that had allowed me to see Cliff, not Max, who was pressed into a corner of the tunnel, a fist jammed into his mouth, and eyes wide with terror.

The lead zombie lurched forward and the whole bizarre situation snapped from dream to reality. I turned, grabbed my camera and tripod in two hands, spun back and whipped the tripod up between the zombie's legs. I'm not quite sure what possessed me to think the tripod was an effective weapon. Did zombies even have gonads?

I may have shouted, "For Queen and Country!" But it's all a bit vague. Frankly, I may have gone a little mad. I do remember turning on my torch and yelling at Cliff, "Run or be eaten!" before bolting in the opposite direction. Which in the grand scheme of things didn't make things better as the zombies were everywhere.

How we'd gone from an abandoned subway station full of imaginary spooks to a tide of zombies down almost every tunnel we turned, I don't know. You'd think a tide of zombies would be hard to miss as you conspicuously took photos in the light of two flashlights that doubled as truncheons. In any case, Cliff and I chased each other down dusty tunnels for far longer than any two sane people should have.

It was when we burst in on ten vampires having a candlelit dinner in an derelict room that my plausibility-metre broke. Because while zombies by themselves were completely plausible to my already terrified brain, having both zombies *and* vampires existing at the same time was pushing things a little too far. Even my lizard brain grudgingly admitted there was just *no way* they could both exist.

In my mind, vampires and zombies somehow nullified each other, lifting the fog of terror to reveal dodgy costumes and streaky make-up. Even if I hadn't realised terror was taking me for a ride, the conversation that followed would have set things straight pretty quickly:

"Ah human guestssss," lisped a vampire around plastic teeth, "You have arrived jussst in time…"

A groaning zombie entered via the same door as Cliff and I.

The vampire, jumped to his feet baring his teeth. In a thick cockney accent he said, "Oi Mate, this is our room, bloody well piss off would ya? You're ruining it."

Dropping his arms the zombie stood back, human expression filling his vacant face. "Alright, just chill out, man. I'm going. Don't know why you'd want to eat dinner with dentures when there's a kickass Zombie Walk going on though." He shrugged, turned and assuming a zombie pose, he staggered back out into the tunnel with energetic groans.

"I need a drink," I said, snatching a glass of red off the table.

"There's enough blood for everyone," chanted the vampire half-heartedly as he re-took his seat.

Fiery red wine burnt its way down my throat. "If blood tastes like red wine then no wonder you drink the stuff," I coughed. "You're all insane by the way. Maybe it's these tunnels, but I am definitely the most sane person in this entire subway system. You can tell this because I'm the only one not wearing a cape."

The table of vampires watched politely as I downed the entire glass of wine. Looking back, I probably looked like a crazy hobo who'd rolled in a pile of dirt.

"More?" asked a particularly pale female vampire.

I nodded and another vampire pulled an extra chair from a dark corner. "Bob couldn't make it," he said when I just stared at it, like it might eat me. "You really should sit down before you fall over."

Like a zombie myself, I shuffled forward and collapsed into the chair, one hand gripping my tripod and camera, the other clutching the glass.

"Sorry," said Cliff, reaching into his pocket and pulling out a notepad and pen. "She's had a bit of a scare, this is her first Halloween and she's not taking it very well. I'm a writer, we're down here for a story. Mind if I ask you a couple of questions?"

And that's how I spent my first Halloween running from zombies and having dinner with vampires.

It's also how I managed to get my best fashion and assignment shots of the year. Or I suppose how Cliff managed to get my best shots, as he was the one who convinced half a dozen zombies and vampires to don Dom's suits and pose in front of the brightly painted wall that proclaimed, 'We Own The Night'.

All I can say Cliff, is nice save.

Nice save, your gonads are safe.

For now.

[Comment . Like . Share]

Kathy Bloomingdale and **87 others** like this.

Cliff Wheeland My gonads are wiping their metaphorical foreheads as we speak. I see this less as a save and more as giving you triple what you expected. No! Quadruple. Not only did you get to see a subway station no New Yorker has seen in over fifty years, but you get paid freelance newspaper rates and can now afford your Broadway addiction for another month. Plus you got an authentic Halloween experience, and *amazing* photos for your portfolio. I should be getting four times the brownie points, really. I'm certain my gonads will be safe in your hands as soon as you realise my logic. *Posted Thursday 1st November at 10:20* [Comment . Like]

> **Jack Fox** I think we can safely say those zombies did indeed have gonads. I would put mine in your hands any day, Maddie,

wink wink. *Posted Thursday 1st November at 10:31* [Comment . Like]

Cliff Wheeland Ah, my last sentence was a poor choice of words. Sorry, the word bag isn't working today. *Posted Thursday 1st November at 10:37* [Comment . Like]

Josh Annelli A man should never challenge a gonads threat. I know. I lived in a womb with certain ball breakers for nine months. They're not shy at tapping the turkey. *Posted Thursday 1st November at 10:40* [Comment . Like]

Madeline Cain Queen of the Night I'll pass, thanks Jack. I don't need to know about the incest that goes on in your life, Josh. By the way, Cliff, *not* the best Halloween experience ever. *Posted Thursday 1st November at 10:41* [Comment . Like]

Cliff Wheeland Aww, come on, a Halloween that pays you *and* allows you to say 'cheese' while wearing plastic vampire teeth? How can that not be the most awesome experience ever? I count it as my best by far. How about I make it up to you with a trip to a Broadway show? That one Kevin refuses to see, with the British accents. *Posted Thursday 1st November at 10:45* [Comment . Like]

Madeline Cain Queen of the Night To prove that I am the bigger person in this relationship, I shall graciously accept. *Posted Thursday 1st November at 10:46* [Comment . Like]

Cliff Wheeland Because you haven't been paid yet. *Posted Thursday 1st November at 10:48* [Comment . Like]

Madeline Cain Queen of the Night That in no way factored in my decision. *Posted Thursday 1st November at 10:48* [Comment . Like]

Cliff Wheeland Is now a bad time to mention that you didn't yell, "For Queen and Country," but ,"Mother cupcake! Every man for himself!" Because that's how I remember that scene going down. *Posted Thursday 1st November at 10:49* [Comment . Like]

Kathy Bloomingdale Let me just air out that gonads threat for you, Maddie… *Posted Thursday 1st November at 10:52* [Comment . Like]

Cliff Wheeland But then again, I was a little disorientated. *Posted Thursday 1st November at 10:53* [Comment . Like]

Josh Annelli Annnnnndddd safe! *Posted Thursday 1st November at 10:53* [Comment . Like]

Cain Michaels That's what you get for dissing pumpkin pie and Halloween; Zombies hunting your skinny white girl ass down! *Posted Thursday 1st November at 11:14* [Comment . Like]

Richard Arnoou Who you fooling? You ain't black! *Posted Thursday 1st November at 11:24* [Comment . Like]

Madeline Cain Queen of the Night I'd just eaten a piece of pumpkin pie, they were probably hunting me down *because* of that. Even the undead know there's something funky going on when you add sugar to vegetables. Same thing probably would have happened if I ate carrot cake. *Posted Thursday 1st November at 11:39* [Comment . Like]

Kevin Doherty Babe, how can you *not* like the dummy movie? Or the undead?? Fighting something that can't die, it's like the ultimate adrenaline rush! You wouldn't mind telling me how you get down there would you? It would make the ultimate filming back drop for the latest commercial I've landed. *Posted Thursday 1st November at 12:20* [Comment . Like]

Victoria Zeng Yes, how did you get out? What happened to

Max? Did any zombies get hit in the face by a train on their way out? *Posted Thursday 1st November at 12:30* [Comment . Like]

Madeline Cain Queen of the Night Sorry guys, I don't know where the entrance was, blind folded remember? 'Max' wouldn't let us take the zombie way out, said we'd be the most likely ones to 'blow the cover' of the place. To my knowledge no one was hit in the face by a train, but then again, not sure how I would be able to tell with all the undead walking about. Also, I'm going to go out on a limb here and say horror movies make me want to wet myself. *Posted Thursday 1st November at 12:34* [Comment . Like]

Nadine Cain Oh darling, how deliciously terrifying! At least you only found undead and not real-dead. I have to ask, what is a zombie walk? I remember that fang thing when you were little; you almost gave yourself heat stroke in the middle of summer, all wrapped up like a mummy. You do have the most active imagination. In saying that, I can't believe you let a stranger talk you into following him into a dark train tunnel. Where was your overactive (and sensible) imaginative abilities then? Do we need to have the stranger danger talk again? *Posted Thursday 1st November at 12:51* [Comment . Like]

Kim Enuik Any adventure starting with, 'We are meeting an anonymous urban adventurer,' should probably be rethought. Especially if he blind folds you… *Posted Thursday 1st November at 12:54* [Comment . Like]

Madeline Cain Queen of the Night I'm hoping you're joking about the stranger danger thing. Besides, Cliff was there with a twenty ton flashlight, it would have been fine, with his skin colour Max wouldn't have even seen him coming. I get the feeling Cliff does this a lot. *Posted Thursday 1st November at 12:55* [Comment . Like]

Kim Enuik Does what a lot? Scares people by jumping out of the shadows? *Posted Thursday 1st November at 12:55* [Comment . Like]

Madeline Cain Queen of the Night No, deals with anonymous sources of dubious origins. *Posted Thursday 1st November at 12:56* [Comment . Like]

Nadine Cain I don't believe skin colour is an accurate assessment of defensive capabilities. *Posted Thursday 1st November at 12:56* [Comment . Like]

Madeline Cain Queen of the Night It is if you're the Invisible Man. *Posted Thursday 1st November at 12:57* [Comment . Like]

Nadine Cain Not amused young lady. *Posted Thursday 1st November at 12:58* [Comment . Like]

Madeline Cain Queen of the Night Aw Mum, come on, laugh. I promise all is good, and that Cliff is a black belt. I love you heaps, I'll call on the weekend. *Posted Thursday 1st November at 12:58* [Comment . Like]

Jarrah Annelli Wow! I would love to see this subway station, it sounds amazing! *Posted Thursday 1st November at 13:08* [Comment . Like]

Jade Annelli I totally agree on the whole plausibility-meter thing, zombies and vampires just cannot co-exist. It's too many undeads in the same universe. For a start they're at completely opposite ends of the colour spectrum. Who knows what would happen if they bred? *Posted Thursday 1st November at 13:21* [Comment . Like]

Kathy Bloomingdale I would have taken that over dog whispering any day. *Posted Thursday 1st November at 13:25* [Comment . Like]

Tim Gleeve I wouldn't have, longest laugh-cry I've had in years, that was. *Posted Thursday 1st November at 13:35* [Comment . Like]

Kathy Bloomingdale No one asked you. *Posted Thursday 1st November at 13:42* [Comment . Like]

Tim Gleeve Holy shit! You saw all that artwork?? *Posted Thursday 1st November at 14:18* [Comment . Like]

Madeline Cain Queen of the Night Yep. *Posted Thursday 1st November at 14:24* [Comment . Like]

Tim Gleeve I've been tracking rumours around the internet for months and you just stumble on it by chance!? Oh Lord, why do you hate me so much? Why do you grant this unappreciative woman a look at this hall of hallowed illustration and not Mwah? *Posted Thursday 1st November at 14:26* [Comment . Like]

Madeline Cain Queen of the Night Because you just referred to yourself as 'mwah'. Which is wanky, even to God. For that comment, I'm going to rub it in and say except for the creepy statue thing, it was the most amazing art exhibition I've ever seen. *Posted Thursday 1st November at 14:39* [Comment . Like]

Tim Gleeve Oh cruel world! *Posted Thursday 1st November at 14:39* [Comment . Like]

Mike Cain Max reminds me a lot of me. Except I wouldn't have freaked out over zombies. I'd have given them a round-house kick to the face. In fact, I would have yawned as I did it. Though dressing up like Dracula and scaring kids away for their candy *does* sound like fun. *Posted Thursday 1st November at 14:50* [Comment . Like]

Madeline Cain Queen of the Night Liar. You would have run away screaming and high-fived a wall with your face. Then Mum's unconscious/dead body vision would be fully realised. *Posted Thursday 1st November at 14:53* [Comment . Like]

Mike Cain A small price to pay to watch you freak out because of a statue. *Posted Thursday 1st November at 14:55* [Comment . Like]

Madeline Cain Queen of the Night You and Max are the same soul split in two. *Posted Thursday 1st November at 14:55* [Comment . Like]

Richard Arnoou I'm not sure you tried your hardest on the Dom front. But then again, I probably would have given up the attempt too when I realised I could get him to bump Cain out of the picture. *Posted Thursday 1st November at 15:10* [Comment . Like]

Madeline Cain Queen of the Night Hey man, you weren't in the trenches, you don't know how much pressure it is, day in, day out, under the intense scrutiny of the mob and feds. I'm just small fry, trying to make it in a big fish pond. *Posted Thursday 1st November at 15:20* [Comment . Like]

Kathy Bloomingdale Well that post has Cliff written all over it. *Posted Thursday 1st November at 15:22* [Comment . Like]

Madeline Cain Queen of the Night Stop playing with my account, Cliff! *Posted Thursday 1st November at 15:27* [Comment . Like]

Cliff Wheeland Stop leaving it open for all to hijack, Ms Cain. And stop leaving yourself open for trouble with Dom. Be assertive. *Posted Thursday 1st November at 15:29* [Comment . Like]

Madeline Cain Queen of the Night Since when did you become my conscience? *Posted Thursday 1st November at 15:30* [Comment . Like]

Cliff Wheeland Since it became a possibility that Cain may 'disappear' when Richard hijacks your Facebook feed to order a hit. *Posted Thursday 1st November at 15:32* [Comment . Like]

Richard Arnoou *Grin* Thanks for the idea, Cliff. *Posted Thursday 1st November at 15:32* [Comment . Like]

Madeline Cain Queen of the Night You are now an accessory to murder my friend, not me. *Posted Thursday 1st November at 15:34* [Comment . Like]

Mike Cain likes the pages **TV Sex Scene + Parents In The Room = Awkward** and **New Moon: A Girl's Choice Between Bestiality & Necrophilia.** [Like]

41 Friends posted on your Wall for your birthday. *7th November 2012.*

Kathy Bloomingdale To one of my oldest and dearest friends. I know we're an ocean apart, but I can still see your grey hairs from here. I've sent you hair dye so you can have a merry birthday without barbs about your age. Xo. [Unlike . Comment]

Tim Gleeve Grrrr, Kathy beat me to it, but happy birthday you old geezer. I hope you have a great birthday filled with friends who aren't as awesome as us, but at least give you cake. [Unlike . Comment]

Kim Enuik HAPPY BIRTHDAY. Let there be cake! So much cake! [Unlike . Comment]

38 more comments [View]

Madeline Cain Queen of the Night Thank you Mama for the amazing birthday care package! I've purchased a massive lock for my suitcase so I can hide all the nom-noms away from the reptilian terror.

Tim Tams, Caramello Koalas and Fruit Chocs, I'm in heaven! *Posted Saturday 10th November at 19:00* [Comment . Like]

> **Nadine Cain** Pleasure, darling. Happy Birthday!! We miss you soooooo much! *Posted Saturday 10th November at 21:13* [Comment . Like]

> **Mike Cain** You know what the best part about your birthday was? We still had cake, and only had to share it between three. Boo yeah! *Posted Saturday 10th November at 21:29* [Comment . Like]

Tim Gleeve Spring, you suck. Why can't you go anywhere without that bully, Summer, trailing behind you? *Posted Monday 12th November at 09:24* [Comment . Like]

> **Kathy Bloomingdale** I agree! One should have to dread the approach of Spring. *Posted Monday 12th November at 09:54* [Comment . Like]

> **Madeline Cain Queen of the Night** Are you both vampires? I have an opening… *Posted Monday 12th November at 11:47* [Comment . Like]

> **Tim Gleeve** I am a mushroom. *Posted Monday 12th November at 12:00* [Comment . Like]

Derek Chan God dammit! Forgot to insure my brain against stress/ exam related meltdowns… *Posted Wednesday 14th November at 18:47* [Comment . Like]

> **Madeline Cain Queen of the Night** Mate, you really have to stop leaving it to the last minute. Or get food poisoning and apply for a sup-exam. Or become an IT consultant like Tim. *Posted Wednesday 14th November at 18:54* [Comment . Like]

> **Tim Gleeve** How did I become option two after *food poisoning*?? *Posted Wednesday 14th November at 19:12* [Comment . Like]

Madeline Cain Queen of the Night If you were normal, you wouldn't have to ask that question. *Posted Wednesday 14th November at 19:19* [Comment . Like]

Kathy Bloomingdale Meltdown? I've already contaminated half of Adelaide with my radioactive waste. *Posted Wednesday 14th November at 20:00* [Comment . Like]

Madeline Cain Queen of the Night Um… *Posted Wednesday 14th November at 20:01* [Comment . Like]

Kathy Bloomingdale Alright, that came out wrong. But you know what I mean. Freaking out. Words. Won't. Come. *Posted Wednesday 14th November at 20:16* [Comment . Like]

Madeline Cain Queen of the Night I had a dream last night that I was visiting Iceland. I think the cold may be getting to me. *Posted Saturday 17th November at 10:36* [Comment . Like]

Cliff Wheeland Ah, what you're feeling there is the cold from the Rockefeller ice skating rink that opened several weeks ago. It's calling to you. "Let Cliff take you ice skating…. Let Cliff take you ice skating…" *Posted Saturday 17th November at 11:00* [Comment . Like]

Madeline Cain Queen of the Night I will soon, promise! It's just I have to finalise this submission for the fashion internship, and start organising my contribution for the final year gallery for college. December is coming too soon, I'm freaking out! I still have all the New York Christmassy things to do too. *Posted Saturday 17th November at 11:06* [Comment . Like]

Tim Gleeve likes the pages **When Ash From Pokemon Turns His Hat Around, You Know Shit's Going Down** and **I Wouldn't Steal A Car, But I'd Download One If I Could.** [Like]

You Want To Pay Me HOW Much For Kevin?.....[New Message]

[Back to messages. Mark as unread . Report spam . Delete]

Between **Kathy Bloomingdale, Cliff Wheeland, 3 others** and **You.**

Madeline Cain Decoy 18th November 2012 at 10:00

Normally I'd Facebook Note this sort of madness but this time I could actually get someone into trouble. And I don't want to get her into trouble because she saved our bacon the other night. The other reason I don't want to publically post this is because Kevin has been reading *all* my posts recently and I would prefer not to start an excuses battle with him in full view of everyone. I'm not quite sure what to do about it.

Tim Gleeve 18th November 2012 at 10:01 [Report]

Is this going to be another face-crotch moment? I'm all ears. Where's the rest of the New York cohort?

Cliff Wheeland 18th November 2012 at 10:01 [Report]

Inviting the rest of clan is kind of like inviting the Mad Hatter to your tea party. The last time we all had a conversation it took hours. That was real life, no typing involved. Also, you kind of came out of it feeling a little schizophrenic. Best keep it small.

Madeline Cain Decoy 18th November 2012 at 10:08

There are zero crotches involved! No, this is to do with my little tabloid photography outing, and Kevin, obviously.

To set the scene, I get a call from Jarrah and Jade this week saying they wanted to do some tabloid photography before they started eating dust mites. We'd planned to do it in September but Fashion Week pushed it back further than we anticipated.

Jarrah Annelli 18th November 2012 at 10:09 [Report]

That's funny, my bank balance seems fine to me. But I do recall a certain mobster calling someone to see if she needed a little 'help' with anything and she dropped a hint about requiring tabloid tip offs. To which he had apparently replied, 'I'll get my boys onto it'.

Jade Annelli 18th November 2012 at 10:11 [Report]

Indeed. Would you be aware of this, dear Madeline? Even after said person said she was 'done' getting into situations with potential mobsters?

Madeline Cain Decoy 18th November 2012 at 10:12

Alright! I was getting to it. Don't I get some artistic license? So I haven't cut myself off completely from Dom yet. But the FBI need me, to help them track his movements.

Cliff Wheeland 18th November 2012 at 10:12 [Report]

Sure they need you. As bait. You're smart enough not to play their game. I can't believe you gave Dom your number.

Madeline Cain Decoy 18th November 2012 at 10:13

I didn't give it to him, he got it from Giovanni's employee files.

Kathy Bloomingdale 18th November 2012 at 10:13 [Report]

You don't find that creepy?

Madeline Cain Decoy 18th November 2012 at 10:15

Of course I find it creepy, but the FBI are right outside my door, why worry? I just *happened* to mention the next photographic experiment I wanted to do. He made the leap to helping me all on his own.

Kathy Bloomingdale 18th November 2012 at 10:15 [Report]

That still doesn't count as distancing yourself.

Madeline Cain Decoy 18th November 2012 at 10:17

Look, it doesn't matter how it happened. Geez. If I'd known you'd be such sticklers for chronology I wouldn't have added you to the conversation. However it happened, in whatever order, the long and short of it was I was given a lead, and like the tabloid photographer I was pretending to be, I took it.

Jade Annelli 18th November 2012 at 10:19 [Report]

The tip Dom gave us was a doozy.

Jarrah Annelli 18th November 2012 at 10:19 [Report]

We should have known things were going to get weird when Maddie dropped the name.

Madeline Cain Decoy 18th November 2012 at 10:20

Kyle Langhorn. She was going to be at the W New York – Times Square, a particularly swanky hotel in, you guessed it, Times Square. Actress, goddess, and recluse, she is rarely found in public and is a privacy nut. She goes Michael Jackson crazy and walks around with full face veils not to be noticed. So snapping a photo of her is a big scoop for a tabloid photographer. Her partner is from here and New York seemed to be the only place, other than red carpet events, that anyone could snap a photo.

Jade Annelli 18th November 2012 at 10:21 [Report]

Regular paparazzi are obvious with their massive cameras but we have a different style that spoils no-one's day and gets us the photos we need. We can get up close without anyone throwing a punch at us.

Jarrah Annelli 18th November 2012 at 10:21 [Report]

We're girls, we don't like to get physical.

Cliff Wheeland 18th November 2012 at 10:21 [Report]

For those of you who were unaware, Jade and Jarrah have a series of spy cameras crafted to look like accessories, with remote shutter buttons on large, fake rings. It's very Maxwell Smart. Those poor New York celebrities need to learn to doubt a pretty face.

Jarrah Annelli 18th November 2012 at 10:22 [Report]

So sweet of you to say.

Madeline Cain Decoy 18th November 2012 at 10:22

So we don a combination of spy-camera brooches, handbags, hats and sparkly forehead headbands. Then we practised using said equipment so we would get the framing right when it came time to get the money shots.

Jarrah Annelli 18th November 2012 at 10:23 [Report]

Truth is, we looked classy and the cameras work!

Jade Annelli 18th November 2012 at 10:23 [Report]

When you weren't cutting off people's heads.

Madeline Cain Decoy 18th November 2012 at 10:24 [Report]

I felt part mysterious and part like I had a neon sign on my head that flashed 'Paparazzi!' Anyway, we arrive at the hotel which has various bars, lounges and restaurants dressed up like Christmas decorations, all glitter and primary colours. Deciding we'd be less conspicuous wandering alone 'looking for our friends', we split up.

Jade Anneli 18th November 2012 at 10:25 [Report]

I take offense to the fact you put 'friends' in inverted commas.

Jarrah Anneli 18th November 2012 at 10:25 [Report]

Tabloid 101, a single pretty girl is helpless, a group is a nuisance. Also, the sooner we found Ms Langhorn, the sooner we could set up near her, cocktails in hand, for a night long stake out of awesome.

Madeline Cain Decoy 18th November 2012 at 10:25

Not quite sure how hours of watching someone else eat and party is considered awesome, but ok. So we split, with strict instructions to Jade not to fan girl out and scare off our quarry.

Kathy Bloomingdale 18th November 2012 at 10:26 [Report]

Just be thankful Tim wasn't there, or else you may have had a security team escort him out as a suspected stalker.

Tim Gleeve 18th November 2012 at 10:27 [Report]

If you've got one chance to waylay science fiction's hottest babe, you take it without shame.

Madeline Cain Decoy 18th November 2012 at 10:38

Sorry to disappoint, but she's lacking in electrified toaster components... We split between the restaurant, bar and exercise area, dotted across various hotel floors. I got the public bar near the lobby, a sleek black, red and white cocktail area with wide lounges, low tables and plenty of atmosphere. I was wondering for a moment if I was forever doomed to lurk in rooms that look like the inside of a tomato when I spotted Kyle perched by the bar.

Her blond hair was curled up neatly in a high bun, glittering, chandelier style earrings hung from her lobes, and a body hugging white dress stopped mid-thigh and ended in golden cuffs near the wrists. She was stunning and being chatted up by a geek who looked very much like Tim: tall, gangly, bespectacled and ill at ease with society but swallowing all that to add a harassment charge to his name.

I got photos of the whole pantomime, from my 'vintage' camera broche. Him suddenly lurching forward to kiss her, her turning her check at the last second, her foot jerking upwards as she over balanced on her stool and flicked him square in the groin and finally security dragging the hunched over fan out the door.

Not sure what headline would go with that, though I'm thinking something along the lines of, 'Why Kyle *really* doesn't go out in public', 'Fan attacks actress', 'Haughty actress snubs fan', or, 'Actress attacks fan for kiss'. Either way, it didn't matter to me, as long as the photos came out clear and the magazines gave us enough cash to be able to live in our own 5th Avenue mansion.

Taking longer than expected, I hurried back to our meeting place in the foyer. But when I arrived the only one who was there was Jade, her shimmering red hair shifting to and fro as she bounced on the balls of her feet. I flashed her a massive grin which she returned with an overenthusiastic wave.

"Get ready to hug me!" we both said. Then, in unison, "Why? Who'd you see?"

I help up my hand to stop the ridiculous repeat-a-thon. "Alright, enough of this. We're not children."

"Sorry. You go first."

"I found her! She kicked a guy in the nuts in the bar. Not on purpose, but you can't tell that from the photos. The 'loids will love it!"

I trailed off as Jade shook her head. "'Fraid that wasn't her, Maddie. She was most definitely at the restaurant, a little too 'happy' on the red wine if you get my meaning. She kept standing to hug the waiters for giving her food. I got super close, it was definitely her—"

"I found her!" shouted a happy Jarrah as she bounded towards us.

"I think not. *I* found her," replied Jade.

Jarrah cocked her head to the side. "That's odd. Because I've got a whole string of photos proving *I* found her, on the phone in the gym looking like she'd gotten some *very* bad news."

"If she was there then how could she have been in the super swish restaurant undressing the waiters with her eyes?"

The girls glared at each other. "It wasn't her!"

Jade Annelli 18th November 2012 at 10:39 [Report]

It was a glaring party, but we weren't the only ones giving evil eyes.

Jarrah Annelli 18th November 2012 at 10:39 [Report]

When Maddie insisted she found her I thought we'd have to abandon the building to find a computer.

Tim Gleeve 18th November 2012 at 10:40 [Report]

Ah, you needed an expert like me to pick the true Kyle Langhorn. Did you fight? Please tell me security had to pull you apart.

Kathy Bloomingdale 18th November 2012 at 10:41 [Report]

Don't pull them into your bizarre fantasies, Tim. They're women with brains, not porn machines.

Jade Annelli 18th November 2012 at 10:39 [Report]

One hundred points for Kathy. No, we did what every woman does when faced with women who are hotter than them. We compared what each one was wearing.

Jarrah Annelli 18th November 2012 at 10:41 [Report]

All wearing exactly the same clothing as Maddie's Kyle. Even the one in the gym. Bizarre.

Cliff Wheeland 18th November 2012 at 10:42 [Report]

Unless she had a transporter, or a time machine, or was somehow a very cleaver magician, there was no way each of you could have spent fifteen minutes watching the same person.

Madeline Cain Decoy 18th November 2012 at 10:43

Exactly! Something was missing. We were a pineapple short of a fruit salad, a joker short of a full deck, a lead singer short of a band. Until the wonderful amazing Natalie West showed up.

Kathy Bloomingdale 18th November 2012 at 10:44 [Report]

Isn't she the wedding photographer? The little one with the beehive hair-do?

Jade Annelli 18th November 2012 at 10:44 [Report]

She's cool, the most enthusiastic photographer I've ever met. Ever.

Jarrah Annelli 18th November 2012 at 10:44 [Report]

She leaves and you kind of feel like you've face planted into the top tier of a wedding cake and thrown the rest at the bride and groom.

Tim Gleeve 18th November 2012 at 10:45 [Report]

If I remember rightly, you were stupidly excited because she wanted to buy one of your photos, cash under the table.

Madeline Cain Decoy 18th November 2012 at 10:45

Yes to all. Except maybe the cake thing, not sure what's going on there, Jarrah, but I'm staying away from your wedding…

Jade Annelli 18th November 2012 at 10:48 [Report]

Wait! Let me get the next part!

So, Ms West practically squeals, "Madeline? How delightful to see you! Why are you here? How's Jason? I saw those amazing chameleon photographs you did for the fashion festival, very cheeky!"

She was like a steam roller, not letting anyone respond before the next question popped out. She swooped in to kiss Maddie on both cheeks while expertly managing not to crush the two cameras hanging from her own neck.

Jarrah Annelli 18th November 2012 at 10:49 [Report]

I'm surprised she didn't keel over, those cameras were massive! And she's so tiny! She must have invisible muscles. Maybe she drinks Gummy Berry Juice?

Jade Annelli 18th November 2012 at 10:50 [Report]

You know you can't stop Maddie from telling a story, even when we could lose our photographic subject at any moment. I wanted to gag her as she started gushing about her photographer experiments and the tabloid photography we were 'attempting'.

Jarrah Annelli 18th November 2012 at 10:52 [Report]

Thank God you didn't! If Maddie hadn't blabbed we wouldn't have gotten the *real* story.

Maddie's all like, "This has been the weirdest one yet because we found her, but in three different places at the same time. I feel like I'm taking crazy pills."

"Oh no! You're not going crazy." Natalie laughed.

Jade Annelli 18th November 2012 at 10:52 [Report]

No, she whooped! And slapping her thigh like it was a ho-down. She was definitely a country girl once.

Madeline Cain Decoy 18th November 2012 at 10:53

Hey now, no poking fun. She saved us!

Tim Gleeve 18th November 2012 at 10:53 [Report]

For Christ sake this isn't a segment of This Is Your Life. Get on with it before I beat you with a cucumber!

Madeline Cain Decoy 18th November 2012 at 10:57

Hope that's not a euphemism for something. Right, fine.

Catching her breath she said, "Heck, there are probably more than three, there are probably ten of them around here."

"Don't tell us we-"

"Stumbled on a look-a-like competition!" said the girls.

"Ain't no magazine gonna pay for photos of impersonators."

"No, no!" Natalie waved her hands in a 'calm down' gesture. "They're decoys! To throw people off the scent!"

Jarrah cocked her head to the side. "How do you know that? Are you on a job here? Is there a wedding?"

Tim Gleeve 18th November 2012 at 10:58 [Report]

Seeing through the smoke screen to the lingerie, I like it. Maybe Kathy's Mum should recruit *you* as the family psycho.

Kathy Bloomingdale 18th November 2012 at 10:58 [Report]

Psychiatrist, Tim. Psycho's are Alfred Hitchcock wannabes.

Madeline Cain Decoy 18th November 2012 at 11:01

A-herm!

Natalie's eyes widened and she put a clichéd hand across her mouth. "Oh dear, I've said too…" Then her gaze fell on me. She tapped a finger against her chin. "Where are *your* cameras?"

"Hidden," chimed Jarrah and Jade. The girls pointed to their hats and hairbands, and I pointed to my broche and bag.

"I think we can work something out," she said slowly. "I'll help you out, but first, you have to promise to help me out of a pickle."

Cliff Wheeland 18th November 2012 at 11:01 [Report]

She really said 'pickle'?

Madeline Cain Decoy 18th November 2012 at 11:06

Yep. Like I said, she's a bundle full of energy and sweetness.

"What sort of pickle?" I said.

Jarrah muttered, "I bet you it's a wedding."

Natalie spread her hands. "I'm flat out, I can't cover every wedding I've been offered this year. I've had to hire contractors to shoot for me. There is one wedding that is so big it requires two photographers and one of my contractors has bowed out. I need someone to fill the space. Your portrait at the show tells me you have a great eye for framing love. Not everyone does. If you're really serious about trying every type of photography…"

She wiggled her eyebrows. "You'll also get paid."

Tim Gleeve 18th November 2012 at 11:07 [Report]

Are you serious? An eye for framing love? How difficult is that? You just point at people kissing or holding hands and hey presto, you've got a photo for the album. Heck, Kathy could have filled in for her.

Madeline Cain Decoy 18th November 2012 at 11:07

Wow Tim, it's so nice to know you hold what I do in such high regard. Saved the world from your laptop yet?

Jade Annelli 18th November 2012 at 11:08 [Report]

What I want to know is what you were thinking about while you stood there for a minute biting your lip. Hell, you said yes to learning from *Cain* and we warned you about the crazies he photographs. Doing a wedding should have been a shotgun decision for you.

Madeline Cain Decoy 18th November 2012 at 11:10

If you must know, I was thinking about the looks of disgust on my idols as they talked about avoiding wedding photography like avoiding acne. People look down on a wedding photographer like they're some poor loner stuck in wedding-land because they can't find a boyfriend. The whole conversation put me off the idea of doing it. Who wants to be considered the single celled organism of photographers? I've had enough of that with pizza delivery.

Anyway, I realised that I was being silly and I wasn't committing to anything (wedding pun!) by trying it.

Jarrah Annelli 18th November 2012 at 11:12 [Report]

It disturbs me that the more immediate I-need-you-to-do-this-thing-otherwise-I'm-not-going-to-tell-you-where-the-real-actress-is, didn't factor in your thinking. None of us were getting paid if you didn't agree. Frankly, I was going to pimp you out if you said anything other than, 'yes'.

Kathy Bloomingdale 18th November 2012 at 11:12 [Report]

Maddie, it's not like you to care what anyone else thinks.

Madeline Cain Decoy 18th November 2012 at 11:14

That was before a kid tried to pay me for pizza in marshmallows and the parents were all like, 'You too good for marshmallows?' To which I replied, 'Marshmallows are not a valid currency and just because I'm delivering pizza does not mean I'm a fry short of a Happy Meal.' When all sugarcane on the planet has mysteriously disappeared leaving only processed sugars, then and only then, would I accept marshmallows as payment.

So yes, being looked down on with scorn worried me, particularly because I want *nothing* to ruin my chances of getting that fashion photography internship. I don't know what you're complaining about. I said yes, didn't I? Who cares *how* I got there.

Tim Gleeve 18th November 2012 at 11:14 [Report]

Touché...

Madeline Cain Decoy 18th November 2012 at 11:17

On with the story.

Natalie shrieked and clapped her hands. "Madeline you're the best! Thank you!" She gave me an enthusiastic hug around the middle (yes, she really is *that* short) and then stepped back to view us with a critical eye. "Are you certain no one can tell those are cameras? It can't get out that I passed on the location of my client's wedding to paparazzi."

"Knew it!" said Jarrah.

Jade gave a flippant wave. "Don't you worry. We've perfected the art. What turns celebs into cell phone throwing paparazzi killers is when they *know* you're pap. They get nervous. If you just look like normal people who've stumbled on them in the street then everyone's happy. We don't ruin their special time and we get photos we can use. Watch."

The girls sashayed to the end of the lobby and turned. They walked back towards us giggling, smiling and making eye contact, turning their heads as they passed and whispering before finally walking backwards and high-fiving.

On their return Jarrah said, "We now have about a hundred photos of you."

Jade Annelli 18th November 2012 at 11:18 [Report]

She was impressed.

Jarrah Annelli 18th November 2012 at 11:18 [Report]

As she should be.

Madeline Cain Decoy 18th November 2012 at 11:19

Whereas I was flipping out like a miniature Poodle on Redbull. There's no way I'm as graceful or as natural as you two.

Jade Annelli 18th November 2012 at 11:20 [Report]

Your stunned mullet look was amazing, it made us look like we'd just stumbled on the wedding by accident rather than design.

Cliff Wheeland 18th November 2012 at 11:20 [Report]

So I take it Natalie felt it safe to tell you what hall you should be in and at what time?

Tim Gleeve 18th November 2012 at 11:22 [Report]

Did she also tell you in which direction you should walk and how you should walk and if you should call her Your Highness? I can't believe you girls let a pint-sized Barbie out manoeuvre you. She wasn't ruthless enough, I would have contracted you all into wedding servitude before

I released the location of Manhattan's best kept secret wedding. Would have paid you in marshmallows too. Perhaps the world's best kept secret wedding, because I didn't even know she was *engaged!!* Frankly, the world is now dead to me. Women are now dead to me.

Kathy Bloomingdale 18th November 2012 at 11:23 [Report]

I'm pretty sure toasters and butterflies already guaranteed that.

Madeline Cain Decoy 18th November 2012 at 11:25

It was more secret spy then that, Cliff. We had a whole system worked out, she had my phone number dialled up and ready to go in her pocket. All she had to do was hit the send button when they were on their way out the door after the ceremony. That way we wouldn't be suspiciously loitering in the hallway outside. It was very cloak and dagger. We may have even assigned ourselves code names...

Jade Annelli 18th November 2012 at 11:27 [Report]

It was perfect, *she* was perfect in a lace layer cake dress with that bald banker next to her. Put in a line-up I'd select Tim over him but I guess money talks. We were in the hallway, the guests were in the hallway (only *ten* of them, can you believe?! When I get married I'll have at least three hundred)...

Jarrah Annelli 18th November 2012 at 11:27 [Report]

They lingered, kissing and showing off their rings and hugging.

Jade Annelli 18th November 2012 at 11:28 [Report]

We slowly made our way through, keeping our promise to Natalie to look like lucky hotel guests that just happened to be there.

Jarrah Annelli 18th November 2012 at 11:28 [Report]

Well, except Maddie, who looked like she was a zombie. I think the effort of being 'inconspicuous' got to her.

Cliff Wheeland 18th November 2012 at 11:29 [Report]

So when you saw the real thing did the decoys *really* look like her?

Jade Annelli 18th November 2012 at 11:30 [Report]

Like they'd been cloned in a parallel universe. Surely I'd have heard if she was an identical quintuplet right? It was over so quick I had to step on the urge to go looking for her decoys.

Madeline Cain Decoy 18th November 2012 at 11:31

It was intense. Natalie winked at us and that was it, in five minutes we had just taken the tabloid photographs of the year. Or so I thought.

Jade Annelli 18th November 2012 at 11:31 [Report]

Who knew wedding photographers were such good sources! That makes them good eggs in my book.

Jarrah Annelli 18th November 2012 at 11:32 [Report]

Indeed, we got to the editor and knocked off in plenty of time to prepare for our double date with Fred.

Jade Annelli 18th November 2012 at 11:32 [Report]

Oooh, I liked Fred, he saw straight through us. That's never happened before.

Madeline Cain Decoy 18th November 2012 at 11:34

Ok ladies, back to the conundrum at hand.

So you'd think amazing photos of not only the wedding but the elaborate deception would have been the end of the craziness for the night but no. Not even close. Because who do we see as we walk down the street towards Jarrah and Jade's tabloid office of choice, but Kevin. In a restaurant. With a mystery blond with the legs of a giraffe and cleavage with its own gravity well. I would have completely missed them but for the eagle eyes of Jarrah. And thus begins the game of – What Is Kevin Up To?

Tim Gleeve 18th November 2012 at 11:34 [Report]

With your host, Jarrah Annelli!

Jarrah Annelli 18th November 2012 at 11:35 [Report]

Thank you! Just call me Eagle-eyed Jarrah.

Cliff Wheeland 18th November 2012 at 11:36 [Report]

Did you just say you saw Kevin having dinner with another woman? That's it, I'm going to become one of those cliché crime writers who actually goes into a rage and kills someone.

Jade Annelli 18th November 2012 at 11:36 [Report]

Ah but wait! There's more! It gets better…

Madeline Cain Decoy 18th November 2012 at 11:38

I don't know about better, but crazier, yes. I paparazzi the shit out of him, the private detective of my own case. I was going to shove the evidence in the face of that Southern Drawling Game Show Wannabe. He was going to tell me what the puck was going on or I was going to spray tan him, tie him down and release a chameleon.

Jarrah Annelli 18th November 2012 at 11:39 [Report]

She was taking the same shots over and over but getting slightly more aggressive with each push on her shutter button ring.

Jade Annelli 18th November 2012 at 11:40 [Report]

Those cameras are *not* cheap, we couldn't have you breaking them.

Jarrah Annelli 18th November 2012 at 11:40 [Report]

So we mobbed her.

Tim Gleeve 18th November 2012 at 11:42 [Report]

You know, Maddie, men do have friendships with another gender we like to call 'women'. If there is no hand holding, kissing or drinking alcoholic shots off each other's abdomen, then surprisingly enough, it's fine. You don't see Kevin having a cow when you and Cliff do one of your Broadway evenings. Sure, take a photo or two and later be all, 'One of my friends was paparazzi-ing and took this, what's going on?' But don't go all psycho rabies girl on him and assume that just because he's good looking he's also a cheater.

Kathy Bloomingdale 18th November 2012 at 11:43 [Report]

Wow. That is the most sensible advice to ever come from your brain.

Tim Gleeve 18th November 2012 at 11:44 [Report]

Girls, when they get together and mix hormones they jump to conclusions. Someone's got to inject a bit of testosterone and common sense into this conversation. Have you spoken to him?

Madeline Cain Decoy 18th November 2012 at 11:44

Yes...

Tim Gleeve 18th November 2012 at 11:44 [Report]

I was right, wasn't I?

Madeline Cain Decoy 18th November 2012 at 11:45

That he wasn't cheating? Apparently.

Cliff Wheeland 18th November 2012 at 11:45 [Report]

You went up to him while he was having dinner, didn't you? Atta girl!

Madeline Cain Decoy 18th November 2012 at 11:46

Maybe...

Tim Gleeve 18th November 2012 at 11:46 [Report]

So even when you were mobbed by two women you still managed to slip out and march to the table. The FBI shouldn't be following you, they should be hiring you. What happened?

Jarrah Annelli 18th November 2012 at 11:47 [Report]

Thankfully she didn't start with, 'You arsehole', which was always a possibility, and went for the more traditional, "Keeeevvvvviiinnnnn, fancy seeing you here.'

Madeline Cain Decoy 18th November 2012 at 11:48

After his initial surprise (which, yes, I had initially determined it to be *guilt*) he introduced the woman as a Hollywood Producer and me as his girlfriend. Then he described me as his Muse and asked if I'd join them in two hours after they'd had a 'very important' meeting.

Jade Annelli 18th November 2012 at 11:49 [Report]

An invitation which we helped her politely decline.

Madeline Cain Decoy 18th November 2012 at 11:50

You can't deny he was up to something. He only gets the look of puppy-dog excitement when something big is happening or he's got an amazing idea he has to get down before he poops his pants. If you'd just let me weasel my way into the meeting I would know. You would know.

Tim Gleeve 18th November 2012 at 11:52 [Report]

The only thing you were going to weasel your way into was a pissed off boyfriend. If he's in a business meeting then why bother pestering him about it? He'll probably bore you with new nightmare game show combinations.

Madeline Cain Decoy 18th November 2012 at 11:54

Because he won't tell me!! "Nothing's set in stone yet babe, I don't want to jinx it. I'm super superstitious. I don't want you to get excited over nothing." Gah! If she's pitching him as the next Bachelor, she's going to find her boobs up near her ears!

Jarrah Annelli 18th November 2012 at 11:55 [Report]

I had no idea he'd gotten so popular.

Jade Annelli 18th November 2012 at 11:56 [Report]

No kidding, the editor went bananas over those photos. Trying to stop Maddie going bananas in return was an intense exercise in mind control though.

Tim Gleeve 18th November 2012 at 11:57 [Report]

Hold on, why did you show Maddie's jealous boyfriend-fake-cheating-evidence to the editor? Seems unprofessional and slightly obsessive. I thought I was the obsessive one in our little threesome.

Madeline Cain Decoy 18th November 2012 at 11:57

Tim, never refer to us as a threesome again. It wasn't on purpose. I wasn't foaming at the mouth for boyfriend revenge.

Jade Annelli 18th November 2012 at 11:58 [Report]

We went straight to the editor with the wedding shots (she works *very* late). We just loaded the SD cards onto the computer without thinking. She starts clicking through when suddenly she stops and says, "Is that Kevin Doherty?"

Jarrah Annelli 18th November 2012 at 12:00 [Report]

She was almost shaking with pent up joy. "Doesn't he have a girlfriend? Is that her?"

Maddie snaps, "No, it's not."

But before she can start proclaiming her level of attachment to Kevin – which, trust me Mad, in your rage voice would have sounded like you were a stalker – I jumped in with, "She's a mystery blond."

I'm concerned about your bank balance, even if you aren't. But it turns out she didn't need to be talked into buying the picture. In fact, she paid double.

Tim Gleeve 18th November 2012 at 12:01 [Report]

Double what? Demerit points? Double Ds? Double the amount of ice-cream cones?

Madeline Cain Decoy 18th November 2012 at 12:02

Double the money she offered for the wedding and decoy shots. For ONE PHOTO OF KEVIN! What the hell is going on??

Cliff Wheeland 18th November 2012 at 12:02 [Report]

His show is a hit.

Madeline Cain Decoy 18th November 2012 at 12:03

But how? You all saw the first couple of episodes. They were terrible, he was ridiculed. Then he started using inspiration from my life and they were just as terrible and embarrassing.

Tim Gleeve 18th November 2012 at 12:04 [Report]

For you maybe, but to the rest of humanity, it was hilarious.

Jade Annelli 18th November 2012 at 12:05 [Report]

Wish I'd taken a couple of shots of Kevin, potentially when Maddie stormed over to the table, maybe I'd have gotten triple.

Cliff Wheeland 18th November 2012 at 12:06 [Report]

Tabloids have weird ideas on fame, people like Kevin whisk the lime light away not necessarily because they are a high brow celeb, but because they are a viral sensation.

Madeline Cain Decoy 18th November 2012 at 12:06

Is it weird? That he got so famous without me noticing? Am I a bad girlfriend?

Tim Gleeve 18th November 2012 at 12:07 [Report]

Yes. But at the same time it's weird that he used your life to make him famous. Why didn't I jump on that train when I had the chance?

Kathy Bloomingdale 18th November 2012 at 12:09 [Report]

We never realised she had marketable potential. I mean, you've always been a klutz, but it's only since you entered the melting pot of New York that you've become Muse real estate. I'm as surprised as you. I've watched all Kevin's episodes and had no idea he was this popular either. Though it's no wonder Tim knows, he lives on the forum boards.

Tim Gleeve 18th November 2012 at 12:11 [Report]

I sure do. Kevin entered meme territory months ago, once you crack that, viral fame is made. I say, if he's making money off you, you should be able to make money off him. You could finally have a steady income. He need never know…

Madeline Cain Decoy 18th November 2012 at 12:15

I took the money, but I'm leaving the tabloid photography to the girls.

I don't know how they can stand spending nights working a job for unknown sums only to be piped at the post by an amateur taking photos of her boyfriend. Without my Kevin photos who knows how much more we'd have gotten for those wedding shots. Next week Kevin's name could be dirt and I'd have to hide in the bushes trying to nab photos of Hugh Jackman. No thanks. Celebrities have big enough heads without me adding to the hype.

Tim Gleeve 18th November 2012 at 12:16 [Report]

Besides, what if celebs start turning to decoys as a trick of the trade? What if clone technology becomes available? You could spend your life running after clone-a-likes.

Madeline Cain Decoy 18th November 2012 at 12:18

Somehow, not as worried about that as Kevin's secret meeting. Soz. Well Tim, as always, it's been an unhelpful conversation.

Jade Annelli 18th November 2012 at 12:19 [Report]

But a satisfying one for me! I was hoping I'd get embroiled in one of your adventures.

Tim Gleeve 18th November 2012 at 12:19 [Report]

I made Jade pinky swear to share it with me if she did.

Madeline Cain Decoy 18th November 2012 at 12:21

You two still pinky swear? What next? Are you going to braid each other's back hair? Wait, how have you guys become chummy enough to pinky swear?

Jade Annelli 18th November 2012 at 12:21 [Report]

Online gaming.

Tim Gleeve 18th November 2012 at 12:22 [Report]

This woman is a kick arse warrior in WOW.

Well, thanks guys, you're the worst jealousy creators a guy could ever wish for. Not that this farce hasn't been a blast, but it's time for a little Tim Time. Peace out.

Tim Gleeve has left the conversation.

Madeline Cain Decoy 18th November 2012 at 12:23

Why are we friends with him?

Jade Annelli 18th November 2012 at 12:25 [Report]

He's like malaria, he gets into your blood stream and never leaves. Got to dash. I wouldn't worry about this Kevin thing. He's the worst at keeping secrets. It will come out soon.

Jarrah Annelli 18th November 2012 at 12:26 [Report]

Whether he wants it to or not. A couple of paparazzi photos always brings the publicity statements out sooner. See you in class!

Jade Annelli has left the conversation.

Jarrah Annelli had left the conversation.

Kathy Bloomingdale 18th November 2012 at 12:27 [Report]

If you'd kept in touch a little more you wouldn't have been surprised about Kevin. Tim would have told you. He's a good egg like that.

Madeline Cain Decoy 18th November 2012 at 12:28

Yeah, I miss the egg head. But don't tell him, he has enough of a God complex as it is.

Cliff Wheeland 18th November 2012 at 12:28 [Report]

I'll see what I can get out of Kevin when I see him next. Will let you know.

Madeline Cain Decoy 18th November 2012 at 12:29

Thanks. Don't punch him just yet. I want to give him a chance to explain himself.

Cliff Wheeland 18th November 2012 at 12:29 [Report]

Will see what I can do ?

Jack Fox liked the page **Terrorists Have Two Eyes, Pandas Have Two Eyes. Coincidence? I Think Not.**

Diane Lynal The best way to find out if you can trust someone… is to trust them. *Posted Monday 19th November at 09:17* [Comment . Like]

> **Tim Gleeve** It's certainly the quickest, also, the most dangerous. The police would advise you to get to know someone first and potentially text your friends with their license plate number… *Posted Monday 19th November at 09:51* [Comment . Like]
>
> **Diana Lynal** With your heart, Tim! I'm trying to learn to love again, you're not helping. *Posted Monday 19th November at 09:55* [Comment . Like]
>
> **Tim Gleeve** If you believe helping is agreeing to an overgeneralise piece of advice, then by all means, I agree. Go get 'em! *Posted Monday 19th November at 09:58* [Comment . Like]

Adam Goldbloom has invited you to use **Farmville.** [Join . Comment]

> **Madeline Cain Decoy** Mate, you need to find a better hobby. *Posted Monday 19th November at 16:24* [Comment . Like]

> **Tim Gleeve** Or a girlfriend. *Posted Monday 19th November at 16:52* [Comment . Like]

Harry Lee More power to your elbow, I say. *Posted Tuesday 20th November at 11:40* [Comment . Like]

> **Tim Gleeve** Is that a tennis term, or a euphemism for something? *Posted Tuesday 20th November at 11:46* [Comment . Like]

> **Harry Lee** I'm going to be annoying and assume your question is rhetorical. *Posted Tuesday 20th November at 11:51* [Comment . Like]

Madeline Cain Decoy Apparently it's shirts-off-Friday on my apartment floor today. Love it when the boyfriend plus newly buff neighbours casually pretend to chat while really showing off their guns to each other. That's it boys, air your differences… *Posted Tuesday 20th November at 20:15* [Comment . Like]

> **Cliff Wheeland** I'll have you know I was working on getting information. It's a known fact that men let their guard down when they feel they're in a locker room setting. If you hadn't distracted Kevin by appearing and answering all his dog whispering/zombie questions I would've had something! Have you been avoiding him? Sounds like he's been starved of his Muse… Soooooo, you think I'm buff? *Posted Tuesday 20th November at 20:24* [Comment . Like]

> **Madeline Cain Decoy** Of course I haven't been avoiding him; I've just been changing the subject every time my misadventures

come up. I put them on Facebook and am done talking about them, you know? Don't get cocky, there were six of you on the landing, you all had your shirts off, you were all showing muscle. It worries me you actively try to get men off their guard by taking off clothes around them. Hang around locker rooms shirtless often, do you? Like it? Wanna try a little pants-off-Friday in the locker room too? Hope that's not what you're wearing to the musical tonight. *Posted Tuesday 20th November at 20:35* [Comment . Like]

Cliff Wheeland I reject your insinuations and instead berate you for ogling men other than your boyfriend and then taking one (*other* than your boyfriend) out on the town. *Posted Tuesday 20th November at 20:38* [Comment . Like]

Madeline Cain Decoy When the choice is between watching yet *another* movie on grid iron, or going to a musical I've been dying to see for months, there is no contest. I'll pick the neighbour who gets shirtless for my cause, any time. *Posted Tuesday 20th November at 20:43* [Comment . Like]

Kathy Bloomingdale Just accidentally greeted a young boy and his Mum with, "Hello ladies." Then I caught him dancing at himself in the mirror. You go gurl. *Posted Wednesday 21st November at 12:00* [Comment . Like]

Madeline Cain Decoy Sure that wasn't a Back To The Future visit by Tim's twelve-year-old self? *Posted Wednesday 21st November at 12:10* [Comment . Like]

Tim Gleeve If it was, and I'm not confirming or denying anything, the boy would have clearly been practising his Superman arms, not dancing. *Posted Wednesday 21st November at 12:14* [Comment . Like]

Kathy Bloomingdale Shame, men who can dance turn me on.

Take Hugh Jackman for example *swoon*. *Posted Wednesday 21st November at 12:16* [Comment . Like]

Tim Gleeve On the other hand... *Posted Wednesday 21st November at 12:18* [Comment . Like]

Madeline Cain Decoy Eeew, get a private message! *Posted Wednesday 21st November at 12:20* [Comment . Like]

Kyle Traybna Dear Mr Fish, thanks for being my friend while I'm home alone, even though you stink. *Posted Wednesday 21st November at 13:36* [Comment . Like]

Mike Cain Me fail English? That's unpossible. *Posted Wednesday 21st November at 13:41* [Comment . Like]

Cliff Wheeland You need to take that back before it makes it into the Oxford Dictionary. Take it back NOW! *Posted Wednesday 21st November at 13:52* [Comment . Like]

Mike Cain Soz bro, that's the haps these daze. *Posted Wednesday 21st November at 13:53* [Comment . Like]

Madeline Cain Decoy I think I just heard Cliff's head explode. Did you fail English? *Posted Wednesday 21st November at 13:56* [Comment . Like]

Mike Cain No, just rubbing people the wrong way. It's research for my English assignment ? *Posted Wednesday 21st November at 13:57* [Comment . Like]

Madeline Cain Decoy Oh paycheck, why you no stay in bank? *Posted Wednesday 21st November at 15:14* [Comment . Like]

Kevin Doherty -> Madeline Cain Decoy Hey babe, it's been a while since we've been on a date and I have a perfect excuse for one, a celebration! Pick you up at eight? *Posted Thursday 22nd November at 17:31* [Comment . Like]

Madeline Cain Decoy I'm always up for a celebration (you know you don't need an excuse to schedule a date, right?). See you soon ? *Posted Thursday 22nd November at 17:44* [Comment . Like]

Showdown.....[New Message]

[Back to messages. Mark as unread . Report spam . Delete]

Between **Kathy Bloomingdale** and **You.**

Madeline Cain ? 22nd November 2012 at 22:48

I can't believe I just did that. More to the point, how could *he* do that?? How did I not see it coming??

Kathy Bloomingdale 22nd November 2012 at 22:52 [Report]

He? He who? See what?

Madeline Cain ? 22nd November 2012 at 22:53

Kevin. I just broke up with him.

Kathy Bloomingdale 22nd November 2012 at 22:53 [Report]

What?! Why? Is this to do with that Hollywood woman? Are you ok??

Madeline Cain ? 22nd November 2012 at 22:54

It's just, I'm feeling so *bizarre.* It's like a giant kick in the pants has woke me up from a stupor. I didn't even realise how I felt until he told me we were moving to LA and then he chose this *thing* over me...

Kathy Bloomingdale 22nd November 2012 at 22:55 [Report]

Honey, you're not making any sense. First you said you broke up and now you say you're moving to LA? Is there a beginning to the story? Can you start there maybe?

Madeline Cain ? 22nd November 2012 at 22:59

Shit yeah there's a beginning! When he had dinner with that long-legged tramp and she offered him his own bloody show in LA! I told you guys something was going on.

Then, on our date he decided to break it to me by saying, "Guess what babe? We're moving to LA. I have my own national show."

No, "Hey babe, I've been given the opportunity to have my own national show, how do you feel about that?" No, "I really love you and I want you to come with me." He just *assumes* that I am going to drop everything to come with him.

Kathy Bloomingdale 22nd November 2012 at 23:02 [Report]

I know you don't like being told to do things, honey. It's the quickest way for someone to get on your bad side. But at the same time, a couple of months ago, you would have said it was romantic to have your boyfriend wanting you in his life, incorporating you into his plans. That's what you wanted in a guy, right? Hot body/cares about you?

Madeline Cain ? 22nd November 2012 at 23:03

See if you like being told a major life decision has been made for you! He didn't want me for me in LA, he wanted me because I provide the material for his precious show. So he can be famous! He didn't even contemplate how I was going to be able to stay in the country.

Kathy Bloomingdale 22nd November 2012 at 23:04 [Report]

I'm not going to be any help unless I know the whole story. How about you take me through what you both said. That way I know whether I should help by being a mediator or dive right in to calling him a douche-face.

Madeline Cain ? 22nd November 2012 at 23:12

Ha! Clueless self-absorbed douche-face is more accurate. This is basically how the conversation went, in a dark, smoky little Korea Town restaurant where you pay $20 a head to cook your own meal:

"Guess what babe? We're moving to LA. I have my own national show."

I snorted water through my nostrils. "Wow, you got a job in LA? When do you –"

"A national job! It starts in December. This will make my career, babe. And I need you there."

"Me? But, I can't just… it would be really hard for me to—"

"Sure you can babe. You have to, you're my Muse, I need you."

"But if I go with you I'll lose this internship. It's an amazing opportunity for *me*. Not to mention I need it to get a Green Card so I can stay in the country. The only other possible way I could get one is if you married me."

The I've-just-swallowed-a-chilli look would have been funny if he was being teased by one of his football mates. But here I was just thinking out loud, and he looked like I'd just proposed on one knee wearing a moustache.

I'd thought these last couple of months I was just being silly, that I was blowing things out of proportion, but right then it really hit me. "Are you asking me to come with you because you're in love? Or because I'm your Muse?"

He looked at me, eyes wide.

You'd think I would have gone Godzilla on him, yelling and hurling raw meat ala the French chef from our first date. But somehow, it didn't make me angry, it just made me really sad. Sure, I knew we didn't mesh exactly, but he was still sweet, eager to kiss me on the mouth, effortlessly generous and heck, a week wouldn't go by where he wouldn't make some effort to let me know I was in his thoughts even though I wasn't in his schedule.

"Look," I said, "If I went with you to LA, I'd have to go home in ninety days, those are the rules of *your* country. I'm not marrying someone I've only dated for five months."

He visibly relaxed. I couldn't help mentally adding, *and who always suggests movies I hate, and uses my life for comedy material.*

"I'm not ready to go home yet, and I've got a good shot at this internship. Why not stay here with your current show, and me?"

He took my hand, and looked at the ceiling. "I really like you, you're sweet and fun, the total opposite of Shapelle. But I have to go to LA, I can't let the opportunity go by. Please, come with me. I… I don't know about love, but I do know it would be better with you there. Surely we can figure out some way you could stay. I'll make them put it in my contract or something."

I smiled at that, but asked, "To be clear, you're choosing LA?"

He looked at our hands, his expression a little lost. Clearly, the conversation wasn't going how he thought it would. "Yes."

He still hadn't answered the Muse question.

"Well, that's it then." Squeezing his hand, I let go.

Kathy Bloomingdale 22nd November 2012 at 23:13 [Report]

Geez, he chose LA over you? I'm sorry, Mad.

Madeline Cain ? 22nd November 2012 at 23:13

Which is why he's obviously a dickhead.

Kathy Bloomingdale 22nd November 2012 at 23:13 [Report]

Obviously. And a clueless self-absorbed douche.

Madeline Cain ? 22nd November 2012 at 23:15

But I can't hate him. For all his exasperating boy logic, he did try. It's just, him trying made me realise how much I didn't want it, how much it wasn't *working*. It'd be easier if I could hate him. Then I wouldn't have this ridiculous relief/guilt feeling.

Kathy Bloomingdale 22nd November 2012 at 23:16 [Report]

He may have tried but I think it was for selfish, dickheady reasons. It's just *he* didn't realise it until you pointed it out. What was making you ignore all the awkward Muse stuff?

Madeline Cain ? 22nd November 2012 at 23:18

I was in love with the idea of a foreign romance and a good looking guy actually *liking* me. Like, the type of guy other girls eye off in the street.

But I want to know a guy likes me for me, not so he can use me as a template to create some story. Being a muse makes you feel less precious and more used.

Kathy Bloomingdale 22nd November 2012 at 23:19 [Report]

That's reasonable; you shouldn't have to doubt why someone's with you. If it makes you feel any better, you're not my muse.

Madeline Cain ? 22nd November 2012 at 23:19

Kindest back-handed compliment you've ever given me.

Kathy Bloomingdale 22nd November 2012 at 23:23 [Report]

I don't know where you get the idea that good looking guys shouldn't like you, you're amazing. You roll with the punches, you dive right into the action, life's an adventure with you. What you need is someone who will go out to Broadway with you, watch bad eighties action movies with you, who will laugh at your latest crazypants situation and then join in the mayhem. You definitely need someone who's as intelligent as you. Which jerk-face never was. I can think of a dozen guys who'd fit the bill better then Kevin, and they're just as good looking. Truly. People can be nice, but it doesn't mean they're your One. When you find him, he'll be your best friend.

Madeline Cain ? 22nd November 2012 at 23:25

I'm glad you can think of a dozen, the only one who even comes close to your description is Cliff. Maybe you can introduce me to these mysterious men one of these days.

Ugggghhh, I can't do this anymore. I'm done. I just need to chill with the lizard and eat a butt-ton of chocolate.

Kathy Bloomingdale 22nd November 2012 at 23:26 [Report]

Do I want to know how much a butt-ton of chocolate is?

Madeline Cain ? 22nd November 2012 at 23:27

Enough to get me through the next two days and this Macy's Thanksgiving Day Parade I signed up for with Victoria. I can't wait to put myself in the way of chaos, anything to stop me from feeling like an emotional version of an Esher painting.

Kathy Bloomingdale 22nd November 2012 at 23:28 [Report]

Wish I was there. Remember, it was the right thing to do. What you're feeling now is that horrible muddle you get when things have ended when you didn't expect them to.

Madeline Cain ? 22nd November 2012 at 23:30

How did you manage to nail it on the head like that? That's exactly it!

I knew on some level it wasn't working. I'm sad it's ended but not devastated. I'm guilty because I feel like I should be worked up, not relieved, and what I'm feeling is my brain trying to fit itself into this new situation. This horrible, full body reaction makes *sense* now!

Kathy Bloomingdale 22nd November 2012 at 23:31 [Report]

What can I say, I have a gift which I hide from family and wield only for girlfriends. Told you once I had the whole story I'd be helpful.

Madeline Cain ? 22nd November 2012 at 23:32

Thanks, Kath.

Kathy Bloomingdale 22nd November 2012 at 23:32 [Report]

Eat Chocolate.

Kathy Bloomingdale -> Cliff Wheeland You're on. Don't be a dickhead and make the first move. *Posted Friday 23rd November at 08:00* [Comment . Like]

> **Cliff Wheeland** I'd never. *Posted Friday 23rd November at 08:43* [Comment . Like]
>
> **Kathy Bloomingdale** Letting loose your big 'making it up to the park' gesture wouldn't go astray right now… Whatever that is. Don't forget to let the park know about the whole secret life thing. The park's not too keen on secrets at the moment. *Posted Friday 23rd November at 08:49* [Comment . Like]
>
> **Cliff Wheeland** Patience young grasshopper! All will be revealed two weeks before Christmas. *Posted Friday 23rd November at 08:53* [Comment . Like]

Kathy Bloomingdale Fine, but if you screw this up like douche-face, I'm going to castrate you. *Posted Friday 23rd November at 08:54* [Comment . Like]

Cliff Wheeland Australian women are very violent towards male genitalia… *Posted Friday 23rd November at 08:57* [Comment . Like]

Madeline Cain ? "So let's get down to facts. You're a babe and it's their loss…" Classmates make my day ? *Posted Friday 23rd November at 11:22* [Comment . Like]

Josh Annelli I only speak the truth. *Posted Friday 23rd November at 12:20* [Comment . Like]

Victoria Zeng *Hugs*. *Posted Friday 23rd November at 12:32* [Comment . Like]

Jamie Anderson Life, you finally get your day in the sun and then… sand ninjas. *Posted Friday 23rd November at 16:44* [Comment . Like]

Mike Cain Mwahahahaha. *Posted Friday 23rd November at 16:50* [Comment . Like]

Madeline Cain ? That's why I never go to the beach with him. It's like sand turns him insane. Well, more insane than normal. *Posted Friday 23rd November at 16:55* [Comment . Like]

Mike Cain All I can say is, there's a fine line between a tan and looking like you rolled in Doritos. I'm just helping a sista out, y'all. *Posted Friday 23rd November at 17:00* [Comment . Like]

Kate Nikle likes the pages **Dear Noah, You Said The Ark Wasn't Leaving Until Five. Sincerely, Unicorns,** and **Hi, I'm Troy McClure. You're Reading This In My Voice** and **50 other pages.** [Like]

Madeline Cain Fashion Star? *Happy dance* I've been short listed for

Sorella's fashion internship! "You have been given early notification of your interview based on the strength of your application." Interview is next week. *Posted Saturday 24th November at 19:19* [Comment . Like]

> **Cain Michaels** Guess I'll be seeing you there. *Posted Saturday 24th November at 19:26* [Comment . Like]

> **Madeline Cain Fashion Star?** May the best woman win! *Posted Saturday 24th November at 19:33* [Comment . Like]

Mike Cain I intend to live forever. So far, so good. *Posted Saturday 24th November at 21:20* [Comment . Like]

> **Madeline Cain Fashion Star?** As long as you can resist tangoing with law enforcement I'm sure that will work out great. Remember, the police never think it's as funny as you do. *Posted Saturday 24th November at 21:40* [Comment . Like]

Kathy Bloomingdale Off to the beach! As such, I'm taking a Facebook holiday. See you all in 24 hours and red as a fire engine. *Posted Sunday 24th November at 08:11* [Comment . Like]

Lulu Tanaki likes the page **Nappy All Changed Then BAM, Poop Face!** [Like]

Kim Enuik -> Madeline Cain Fashion Star? Did I just see that? *Posted Sunday 25th November at 11:30* [Comment . Like]

Cain Michaels -> Madeline Cain Fashion Star? Wow, you're not the kind of girl who walks through doors are you? You crash into them kamikaze style. *Posted Sunday 25th November at 11:31* [Comment . Like]

Cliff Wheeland -> Madeline Cain Fashion Star? I recorded that for you. Your future children are welcome. *Posted Sunday 25th November at 11:32* [Comment . Like]

Nadine Cain -> Madeline Cain Fashion Star? Madeline, Michael said he saw you on the news. Is everything alright? *Posted Sunday 25th November at 11:52* [Comment . Like]

Mike Cain -> Madeline Cain Fashion Star? Oh sister dear, please correct me if I'm wrong, but did I just see you on the evening news taking out a news anchor dressed as a turkey? *Posted Sunday 25th November at 13:30* [Comment . Like]

Tim Gleeve I'm sorry, what? Was Maddie the turkey? Or the news anchor? *Posted Sunday 25th November at 13:47* [Comment . Like]

Mike Cain I wish I could say Madeline, but no, it was the news anchor dressed as the turkey. From what I could see, Maddie was on the back of a motorbike (bad idea under most circumstances) which then inexplicably swerved and resulted in her launching herself at the news anchor, and the motorbike driver taking out one of guys holding the anchor line for a giant balloon. *Posted Sunday 25th November at 13:54* [Comment . Like]

Madeline Cain Fashion Star? OH MY GOD IT WAS ON AUSTRALIAN NEWS?? Why me? Why couldn't Victoria have been the one to take out a turkey on *international TV*?! *Posted Sunday 25th November at 14:40* [Comment . Like]

Jade Annelli What I want to know is how you found yourself hanging like, a hundred feet in the air from a Snoopy balloon? *Posted Sunday 25th November at 14:44* [Comment . Like]

Madeline Cain Fashion Star? Ok now, stop that. That's how these ridiculous rumours start. I wasn't hanging a hundred feet in the air, it was six feet, tops. I didn't *launch* myself at the news anchor, I was on the back of a media bike and we hit a pot hole. I *fell* off. It just so happened I feel off onto someone dressed as a turkey doing a live broadcast. *Posted Sunday 25th November at 14:50* [Comment . Like]

Tim Gleeve That's how *legends* start! This has got to be one of the most awesome things you've even landed in. And this time someone recorded it for me to watch!! *Posted Sunday 25th November at 14:53* [Comment . Like]

Mike Cain I don't know if I believe you when you say you lucked onto a comfortable landing. There has to have been some premeditated, directional falling. *Posted Sunday 25th November at 14:57* [Comment . Like]

Jade Annelli Again, hanging in the air from a giant balloon...how? *Posted Sunday 25th November at 14:57* [Comment . Like]

Victoria Zeng Maddie was being a hero! She'd helped the news anchor back to his feet and the camera man was pointing behind them, and Maddie turned and like the hero she was she ran and leapt and grab the rope of the unconscious balloon holder to stop it flying away. It was the best thing I've ever seen! It's a shame she lost her shoes when she was lifted into the air. *Posted Sunday 25th November at 15:00* [Comment . Like]

Nadine Cain I'm glad you're alright! What were you thinking? That balloon holder was at least three times your size. *Posted Sunday 25th November at 15:10* [Comment . Like]

Madeline Cain Fashion Star? It was an instinctual reaction, thinking didn't come into the equation. People were yelling, one guy was already being lifted into the air, I just wanted to help. If only I'd some sort of harness, I'd have gotten at least a hundred more photographs for Jason's Bird's Eye View assignment. *Posted Sunday 25th November at 15:15* [Comment . Like]

Josh Annelli How is it you've been in the right place at the right time with *all* these assignments? It's not fair. *Posted Sunday 25th November at 15:17* [Comment . Like]

Mike Cain It was like you thought you'd try out for Cirque du Soleil only to spin around in some kind of aerial interpretive dance. *Posted Sunday 25th November at 15:19* [Comment . Like]

Nadine Cain Enough, Michael. I'm very proud of you darling, that was a very brave thing to do. If you could get that lovely boy, Cliff, to send his recording, I'd love a copy. *Posted Sunday 25th November at 15:22* [Comment . Like]

Victoria Zeng It only took them five minutes to get her down. *Posted Sunday 25th November at 15:25* [Comment . Like]

Kim Enuik Have to say, I'm pretty jealous they got you down in a fire engine. Lucky there was one in the parade, hey? *Posted Sunday 25th November at 15:27* [Comment . Like]

Madeline Cain Fashion Star? Next time you're welcome to it, I'll just watch from the crowd. I would say, 'Not a chance,' Mum, if I didn't already know it was on YouTube. Uggghhh! At least this is my last portfolio experiment, *and* last assignment. There's nothing more specky than a bird's eye view from a Snoopy balloon. *Posted Sunday 25th November at 15:30* [Comment . Like]

Kathy Bloomingdale I go away for ONE DAY and come back to this. *Shakes head*. I can't leave you alone for one minute, can I? *Posted Monday 26th November at 10:10* [Comment . Like]

Jarrah Annelli It's the end of November which can only mean one thing: attractive men surface from under hideous moustaches! Hurray! *Posted Tuesday 27th November at 14:30* [Comment . Like]

Madeline Cain Fashion Star? At Rockefeller Centre waiting for the light-up of the big tree! With- **Cliff Wheeland.** *Posted Wednesday 28th November at 20:45* [Comment . Like]

Kathy Bloomingdale What's the weather like? *Posted Wednesday 28th November at 21:00* [Comment . Like]

Madeline Cain Fashion Star? It's F to the Reezing, but amazing! Will tell you about it soon. I've had a Christmas epiphany! *Posted Wednesday 28th November at 23:36* [Comment . Like]

Christmas Epiphany……[New Message]

[Back to messages. Mark as unread . Report spam . Delete]

Between **Kathy Bloomingdale** and **You.**

Madeline Cain Fashion Star? 29th November 2012 at 10:00

I have to thank you, Kathy. It was your psychoanalysis that made this happen. I just had the best night!

Kathy Bloomingdale 29th November 2012 at 10:09 [Report]

Great… what did I do?

Madeline Cain Fashion Star? 29th November 2012 at 10:11

I've been thinking about everything we talked about, why I was feeling so weird, why I'd held onto something that wasn't working for so long, what I really deserved. As soon as you helped me stop obsessing about Kevin I was finally able to think!

I was at Rockefeller Centre last night for the tree lighting ceremony. Cliff took me to, 'take my mind off things'. Off Kevin, off the parade, off obsessively practising interview questions.

Kathy Bloomingdale 29th November 2012 at 10:15 [Report]

Yay you! You're starting to enjoy New York again. For a while there you were just working and spending time in Kevin's apartment, weren't you? I'm glad I helped you figure out how you fit into life again. All in a day's work for your tag team best friends Kathy and Cliff!

Madeline Cain Fashion Star? 29th November 2012 at 10:16

That's not the end of the story! This is better than getting my New Yorker on.

Kathy Bloomingdale 29th November 2012 at 10:17 [Report]

Here I was thinking you were going to shower me with gratitude and affection. Fine, I'll play the guessing game. Tell me more.

Kathy Bloomingdale 29th November 2012 at 10:20 [Report]

Ok, either you've gone offline or you're writing me an essay…

Madeline Cain Fashion Star? 29th November 2012 at 10:25

So there we were on the sloping path between two buildings, looking across the skating rink to the massive spruce tree in Rockefeller plaza, huddled together in a packed crowd waiting impatiently.

I must have been shivering pretty hard because Cliff said, "You alright there, Aussie? Cold? Are you still enjoying yourself?" Reaching an arm over my shoulder, he rubbed my arms vigorously earning death stares from the surrounding public he almost elbowed in the face.

"After the craziness of the last few weeks this is exactly what I needed. Thanks heaps."

"What are friendships for, hey? Relationships and television escapades come and go, but friends stick around like a bad smell. Ten times out of ten if you find yourself in a jail cell they're right there with you. Their mission in life is to let you be yourself and make sure you have fun doing it." His teeth flashed a band of white in the dark. "Let's go ice-skating after; it'll just be like old times."

"Except less butt on ice action."

We grinned at each other while the crowd started counting erratically down from ten. As Cliff joined in I couldn't help thinking how he always had time for me, how he'd led my classmates like an army to the FBI headquarters to get them to release me, how he spent three months playing tour guide, the number of Broadway shows he'd seen with me, and the awesome advice he'd give on everything from making friends with Kim to handling bribery. I remembered how much it sucked being cut off from him for the summer; it hurt ten times more than avoiding Kevin these past two weeks.

What did it say that I felt being away from my best mate more keenly than I did having split from Kevin? Why did the thought of me moving out of my student housing and away from Cliff make my stomach drop more than the knowledge Kevin was definitely moving to LA?

What you said about the One being your best friend flashed through my head again. Looking at Cliff I realised how much I liked him, *really* liked him. Wanting to snuggle closer to him felt as natural as breathing.

Without a thought I slid around in front of Cliff, stood on my tip toes, and pulling his face to mine, I kissed him.

Then the lights came on and the choir sang.

Kathy Bloomingdale 29th November 2012 at 10:26 [Report]

I'm sorry you did what?!

Madeline Cain Fashion Star? 29th November 2012 at 10:27

I kissed him. It was amazing. Not sloppy or awkward but warm and tasty.

Kathy Bloomingdale 29th November 2012 at 10:28 [Report]

Two weeks after... Geez, sorry for being a wet rag, it's just the 'without thinking' bit has got me worried. You know, that the moment swept you away, that you're not doing it for the right reason.

Madeline Cain Fashion Star? 29th November 2012 at 10:33

Argh! That was a poor choice of words, what I meant was I didn't hesitate; I didn't even need to question the impulse because I knew exactly how I felt.

Cliff had exactly the same reaction as you. "Woah, Maddie! Did you really mean to… If that was just a Christmas spirit thing that's cool, it's just…ah… it would be nice to know where that came from."

I stepped back to better see his face and immediately feel the need to step closer again. That's what proved it to me. "I meant it."

A slow, sweet smile infused his face. "Well alright then." He pulled me in, hugging me tight to his chest.

"You only get one of those a night." My voice came out muffled against his chest, barely audible against the choir's 'Joy to The World'.

"Sorry, what?"

"You only get one of those a night," I repeated. "Until jobs and plans work themselves out. I'm not a hussy."

"I would never say such things. You should probably turn around anyway; you're missing an epic light show."

Kathy Bloomingdale 29th November 2012 at 10:34 [Report]

Well that's different. Gosh, I'm so happy for you! I always thought you two matched. He's liked you for so long, did he tell you?

Madeline Cain Fashion Star? 29th November 2012 at 10:35

Really? No he didn't. Well *that* makes me feel like a moron. They should call me Madeline Cain the Epically Clueless.

Kathy Bloomingdale 29th November 2012 at 10:35 [Report]

We do.

Madeline Cain Fashion Star? 29th November 2012 at 10:36

But that's why I like him so much. He continued to show me the most awesome time, I suppose it was a date, and he never once tried to steal another kiss.

Kathy Bloomingdale 29th November 2012 at 10:36 [Report]

That's odd. What sort of a boy is he?

Madeline Cain Fashion Star? 29th November 2012 at 10:38

My boy ? I feel like everything is working out the way it should, the grand plan is falling into place. My flight home for Christmas won't be the end of my overseas adventure; it will be the start of a brief visit that will end back in New York, where everything is coming up Madeline! The Universe is setting it all up, bring on the interview!

Kathy Bloomingdale 29th November 2012 at 10:39 [Report]

I can't say I'm not going to be *devastated* if you get this job, but if anyone deserves it, it's you. I'll be beaming you all of my good luck vibes. Congrats on you and Cliff, I'm super excited.

Madeline Cain Fashion Star? 29th November 2012 at 10:40

Couldn't have gotten there without you.

Kathy Bloomingdale -> Cliff Wheeland Well played, Sir. And once the internship thing is resolved? *Posted Thursday 29th November at 11:43* [Comment . Like]

Cliff Wheeland The final stage of the plan will be enacted.

Fingers crossed. *Posted Thursday 29th November at 11:54* [Comment . Like]

Kathy Bloomingdale Fingers crossed, buddy. *Posted Thursday 29th November at 12:12* [Comment . Like]

Tim Gleeve On a scale of one to Australia, how insane is your weather? *Posted Friday 30th November at 13:32* [Comment . Like]

Madeline Cain Fashion Star? What's going on at home? I'm freezing my delicates. It's nearly 8am and apparently it's minus six degrees. Thank God for Antarctic quality long johns. #NotFreezingToDeathIsMyFavourite. *Posted Friday 30th November at 14:00* [Comment . Like]

Tim Gleeve In Adelaide we've had a week long heat wave, New South Wales has just experienced record floods and we have two cyclones/hurricanes/typhoons in the north. Fingers crossed that doesn't land you in an airport in China on your way home. *Posted Friday 30th November at 14:14* [Comment . Like]

Madeline Cain Fashion Star? I'm finally in a country where the weather and Christmas carols match! *Posted Friday 30th November at 18:00* [Comment . Like]

Cliff Wheeland and **three others** like this.

Kim Enuik They're not 'Suggested Friends,' they're people I'm intentionally avoiding. *Posted Saturday 1st December at 09:20* [Comment . Like]

Madeline Cain Fashion Star? Stop avoiding your parents! *Posted Saturday 1st December at 11:10* [Comment . Like]

Kim Enuik I'm not doing it out of maliciousness but self-preservation; there's too much incriminating evidence on here! *Posted Saturday 1st December at 11:16* [Comment . Like]

Mike Cain I got arrested in town the other day. *Posted Saturday 1st December at 15:40* [Comment . Like]

Madeline Cain Fashion Star? What?? Why? *Posted Saturday 1st December at 16:01* [Comment . Like]

Mike Cain Possession of guns. *Flexes*. *Posted Saturday 1st December at 16:09* [Comment . Like]

Madeline Cain Fashion Star? You're such an arse. *Posted Saturday 1st December at 16:14* [Comment . Like]

Derek Chan likes the page **Growing Your Beard During Exams For Extra Wisdom** [Like]

Kyle Traybna That pimple was so epic I had to share on YouTube. *Posted Sunday 2nd December at 08:13* [Comment . Like]

Kathy Bloomingdale No, no you didn't. *Posted Sunday 2nd December at 10:15* [Comment . Like]

Claire Holderness #MustNotHaveMcDonaldsForDinnerAgain #NoMatterHowMuchIWantABigMac #Mmm *Posted Sunday 2nd December at 18:50* [Comment . Like]

Tim Gleeve Who are you kidding, you'd just get wasted and do a McNugget run #StayStrong. *Posted Sunday 2nd December at 18:58* [Comment . Like]

Ken Holderness #MissYourFace. *Posted Sunday 2nd December at 19:04* [Comment . Like]

Madeline Cain Melt Down Holyshitholyshit! Shapelle was in my internship interview. WTF!? This is bad. *Posted Monday 3rd December at 13:30* [Comment . Like]

Tim Gleeve The model who tried to brain you with souvenirs while Kevin played King Kong?? Did she decide on a career change? *Posted Monday 3rd December at 13:41* [Comment . Like]

Cliff Wheeland You didn't say she was there for *an* interview, you said she was in *your* interview. Why would she be in yours? *Posted Monday 3rd December at 13:44* [Comment . Like]

Madeline Cain Melt Down She's one of Sorella's clients! *The* major client I'm guessing because she was the only 'client' there. Oh my God, why would you allow your clients to dictate the staff you hire?? I'm not going to get this internship. What the hell am I going to do?! *Posted Monday 3rd December at 13:49* [Comment . Like]

Kathy Bloomingdale Was she professional? Did she make trouble? How much sway can a model have? It's not like she's the only client. I mean, Sorella sounds like she has very strong opinions of her own, she would want the best. *Posted Monday 3rd December at 13:52* [Comment . Like]

Madeline Cain Melt Down But what if there are two applicants of equal skill and one is a major problem for a client? What then?! All she did was stare, stare and make doodles. *Posted Monday 3rd December at 13:54* [Comment . Like]

Cain Michaels Really? I think she was in my interview too. You couldn't get her to shut up. *Posted Monday 3rd December at 13:55* [Comment . Like]

Cliff Wheeland When do you hear who got it? *Posted Monday 3rd December at 14:00* [Comment . Like]

Cliff Wheeland Maddie?? *Posted Monday 3rd December at 14:20* [Comment . Like]

Cain Michaels It is with surprise that I announce I'm now an intern under one, Ms Sorella Fontaine. Doesn't feel as awesome as I thought it would, I get the feeling I was the second fiddle... *Posted Tuesday 4th December at 11:20* [Comment . Like]

Richard Arnoou Congrats, Bud. And hey, Sorella wouldn't have hired you if your pictures were crap. I applaud you for not pissing off the right people like you piss off the rest of us... (jokes). *Posted Tuesday 4th December at 11:22* [Comment . Like]

Josh Annelli High five, mate. However it happened you'll show them they picked good. Don't worry, she won't hold it against you, you just have to give her time. *Posted Tuesday 4th December at 11:26* [Comment . Like]

Victoria Zeng Got to be in it to win it. Bet you dressed so fabulously at the interview they couldn't resist. *Posted Tuesday 4th December at 11:28* [Comment . Like]

Jade Annelli Glad the internship was kept in the family and didn't go to some jumped up University student. They always think they're better than us! But you showed them! (Josh is right, just stay off her radar until the End of Year Show, it will be like nothing ever happened. Hopefully). *Posted Tuesday 4th December at 11:31* [Comment . Like]

Jarrah Annelli Congrats! Don't let a stupid model sully your win. Be the awesome fashion photographer we know is inside. *Posted Tuesday 4th December at 11:33* [Comment . Like]

Madeline Cain Melt Down Why do people not understand?! The amount of fucks I want to give about this is zero. *Posted Tuesday 4th December at 21:00* [Comment . Like]

Tim Gleeve Each person values a unit of 'Fuck' differently... *Posted Tuesday 4th December at 22:10* [Comment . Like]

Josh Annelli On special days do you give twice the amount of fucks? Which still equals zero?? *Posted Tuesday 4th December at 22:15* [Comment . Like]

Tim Gleeve Good point, that zero still cancels everything out. *Posted Tuesday 4th December at 22:18* [Comment . Like]

Kim Enuik On a scale of one to Voldemort, how badly do you want revenge? *Posted Tuesday 4th December at 22:22* [Comment . Like]

Josh Annelli Come on, Maddie. Rant at us. It will make you feel better. *Posted Tuesday 4th December at 22:27* [Comment . Like]

Don't Give Up…..[New Message]

[Back to messages. Mark as unread . Report spam . Delete]

Between **Kathy Bloomingdale, Tim Gleeve** and **You.**

Kathy Bloomingdale 5th December 2012 at 11:40 [Report]

Speak to us. You won't answer texts, you won't take phone calls, you can't just sit in your apartment drunkenly pouring you and the chameleon wine. Look, we can turn this around. It's only too late when you give up.

Tim Gleeve 5th December 2012 at 11:45 [Report]

Coming home wouldn't be too bad, right? Hell, you wouldn't need to convince Kathy and me, we'd move to Sydney or Melbourne with you in a heartbeat. We can stop all this Facebook nonsense and tease each other in person.

Kathy Bloomingdale 5th December 2012 at 11:47 [Report]

What about Jason? Surely he has options for his students when they leave. With so few a year you can't tell me he's not able to pull some strings.

Madeline Cain Melt Down 5th December 2012 at 11:51

It's so, so stupid! It's not possible for six months of hard work to go down the drain like that! No, how it works, is you put in the hard work, you throw everything into that goal and you win it on your merits. The top person gets the top job. It's bloody simple. You don't lose it because you accidentally took a photo of some *woman* who makes assumptions based on her own twisted perception of reality.

How can the Universe betray me like this!? How can I get handed some of the world's most expensive clothing, have every fashion shoot go so smoothly, be directed so clearly down one path to be cut down at the last? Only weeks after realising I'd wasted five months on the wrong guy. It felt like Cliff was my reward after all that stupid agonising, but now 'us' is an impossibility! What was the point of it happening in the first place, huh? If I never had a chance of being able to stay? Riddle me that.

Go on, shower me with your wisdom!

Kathy Bloomingdale 5th December 2012 at 11:54 [Report]

Honey, some things in life are just out of your control. You could never have predicted Shapelle would being there, you could never have predicted you would ever *see* her again. If you'd found out about Shapelle earlier then what would you have done? Just given up? Of course not, you would have moved forward trusting Sorella's integrity. You couldn't have predicted her reaction to Shapelle's pressure.

Madeline Cain Melt Down 5th December 2012 at 11:58

Well I know now; Sorella's a God damn coward. "This is one of the best portfolios I've seen in years… Jason recommends your work so highly."

Yeah? Well why didn't you hire me, twit?! Don't give me hope and then scurry away with your tail between your legs for a treat from the blond haired witch!

Kathy Bloomingdale 5th December 2012 at 11:59 [Report]

Well, now you know your idols have faults and pressures too. You don't know what Sorella's financial situation is like; those at the top constantly have to battle not to get knocked over.

Tim Gleeve 5th December 2012 at 12:01 [Report]

What if Sorella was threatened by how good you were? Did you ever think of that? I know it doesn't help you right now, but it's worth considering her reasons were selfish. For every backward thinking starlet, there's a forward thinking competitor who'll see the value of surrounding themselves with people as good, if not better, than them.

Kathy Bloomingdale 5th December 2012 at 12:03 [Report]

Look at where you are! You have a massive portfolio of fashion work *and* work from half a dozen different photography types and styles. You have a pretty piece of paper from one of photography's most prestigious colleges, and high praise from your award-winning teacher. You didn't have that six months ago. And you didn't have a resourceful guy who has every intention of keeping you in the US so he can kiss you more than once a night.

Tim Gleeve 5th December 2012 at 12:04 [Report]

It's not like you're obsessed with fashion, right? Actually, this is probably the bullet that saved your life. I mean, do you *really* want to spend your days working with a box of cats like Shapelle?

Madeline Cain Melt Down 5th December 2012 at 12:06

No, but that's not the point. The point is I was robbed blind! Without this internship I don't have a job. I can't stay in the US. End story. Sure, I couldn't pick an aqua skirt from a cerulean one or the arse-end of a fez from the front, but it was the only gig that didn't get me constantly parodied on a B-rated American game show.

Kathy Bloomingdale 5th December 2012 at 12:08 [Report]

I think what Tim is saying is it wasn't your passion. You shouldn't just pick your career because it's the least chaotic, you should pick it because it gets you excited to be at work. Besides, you're far away from the boyfriend who kept you around for material, it doesn't need to colour your experiments anymore.

Madeline Cain Melt Down 5th December 2012 at 12:09

But that's the thing Kathy, none of my experiments have been overwhelmingly positive! Nothing in the past six months stands out as something I want to dedicate my life to. I don't know what I want to do. It's the end of Jason's course and I still have no idea. I'm going to lose my best chance! God, all I want to do is take photos. Why won't life just let me be?

Tim Gleeve 5th December 2012 at 12:11 [Report]

Why not just apply for jobs for now? Show your portfolio around, get noticed. You can still do you own photography while holding down a day job. There are still loads more types of photography to try, you were only sampling this past six months. As long as you keep putting yourself out there, you keep making opportunities for yourself.

Madeline Cain Melt Down 5th December 2012 at 12:12

It's almost Christmas, Tim. Why would anyone hire in the next three weeks? It's too late, there's no way I can land a job before I come home.

Kathy Bloomingdale 5th December 2012 at 12:14 [Report]

You're probably right, but you're trying wedding photography in two weeks, who knows what could come from that, and there will be potential employers at your End of Year Show. At the very least you'll have a little nest egg from this wedding gig to be able to come back to the US in the New Year and apply for as many jobs as you want.

Madeline Cain Melt Down 5th December 2012 at 12:16

Urgh! That stupid photography gig, I forgot all about it. The last thing I need is to get a job where I'm ridiculed by professional photographers everywhere. Now I have to waste a day watching happy couples be happy while dealing with having to leave my own potential boyfriend.

Tim Gleeve 5th December 2012 at 12:19 [Report]

Which professional photographers? Those po-faced ones you met at the Ball? They're the ones who did the cowardly about-face remember? Well, at least Sorella did. Do you really trust their advice? Who gives a flying fart in space about what they think. The one who's never steered you wrong is Jason. He's the one you need to talk to; he's the one whose opinion should matter. Tell him what you want, tell him the trouble you're having deciding and ask him what you should do.

Madeline Cain Melt Down 5th December 2012 at 12:20

He's been away for weeks. He won't be back in the country until the day before the gallery.

Kathy Bloomingdale 5th December 2012 at 12:23 [Report]

Which is what, less than a week away? Not much is going to happen before Christmas, you said so yourself. At least do this wedding thing for the money, then you have the option to fly back and apply for a bunch of other jobs.

Besides, Tim is right, you don't want to be spending day in, day out, with a stick figure like Shapelle. You'd punch her in the face and then you'd be in jail and that's a little harder to come back from than a career change.

Madeline Cain Melt Down 5th December 2012 at 12:23

Ha! Probably.

Tim Gleeve 5th December 2012 at 12:27 [Report]

If I was there I'd help you, then the only modelling she could do is as a panda ? Right, so the PLAN:

- Suck it up and have fun eating someone else's wedding cake.

- Put together the best End of Year Show photograph collection ever.
- Speak to Jason at show about smoozing for you.
- Tell plan to Cliff so you can use his desperation to keep you there to your advantage.

Have I missed anything?

Kathy Bloomingdale 5th December 2012 at 12:28 [Report]

Take Sorella off the Christmas Card list.

Tim Gleeve 5th December 2012 at 12:29 [Report]

Ah, quite right. Also, number 6: Pray for snow so you can go make snow angels in Central Park. I think that's everything.

Madeline Cain Melt Down 5th December 2012 at 12:30

Good plan. And thanks. For the plan, for pounding on my digital door only to have me snap at you, just, thanks. I've got a number 7: Talk to Cain so he doesn't feel like an arsehole at Christmas.

Tim Gleeve 5th December 2012 at 12:31 [Report]

That's the Christmas Spirit.

Madeline Cain Melt Down 5th December 2012 at 12:31

Wow, did you seriously just write that? Do you have a temperature?

Kathy Bloomingdale 5th December 2012 at 12:32 [Report]

It's the heat, it's addled his brain. Now go and hang out with someone that makes you happy.

Tim Gleeve 5th December 2012 at 12:33 [Report]

Or set loose Duncan in a crowded place and see what happens. Either one will bring a smile.

Madeline Cain Melt Down 5th December 2012 at 12:33

Oh, Duncan...

Mike Cain -> Madeline Cain Melt Down This is me giving you permission to run riot this month. Screw all those pansies you were trying to impress. I'm the only one that matters. Make me proud. *Posted Tuesday 4th December at 17:15* [Comment . Like]

> **Tim Gleeve** Because soon it will be January and you'll have to have your professional face on. Trust me, the professional face kills fun. *Posted Tuesday 4th December at 17:23* [Comment . Like]
>
> **Madeline Cain Melt Down** We certainly can't let professionalism ruin Christmas, can we? That explains your slowly declining personality and sexual prowess, Tim. The only time I ever tried to make you proud, Mike, I ended up in hospital with a broken arm. It is unlikely I will attempt this endeavour again within the next decade. Though with the New York/Madeline mix who knows what unforseen solar flares will ensue. *Posted Tuesday 4th December at 17:29* [Comment . Like]

Lulu Tanaki You're the average of the three people you spend the most time with. *Posted Wednesday 5th December at 08:45* [Comment . Like]

> **Ray Star** Two of yours are under ten... *Posted Wednesday 5th December at 08:59* [Comment . Like]
>
> **Madeline Cain Melt Down** That makes you 33% Ninja Turtle. *Posted Wednesday 5th December at 09:11* [Comment . Like]

Natalie West has send you a **Friend Request.** [Accept . Ignore]

> **Natalie West** Hi, Madeline! Thought this would be the easiest way to update you on the gig in a couple of weeks. *Posted Wednesday 5th December at 11:42* [Comment . Like]

> **Madeline Cain Melt Down** Sounds like a plan. *Posted Wednesday 5th December at 12:02* [Comment . Like]

Cliff Wheeland Apparently, Madeline has yet to apply Mike's disable-Laani instructions. Either that, or Laani is really alive. "Do you have mental deodorant? That way I don't have to marinade in this conversation." *Posted Wednesday 5th December at 14:15* [Comment . Like]

> **Kathy Bloomingdale** She's really alive. She's absorbed so much hostile personality that you're going to have to perform an exorcism to get rid of her. Shall I order you some holy water from exorcisms.com? *Posted Wednesday 5th December at 14:23* [Comment . Like]

> **Mike Cain** I feel it's less Maddie forgetting to disable her and more Maddie recommissioning her for Christmas chaos fun times. *Posted Wednesday 5th December at 14:40* [Comment . Like]

Claire Holderness Why aren't #Internet junkies called Spiders? It's the World Wide *Web* after all. #DeepPondering #EnglishIsWeird #BrainAboutToExplode #LetsEatCakeInstead. *Posted Wednesday 5th December at 17:20* [Comment . Like]

> **Tim Gleeve** You don't understand,Woo. It doesn't matter if we are 'online' or 'offline', we are all in the matrix. #TheMatrixIsReal #ITookTheRedPill #SeeingBlackCats. *Posted Wednesday 5th December at 17:25* [Comment . Like]

> **Claire Holderness** #Shudder

#InternetJunkiesAreDefinitelySpiders #JustAsCreepy *Posted Wednesday 5th December at 17:35* [Comment . Like]

Madeline Cain Melt Down I took Duncan for you, now you have to do something for me. *Posted Wednesday 5th December at 20:00* [Comment . Like]

Kim Enuik I didn't realise it was an exchange of favours. *Posted Wednesday 5th December at 20:10* [Comment . Like]

Madeline Cain Melt Down Oddly enough, not everyone is jumping over themselves for the company of your scaly friend. I need a carry boy, I've got a stack of prints I need delivered before I leave the country. You can bring the lizard if you want. As long as the lead has been fixed. *Posted Wednesday 5th December at 20:13* [Comment . Like]

Kim Enuik What do I look like, a walking shelf? *Posted Wednesday 5th December at 20:14* [Comment . Like]

Madeline Cain Melt Down I'm going to be gone in two weeks. Do you really want to deprive Duncan of his last few chances for an outing with his beloved housemate? *Posted Wednesday 5th December at 20:17* [Comment . Like]

Kim Enuik Fine. Forced into slavery by my own chameleon. *Posted Wednesday 5th December at 20:18* [Comment . Like]

The End of Year Show & Well Endowed Family Drawings

NOTES > My Notes [Write a note]

By **Madeline Cain Experimental** Friday, 7th December 2012 at 22:53

It makes sense Jason would be there for my final bon-voyage screw up. It also makes sense he'd be the one to tell me a story that makes my past six months of fretting seem like a waste of energy.

Like all my screw ups of the past year, this one snuck up on me in that insidious way which ends in me discovering it in front of an audience. So I feel the story needs to be told in the same way, with the unknowing set-up first, and the discovery last.

Several days prior to our end of year gallery, you'd have seen me and my packhorse, Kim, visiting several of my clients including the dog whisperer, the burley Macy's parade crew, Madison Square Garden (AKA 'lip-sync' stadium) and last but not least the woman who voluntarily offers to entertain little terrorists commonly known as children. The day-care centre was our last stop on this ice-age of an afternoon before we retreated to the tropical heating of the gallery to hang my prints for the show. Predictably, Kim wasn't taking this tramping through the elements well.

"All I'm saying is, is it really that hard to get a tray with wheels, or hire a taxi or use some other method that *doesn't* involve me slowly losing limbs to frost bite? Any of those options seem more logical than the subway plus human slave equation." Kim cursed as his shoe broke through a thin layer of ice and into a puddle. He hopped down the sidewalk toward the day-care entry trying not to drop the pile of plastic covered prints. "I can't feel my fingers; I haven't felt my toes for at least an hour. If it gets to the point where I can't feel my penis, you're on your own, paying back a favour be damned. I plan on giving Duncan brothers and sisters in the future."

Jumping the offending puddle I said, "Dude, what sort of sperm are you packing? Are you planning full lizard children or half breeds?"

"It's too cold for smartasses. You know what I meant. It's too cold to do anything, including bringing Duncan on this expedition. Whose stupid idea was that—"

"– Yours."

"– I'm glad he hasn't poked his head out of this jacket, he'd be a reptilian popsicle. I bet he's not getting enough oxygen either."

Thinking back, it was probably for this reason that Kim didn't attach the lead to Duncan's harness like he should *any time he leaves the apartment.* Knowing Kim, he felt like he'd been mean enough. And I bet Duncan took full advantage, looking woeful and stationary when Kim first pulled him out into the warm foyer of the school. Then he zipped off when a child tugged on Kim's jacket, offering him a bite of a half-eaten crayon.

By the time Kim abandoned my gallery prints on a table to go hunting his escapee, I was in the office with Miriam, the school head. I feel this means I cannot be held accountable for the events that followed. It's all Kim's fault. I wouldn't get into half these mishaps without you and Duncan. You're my chaos sidekicks.

So keeping that final scene in mind, let's flash forward to the End of Year Show. The walls of the ground floor gallery and the classroom above were covered (tastefully) with the best photos from the seven of us. It was an eclectic range of portraits, street photography, fashion, landscape, 3D (yep, the carriage from first semester made the cut) and 'abstract'. Each photo was up for silent auction and both rooms were packed with people who came in looking like the Michelin Man only to divest their layers and emerge tastefully dressed butterflies. Half the crowd felt like friends, with various members of the Little Y's coming to say hello, as well as neighbours from our apartment floor. Even the four odd ball university students I deliver pizza to once a month dropped in to wish me a very happy 'evening of business'.

Despite the festive atmosphere I spent the first half of the Gallery in a fog of self-doubt and despair. For those of you who don't know, the fashion photography internship I'd been working so hard on for the past six months had been snatched from my grasp by a model we all know, and should spit on if we ever see her in public (or fling poo at, whichever is handier at the time). It left me with a sizably shrunken confidence and a trail of bizarre photographic experiments, none of which screamed 'choose me as a career!' The one person I desperately wanted to talk, Jason, had had his plane delayed and it looked unlikely he would even make it to the Show let alone NYC that night.

While the bids on my photographs weren't any less than those of my classmates, no one was handing me their card either and I was finding it harder and harder to keep up a witty and charming façade for potential employers.

So when a voice behind me asked, "Why are half your End of Year photos fashion?" it took all my inner strength not to turn around swinging.

Lucky, as behind me stood Jason, salt and pepper hair fashionably mussed, head cocked to one side as he studied them.

"Jason! You made it!"

He gave a crooked grin. "Only for the last half hour, but at least I made it before closing time!" He pointed at a particularly realistic zombie. "Don't get me wrong, the fashion ones are great, but they're not your best work."

My shoulders slumped. "Just as well I didn't get Sorella's internship then. It makes dedicating half a year to it seem pretty pointless."

His eyebrows jumped up. "That surprises me, because they *are* good. But what you said about it being pointless isn't quite right. Dedicating yourself to learning a new skill is never a waste. You should never stop learning new things, and you shouldn't *not* learn them just because you think they'll be irrelevant to your main goal. That's how true creatives thrive, by pulling together connections between things that have never been connected before. It's the power of art, of new perspectives. You're good at that and I don't think fashion allows you to put that skill into full effect."

"So I dedicated myself to something that isn't right for me *and* I've lost my best chance at a career, figures," I said.

He frowned, then taking me by the arm he lead me into the

corridor, unlocked a small door across the hall, and drew me inside. He sat down on an antique velvet lounge and cross his ankles. "That's better. Now what's this nonsense about losing your best chance?"

So I told him as I paced, of my conversation with his peers at the ball, the hodge podge experiments I had attempted over the past six months, about having as much of an idea about what I want to do as a penguin has of how to bungee jump. "I have hundreds of photos but *still* no idea of what I want to specialise in. I feel like I'm trapped in one of those mirror mazes where you can't figure out which 'you' leads to the exit."

Jason snorted, shaking his head. "Maddie, I respect my peers very much, but God do they spin a lot of bullshit."

"Excuse me?"

He leaned forward, elbows on knees. "There's no right way to make a career in life, what works for one person is completely the wrong way to go about it for the next. No event, no opportunity, no talent is reproducible from person to person, even one person can't reproduce what they did exactly as they did it before with the same results. You don't *have* to choose a specialisation right away; you have decades to play around. This course is not going to be your only opportunity, and it certainly won't be your best, though I'm flattered you think so." He stood up and crossing the space between us put an arm around my shoulders, shaking them. "You silly goose. You're barely at the start of your twenties; someone has to tell you you'll have more than one job and one passion in your life time!"

"But you can't make anything resembling a living jumping from one thing to the next," I said. "You need something to support yourself."

Jason held me at arm's length. "Yes, you need to make money. Some people do portraits, some people do fashion, and some people do weddings. But while you have that job you keep doing the photography *you* like, you keep experimenting with new things. The job will sustain you while you search for what you really love. Your portfolio is stellar; you already have a body of work that could get you half a dozen jobs in different fields. The key thing to remember, is you don't have to stay in them forever and the opportunities that present themselves outside that job won't be any less. You can always build your portfolio when you find that thing that makes your heart beat quicker. Okay?"

I nodded, sniffing.

"Ah, come here." He collected me in a big bear hug. "You should have come to me sooner. If you want to stay in New York I've got a dozen contacts I can introduce you to in the New Year. If you want to go back to Australia, I've probably got half a dozen contacts there too."

"Thanks." I gulped by his ear.

"Bet they didn't tell you I didn't start my photography career until I was thirty-five."

"Really?" I stepped back and he gave me a wink.

"Yep. Before then I was a tour guide. But you can't be one of those forever, your gut starts rebelling against the tequila parties. Tried office work for a while but I missed the travel. Wasn't really good a taking direction from a boss either."

I tried to imaging the refined man before me leading a party hungry Contiki tour around Europe, but all I managed to do was imagine him in increasingly bizarre Hawaiian t-shirts. I shook my head to dispel the disturbing images. "Thank you so much. I'm coming back in January to see what I can do about finding a job; I'm not ready to leave yet."

"We'll work something out then; I don't leave my students in the cold. Well, not unless there's an airport delay."

A loud knock on the door interrupted us and a middle aged man with a wispy beard poked his head around the doorjamb. "Ah, Jason, there you are! Just want to say a quick goodbye before I freeze to death waiting for a cab."

The man's eyes caught mine and he grinned opening the door wider. "I won one of your portraits, young lady," he said pulling a sheet out of the paper bag in his hand before dropping it back in. "Very eye-catching, can't wait to show the wife."

Jason's face was carefully blank as he shook the man's hand. Alone again, Jason and I look at each other.

"Did he just say he had the winning bid on one of my photos and show us a crayon drawing?"

Nodding, Jason added, "Is it just me, or did the man in that drawing appear to be very well endowed?"

"As in third leg endowed," I confirmed.

"As in tripod," Jason reiterated. "Any idea what's going on there?"

I went to shrug, then caught sight of Kim out the corner of my eye and groaned instead. "Oh crap."

I dived across the hall into the gallery space, collecting Kim by the collar of his jacket on the way. The Gallery was almost over and dozens of winning bidders lined up with their prints for wrapping or bagging by Jason's staff.

"Hey, what's the big rush?" asked Kim, shrugging himself out of my grasp.

"You want to tell me what happened at the day-care the other day while I was with Miriam?" I snapped.

At that moment three of the bidders standing where my prints had been hanging, all held them out to look at the print they'd purchased. On the back of each was a drawing in a rainbow of crayon, depicting happy stick figure families. You could tell exactly how many boys were in each family by the long appendage draw between the legs of each male stick figure.

"I *knew* I hadn't left them in a mess when I went looking for Duncan. Damn kids!" muttered Kim.

Jason on the other side of me was bent over double, absolutely pissing himself.

And thus ends my reign of chaos on New York City for 2012. With innocent photographic buyers ending up with not-so-innocent pictures of stick figure families with massive wangs.

At least my talk with Jason showed me it wasn't the end of the world.

[Comment . Like . Share]

Cliff Wheeland and **90 others** like this.

Nadine Cain I seem to recall you and Michael doing similar drawings when you were younger. Your father and I were mortified (well, your father's reaction was closer to Jason's). I was terrified they'd think we were running a nudist colony in our backyard and call welfare services to take you away. Looking back on it, I wish I'd kept a couple for your 21st birthdays… Of course it's not the end of the world if you don't get that internship, darling! I feel partly responsible for your heartache over the past couple of weeks, I know I've been on you to get a stable job, I worry about you, but I didn't *mean* it. Jason is right, you're amazing and there are a million jobs waiting for you. Maybe in Australia… A Mama can always dream to have her darling close. *Posted Saturday 8th December at 07:40* [Comment . Like]

> **Madeline Cain Experimental** Thank God we lost those; otherwise I'd have to get Mike to concoct some sort of fire in which all our childhood drawings perish. Thanks Mum, your support means a lot. I'm going to see how the Universe and I go in New York first. If that doesn't work out I'll turn my sights to home. We can talk all about that when I get home for Christmas. *Posted Saturday 8th December at 09:05* [Comment . Like]
>
> **Mike Cain** I would probably superglue them to an anvil and throw them into a volcano, fires don't destroy all the evidence. *Posted Saturday 8th December at 09:20* [Comment . Like]
>
> **Nadine Cain** Always darling, you deserve to have all your dreams come true. *Posted Saturday 8th December at 09:23* [Comment . Like]
>
> **Madeline Cain Experimental** Á la Lord of the Rings, I like your brain, bro. *Posted Saturday 8th December at 09:29* [Comment . Like]

Mike Cain I'm assuming for these stick figures to have a 'third leg' they would have to be drawn naked? *Posted Saturday 8th December at 09:40* [Comment . Like]

Madeline Cain Experimental Belly button, snail trail and all. *Posted Saturday 8th December at 09:43* [Comment . Like]

Mike Cain Those kids are anarchists in the making. I hope they have a role model as good as me one day. *Posted Saturday 8th December at 09:45* [Comment . Like]

Madeline Cain Experimental *Shudder* I hope you develop a fear of flying so you'll *never* meet. *Posted Saturday 8th December at 09:46* [Comment . Like]

Kathy Bloomingdale Kids, all they want is to be naked. *Posted Saturday 8th December at 09:52* [Comment . Like]

Tim Gleeve Bet those photographs will go for thousands of dollars on EBay one day, you should have kept some. Tell me you didn't chase after people with an eraser. *Posted Saturday 8th December at 09:54* [Comment . Like]

Madeline Cain Experimental No chasing them with an eraser, there was no way I was having *that* conversation. "Sorry Sir, you've got an accidental doodle of a doodle on your picture, let me wipe that off for you." *Posted Saturday 8th December at 09:55* [Comment . Like]

Tim Gleeve There will be some very confused New York picture framers... *Posted Saturday 8th December at 09:57* [Comment . Like]

Kathy Bloomingdale The drawing debacle aside, I'm glad you spoke to Jason. See, we told you he was the best person for a pep talk. Things will work out. *Posted Saturday 8th December at 09:59* [Comment . Like]

Kim Enuik It is not all my fault! *Posted Saturday 8th December at 10:11* [Comment . Like]

Jade Annelli It totally is. *Posted Saturday 8th December at 10:14* [Comment . Like]

Jarrah Annelli Sorry mate, but the only other person you can blame that on is a lizard. *Posted Saturday 8th December at 10:16* [Comment . Like]

Josh Annelli Or lack of teacher supervision. But mostly you. *Posted Saturday 8th December at 10:17* [Comment . Like]

Richard Arnoou Blaming a lizard just makes you look petty. Own up to it now, and when they're worth thousands on EBay you can claim you made Maddie famous. *Posted Saturday 8th December at 10:18* [Comment . Like]

Cain Michaels Take blame now for glory in the future. *Posted Saturday 8th December at 10:19* [Comment . Like]

Victoria Zeng Wish I'd thought of doing that. Adding a secret picture to the back. *Posted Saturday 8th December at 10:20* [Comment . Like]

Josh Annelli Me too. Probably minus the massive bananas though. *Posted Saturday 8th December at 10:20* [Comment . Like]

Cliff Wheeland I saw those! Here I thought they were some sort of secret art exhibition. I didn't realise they all came from you, though I should have guessed. My two prints also appear to be sporting one well-endowed dog and a five legged horse... *Posted Saturday 8th December at 10:43* [Comment . Like]

Madeline Cain Experimental Geez, you couldn't have given me a bit of a nudge-nudge-wink-wink earlier? Nice to know you've got my back after half a dozen people have walked off with double the fun. Definitely hang onto those, they'll probably be worth triple. *Posted Saturday 8th December at 10:46* [Comment . Like]

Cliff Wheeland You were sorting out your future, I didn't want to interrupt. Keeping you in NYC is worth far more than pointing out some overly exaggerated finger paintings. *Posted Saturday 8th December at 10:48* [Comment . Like]

Madeline Cain Experimental Glad you think so ? *Posted Saturday 8th December at 10:49* [Comment . Like]

Kate Nikles likes the pages **I Wish Music Played In Epic Moments of My Life & Not Just In The Movies** and **I Find It Awkward Eating Bananas In Public.** [Like. Comment]

Tim Gleeve I'm gonna eat your soul. But in a nice way. And you're going to like it. *Posted Saturday 8th December at 12:50* [Comment . Like]

Madeline Cain Experimental I'm hoping this is some sort of new video game and not you joining a religious cult… *Posted Saturday 8th December at 13:10* [Comment . Like]

Tim Gleeve You'll never know unless you come home. *Posted Saturday 8th December at 13:15* [Comment . Like]

Madeline Cain Experimental That's not the major draw card you seem to think it is. *Posted Saturday 8th December at 13:18* [Comment . Like]

Victoria Zeng I'm not convinced I took my bag with me when I left the subway. The panic is only being kept in check because I'm not sure I left the house with a bag at all. Hellllooooo December! *Posted Sunday 9th December at 14:00* [Comment . Like]

Madeline Cain Experimental Definitely blame December for the craziness. Do what I'm doing and save your professional face for January. *Posted Sunday 9th December at 14:25* [Comment . Like]

Madeline Cain Experimental I can safely say I've managed to fit a lot of crap in this room. *Posted Sunday 9th December at 17:30* [Comment . Like]

Nadine Cain You always were a hoarder, my love. *Posted Sunday 9th December at 17:42* [Comment . Like]

Madeline Cain Experimental Gee Mum, thanks for making me feel like you were standing in the doorway as you said that. It's like we live in the same house again. *Posted Sunday 9th December at 17:50* [Comment . Like]

Nadine Cain Can't come soon enough. *Posted Sunday 9th December at 17:52* [Comment . Like]

Ray Star While I have past, present and future plans chasing each other in my head as I hurry to get my children shoed, the kids are busy being present.

Me: *Angry face* "Why aren't your shoes on?"

Mr D: "I found a caterpillar."

Sigh. Can't argue with that. Brings me back to what's important in life. *Posted Monday 10th December at 11:25* [Comment . Like]

Madeline Cain Experimental Bugs? *Posted Monday 10th December at 11:50* [Comment . Like]

Cliff Wheeland -> Madeline Cain Experimental I have a surprise for you. I think you'll find it sufficiently fulfils the requirements of the 'Making It Up To Maddie' pact I made mid-year. I've been working on it for months. Want to see? *Posted Monday 10th December at 14:30* [Comment . Like]

Madeline Cain Experimental Coming over right now! *Posted Monday 10th December at 14:32* [Comment . Like]

Madeline Cain Experimental Holy heck, did anyone else know Cliff was a published author?? *Posted Monday 10th December at 16:00* [Comment . Like]

Josh Annelli Really? Why doesn't he come up on the Google Machine? *Posted Monday 10th December at 16:29* [Comment . Like]

Madeline Cain Experimental He publishes under a pen name, to help sales. Cliff's other, more literary life, is as the one and only Henry Jackson. *Posted Monday 10th December at 16:35* [Comment . Like]

Jim Klien Why didn't you tell us you knew Henry Jackson personally!? We could have had him over to the Little Y's. You've been holding out on me, girlfriend! *Posted Monday 10th December at 16:45* [Comment . Like]

Madeline Cain Experimental I promise you I haven't, Audrey! I didn't know. He was at the gallery opening too! *Posted Monday 10th December at 16:49* [Comment . Like]

Jim Klien Foiled again! *Posted Monday 10th December at 16:51* [Comment . Like]

Kim Enuik Huh, I always said he was too cashed up to be a student. Remember that carriage ride in the park? That shit is expensive! *Posted Monday 10th December at 16:54* [Comment . Like]

Jade Annelli That's weird, why are you taking a writing course, Cliff? According to Wikipedia you're the star of over five books. *Posted Monday 10th December at 16:57* [Comment . Like]

Kim Enuik Commiserations on the last one though, Bud.

Sounds like the publishers were riding you too hard to let you do your thang properly. *Posted Monday 10th December at 17:00* [Comment . Like]

Jarrah Arnoou Check out the one star review on the last one: 'The clichés in this book reek like the arse end of a baboon.' *Posted Monday 10th December at 17:12* [Comment . Like]

Cliff Wheeland *Shrug* a minor setback. I needed a bit of inspiration, so here I am! You'll get it once you read the book ? *Posted Monday 10th December at 17:20* [Comment . Like]

Kathy Bloomingdale -> Cliff Wheeland So the book's your grand gesture. Why? Is it dedicated to Maddie or something? *Posted Wednesday 12th December at 12:13* [Comment . Like]

Cliff Wheeland It's more than dedicated to her! She's the main character and she's kicking ass! What better way to say, 'this is how much you mean to me', than showing her that even when she's not around she's all I can think about. All I can write about! *Posted Wednesday 12th December at 12:24* [Comment . Like]

Kathy Bloomingdale Please tell me you're joking. *Posted Wednesday 12th December at 12:28* [Comment . Like]

Cliff Wheeland Huh? What do you mean? *Posted Wednesday 12th December at 12:30* [Comment . Like]

Kathy Bloomingdale Oh my God, you're not joking. Do you have any idea why Maddie and Kevin broke up?? I mean other than the fact that they were completely different people and he was moving to LA. The reason why *she* believes they had to break up? *Posted Wednesday 12th December at 12:33* [Comment . Like]

Cliff Wheeland No. Call me silly, but I thought it best not to discuss her ex this close to the break up. That's not really the done thing when you're trying to woo a girl. *Posted Wednesday 12th December at 12:35* [Comment . Like]

Kathy Bloomingdale Idiot. Why would you never ask me?? Maddie's main reason was because she thought Kevin was using her, to get material for his show. She didn't know if he actually liked her or if he was just keeping her around for inspiration. Dude, how could you not have asked?? *Posted Wednesday 12th December at 12:40* [Comment . Like]

Cliff Wheeland Oh no. Nononononono! I've got to go. *Posted Wednesday 12th December at 12:41* [Comment . Like]

The Book.....[New Message]

[Back to messages. Mark as unread . Report spam . Delete]

Between **Cliff Wheeland** and **You.**

Madeline Cain Ex-Muse 12th December 2012 at 13:30

Is this some kind of joke? The famous author 'slumming' it with the students to get his latest plot line?

Cliff Wheeland 12th December 2012 at 13:32 [Report]

Let's not do this through Facebook. Open your front door and talk to me.

Madeline Cain Ex-Muse 12th December 2012 at 13:34

What, so you can throw your bullshit words at me? Get a reaction out of me so you can use it to make your main character more vivid? That's your job as an author, isn't it? To get your character up a tree and throw rocks at them? Well I'm done with that shit.

Cliff Wheeland 12th December 2012 at 13:38 [Report]

Maddie, it's not like that, I didn't know how much you hated it, I thought I was being romantic. I thought it would show you how much you mean to me. I wasn't trying to… to *steal* you. I wanted to show how much you influence who I am. In a good way. In a way I don't ever want to change.

Madeline Cain Ex-Muse 12th December 2012 at 13:39

I smell the shit of the bull. Have you been the only person on the planet not to have watched 'Your Job Or The Money'? I'm thinking of starting a petition to rename it the 'Let's Make Fun Of Madeline Cain' Show.

Cliff Wheeland 12th December 2012 at 13:40 [Report]

Actually, yes. I am one of *many* who hasn't watched it. When have you known me and Kevin to be on speaking terms long enough for me to dedicate five minutes to being near him let alone watching him for a full half hour? I'm not him.

Madeline Cain Ex-Muse 12th December 2012 at 13:41

That's funny, because I could have sworn you and him have a great deal in common: a) you like to keep me around for your inspiration and; b) you both like to exploit 'quirkiness'. Same aim in my book.

Cliff Wheeland 12th December 2012 at 13:43 [Report]

I didn't set out to exploit anything! Sure, I came to NYU for inspiration, I work best immersing myself in the culture and surroundings I'm writing about. That's why the previous book bombed, because I stopped doing the thing that made my work unique, I sat at a desk and favoured keyboard bashing over getting into the thick of things.

Madeline Cain Ex-Muse 12th December 2012 at 13:44

So that's what the fake dead body in the elevator was for. Good to know you were experimenting on humans other than me.

Cliff Wheeland 12th December 2012 at 13:45 [Report]

I didn't plan for this. You threw down that challenge in the elevator and I tried to meet it the only way I knew how, with words and stories. You unblocked me; you made it possible for me to be creative again.

Madeline Cain Ex-Muse 12th December 2012 at 13:46

Aren't I just a fan-bloody-tastic physiologist? I'm glad your best-selling bullshit is flowing again.

Cliff Wheeland 12th December 2012 at 13:46 [Report]

Maddie…

Madeline Cain Ex-Muse 12th December 2012 at 13:47

So do you actually like me? Or do you just keep me around to write more blockbusters?

Cliff Wheeland 12th December 2012 at 13:49 [Report]

How can you even ask that? I wasn't looking for you, but you appeared and you were amazing. It's no wonder you crept into my work. I know Kevin's a dick, but I'm not him. Now that I know, I will never do it again. You have my word.

Tell me what I can do to make it up to you, and I'll do it.

Madeline Cain Ex-Muse 12th December 2012 at 13:51 [Report]

What I *need* is a break, a break from all of this, from artists, from dating. I'm sick of second guessing peoples' motives. I need you to leave me alone for a while.

Cliff Wheeland 12th December 2012 at 13:52 [Report]

Is this one of those 'don't call me I'll call you' scenarios?

Madeline Cain Ex-Muse 12th December 2012 at 13:53 [Report]

Call it whatever you want. Just let me figure out what it is I want to believe on my own time.

Cliff Wheeland 12th December 2012 at 13:54 [Report]

Fine, we'll do it your way. Take all the time you need. But know that I won't wait forever. There's only so many times a man can be called a liar by the woman he loves before he folds.

Cliff Wheeland 12th December 2012 at 13:59 [Report]

Ok, I guess that means the time starts now. Bon voyage, sweet Madeline.

Madeline Cain Ex-Muse We now live in a society where pizza gets to your house before the police. I think I can safely say I won't miss this delivery job when I leave next week. Goodbye Giovanni and thanks for all the crazies. *Posted Thursday 13th December at 20:11* [Comment . Like]

> **Kathy Bloomingdale** Was it serious?? *Posted Thursday 13th December at 20:33* [Comment . Like]

> **Madeline Cain Ex-Muse** Let's just say people are a little too gun happy in this country. *Posted Thursday 13th December at 20:38* [Comment . Like]

> **Kathy Bloomingdale** Oh my. *Posted Thursday 13th December at 20:44* [Comment . Like]

Mike Cain I believe Mario is actively trying to encourage children to take psychotropic mushrooms. And take question marks up the butt. But mostly mushrooms. *Posted Thursday 13th December at 22:50* [Comment . Like]

> **Tim Gleeve** You look too deeply into children's games. *Posted Thursday 13th December at 23:05* [Comment . Like]

Mike Cain Do I, or am I the only teen able to fight subliminal messaging? *Posted Thursday 13th December at 23:15* [Comment . Like]

Tim Gleeve Seems a sucky super power to me. *Posted Thursday 13th December at 23:18* [Comment . Like]

Mike Cain Better than the power to instantly repel women with your bug collection. *Posted Thursday 13th December at 23:22* [Comment . Like]

Madeline Cain Ex-Muse When I play video fight games I press random buttons and hope for the best... *Posted Thursday 13th December at 23:25* [Comment . Like]

Cliff Wheeland People who investigate the strange noises in horror movies deserve to die. *Posted Friday 14th December at 09:05* [Comment . Like]

Kim Enuik Amen. *Posted Friday 14th December at 11:11* [Comment . Like]

Kyle Traybna If 'I can't believe it's not butter' is not butter, then what the hell is it?? *Posted Friday 14th December at 15:30* [Comment . Like]

Tim Gleeve It is the opposite of butter. *Posted Friday 14th December at 15:38* [Comment . Like]

Kyle Traybna What, bread? *Posted Friday 14th December at 15:40* [Comment . Like]

Tim Gleeve No, yellow air. *Posted Friday 14th December at 15:50* [Comment . Like]

Kathy Bloomingdale Six million sperm and you two were the fastest? *Posted Friday 14th December at 15:55* [Comment . Like]

Kate Nickles likes the page **Checking Your Symptoms On Google**

& Accepting You're Going To Die and **25 other pages.** [Like . Comment]

Madeline Cain Ex-Muse One last sleigh ride, one last ice skate, one last visit to the Rockefeller Christmas Tree, and one last tramp under the Christmas decorations in mid-town. Thanks to all the friends who matter, making it an amazing day before I do my final gig and skip country. *Posted Friday 14th December at 21:12* [Comment . Like]

> **Jade Annelli** We'll miss you! If you're ever in London don't forget to come and make our lives interesting! *Posted Friday 14th December at 21:20* [Comment . Like]
>
> **Jarrah Annelli** Screw NYC, London is where it's at. You know you wanna. *Posted Friday 14th December at 21:24* [Comment . Like]
>
> **Madeline Cain Ex-Muse** I know I want to go *everywhere.* I am definitely planning to bring my own brand of special to you at some point. Besides, I promised another friend I'd come say hi. *Posted Friday 14th December at 21:27* [Comment . Like]
>
> **Cain Michaels** See you back here in a month. Feel free to stay at my pad while you do your industry smoozing. *Posted Friday 14th December at 21:29* [Comment . Like]
>
> **Madeline Cain Ex-Muse** You're already doing enough smoozing for the both of us. Besides, I think Duncan would be hurt if I didn't sprinkle coco across the bench and then crash in his bedroom. *Posted Friday 14th December at 21:33* [Comment . Like]
>
> **Kim Enuik** Don't forget, if you're back for good I call dibs on being your housemate. And no, you don't get a choice. *Posted Friday 14th December at 21:35* [Comment . Like]

Madeline Cain Ex-Muse Never thought I had one. *Posted Friday 14th December at 21:37* [Comment . Like]

Worst Stereotyping Ever – The Breakdown Of A Wedding

NOTES > My Notes [Write a note]

By **Madeline Cain Cakeface** Sunday, 16th December 2012 at 09:41

Now I truly understand the term Bridezilla. Yes, the bride is responsible for all the beauty of a wedding, she has slaved over the details and arrangements, location and style, shaved and waxed areas that should never be shaved and waxed. She's the living epitome of beauty and grace and perfection as she glides through her day. But she's also willing to let it all go to get the bastards that ruined it.

Previously I declared that the gallery was my final act of embarrassment for 2012. I should learn not to count my chickens before they hatch. Let this be a lesson to all of you that stereotyping is a stupid thing to do. Particularly stereotyping that involves the Federal Bureau of Investigation.

After the shit storm that was last week, I was not in the best mood for a wedding or picking up a camera – unless it was to bludgeon people who wanted to cheer me up. Did I feel the need to follow Shapelle and *actually* blackmail her? Yes. Did I resist? Barely. But I had committed and there was no backing out. So myself and Daniel, the second photographer, went on a trip to Long Island and a function centre in the Hamptons.

There were two of us there to photograph a wedding that was so large it could have doubled as its own nation. I wondered how much they were spending on photographers if they could afford to scatter diamond and crystal around the venue like it was glitter from a $2 store.

The scene was just as you'd expect from watching any movie involving rich white people and the Hamptons. The sumptuous mansion overlooked a massive green lawn and a grey blue ocean that only hairy men and whales dared swim in due to its bone shattering coldness. Two marquees were set up on the lawn complete with lit braziers and portable heaters to make sure everyone didn't freeze in their chairs. One marquee was lined with rows of chairs for the ceremony, the other was full of round tables and a dance floor for the reception. Being winter and almost Christmas, the whole place had the feel of an ice palace: massive crystals in the shape of snow flakes and stars, spruce trees covered in shimmering baubles and 'icicles', and Bridezilla, the majestic Snow Queen in a long sleeved, high neck dress covered in crystal beads that chimed as she moved. But unlike a Snow Queen, she knew how to throw a party.

From the first glass of champagne thrust into my hand as I entered the dressing suite at 8am, I knew the day was going to be a lot more entertaining than kids in onsies or zombies in un-wrinkle-able tuxes. I wasn't until I exited the room two hours later – with several hundred photos of the bride and her bride's maids preparing – and ran into Agent Smith dressed as a function centre steward that I realised the fun and games were just beginning. Professional in her undercover role, Smith didn't bat an eyelid as I gapped at her. Probably worried I'd give the game away, she jerked her head over her shoulder and murmured an apology before continuing down the hall. Who should be there, front and centre, though we were almost two hours away from New York City at an unknown person's wedding, but Dom.

How was that possible? Bridezilla didn't have a mob vibe about her but here was Dom at the far end of the hall, face red, gesturing wildly at a security guard, who on closer inspection appeared to be Agent Brown. With a blank expression the Agent pointed directly at me, hand hovering over a bulge near his hips. With an exaggerated *thank you*, and a rolling of his eyes Dom headed my way.

I flashed my panic-eyes at Agent Brown, hoping my expression conveyed a great big, *WTF Man?* Brown held up his hand in a 'stay' position, the other hand resting against what I assumed to be some sort of weapon.

It wasn't until Dom was several metres away that recognition crossed his features. "Sugar! What are you doing here?" He side stepped to the left, reaching for the handle to the dressing room and Agent Brown made a harried slashing motion with his hand.

As though my body were no longer my own I found myself between Dom and the handle, a big car-salesman smile on my face. "Sorry, Dom. The bride said no one in until after the ceremony." His eyes narrowed, and my heart jumped. Not sure if it was the stereotyping that projected the 'don't mess with me' attitude, I continued in that absurdly bright tone, "She wants to surprise everyone. If it makes you feel any better she's not letting anyone out."

He lifted one thick, black eyebrow.

"Well, except me," I stammered, "I'm supposed to take photos of all the place settings and icicles and... sea foam. For photographic ambiance... you know, for-"

"Stop," he said, holding up a hand. "Fine. Let Miranda have her little princess moment. But tell her we have business to discuss *soon*. Think you can pass the message on?"

Geez, who in New York *didn't* have business to discuss with Dom? "Of course." I grinned so hard you could almost hear my teeth creak.

He sighed, running a hand over his greased back hair. "Thanks Sugar, I know you've got my back." He clapped a hand on my shoulder before striding back down the corridor.

He had no idea how wrong he was.

"You should probably go and do that ambiance thing," murmured Agent Brown edging down the hall after Dom.

"I made the bloody thing up," I snapped.

He shrugged. "He's hanging around this wedding like a mouldy odour, which means he's going to notice if you don't. Something big is going down and you don't wanna tip our hand. You're committed to whatever bullshit you spun into gold, so hop to it."

Well that was just peachy, I now had to fulfil a completely imaginary task while also trying to fit in the real and necessary job of checking the lighting in the marquee into my tight schedule. And probably have to resist the urge to check every chair in the place for bombs. Why I didn't tell Dom the *actual* job I'd was going to do I don't know, but slashing motions from Federal agents do much to freeze the rational mind.

So I dashed from one ornament to the next, hoping I had enough shots to prove 'ambiance' if quizzed by Dom, before hurriedly checking the marquee lighting and arriving at the dressing suite with less than a minute to spare.

A dozen expectant heads turned my way when I entered. Then, when they saw my ugly mug, they sagged back to their previous positions.

Bridezilla, Miranda, frowned. "Have you seen Dom?"

Surprised to see her disappointment at lack of Dom-ness, I open and shut my mouth several times before asking, "Is he part of the bridal party?"

She snorted waving a hand. "Oh goodness no! He's my designer. Discovered this dress and helped me organise this whole day."

My insides did a little jig. "Dom? Really??"

"Yes, who else?"

I shrugged, struggling to understand.

"He's only tipped to be the next in line to take over the top stylist job at 7th Avenue Magazine. That man will rule the fashion world one day and I'll be able to say he was the one who did my wedding. A strategic move if I do say so myself," she said, fluffing up her hair.

Holy radioactive monkey testicles. Magazine fashion stylist.

Not mobster.

Climbing the fashion industry ladder like a Boss.

Not a shady underworld figure.

Sweet baby cheeses, I'd set the FBI on a stylist!?

It was all completely innocent: the clothes, the appearance at Fashion Week, designers owing him 'favours', the offer to bump any competition from other fashion photographers. Everything suddenly *fit.* I'd been concocting wild theories based on what? I felt like a unicorn who'd just tried to head butt a rhino; I'd put a whole task force into action to watch a man who dressed life sized Barbie dolls for a living.

This was sooooooo getting me deported.

I still had no explanation for the penis-gun incident though. Was the fashion industry more dangerous then I realised? Rivals ordering hits on people who were headed for the top job??

But if we removed that incident from the equation what did we have? A bloke who slicked back his hair and thought he was the best thing since Robert Downey Jr.

I needed to find the Agents *immediately* to stop whatever drastic measures they were putting in place.

A loud knock sounded. "They're ready," called a muffled voice.

Miranda's face paled slightly as I'm sure my own did.

"Don't worry, the stylist has done an amazing job," assured a bride's maid.

"Then I guess Dom will have to be as surprised as the rest of them," said Miranda, standing up and shaking herself out like an athlete.

Bugger it, I thought, shrugging, *the FBI are professionals. If anything happens it will be quiet and in some tucked away corner where the public won't get hurt. Plenty of time to fix this thing.*

I should know better than to tempt fate with such obvious bait. I should also probably have told the bride about Dom's need to discuss 'business'…

But suddenly time was not my own and I was glued to that camera like I'd grown a fifth limb. Concerns of fake mobsters and overzealous FBI agents faded into the background as I captured one of the happiest events I've attended this year. The crowd was well lubricated with pre-wedding alcohol, smiling appeared mandatory (but natural), and clichéd tears of joy were expected.

There's something about the energy of a wedding that buoys you up, and turns you into a photographic gymnast. The last time I knelt, bent and reached that way I was in a dance recital, twelve and dressed in lurid pink. That colour probably turned most of the audience spontaneously gay.

I found myself playing with shots like I hadn't done in months, and happily gaining bruises if it meant getting that perfect shot captured. The ceremony was a frantic snap-a-thon followed closely by clichéd but adorable, 'official' photo session on the beach.

Two champagnes later, and a brief interlude for the bride and groom to change, and finding Agent 'Brow-Smi' didn't seem quite the urgent task it had been. I hadn't seen either Agent in several hours, and Dom had been a ghost, overseeing but never truly there.

The wedding party and well-wishers had moved into the banquet marquee. Chandeliers cast an atmospheric glow and the cold was kept at bay by white canvas walls that had been rolled down to trap the heat and block the wind. A crystal tinkle of a spoon-struck wine glass filled the air and the Best Man stood, looking dashingly handsome and debonair. I immediately captured two hundred and five photos of him on my camera.

Dom materialised like a magician on the edge of the dance floor, a beacon to undercover agents everywhere. He looked like a dwarf next to the glittering five-tiered monstrosity of a wedding cake. I'm pretty sure that cake would've cost at least two months' rent.

As the Best Man told his introductory joke and made mention of some particular childhood memory, Dom, with a look of intense concentration on his face, raised his arm to shoulder height pointing something square and black directly at the groom. The Best Man looked over his shoulder expectantly, Dom's index finger twitched and a loud *bang* echoed from the back of the marquee followed by an even larger BANG.

Myself and half the crowd jump. Children abandon parents, and parents abandon grandparents as half the attendees attempt to shove each other out of the way to dive under their tables.

The confusion on the Best Man's face is almost as comical as the horror and rage on Dom's as he jabbed his arm repeatedly towards the groom, finger twitching. Each twitch was accompanied by a delayed double bang.

It's unclear at what point the Agents decided to finally play their hand. But if they'd waited several more seconds they would have seen attendants hurriedly rolling up canvas walls on the beach side, and the Best Man very clearly and obviously repeating his previous punch line while staring daggers at Dom.

I found out much later that the 'business' Dom had wanted to discuss with Bridezilla included which of two remotes he needed to use to control the projector screen for the Best Man's inappropriate photo essay on the groom, and which was to set off fireworks as the newly wedded couple had their first dance.

Dom had the misfortune of choosing incorrectly, as demonstrated several seconds later by the burly Agents Brown and Smith crash-tackling him into the cake.

Faster than you can say the word 'bomb' several moist (and tasty) projectiles hit me as the cake exploded like a silver and white supernova, showering wedding guests up to three tables back from the dance floor. A stunned silence followed. Some may have sworn they heard crickets.

That was until Bridezilla broke a chair over Agent Brown's head. Then suddenly it was like a football match, fans of the bride shouting for 'a solid kick in the tomatoes' and food flying everywhere (any chance for a food fight, hey kids?).

Grabbing a handful of Agent Smith's tangled and cake covered hair, Bridezilla hauled her out onto the dance floor shrieking, "I've been starving myself for three months to eat that cake!" Then, with all the skill of a pro-wrestler, Bridezilla body slammed the second member of the FBI.

The shock of seeing a waif of a woman take out two FBI agents is on my list of the top ten most hilarious thing I've ever seen. Yet, somehow, bizarrely, even though I was merely a spectator to these messed up events, it was all my fault. It got me thinking, if this was the trouble I could cause just by existing, what sort of trouble could I cause if I learn how to do this on purpose?

Actually, you know what? It's all YOUR fault. The thought that Dom was a mobster hadn't even entered my mind until one of you suggested it and the rest ran off with the idea like it was a diamond encrusted Batman cape. You should all be ashamed of yourselves. Your stereotyping ruined Bridezilla's wedding.

The End by Madeline Cain.

[Comment . Like . Share]

Kathy Bloomingdale and **97 others** like this.

Mike Cain How come Aunty Jenny's wedding wasn't that awesome!? Man, it would almost be worth being you just so I could watch the breakdown of a human-being in fast forward. I'd be able to orchestrate this on purpose no problems. *Posted Sunday 16th December at 11:00* [Comment . Like]

> **Madeline Cain Cakeface** Yes, I'm certain it would be a natural talent that Mum would be oh so proud of. Putting you near a wedding would break the universe. Am I causing enough Christmas chaos for you? *Posted Sunday 16th December at 11:12* [Comment . Like]

> **Mike Cain** My little sis is all grown up *sniff*. *Posted Sunday 16th December at 11:14* [Comment . Like]

Victoria Zeng Go Bridezilla! Don't let no-one mess with your wedding! Sharpen your stilettos and show them who's boss. *Posted Sunday 16th December at 11:42* [Comment . Like]

> **Jade Annelli** Bugger Bridezilla, it should have been the bride's maid watching her back. Destroying wedding ruiners is part of the job description along with decent hens' night strippers and loss of memory between 1 and 6am. *Posted Sunday 16th December at 11:49* [Comment . Like]

> **Cain Michaels** You can't tell me you wouldn't have done the same thing if it was your wedding. Except you would have destroyed them by force feeding them cake. *Posted Sunday 16th December at 11:54* [Comment . Like]

> **Josh Annelli** How come all the hot, women wrestlers are taken in this world? She uses chairs as fighting props *and* sucker punches? That's the woman for me. *Posted Sunday 16th December at 11:57* [Comment . Like]

Richard Arnoou You mean when she's divorced and has one kid she'll be the woman for you… *Posted Sunday 16th December at 11:59* [Comment . Like]

Josh Annelli *Sharpens the razor and drops a few sleeping pills into Richard's coffee*. *Posted Sunday 16th December at 12:03* [Comment . Like]

Victoria Zeng I wonder if it's illegal to take out an FBI agent if they started it first? *Posted Sunday 16th December at 12:05* [Comment . Like]

Cain Michaels Depends on how many times she went for the body slam. *Posted Sunday 16th December at 12:05* [Comment . Like]

Jarrah Annelli I think we should call her Ninja Bride. She gets her superpowers from starvation and cake depravation. Bet Dom looked like a walking Mr Whippy cone. *Posted Sunday 16th December at 12:07* [Comment . Like]

Kathy Bloomingdale See, you had fun! Those bimbos at the ball had no idea what they were talking about. I bet you got more interesting photos than that Daniel guy too. By the sounds of things you'll end up with a tidy pay cheque which means not only do you have fun on your side but money. Something to think about when applying for jobs next year. (So, the cake tasted like?). *Posted Sunday 16th December at 12:16* [Comment . Like]

Tim Gleeve Wedding photographers clearly keep the whole being-able-to-drink-on-the-job thing on the down low. Because if the rat-pack knew, I'm pretty sure they'd be doing it rather than giving you judgy-eyes. *Posted Sunday 16th December at 12:19* [Comment . Like]

Madeline Cain Cakeface I think the alcohol was unique to that particular event, sorry to say. I do not condone drinking on the job children (But if you have to, champagne makes everything happy). I had an amazing time, Kathy, surprisingly, and not because I saw ten Funniest Home Videos packed into thirty seconds. The ambiance thing, though it was initially a load of bullshit, ended up working really well. According to Natalie my photos were five times better than Daniel who is supposed to be a professional. (Tasted like raspberries, honey and chocolate – yum!). *Posted Sunday 16th December at 12:23* [Comment . Like]

Nadine Cain Shame on the FBI for using you as a human barricade in the first place! Well they got their comeuppance with a good old fashioned dose of karma. Karma always wins, especially when dressed in white and wearing a shiny new ring. It's a weight off my chest that this Dom fellow is about as likely to get you shot as he is to mix fluoro pink with brown. A fashion mogul, hey? You make sure you stay in touch with him, I want my front row fashion week seats. Some new clothes for your Mama would be nice too… *Posted Sunday 16th December at 12:40* [Comment . Like]

Tim Gleeve Told you the FBI didn't have your best interests at heart. It's probably best you're skipping town over Christmas ? *Posted Sunday 16th December at 12:48* [Comment . Like]

Nadine Cain Yes, you're home soon!!! I can't wait! Only three days to go! *Posted Sunday 16th December at 12:49* [Comment . Like]

Tim Gleeve I always thought Dom sounded more like a whoopsie than a mobster. No self-respecting mobster would be found with half a dozen animal onsies for kids. *Posted Sunday 16th December at 12:52* [Comment . Like]

Kim Enuik What I want to know is what have you done with your inner Nancy Drew? Considering Dom's most heinous crime of the century was probably introducing Jeggings, why was he being shot at? I'm dying of curiosity over here. *Posted Sunday 16th December at 12:57* [Comment . Like]

Jade Annelli Maybe he called her a skank? *Posted Sunday 16th December at 12:59* [Comment . Like]

Jarrah Annelli Maybe he drop-kicked her pet out the window because she was taking shitty photos? *Posted Sunday 16th December at 13:00* [Comment . Like]

Richard Arnoou Maybe the smell of his hair gel offended her? *Posted Sunday 16th December at 13:02* [Comment . Like]

Victoria Zeng For making her wear high heels? I'd understand that killer rage. *Posted Sunday 16th December at 13:03* [Comment . Like]

Madeline Cain Cakeface None of the above! It took a bit of digging but I'm proud to say my Nancy Drew is alive and kicking mystery-solving-butt. Dom had made some sort of boast at work about being able to get into The Dragon's Den, and Ivana, his rival, had used Camilla as bait to convince him to get them into the club. Turns out Camilla had a boyfriend vendetta, or should I say ex-boyfriend vendetta. So Andre what's-his-name, the TV star, arrives by limo at the club and she takes aim, only you-know-who was in the way. Badabing-badaboom yours truly knocked her out with a handbag and no one died. Success! *Posted Sunday 16th December at 13:10* [Comment . Like]

Tim Gleeve Well, that was a letdown. *Posted Sunday 16th December at 13:11* [Comment . Like]

Mike Cain There have been a lot of 'unconscious' moments for the extras in your stories. I reckon you just roofied them all and jazzed it up to sound more exciting. *Posted Sunday 16th December at 13:13* [Comment . Like]

Kim Enuik So Dom got played and you raked in the spoils.

Why does life throw me lemons while you get cupcakes? *Posted Sunday 16th December at 13:15* [Comment . Like]

Madeline Cain Cakeface Well, when you're wearing said cupcakes on your face it's kind of hard to see it as a plus. I'm sorry my storytelling skills were not up to your exacting standards, Tim. How about we swap, I'll be the computer geek that makes memes of my brother and you can be in a story full of certifiable insanity. *Posted Sunday 16th December at 13:18* [Comment . Like]

Josh Annelli You love it. You wish you were the one tackled into the cake. *Posted Sunday 16th December at 13:19* [Comment . Like]

Madeline Cain Cakeface Ah, you caught me. Bathing in cake is the new mud-bath. *Posted Sunday 16th December at 13:20* [Comment . Like]

Tim Gleeve Checking the fridge every ten minutes to see if any food has magically appeared. Still empty and smelling slightly of bananas. *Posted Monday17th December at 16:22* [Comment . Like]

Madeline Cain Cakeface Second to last day in NYC and what do I do? Waste half of it showing clients all the photos not involving cake. Hopefully they buy every one of my two thousand photos and I become an overnight millionaire! *Posted Tuesday 18th December at 16:55* [Comment . Like]

Kathy Bloomingdale I'm sure it will be a smash :p *Posted Tuesday 18th December at 17:10* [Comment . Like]

Madeline Cain Cakeface I thank God every day that you

decided to study costume design over stand-up comedy. *Posted Tuesday 18th December at 17:20* [Comment . Like]

Nadine Cain Good luck beautiful! Make your last day count! *Posted Tuesday 18th December at 17:22* [Comment . Like]

Mike Cain likes the page **Wearing Your Batman Cape Under Your Clothes In Case Shit Goes Down.** [Like . Comment]

Claire Holderness Just ate vegetarian for the second night in a row, turned out pretty awesome. #AlrightItWasAnAccident #AdultingLikeABoss #Wait #WhatDoYouMeanBaconsNotAVegetable. *Posted Tuesday 18th December at 19:22* [Comment . Like]

Tim Gleeve Depends on how you define a vegetable. *Posted Tuesday 18th December at 19:45* [Comment . Like]

Kathy Bloomingdale In every definition of vegetable there is one thing you can be certain of, no mention of the word bacon, ham, pig or swine. *Posted Tuesday 18th December at 19:49* [Comment . Like]

Madeline Cain The Grown Up I don't want to alarm anyone, but thought you should know **Natalie West** just offered me a job. And I think I might say yes. *Posted Wednesday 19th December at 12:04* [Comment . Like]

Kathy Bloomingdale WHAT!? Spill. Details. Now. *Posted Wednesday 19th December at 12:20* [Comment . Like]

Tim Gleeve What happened to never taking a job where the photographic goon squad look down on you? *Posted Wednesday 19th December at 12:26* [Comment . Like]

Kathy Bloomingdale Tim! What the hell? *Posted Wednesday 19th December at 12:27* [Comment . Like]

Tim Gleeve *Shrug* someone's got to play Devil's advocate. *Posted Wednesday 19th December at 12:29* [Comment . Like]

Madeline Cain The Grown Up Natalie is run off her feet; she can't accept every wedding offered. She wants to expand, and she was so impressed with the other day (FBI dance spectacular and all) that she wants to do it with me. She said my work is miles ahead of Daniel, who's the 'professional'. Jason's right, Sorella and the other's whole act is bullshit. I had an amazing time at that wedding and I want to see where it takes me. Plus, not only is our base in New York, but there'll be some cross country travelling added to the mix. That's worth saying yes, I think. *Posted Wednesday 19th December at 12:38* [Comment . Like]

Tim Gleeve Depends on how good you are at scoring me chicks when I come to visit. *Posted Wednesday 19th December at 12:39* [Comment . Like]

Kim Enuik Thank Saint Nick for that! Was not looking forward to breaking in a new housemate. *Posted Wednesday 19th December at 12:41* [Comment . Like]

Kathy Bloomingdale Sigh, I suppose that means I'll have to come back too. To stop Tim from being arrested for harassment of course. *Posted Wednesday 19th December at 12:44* [Comment . Like]

Madeline Cain The Grown Up Of course. *Posted Wednesday 19th December at 12:48* [Comment . Like]

Jarrah Annelli Congratulations! *Posted Wednesday 19th December at 12:48* [Comment . Like]

Josh Annelli So, client photo showings are not such a bad thing after all. *Posted Wednesday 19th December at 12:49* [Comment . Like]

Victoria Zeng Say yes! Say yes! *Posted Wednesday 19th December at 12:49* [Comment . Like]

Natalie West So does this post mean what I think it means? *Posted Wednesday 19th December at 12:49* [Comment . Like]

Madeline Cain The Grown Up Yes. *Posted Wednesday 19th December at 12:50* [Comment . Like]

Madeline Cain The Grown Up About to get on a big jet plane. But watch out NYC, I'll be seeing you *real* soon! *Posted Thursday 20th December at 09:14* [Comment . Like]

Madeline Cain The Grown Up Merry Christmas and Happy New Year bitches! *Posted Tuesday 25th December at 10:00* [Comment . Like]

Madeline Cain The Grown Up God damn it Mike I'm home for one second and suddenly you're all over my account like a wet flannel! What kind of language is my bloody Facebook in now? Is this German? No, Hindi? DID YOU PUT MY DAMN FACEBOOK INTO HINDI!?! *Posted Tuesday 25th December at 11:32* [Comment . Like]

Enjoyed Madeline Cain: Adventures In Fashion?

Then Sign Up For The Newsletter!

Not only will you get a newsletter full of tales of adventure (I travel a *lot*) competitions, and my latest writing exploits, you'll get two bonus YA short-stories, *and* abusive umbrella message tones (?? oh, you'll understand soon).

Also, one lucky subscriber will be picked out of the hat to have a character named after them in my next novel. Congrats to lucky Claire Holderness who had a character named after her in this very novella!

Just sign up to my irregular author newsletter below (it may come to you monthly, maybe 6 monthly, it's a surprise for both of us! All you need to know is, I'm not into spam) to get your story gifts.

Sign up here! *http://www.cravenstories.com/books-and-more/freebies/reader-freebies/*

If You Enjoyed Madeline Cain: Adventures In Fashion, Please, Leave a Review Online!

Emily really appreciates every reader's support, and is stoked (pick the Aussie!) that you loved the book. If you could help her quit her day job to write more Madeline Cain novels by leaving a review at your favourite ebook retailer or at Goodreads below she would love you forever! Please don't hesitate to email her either!

Review @ Goodreads: *http://tiny.cc/MCGoodreads*

Thank you! And see you at the next Adventure!

Other Books By This Author

Jake's Page: A Short Story and Play

Available in print in all online stores.

Jake Black is almost your average teen, fresh from the high-school farm he jumps at the chance to move from Hobart to Adelaide, with the vague plan of taking engineering at the University. Like many people of his generation who travel from home, he turns to Facebook as a medium to pass on news and keep in touch with family and friends. If only his mother wouldn't call him every day to check on his diabetes. Or use his sister's account to spy on his activities. Perhaps this is why his parents were so eager for him to attend one of the city's residential colleges, where he is surrounded by 200 students who can keep watch.

However college is more adventurous than Jake's parents bargained for. From his first 'ponding' in the courtyard fountain to forced o-week activities such as Goon of Fortune, and being dropped 30km from the city wearing nothing but a g-string and body paint, Jake plunges into college life with the enthusiasm of one finally release from the parental blanket.

Ignoring the inevitable medical impacts of his new life style Jake struggles managing his mother and his new freedom with mixed results on the public Facebook platform.

Jake's Page is a comic yet heart-breaking tale of a young type 1 diabetic, and his Facebook Page, told through status updates, Facebook notes, and Facebook personal messages. This e-book presents the tale as both an short story, and a play.

Original Fantasy: A Practical Guide to Writing Genre

Available in print at all online retailers!

"Emily creates a warm, funny, personable read in this guide book version of our mentorship. I love it. Even if I do come off as a stern and slightly frightening Mage..."

~ Isobelle Carmody

So you've finished your novel and it is Frankenstein's monster.

Don't Panic!

Whether you write fantasy, science-fiction, crime, thriller, YA, or chick-lit, this humorous and helpful guide will hone your skills and lead you through the quagmire of writing original fiction.

Emily Craven details the lessons she learnt during her twelve-month mentorship with award-winning author Isobelle Carmody. Emily has included dozens of examples of her original passages, along with Isobelle's insightful comments.

An award-winning publisher and author in her own right, Emily simplifies and demystifies the complexities of writing and editing your novel.

About The Author

Chocolate. Karaoke. Star Trek. Travel. Books. Puppies. Shaking what your Mama gave you. All of these are some of my favourite things. But when I meet someone, I want to know who they are, not what they like. I want to know what's their story? Why do they get up every morning? Other than, like, needing to have a pee.

Aherm, moving on.

For me, what rocks my world is showing daring creatives how to draw the curious down the rabbit hole with stories, how to use their tales to spark connection, understanding, and create belonging with a wonderland of their making.

Stories entered my DNA as a kid. They were what saved me from lonely lunch times with no friends when my family moved states and I was shoved into a new school mid-year, mid-puberty, mid-awkward-phase. They allowed me to escape to another world of adventure, of struggle (that wasn't mine), of empathy, perspective, and heroes who strived against the bullies, and again and again, picked themselves. Stories showed me how to adapt, to care, to trust myself. They understood me on a level I barely understood myself. I was such a voracious reader I started writing my own books when I was 12 because my favourite authors just couldn't keep up.

Stories were how I survived boredom. Boredom was how I ended up a Star Trek nerd. Every afternoon when I got home from school, my mother commandeered the TV to fuel her Star Trek addiction. The choice was be bored or be obsessed. You could say I was brain-washed a Trekkie and I have no regrets!

That's the only reason I can think of for how I ended up choosing to study Astrophysics. Two years in and something happened that I never in a million years expected. I hated it. I had no idea what else I would even do if I quit. I was good at it, sure, but every six months I would have a mini-break-down in my bedroom, the words of high-school teachers and parents going around and round my head – 'you're too smart for art.' If present me could time travel, I'd go back and slap them all up-side the head, with a loud, 'fuck that noise' for good measure.

How many times have you been told you 'should'? You should do this, you should do that, even though you know that box doesn't fit you?

What I didn't realise at the time was the reason I was so drawn to Star Trek wasn't the science, it was the adventure. A soap opera in space; people working together solving problems, falling in love, and shooting phasers! This was the root of my unhappiness; I was suppressing the biggest part of myself. I didn't want knowledge for the sake of knowledge, I want to create things that connected people. And the way that excited me, that lit a fire in my belly to create that connection, was by creating and sharing stories. Fictional preferably, with a hint of magic, a dash of quirky, and a sneaky side of truth.

I wish I could tell you that when I set my sights on career as storyteller, I shook off that 'should' energy. I did not. While I devoured dozens of courses on writing, publishing, marketing, editing and eBooks, and learnt one of the most important lessons of my life – that what you create alone will never be as good as what you'll create together with the feedback of professionals who aren't you and see your blind spots – I was still doing all the things you should. You should send your novels to traditional publishers, you should write short stories to get a name for yourself, you should have a 'very' professional website where you're 'very serious' and therefore 'competent', as confirmed by your head shot which makes you look like you have sat on a cactus.

I waited a really long time for someone to pick me. And I was lonely, so very very lonely. When a boy who already had a 3-book deal with a major publisher got the only writing grant available in the state to writers under 30, something finally snapped for me. I was sick of waiting; it was time to choose myself. I couldn't be rejected if I was the one creating the thing, right?

It was when I took the conscious decision to step off the beaten path that things changed for me. I created my own opportunities, but in a way that no one else was doing at the time – I created them so that I was making and creating WITH someone else. The power of collaboration runs through everything I do now, from the very first writing and publishing project I created in my little city of Adelaide, which spiralled into a 5-year international endeavour that would turn into the award-winning storytelling app, Story City, and lift up over 300 storytellers across half a dozen creative industries.

In creating my own opportunities, in making things like Story City, my novels, my branding work, I realised I made a place where I belonged, and where hundreds and thousands of others realised they belonged.

The success that I have had today is due largely to the power of story. Of how stories allow you to be understood for you, and to connect beyond yourself. I've won awards, presented hundreds of hours of storytelling workshops internationally, published 6 books, edited and/or published dozens of authors, I am a global entrepreneur of an app that helps you explore and connect to a city and the stories of its people, and I'm part of a 6 person team that brands a handful of high-flying femmpreneurs every year.

While much of that has been because of hard work, talent, and practice, the truth of the matter is I have gotten this far because I have chosen to make things together, rather than alone. To hone my understanding, skills and stories, with outside eyes, because through collaboration I make far more impact than I ever would on my own.

So I say to you pick yourself, don't wait for others to pick you. But also pick doing it together, rather than doing it alone.

Find your people. Band together. And you will make great things.

With This Book You Also Get A Free E-Book Copy!

Just email emily@cravenstories.com with the following to prove your purchase:

- A photo of yourself holding the book PLUS;
- A photo of your name written in pen on the copyright page;
- Mention where you bought the book from.
- What format you would like the book in: .epub (iPad, Kobo, Nook etc), .mobi (Kindle/Amazon) or PDF.

Once Emily receives your email she will personally email you back your e-book copy. She's only human, so give her a couple of days to get to your email. Thank you once again for purchasing the book!

Contact

Facebook: *http://www.facebook.com/EmilyCravenAuthor*

Website (bookmark me!): *http://www.cravenstories.com*

Twitter: *@cravenstories*

Instagram: *@imagesforjoy*

Email: emily (at) cravenstories (dot) com

www.ingramcontent.com/pod-product-compliance
Lightning Source LLC
Chambersburg PA
CBHW050610110726
47899CB00001B/47

* 9 7 8 0 9 8 7 5 0 0 6 8 7 *